SECRETS OF THE DEAD

Secrets taken to the grave cannot remain hidden forever.....

MICHAEL FOWLER

Michael was born and grew up in the once industrial heartland of South Yorkshire and still lives there with his wife and two sons.

He served as a police officer for thirty-two years, both in uniform and in plain clothes, working in CID, Vice Squad and Drug Squad, and retired as an Inspector in charge of a busy CID Department in 2006.

Secrets of the Dead is the third novel in the DS Hunter Kerr series.

Aside from writing, his other passion is painting, and as a professional artist he has numerous artistic accolades to his name. His work can be found in numerous galleries throughout the UK.

He is a member of the Crime Writers Association.

He can be contacted via his website at www.mjfowler.co.uk

By the same author:

HEART OF THE DEMON

COLD DEATH

Acknowledgements

The idea for this story was sparked by an exercise at The Rawmarsh Writers Group, so I am grateful to Margaret Ardron for that. Though, without the help of others this would never have come to fruition. Therefore I have to thank Detective Sergeant Ian Harding, who runs South Yorkshire's Cold Case Unit. He gave me an invaluable insight into their working practices and also some great quotes, which I couldn't resist borrowing.

Once more I owe a debt of gratitude to Stuart Sosnowski, CSI Supervisor, South Yorkshire Police, who never lets me down, no matter how many crime scenes I conjure up in my imagination for him to process.

Also to PC Steve Cook, Task Force, with whom I frequently swap stories in the pub and who gave me the ending for this novel.

I want to thank Liz, not only for her continuing support, but also for spending the time to patiently go through my first edit. Also, to Janet Williamson, who read the finished story and provided advice towards its final edit.

Finally, I have to give special mention to Darren Laws at Caffeine Nights Publishing. Darren has worked tirelessly to support and promote me in the short time-span I have been with them and never loses his patience, no matter how many times I decide to change things after submission. Thank you Darren.

To my loving wife Liz, for all the support and encouragement she has given me over the years, enabling me to write and paint.

PROLOGUE

Barnwell: 14th November 2008.

A sudden wave of panic washed over him and his chest tightened.

Slowing his pace and pausing for a moment, he checked his bearings. It was a long time since he had been in these woods and the memory of that last visit bore no resemblance whatsoever to the area he was currently scanning. In fact, nothing was familiar.

He cursed beneath his breath. He had especially chosen this morning because of the foul weather, but hadn't anticipated it working against him. The veil of early morning fog was thicker than he had expected - he could only just make out his boots, never mind the landmarks he was seeking.

Ten minutes earlier he'd left his car parked in the lay-by, at the edge of the coppice, in almost the same spot as he had done all those years ago, and now he was attempting to re-trace the route he had taken that night. But it was proving more difficult than he'd expected. So much of the terrain had changed. The wood was much denser, and of course, it had been nightfall back then.

If truth be known he wouldn't be here now, had it not been for that letter he had received a week ago. Inside the Sheffield-postmarked envelope had been a single sheet of paper with five words typed upon it -'It's time for the truth'– nothing threatening about the sentence, but to him those words were a shadow of peril hanging over him.

Since then he had slept fitfully. When he had dropped off he had been haunted by images of that night. They had replayed over and over, and no matter how hard he tried to dismiss them, they lurked in the deepest recesses of his mind and leapt out whenever he had closed his eyes. Two days ago, it had led him to kill again.

He'd thought that would put paid to his problems, but he had discovered that there was another loose end to eliminate. Since then, he had dwelt on little else. Finally, last night, he had convinced himself what he needed to do. The next killing was inevitable. Only then would he be able to bury the past.

Before that, though, he had one more important thing to check out.

When he had heard the weather forecast this morning he had immediately realised that today would be his best opportunity; not even the most ardent of dog walkers would be braving the woods in these conditions.

Taking another quick look around, convinced he must be close to the spot, he stepped off the main path and cut deeper into the undergrowth.

Tramping through the dying ferns, he spotted his first landmark and let out a sigh of relief. He was surprised he had not seen it sooner - the laurel bush before him had grown so much; it was almost as big as a tree.

He picked up his pace. The bracken beneath his boots was soft and springy - the moisture-laden atmosphere had flattened the mass, making his trek easier, though he found himself catching his breath and beads of sweat had begun to form on his brow. It was a sign of how much out of condition he was. Always so fit as a young man, the toll of his over-indulgent lifestyle over the years had finally caught up with him.

Stopping in mid-stride, he scoped the way ahead. Silvery tentacles of fog weaved before him, caressing the woodland floor, wrapping themselves around tree trunks, making the search for his second marker harder. He strained to listen. Nothing: everything was so still. Not even birdsong this morning.

He walked on through the damp undergrowth, yawing from his course every dozen or so steps. The manoeuvre had the desired effect, for within five minutes he spotted the oak tree he had been looking for. It was bigger and more majestic than his last memory, but then it had been twenty five years ago. He increased his pace, striding into a small clearing and ran a hand over the bark. Then, turning to his right, he re-fixed his bearings and focused on the spot where he had buried her all those years ago.

A thicket of holly overhung the site.

My secret is even safer.

He smiled to himself. In that moment he felt an overwhelming sense of reassurance and let out a satisfied sigh. Reaching into his coat pocket, he slid out his cigarettes. Shuffling the pack, he removed one with his lips and, cupping his lighter, lit it. Taking a deep breath, while raising his head towards the mist laden sky, he held the smoke longer than normal until he could feel the kick from the nicotine fuzz his brain. Now he was relaxed. Removing the cigarette, he bowed his head and said a silent prayer for himself.

Confident that his business was done here, he took a final drag on his cigarette, nipped the remains and flicked the stub away. Then, taking a last look around, he turned on his heels and began the stroll back to his car.

- ooOoo -

CHAPTER ONE

22nd November.

The relentless ringing of the bedside telephone snapped Barry Newstead from his dreams.

For a brief moment, still half-asleep, somewhere in the depths of his consciousness something was telling him it was the alarm clock, and he was about to smack a hand over the off button when his brain jumped into gear and he realised what the persistent noise was.

Grunting, he forced open his eyes, raised his head from the pillow and looked at the back of his bedside cabinet where the small alarm clock rested.

The green back-lit digits were fuzzy without his reading glasses.

Narrowing his eyes, he could pick out a blurred 22:18 on the clock face LED. He had only been asleep for ten minutes but it felt like hours.

The phone continued to ring and, more asleep than awake, he fumbled around in the dark for the handset. Finally his pudgy fingers coiled around it and he snatched it out of its holder.

Beside him, Susan, his partner, moaned. It had disturbed her too.

Propping himself up on an elbow, he thumbed the receive button. "Hello?"

"Barry, is that you?"

He'd heard that voice before. It seemed a little brittle now, but he thought he could place it from his past.

"Yeah, who's that?"

"Sorry, have I woken you?"

He was just about to swear and give back the affirmative answer when he checked himself.

"No you're okay, I'd only just dropped off."

"Barry, its Jeffery Howson. Do you remember me?"

He could recall the name but he couldn't conjure up a face.

"We were in CID together at district remember?"

A blurry vision flashed inside his head but just as quickly disappeared. The memory was faded. Suddenly the cogs in Barry's brain began whirring, snatching him completely out from his slumber. He was intrigued.

16

"I need to meet with you." The voice broke off. There was a couple of seconds' silence, then the cracked voice continued, "I wouldn't have rung you but it's important, really important."

"Do you know what time it is?"

"I don't mean right now, but I could do with seeing you as soon as possible. I need to get something off my chest. Something I've been holding on to for a long time and I need to speak to someone I can trust."

Another pause. Barry could hear deep wheezing at the other end - a throaty, rasping sound.

The voice came back on, "They tell me you've gone back in the job as a civvie?"

"Yeah I'm a civilian investigator with Barnwell Major Investigation Team. Been there almost six months."

"Yeah, that's what I was told. That's why I need to see you. I remember what you were like in the job; I know I can trust you."

That was the second time he'd used the word trust.

Another short pause as the man gasped for a breath. Then he said, "I need to tell you about the murder of Lucy Blake-Hall back in nineteen-eighty-three. The wrong man was convicted and I know who really killed her. I don't want to say too much over the phone. I need to meet with you."

Now fully awake, tightening his grip on the handset, Barry made a mental note of the arrangements the former detective outlined for the next day and repeated them back to him.

"Do you know Barry, this is such a relief. You're the first person I've told about this. I have carried the guilt of what I have done for far too long and it's time to set the record straight. Especially the fact that I know that Lucy's killer is still free." A short coughing fit followed and then the voice added, "Barry, do you ever think about dying?"

Before he had time to answer, the line went dead.

Barry hung onto the phone for a few seconds, listening to the soft burr of the dialling tone, his eyes studying the gloom of the bedroom while his thoughts mulled over the call. Setting the handset back in its cradle, he reached across and switched on his bedside light. He knew he was going to have difficulty getting back to sleep.

* * * *

23rd November.

Pushing himself back in his seat, Barry Newstead watched as Susan Siddons, all petite, five feet of her, made her way back to him between the knot of people who were queuing at the bar.

It still amazed him that at fifty-one, despite giving birth and indulging in such an unhealthy lifestyle over the years, she still managed to hold onto her teenage size ten figure. And from the way some of the men glanced at her as she brushed past them, she also hadn't lost any of her ability to turn heads.

He knew he shouldn't be surprised. After all, it had been her dainty figure and natural beauty that had first attracted him all those years ago.

Looking at her now, weaving between the small throng towards him, it seemed she had hardly changed since that first day they had bumped into one another. True, her hair was now artificially coloured and cut a lot shorter, and there was a slight kink to the bridge of her nose, the result of a beating from a previous partner, but it didn't detract from her prettiness.

He couldn't help but feel smug. He considered himself so fortunate to get a second chance with Susan. Fate had brought them back together, he had repeatedly told himself over the past few months; she had been a key witness in a recent case and it had given them the opportunity to rekindle their friendship.

As she neared she threw him a beaming smile, followed by one of her mischievous winks.

She's caught me; he had been eyeing her far too long.

That smile of hers brought the memories flooding back.

He'd first met Susan in 1976. He had been twenty-two at the time and had just entered CID as an aide. She was eighteen, embarking upon a career as a journalist with the local paper and had turned up at a stabbing he had been called to. She had dogged him for the story. It had not just been Susan's prettiness and persistence which had captured him, but she has also had an inner quality which he had found hard to resist. He gave her the story and she had become a regular contact with whom he shared information. They formed a clandestine partnership. He would drop a snippet her way or give background to some of the court cases he was involved in and in return she'd give him a lead on a suspect, which would help him clear up local crime.

They soon began to meet in pubs to swap stories, until one night when they'd both had too much to drink and they had ended up back at her flat. From there, the relationship had changed to one which became intimate and sexual.

The first time it had occurred, Barry's conscience had been pricked. He had been about to get married and for months thereafter he had tried to avoid Susan, dealing with her enquiries over the phone.

But they did meet again and the inevitable happened. Barry had been dealing with a nasty rape of a young mum. The rapist had forced his way into the twenty-one year old woman's home and attacked her in front of her two year old son.

Making her own enquiries for the newspaper, Susan had got a lead on the suspect - a fifteen year old, living two streets away from his victim, who had been exposing himself to young girls from his school.

Susan had helped Barry crack the case. They had celebrated their triumph in the pub and after closing time they had jumped into bed together again back at her flat.

For the next couple of years they bounced in and out of each other's lives, though neither of them wanted the relationship to develop any further.

Then, right out of the blue, in 1979 she had telephoned him and made it clear she no longer wanted to see him again. She had met someone else.

Her phone call was a relief. It gave Barry the chance to throw everything back into his marriage, though from a discreet distance he hadn't been able to resist keeping track of her life. He learned of every one of her relationships with men, none seemed to last for longer than six months. Reports came across his desk that she was drinking far too heavily and there had been occasions when police had been called to domestic incidents with some of her partners. She had a habit of falling for the wrong kind of guy.

Barry had also discovered that she had given birth to a daughter and Social Services had been involved because of her regular drunkenness.

In 1985 he had dropped back into her life after a fashion. On an evening shift, the duty sergeant had requested he should join him at her address, uniform had attended as a result of a 999 call. Susan had suffered a vicious beating at the hands of her latest boyfriend.

She was a sorrowful sight and he had offered to take her to casualty for treatment. There, he had stood guard outside the cubicle, listening as the doctor checked her over.

"You're going to be just fine Miss Siddons. We'll clean you up and then send you for an X-Ray," he had heard the doctor say, and then he had caught, "Now if I can just take down a few personal details."

She had hesitated when the doctor mentioned her daughter. It wasn't much of a hesitation, but it was long enough to arouse his suspicions. He had whipped aside the curtain and locked onto her gaze. She had tried to glance away but the look on her face instantly told him he was right.

He had a daughter. Carol was six years old.

The news had rocked him. Speechless and dumbfounded, he had sat beside Susan in the hospital cubicle, doing his best to focus on what she was saying.

She confessed she had ended their relationship because she was pregnant with his child and didn't want to ruin his marriage.

After Susan had sobered up, been given treatment and discharged from hospital, she had apologised and made it clear no one would ever find out.

She had kept her word and allowed him to move on and he became a father for the second time when his wife Jean gave birth to Sarah.

He made regular appearances in Carol's life, supporting her and Susan financially as much as he could, and he always bought presents for birthdays and Christmas. But he was never a father to her like he was to Sarah and knew he would have to carry that millstone around his neck until his dying day - especially after the tragedy.

Carol had gone missing on 12th October 1993; the date was ingrained in his memory. She had sneaked away from the Social Services residential care home, where she had been placed and had simply disappeared without trace.

Because of her background history, every officer who had picked up the file had written Carol off as a runaway, believing that she had fled the area to make her living off the streets. Barry had thought differently. He covertly monitored the case every day for weeks and had picked up the Missing from Home File once uniform had filed it away. Behind the scenes he had worked on it, even defying threats from his Detective Inspector to 'leave it alone' because it was not a CID job. After eighteen months of secretive investigation, he had got no nearer to solving Carol's disappearance. Deep down, he always guessed that his daughter was dead, but he had never shared his suspicions with Susan.

So when the news came of her death, it was not a surprise to him, though the circumstances of her death were.

Five months ago, Susan had got back in touch and told him their daughter's body had been unearthed. She had been brutally murdered and buried in a shallow grave.

Hearing the news had made Barry focus on his life for the first time in a long while. He had been retired from the force for almost six years and in that time had lost his wife to a stroke. With his second daughter married, the past four years had been boring and lonely. He needed to get back into the job; get involved in the murder enquiry and catch his daughter's killer.

Barry contacted his favourite CID protégé, Hunter Kerr - now a Detective Sergeant - heading up one of the squads of Barnwell Major Investigation Team and persuaded Hunter to take him on as a civilian investigator so he could immerse himself in the case. After three months, he had finally discovered her fate. Carol had been the first victim of the infamous 'Dearne Valley Demon.'

He and Susan had buried Carol in a proper grave and supported one another in their grief. Two months ago she had moved into his home and they had begun the slow process of rebuilding their lives.

"Are you sure we're at the right pub?" Sue asked as she picked up her bottle of orange juice and slid into her seat.

"Definitely. The George and Dragon he said to me. It's where everyone in CID meets whenever they're on evenings. Or at least it was in my day."

"And he definitely said he wanted to talk to you about the murder of Lucy Blake-Hall?"

"Yeah he said something about the wrong person being convicted. Why, do you remember it?"

Susan pondered the question. "Hmm," she mused through pursed lips, and continued. "I've forgotten a lot of the finer detail, but I recall the story. It was a case I followed religiously back in the early eighties. I used to follow our crime correspondent around like a little lap dog. I'd pick up all the crime stuff when he was off or on holiday and that was one of the crime stories of the year for the Chronicle." Susan took a sip of her orange through a straw and then nursed the bottle. "From what I remember, Lucy was in her early twenties, married with a kid, a daughter I believe. She was having an affair with a local guy - I can't remember his name now. From what I recall she was last seen arguing with him outside a pub in the town centre and then no one saw her after that. Husband reported her missing, and within days they had tracked down her lover, arrested him and charged him with her murder, but he pleaded not guilty and there was a long court case. He made allegations he had been fitted up by the police but the jury found him guilty. That's it in a nutshell. He got life but he might be out by now, what with sentencing these days." She took another sip at her drink, never taking her eyes away from his. "One thing about the case," she continued, still clenching the straw between her teeth, "And which kept the story running in the Chronicle for quite some time, was the fact that they never found Lucy's body.

Barry slowly nodded his head, "Interesting." He took another look at his watch. "Howson should have been here over half an hour ago. He definitely said half twelve to me."

"Did you say this Jeffery whatever his name is is retired?"

"Jeffery Howson," Barry reminded her. "Yeah, long time ago. He'll be well into his sixties now. He was a senior detective when I went to district CID. He was on another team so I didn't have that much to do with him and can't really remember that much about him but he can obviously remember me."

"Weren't you involved in the Lucy Blake-Hall case, then?"

"No, I had a couple of years away from the department. I went on attachment to Headquarters Serious Crime Squad for a few years." Barry picked up his beer and eyed it. There was a quarter of a pint left. He drained it in several swallows, then set it down, letting out a satisfied sigh as he wiped the residue from his thick, bushy moustache.

"Do you know I wish you'd shave that thing off, it would take years off you."

He set down his empty glass. "This morning you were having a go at me, saying I could do with losing a few pounds. Are you fed up with me already?"

"Now we're an item, I'm going to lick you into shape so you can keep up with me." She twinkled her hazel eyes at him. "Either that, or I'll trade you in for a younger model." She reached across and mussed a hand through his dark mop of unruly hair.

He shrugged away from her and picked up his empty glass. "I think you'd best remember your place, young lady" he retorted with a smirk. "I'm going to get another beer. It doesn't look as though Jeffery Howson is going to show up." Pushing his 6' 1" seventeen stone frame up from the chair he added, "I have to say he didn't sound too good on the phone last night."

He suddenly recalled the chilling last words Jeffery Howson had said before hanging up.

"I hope nothing's happened to him," he mumbled as he made for the bar.

- ooOoo -

CHAPTER TWO

DAY ONE OF THE INVESTIGATION: 24th November.

Hunter Kerr eyed the paperwork littering his workspace. He didn't like it when his desk was messy.

He had arrived in the office early with the intentions of making a dent in the stack of overdue reports, but he'd been here an hour already and somehow hadn't quite clicked into gear even with two cups of strong, sweet, tea inside him. The third cup he'd brewed two minutes ago rested in front of him. He dropped in two lumps of sugar and stirred the steaming contents with the end of his biro. Then he sucked the residue from its top and returned to the task in hand.

Leaning back in his seat, pushing a hand through his dark brown hair, he read over the last sentence he had penned and then glanced up to the ceiling in search of inspiration. He was really struggling with piecing together his report on the sudden death of the young woman whose body had been found in the derelict cellar of a disused pub three days earlier. The main problem was the sheer lack of detail on the front page of the 'Report of Death' form before him.

There was certainly no lack of specifics in the 'Circumstances of Death' section on the reverse of the document. He'd been able to complete that part quite easily. A small team of builders carrying out renovation work had discovered her lying face down on the concrete floor, immediately realising from the bloated face and pungent smell that she wasn't sleeping rough. The foreman had dialled 999 straight away and, except for where one of them had kicked through the bottom panel of the cellar door, they hadn't disturbed anything.

Although he was still awaiting results from toxicology samples taken during the post-mortem, all the indications were that she had died of a heroin overdose. At least a dozen empty syringes surrounded her body. Added to that, the numerous discarded foil wrappings and a couple of spoons which showed signs of being heated over a naked flame, clearly set the scene that the cellar was being used by addicts as a shooting den and she had accidentally ended her life there.

For a brief second, he recalled the first images he had of her, lying amid the detritus of a damp old pub cellar, in the early stages of decomposition and with bits of her missing - vermin had begun to nibble at her purple-coloured bloated flesh. He closed his eyes and shook his head, then returned to focus on the file.

The only reason Hunter had been landed with completing the report was because the Pathologist had picked up on an injury to her right cheek; there was some bruising and the cheekbone was cracked. The cause of that injury was inconclusive, though Hunter had pointed out that she had been found lying face down on hard concrete ground. If the toxicology report came back that it was a heroin overdose, which had caused her premature death, then he could clear its 'suspicious death' status and leave it in the hands of the Coroner.

Before that though, he had to summarise an account of his investigation and that was currently proving difficult because of the sheer lack of information. The sections detailing who she was or where she lived were still blank. Everyone who had attended the scene and viewed the corpse, himself included, had initially thought that the body was that of a young teenage girl, but the autopsy had revealed that the petite form was that of a woman aged between late teens and early twenties. And the fact that she had grey-blue eyes, shoulder length light brown hair, a good set of teeth and the initials 'J.J,' together with a pink butterfly, tattooed upon the lower part of her neck, between her shoulder blades was the sum total of everything they had in terms of identification. There was nothing on the body, or in the cellar where she had been found, which revealed who she was. The Scenes of Crime Officer had done his best to fingerprint the cadaver at the mortuary but it had been the ends of the fingers which rats had nibbled first, making the process extremely difficult. Except for the recent tattoos, all he had to go on to establish her identity, were three items. He looked at the clear plastic exhibit bags at the top of his pending tray. First there was the torn photograph. He'd found that, together with the Christmas card, in the rear pocket of her jeans. The half-picture featured the head and shoulders of a man who looked to be in his early thirties, clean shaven, with thinning dark hair. He thought the face seemed familiar. The Christmas card appeared to be an old one, folded and heavily creased. Inside, it had been simply signed 'Mr X.'

Hunter wondered if Mr X was the guy in the photo.

Then he'd found the worn brass key in one of her front pockets, which he guessed gave access to her home, though looking at the state of the key, and given the circumstances of her discovery, he thought that address was more than likely a sub-let room in a run-down rented house.

He had done a lot of leg-work these past two days and realised zilch for his efforts. He'd reacquainted himself with ex-colleagues and a number of local junkies from his drug squad days, but they hadn't been able to help with either finding her home or giving her a name. And he had uniform trying to track down any dossers who used the derelict pub, but they had so far come up with nothing. He'd decided that if he hadn't got anywhere by the end of the day, he was going to speak to his contact at The Barnwell Chronicle and ask her to run a piece as a last-ditch attempt to identify the body.

The thwacking sound and the sudden appearance of a newspaper landing on top of his paperwork made Hunter jump. He looked up to see his colleague DC Grace Marshall, her slim frame dressed in a light grey trouser suit striding past. He had been so absorbed in the drafting of his narrative that he neither heard nor saw his working partner breeze into the office.

Barry Newstead followed in her wake, looking rumpled as ever. He had his jacket slung over his shoulder, allowing Hunter the view of a white shirt straining over his ample belly. The tail of one side had escaped from the waistband of his trousers and it was open at the collar, from where the two ends of a striped tie dangled at an odd angle from its untidy knot.

As he switched his gaze from one to the other, Hunter couldn't help but smile to himself. They were so far apart when it came to dress and style, and yet complemented each other with their ebullient character and respective work ethic.

"You're a bit of a dark horse, Detective Sergeant Kerr!" Barry arrowed a finger towards the newspaper on Hunter's desk, and shot him a wink as he sucked in his stomach, squeezed himself around his desk and lowered himself onto his chair.

Hunter snatched up the copy of the local weekly Barnwell Chronicle, which had already been opened to one of the inside pages. There, in full colour, he was pictured proudly holding before him one of his recent paintings. Below it was the headline 'A Brush with the Law'. He could feel himself colouring up. A month ago, his journalist contact at the local paper had interviewed him about his recent success within the art world. Two of his seascape oil paintings had been selected for The Mall Galleries 'Royal Society of Marine Artists' exhibition. It had been the most defining moment of his artistic career to date and had brought him an invite to showcase his work with a leading London gallery.

Barry said, "Detective Sergeant Hunter Kerr uses the long arm of the law for more than just collaring criminals."

Hunter caught Barry's smug grin but chose to ignore the gibe. Instead he silently read the opening paragraph of the article.

"Fancy a cuppa?" Grace said, as she edged towards the set of filing cabinets at the far wall, where the office kettle and array of mugs sat. She picked up the kettle, checked there was enough water in it and flicked its switch. Looking back over her shoulder, she offered, "Take no notice of him, he's jealous. I'm very proud of you Hunter. At least someone else has a bit of class in this office."

Hunter lifted up his gaze and caught Grace pulling her highlighted corkscrew curls away from her flawless tawny skin, exposing her high cheekbones. He noted that the summer freckles, peppering her cheeks and spanning the bridge of her nose, were now starting to fade.

Barry's grin widened and he shot out his tongue towards her. "Give over with your brown-nosing wench and get that coffee made."

"Yo's saying that because I is black, or because I is woman, Mr Newstead?" Grace returned, mimicking her father's Jamaican patois and fixing Barry an exaggerated piercing look.

Barry returned a single middle finger salute. "Swivel on that Detective Constable Marshall."

It was her turn to smile. Then she returned to making the drinks, pouring steaming hot water into three mugs.

Hunter shook the tabloid straight and quickly scanned the couple of paragraphs which made up the remainder of the article. His initial embarrassment had subsided; now he beamed inside. He folded the paper and set it aside. He would read it and digest it again tonight when he got home and had more time.

Grace settled a steaming mug down in front of Hunter. "Oh and there's a full-page spread on page five in there about the 'Lady in the Lake' murder. They've covered the case really well."

"I bet you're really pleased with that result, aren't you?" said Hunter, who caught the glint in Grace's eyes as she slumped down into the swivel chair at her desk opposite. He was referring to the guilty verdict given to the brutal murderers of a 23 year old Asian girl whose bloated and battered body had been discovered at the bottom of Barnwell Lake three months ago.

When the job had been called in, Grace had been 'acting' DS while he had been away on a long weekend break with his family and she had taken control of her first murder investigation.

He remembered how admirably she had coped during his absence, both with the investigation and with being in charge of the team, especially given her own personal problems at the time. There had been many times since then when he had lain awake at night, re-running the case in his head, wondering how he would have coped had one of his children been abducted by a known serial-killer. He knew she was still seeing the Force Counsellor, and still suffering the occasional panic attack. And yet outwardly, like now, she continued to display such remarkable resolve and resilience.

She would have made a good actress.

"Chuffed to bits. The judge gave me a commendation as well."

"And rightly so, you deserve it. I hope the gaffer's said something to you?"

"He has actually. Told me a couple of days ago that he'd put me forward for a Chief Superintendent's commendation."

"I can see we're gonna have to get the joiners in to make some wider doors for that big head of yours."

"Huh! Hark who's talking. At least I don't have to suck up to journalists to get an article done about myself." She licked the tip of a forefinger and struck an invisible mark in the air.

Hunter laughed and picked up the tabloid again, flipping back the sheets to page five, where he found a full-page spread outlining the background of their 'Lady in the Lake' investigation, and the subsequent court case, together with a series of photographs depicting the offenders and the scene of the murder. He began to pick his way through the article; he wanted to ensure that the crime reporter had given due credit to the painstaking work carried out by the MIT team on what had been another difficult case.

In the background, one of the phones rang. He heard Grace answer - she had beaten Barry to it despite juggling a mug of coffee. Within a few seconds her voice became excited - the way it did when something was breaking.

He lifted his eyes from the newspaper and watched her making notes on a pad, the handset clamped between ear and shoulder.

A couple of minutes later she set the receiver back on its cradle.

"That was the duty inspector. Uniform are at a suspicious death. A woman made a 999 call ten minutes ago. She's turned up at her father's and found him dead and thinks his house has been broken into. Mike and Bully have just been diverted to the scene."

Grace was referring to the other two members of his team, Mike Sampson and Tony Bullars. Hunter set down the newspaper.

"Got any other details?"

"The address they're going to is listed to a Jeffery Howson. The Inspector believes he's a retired cop."

Barry Newstead launched himself out of his chair, banging his knees on the edge of his desk in the process. He made a pained face. Rubbing the tops of his knees vigorously, he said loudly, "Bloody hell, I never expected to hear that name again so quickly." Then on a softer note, he added, "Mind if I tag along? If this is the Jeffery Howson I think it is, then there's something I need to tell you."

* * * * *

They dashed to the scene on the outskirts of Barnwell, using a series of side streets to avoid heavy traffic on the main thoroughfares. From the back seat of the unmarked CID car, Barry gave Hunter and Grace a potted version of the phone call he had received two days previously from the man who had stated he was retired detective Jeffery Howson.

"Are you sure he said that?" enquired Hunter. He drove one-handed, his other hand flexed around the gear stick, constantly changing up and down as he sped through one small estate after another, weaving between tightly parked cars.

"Positive. I know I was dead to the world when the phone went but I can remember most of what he told me. He wasn't on long anyway. He definitely said he wanted to tell me something about the murder of Lucy Blake-Hall from way back in nineteen-eighty-three and that the wrong man had been convicted."

"And you were supposed to meet him yesterday?" said Grace.

"Yes at the George and Dragon in Wentworth. He said to meet him there at twelve o'clock. I went with Sue and we waited until half two but he never showed up. If this is the same Jeffery Howson, and I can't believe that there'll be two retired cops with the same name in the same location, then I now know why he didn't turn up."

Alarm bells were beginning to sound in Hunter's head. "And it also means that there could be more to that phone call."

A hundred yards in front, Hunter spotted the turning which would take them to the road they wanted. He dropped down a gear and began to indicate right.

The cul-de-sac, which held less than a dozen 1930s style semi-detached houses, had already been cordoned off by the time Hunter, Grace and Barry arrived. Blue and white Police Crime Scene tape fastened between two gate posts stretched across the quiet street. It was a big area which had been isolated, but Hunter knew it was better to start off with a large cordon, which can be reduced, rather than a small one which might need expanding, and which could also get contaminated in the interim.

Someone had done their job right, he thought as he slowed the car and glanced around.

Up ahead, highly visible in a yellow coat, a female Police Officer was standing guard by another barrier of plastic ribbon. An inner cordon had also been established.

Pulling into the kerb and switching off the engine, Hunter took an even longer look at the surroundings. He had not been on this street for years. It was a route he had frequently taken back in his uniform beat days when he had needed some peace and solitude, and he recalled how this road led onto a series of footpaths through a ten acre patch of much-used woodland, which was also the site of an ancient Roman ridge. It was a popular place for dog-walkers and metal detecting treasure hunters. If this was a murder, he thought to himself as he pushed open the car door, they were certainly going to have their work cut out, given the number of people passing regularly through this location.

He studied the parked up cars already here. One of the department's unmarked Ford Focuses, two marked police vehicles, a white SOCO van and a crimson coloured Lexus on personal plates, which he knew belonged to Forensic Pathologist Lizzie McCormack, lined the road outside 12 Woodlands View.

As his eyes again studied the scene, he could see from the activity half way along the street that uniform had already started house-to-house enquiries.

Hunter went to the boot and took out three white forensic suits and three sets of shoe covers. Then, locking the car, he strode towards the scene.

As they approached the inner cordon the uniformed Officer took a step forward in an attempt to head them off.

Issuing her a 'well done' smile, Hunter pulled out his warrant card, held it up long enough for her to get a good look, and then sidestepped her and ducked beneath the tape.

Grace and Barry followed, falling in beside him.

By the gateway of number 12, another high visibility garbed officer stood sentry-like. Hunter flashed his warrant card again and the three walked down the driveway to the side door. It had been wedged open and Hunter immediately noted the damage to the glass panel in the upper section. The corner closest to the key-lock had been smashed, and fragments of glass lay scattered over a portion of the tiled kitchen floor inside. A yellow coloured Scenes of Crime marker - number one - had been placed in the middle of the broken glass and a series of strategically placed forensic foot plates snaked their way into the depths of the house, from where Hunter could hear muffled voices. He recalled the earlier phone call Grace had taken back in the office, especially the part about the daughter believing that the house had been broken into, and he conjured up an image of a hand reaching through the shattered panel and turning the key to let themselves in.

Before stepping inside, Hunter pulled on his forensic suit and shoe covers and slipped on latex gloves.

Grace and Barry donned their own protective clothing and followed him in.

The side door opened into the kitchen, a small area with fitted floor and wall units in dark oak, many of which had lost their polished lustre. Decades-old green and white tiles decorated the walls.

Pushing open an inner door, Hunter traversed over the reinforced foot plates in the direction of the voices.

The lounge was where all the activity was taking place.

The moment he stepped into the room, his sense of smell was immediately assaulted by the fetid and musty mix of stale urine and tobacco. Pinching his nose, he quickly took in the surroundings. The room was untidy and drab. Artexed walls, which he guessed were originally cream in colour, had become stained a dirty brown, and the mahogany furniture, dating from the 1980s, looked tired. Heavy drapes partially drawn across the window blocked out most of the natural light, only adding to the gloom of the room. The fireplace had been fashioned from a patchwork of Yorkshire stone, which spanned across from one alcove into another to make up a low unit, on which perched a large flat screen TV. It was the only modern item Hunter had so far spotted. What did take his eye was the print of the painting 'The Chinese Girl' often referred to as 'The Green Lady,' which hung above the fireplace. He remembered the same print above his own parent's fireplace during the seventies. He had not seen one of these for years and knew that this was now an iconic piece of art.

This is a place which has seen better days, Hunter said to himself.

DC Mike Sampson was the first person Hunter spotted, hands locked into his sides, his squat rotund shape stretching the fabric of his forensic over-suit. He acknowledged their arrival with a nod.

He wasn't the only person in the lounge. Professor Lizzie McCormack was in crouching position, knees bent, taking her weight on the balls of her feet, and examining the head and neck of a lifeless man slumped in an armchair to the left of the fireplace.

As Hunter eyed a dark stain covering the crotch of the man's trousers, he realised why he'd been greeted by the strong stench of urine. Next to the body was an overturned low table and an upturned ashtray, the contents of which had scattered everywhere across the patterned carpet, which explained the tobacco smell. Also on the floor, close by the side of the armchair was the handset of a cordless phone. Its cradle was several metres away and the phone lead had been ripped from the wall socket. Strategically placed crime scene markers earmarked everything Hunter could see. There was little doubt that a major scuffle had taken place.

The dead man had an emaciated look; the facial features were waxen and stretched tight over the skull. Every outline of the bone structure was evident beneath the yellowing flesh.

Wide open eyes were set deep inside dark ringed sockets. The shirt and jumper he was wearing hung off his thin, frail body.

Hunter's initial thought was that the man looked like one of the Belsen victims. The body looked to have been dead for some considerable time and yet Hunter knew that Barry had last spoken with this guy only two days previously.

He also recalled Grace saying the deceased was a retired detective. If that was the case, then this looked like someone who had been out of the game for a long, long time.

"Lung cancer," said Mike Sampson.

Hunter shot his colleague a glance.

"Mind reader eh?" Mike returned a rueful look. "I saw the way you were looking at him. I thought exactly the same when I first saw him. And you can obviously see the cause," he said, pointing at the cigarette butts spilt across the floor.

Mike stepped around the pathologist who was still scrutinising the head and neck of the body. She was peering closely into the eyes of the cadaver.

He continued. "When me and Bully arrived, his daughter was still here. Bully's taken her home by the way she only lives in the next street. He's getting a statement from her about the last time she saw him, and background stuff."

Hunter nodded. "Has she touched anything?"

"No everything's as she found it. She was with her daughter and she pulled her out of the house and rang us straight away on her mobile. She was in a bit of a state, as you can imagine, so Bully's taken her home. Before he took her there though, she told us that it looked as though someone's searched through his stuff." Mike pointed to several books lying across the floor next to a bookshelf. Then he indicated a writing bureau. The writing flap was down and various papers and envelopes were strewn across it, some had fallen onto the floor. "She said she had left the place tidy on Saturday afternoon."

"Does she know if anything's been taken?"

Mike shrugged. "To be honest Hunter, I don't think she's had time to check. We'll have to bring her back here once we've got things sorted and the body's out of the way."

"And she's confirmed that this is her father Jeffery Howson, and that he's a retired detective?" Hunter looked the body over once more. He didn't recognise him. He was thinking he must have already left the job by the time he joined CID. He switched his gaze to Barry, who responded, "Hair's a lot thinner, and he's obviously lost a lot of weight, but I recognise him from my days at District."

"Daughter says he retired as a DC. She can't remember exactly when that was but believes it's over ten years ago now," continued Mike Sampson. "He was diagnosed with lung cancer four months ago - terminal."

"That's not the cause of this man's death though," said Lizzie McCormack, pushing herself upright. Slim and petite, with grey hair and spectacles she bore an uncanny resemblance to the actress Geraldine McEwan and as a result had gained the nickname Miss Marple. "This man's eyes are very badly bloodshot and there is some evidence of trauma around the mouth and nose. I'll be able to tell you a lot more once I've done the post-mortem, but my initial findings are that he has died as a result of asphyxiation. It looks very much like he has been suffocated by someone, or something was used to smother his nose and mouth." The pathologist paused and glanced down around her. Her gaze settled upon a brown cushion on the floor, a foot or so to the side of the chair. It lay beside the upended low table. She stabbed a finger towards it. "I'd have that checked out by forensics. That just may be the weapon." Lizzie turned back to face them. "Oh, I've also found what appears to be extensive bruising to the wrists. Looks as though he's put up a bit of a struggle while being restrained. With a bit of luck, there might be contact DNA from the perpetrator. Will you ensure his hands are bagged and sealed?"

Hunter nodded. "So, am I right in thinking that you're indicating he was held tight by the wrists while being suffocated or smothered?"

"Eloquently summed up, DS Kerr."

"So at least two people carried this out?"

"Nail on the head again. My my, we'll make a detective of you yet."

"I'll take that as a compliment."

"You and I go back too far for it be anything else, DS Kerr." She delivered him a cheery smile as she eased herself up straight. Then, glancing at her wristwatch, she continued. "I've taken an initial core body temperature reading and that indicates to me that he has been dead at least twenty four hours. Once again, I can be a lot more accurate once I do the PM. And if you manage to get things sorted and can get the body down to the morgue inside the next three hours, I can start that late this afternoon." She snapped off her latex gloves, slipped them into her jacket pocket and returned a sideways glance as she made for the exit. "Nasty way to die you know suffocation. Like drowning. Panic, lots of panic. That's what the victim endures. Terrible way to go," she finished, shaking her head as she stepped through into the kitchen and then out of sight.

* * * * *

The disposable shoe covers Hunter was wearing rustled on the linoleum covered corridor as he headed towards the post-mortem suite of the Medico Legal Centre. As he pushed through the double slap-doors into the walk-in freezer area the familiar smell of formaldehyde greeted him, despite the automated deodoriser.

A mortuary technician was just offloading a male body from a gurney into the minus twenty degrees centigrade fridge. Hunter spotted the large sewn-up Y section incision extending from the chest down to the pubic bone of the naked cadaver, a clear sign it had undergone a recent post-mortem. One half of the face was gone - no jaw, no cheek and no eye socket, just a dark mush.

"What happened to him?"

"Suicide. Blew half his head off with a shotgun," the green garbed technician answered as he slid the metal tray supporting the corpse onto a set of rubberised rollers inside one section of the fridge.

"What a mess. Must have been desperate?" Hunter added, taking one last look at the grisly self-inflicted injury as he slipped past.

"Farmer about to be evicted from his farm, I understand. Told his wife he was just going to clean out one of the barns. Must have been a hell of a shock for her, finding him like that."

The tray made a metallic clang as it hit the back of the freezer. As Hunter pressed through a second set of doors leading into the main cutting room, he just caught the sucking sound the solid steel fridge door made as it fastened onto rubber seals, ensuring the body remained airtight until the undertakers arrived to take it away.

The double-doors swung shut behind him. The smell was even stronger in here. He knew that the metallic cloying stench was coming from the stale blood of that last post-mortem, which hadn't yet completely drained away from the hosing down of the static gurney.

The Senior Investigating Officer appointed to the case, Detective Superintendent Michael Robshaw, was already there, with Scenes of Crime Supervisor Duncan Wroe. Before leaving 12 Woodlands View Hunter had contacted the Police Communications room asking for the pair to be updated and requesting that they meet him at the Medico Legal Centre. He had left Grace in charge of the scene, to liaise with forensics, gather the exhibits and pull together evidence, especially to determine if there were any witnesses.

Pathologist Professor Lizzie McCormack was also present. In her green scrubs, she was just snapping on latex gloves in preparation for her examination. Jeffery Howson had already been stripped and now lay on a metal cutting table.

She acknowledged Hunter's arrival with a nod and then in her soft Scottish brogue, began her preamble as she bent over the table scrutinising the corpse. Name, age, height and weight were dictated in clear voice picked up by the in-built recording system.

Hunter was not surprised when the pathologist announced that the body of the retired detective weighed just 7st 8lbs. He could see almost every bone protruding through the yellow waxen flesh; the cancer had eaten away at him.

The pathologist began her examination at the head, hooking an arm beneath the neck and raising it from its table prop.
With her free hand she pinched back the nose, pulled at the lips and ran a finger around inside the mouth. She swabbed inside the nostrils and the mouth and dropped the swabs into clear plastic exhibit phials.

"It's just as I surmised from my initial examination of this body at the house. Clear signs of trauma around the mouth and nose and I've swabbed some trace evidence of fibres from those areas. He's bitten down on his tongue as well, most probably as he's struggled."

She moved onto the arms, down to the hands, removing the plastic forensic bags which had encased them, and individually checked each finger, taking several swabs beneath the nails.

"Can you photograph these please?" she said as she raised the corpse's stick-thin wrist.

Duncan Wroe had been hovering behind Lizzie McCormack, taking the swabs from her, scribbling on the labels of each of the samples she had handed to him and then stacking them on a trolley beside him. He reached down to a lower shelf, snatched up his Nikon digital camera with its macro lens and began shooting off a series of frames as the professor rotated the left forearm.

She followed by picking up the right arm and repeating the process.

"There are clear signs of haemorrhaging into the soft tissue of both right and left lower forearms, especially around the wrist." She pointed out a series of deep purple patterns, which stood out because of the paleness of the flesh around the left wrist.

"Looks as though he put up a hell of a struggle?" Hunter said.

"I thought that myself at first, but these contusions are ever more evident because this man was taking Warfarin. I saw in his notes that he had a heart condition, which was controlled by the drug. The least little knock can look as though he's been in a bar-room brawl. These marks, exaggerated though they may be, look like finger grip marks. He has definitely had his wrists pressed down hard probably against the arms of the chair he was sitting in."

She picked up another two swabs and washed them over the bruised areas.

"There might be trace evidence of DNA if the offender wasn't wearing gloves," she announced, sealing the swabs and handing them over to Duncan Wroe.

For the next hour and forty minutes Hunter watched Lizzie methodically going about her job. Firstly, with a precision steel scalpel, making the standard Y shaped incision into the cadaver's chest, down through the stomach and finishing in the pubic bone region, this enabled her to crack apart the rib cage, providing access to the internal organs. She removed and inspected the heart and lungs carefully, weighed them, sliced into them and examined them again before dropping them into a bucket for a final analysis later. Throughout this, in her soft Scottish voice, she continued with her autopsy dictation.

Part-way into the dissection the removal and the cutting opening of the stomach provided a surprise and significant revelation.

Initially the vile stench caught them unawares and caused each of them to take a hurried step back.

It was some moments before Professor McCormack looked into the contents, but then she cried out, "My my, what have we got here?" Between thumb and forefinger she brought out an inch-long object. It looked to be metal, but was covered in sticky yellow globules of slime. She wiped it into the palm of her gloved hand and then held the object up to the light.

It was a small brass key.

"This was something he didn't want anyone to find."

She passed it to Duncan.

Her blue-grey eyes shifted between Hunter and the Detective Superintendent. "Now if I was a detective, I would be thinking that key had something significant to do with his death," she added, flashing them a smile.

She completed the autopsy at the head, slicing into the lower part of the neck and removing the trachea, before finally removing and examining the brain.

Hunter had watched this so many times over the years and yet he still got a sense of morbid fascination.

Two and a quarter hours had passed before the pathologist set the scalpel back down onto her tool trolley and snapped off one of her surgical gloves.

"To sum up gentlemen, the post-mortem has uncovered petechial haemorrhaging to the eyes and there is determined damage to the external airways around the mouth and nose. Fibres removed from the nasal passages and from the victim's mouth leave me to conclude that asphyxiation is the cause of death, as a result of him being smothered with a cloth covered article. And the injuries to the wrists lead me into believing that you are looking for at least two killers. He was definitely held down while being smothered."

Lizzie McCormack turned, peeled off her other latex glove and dropped the pair into a yellow biohazard bin as she retreated to her office.

Hunter looked at Detective Superintendent Michael Robshaw.

He guessed that right now their thoughts were similar. Some cruel bastard had pressed a cushion over Jeffery Howson's face until he'd stopped breathing.

Why was the retired detective killed? What is the significance of the key found in his stomach, why would he swallow it? Hunter guessed there was an inextricable link between these three questions.

* * * * *

Looking at his reflection in the bathroom mirror, Hunter smoothed a hand over his freshly shaved jaw-line, slowly rotating his head side to side, back and forth. Happy with the result, he rinsed his razor in the hand basin and then raked a comb of fingers through his receding mane.

Ten minutes previously he had been lingering in the shower longer than he normally did and with the water temperature as high as he could stand. It was always like this after post-mortems; a long hot shower was the only way he could rid himself of the smell of death.

He had confined most of his clothing to the washing machine, though his suit jacket hung outside on the clothes line, swinging in the cold late autumn breeze.

Removing the towel from his waist, he dabbed at his damp hair and then fingered his smooth chin thoughtfully. He had a flashback of the earlier post-mortem. He thought he'd seen it all during his years of investigating murders but the discovery of the key in Jeffery Howson's stomach had left him open-mouthed and it had provided a hot topic of conversation upon his return to the office, where he had met up with Grace, Mike Sampson and Tony Bullars who had scaled down their enquiries for that day.

Scenes of Crime and Forensics had made a preliminary examination of the house, but with darkness drawing in, they had secured 12 Woodlands View and planned a full search and inspection in the morning. Prior to clocking off, they'd had a scrum-down with Detective Superintendent Michael Robshaw, giving him an overview of events. Their SIO wanted them in for an 8am briefing and then he had ended with a comment that had Hunter puzzled.

Not only did he remind them he would see them all later - MIT had a curry booked at a local Indian restaurant to celebrate the outcome of the 'Lady in the Lake' case - but added that he had something important to announce.

As Hunter finished drying himself he pondered on the detective superintendent's earlier words.

It must be something of significance, Hunter told himself, *otherwise why would he have felt the need to make the comment?*

His thoughts drifted to the evening ahead.

The Major Investigation Team had been going for a curry on a regular basis since its inception two years ago, and although on this occasion it had been booked to celebrate the successful result from their last case, some of the team, himself included, suggested they invite their respective wives, husbands or partners. There had been a few objections, most notably from Barry Newstead and Mike Sampson, but the majority had agreed upon partners joining.

He smiled at his reflection. He knew it wouldn't be long into the meal before Beth would be kicking his ankles beneath the table. No matter how hard he tried to avoid it, he knew from previous gatherings that before even the first drink was consumed to toast the MIT's latest conquest, talk would soon get around to this latest murder enquiry.

Over the years he had made so many promises to Beth about avoiding such talk, but he seemed to break them almost on every occasion.

If only he could explain the buzz he experienced from doing his job.

There would be one consolation for Beth. She would be rescued part way through the evening by Grace, leaving him to engage in boy's own stuff, while his wife and work partner huddled into a corner, sharing a bottle of wine and chatting.

The sudden peal of music drifting up from the lounge downstairs snapped him out of his thoughts. He recognised the opening track of James Blunt's 'Back to Bedlam' album.

He turned back to the mirror, once again moving his head from side to side, this time checking the few grey hairs at his temples.

The years are creeping up on me, he said to himself, stroking the right side of his hair.

He flexed his pectorals and tensed his shoulders so that the muscle was rippled and defined. The regular workouts at his father's boxing gym kept him in good shape.

"Posing as usual, Hunter Kerr?"

Beth made him jump. She had crept upstairs and he hadn't heard a thing.

She slipped her arms around his naked waist and ran her smooth fingers over his taut abdomen, then dragged her nails across his prominent abs.

For a split-second, his stomach tightened.

Beth leaned into him, resting her head into the crook between his neck and shoulder. The subtle flower fragrance from her perfume drifted over him. She smelt good.

He focused on her face. Shades of brown eye-shadow set off the blueness of her eyes and he loved her cute turned up nose. In the mirror, he watched her kiss the nape of his neck, one side of her bob of fair hair falling across the front of his shoulder.

She caught him looking at her through the mirror and cracked a cheeky smile.

"What are you thinking?"

"I was just thinking to myself what a lucky person Beth Kerr is to be married to such a hunk as me."

"Delusional as well as a poser." Beth said, kissing his shoulder. "I was just thinking we've got a good hour before we need to get ready," she whispered.

Hunter spun around, catching her unawares. He gripped her wrists, quickly pinning them behind her back. Then he kissed her soft mouth.

As he led her to the bedroom, the second track was just striking up.

* * * * *

Barry Newstead leaned into Hunter's ear and said in a hushed voice, "A few years ago celebrating a result was a lot different from this. Do you remember? It was a pie and a pint and a lock-in at the pub and you paid for it with a thick head the next day."

Hunter did remember. Surprisingly, the memories of those nights were as fresh as if they had happened only yesterday. The venue was always the pub at the bottom of the hill, not far from district headquarters, where, after midnight, a couple of the lads would get their guitars out from the boots of their cars and everyone would join in with the drunken revelry; slurred renditions of songs such as 'Whisky Wild Rover,' Black Velvet Band,' and 'Sloop John B', would reverberate around the small lounge. In the small hours everyone would eventually stagger home with croaking voices. And just like Barry had said, the following day he would feel as if his head and guts were going to explode.

"Yeah, good nights eh?" he said. "But things move on."

"Not always for the best if you ask me. I don't know, this bloody job's gone soft," Barry took a long slurp of his beer, demolishing half the pint.

Hunter glanced across at Beth who had already found a seat in the small lounge area by the foyer and was chatting away to Sue Siddons.

The four of them were the first to arrive at the Indian restaurant. Hunter and Beth had got there by taxi. Sue had driven Barry's car. They had arrived simultaneously and given each other a smiling welcome before entering the restaurant.

This was the squad's favourite curry house. They had tried several across the Borough over the past two years but had voted this the best. Not just because of its traditional decor, the low-lit intimate feel and friendly atmosphere - it was more a place for couples than an end of night venue for those who had drunk too much – but also because of its food, freshly cooked in the Bangladesh tradition. And it was quiet enough for the team to gossip among themselves, especially about work.

"I don't know Barry, I quite like these nights out. You get to know more about the person you work with." He took a sip of his own pint of chilled Indian beer in a decorated glass. "Do you know why I think you don't like these evenings Barry?" Hunter deliberately turned his head away, hiding a smile.

"Go on, surprise me," he replied gruffly.

"Because you're afraid of letting your mask slip or someone might reveal your secrets. We might find out that the ruff-tuff brusque detective is really a pussy-cat with a liking for crochet and basket-weaving."

Hunter saw Barry's head whip round. He tried to avoid eye contact.

Barry dug Hunter's arm with his elbow. "Daft pillock!" He took another swill of his beer, then said softly, "anyway, what's wrong with crochet?"

They both cracked a grin.

Grace and her husband David were the next to arrive. David joined them at the bar, while Grace sidled off to greet Beth and Sue.

As Grace drifted towards where his wife and Sue were seated, Hunter couldn't help but follow her with an admiring eye. Grace was not only slim and pretty but she had a real eye for style and fashion. Tonight she had on a brightly coloured print top over a pair of white linen trousers and was holding a suede clutch bag. Knowing his work partner, Hunter was sure there would be at least one designer label to her outfit.

He had known a few lads who had tried it on with her over the years and she had left them with their tails between their legs. Grace had been married for sixteen years and he knew from their many conversations that David and her two daughters, Robyn and Jade, were centre-stage of her world. More so now, given what had gone on before with the 'Demon' case

Hunter shook David's hand and ordered him a drink. David had recently taken on a role as manager of an IT consultancy and Hunter reminded himself to ask him about the job later on in the evening, but he wouldn't dwell on it. Computers were not his thing, though he knew from previous meetings that David was also an avid armchair sports fan with a mutual interest in soccer, so they had plenty to talk about.

Mike Sampson was the next to arrive. He made straight for the bar, acknowledging them with a brief nod as he ordered two pints.

Hunter knew that the first beer would hardly hit the sides before Mike was ready for the second. And he was right. Mike had devoured the pint before the second had been dispensed from the pump.

He clonked the empty glass down onto the dark marble bar and wiped the corners of his mouth.

"Christ, I needed that." He said taking the second drink from the barman while digging into his trousers pocket for cash.

Hunter returned the nod and raised his glass. "Down the hatch."

Mike took another sip of his beer. "I'm taking it easy tonight." He patted his rotund belly. "You know I'm not a lover of alcohol."

His comment caused them to chuckle.

Hunter eyed Mike. He wasn't the biggest of coppers and for as long as Hunter had known him, even in uniform, he had been overweight. But what he lacked in stature he made up for with his sanguine character. He was a good thief-taker, a very good interviewer and he had a dry wit. When you were at a low ebb or there was a dark moment in an enquiry, you could always rely on Mike to lighten the moment, but he was also the consummate professional who did more than his fair share of the workload. Hunter had known Mike frequently come in on his day off to do an hour or two on his paperwork, and then spend an hour distracting others with his gossiping and joke telling. But Mike was also a complex character and very guarded when it came to his personal life. Hunter knew that he loved fishing and shooting, with a wide circle of mainly male friends, and he was very knowledgeable when it came to pub quizzes, but that was where it ended. He had never known Mike to be in a personal relationship.

Mike had always lived at home with his mother until her unexpected death from a stroke three years ago and since then had lived alone. Hunter had been to the house a few times to pick him up or drop him off when they were going out for a drink and a curry and had been surprised when he had seen the interior. Not that it was untidy or dirty, in fact the opposite was true, the house was pristine. But the furnishings, the carpets, even the décor, were statements from the 1960s and '70's. It was stuck in a time warp in an era which belonged to Mike's mum. Nothing had been upgraded or changed. It was almost as if he was leaving it as a shrine to the memory of his mother.

Yet, despite his seemingly lonely home life, Hunter had never seen Mike down in the dumps. He was always the life and soul of both the office and the party and Hunter guessed that by the end of the evening, he would have everyone's attention with another of his funny stories or an array of politically incorrect jokes.

By 8:15pm most of the squad had gathered.

Barry nudged Hunter when Tony Bullars came through the doors, a very attractive raven haired woman on his arm.

Flaxen haired with sparkling blue-grey eyes and chiselled features "very handsome", as Beth had ribbed him on more than a few occasions Hunter knew that Bully had an eye for the ladies and never settled with a girlfriend for very long. He had seen him with this girl on the last two departmental gatherings, though for the life of him he couldn't recall her name. He'd make sure he'd talk with her before the evening had ended.

"Things must be getting serious. Next thing he'll be telling us he's decided to settle down," he said to Barry through one side of his mouth.

Hunter ordered another round of drinks and slipped away from the bar to take Beth a glass of white wine. He noticed that the original group of Sue, Grace and his wife had expanded. DC Paula Clarke and two wives of other squad members had joined and were engaged in light-hearted chat with the occasional laughter. He wondered who the subject of their gossiping was; no doubt Beth would tell him later.

Suddenly, the lounge went quiet. He caught the look on his wife's face, eyes wide and eyebrows raised, her gaze was fixed somewhere over his shoulder. Turning sharply, he spotted Detective Superintendent Michael Robshaw making for the bar. Just as quickly, stepping out from behind him, he saw the flame haired woman, its natural ginger colour subdued by an auburn tint.

She offered a meek smile.

"Well that's certainly killed the conversation," the Detective Superintendent responded good-humouredly, his keen eyes searching out the faces of his team. "I think you've all met DCI Dawn Leggate?"

She strode the short distance to Hunter, hand outstretched. The gesture took him aback.

He felt his insides flutter. Seeing her heavily freckled face brought all the angst and uncomfortable memories flooding back: Memories which, until now, had started to dissipate.

Hunter had last seen the Detective Chief Inspector eight weeks ago in the rear yard of the headquarters custody suite. She and her team were preparing to return to Stirling police station, in Scotland, where she was based, with two murderous villains. He and Barry had helped in their arrest. She had shaken his hand then and he had thought and hoped it would be the last time he would have to see her.

Nine weeks ago, he had discovered something that rocked his world.

The sea-change to his life had started at the end of August, while returning from a weekend away with his family. Driving back from the village of Staithes, along the moors, he had witnessed his parents' car being rammed off the road. They were left badly injured by the driver, who sped away from the scene without stopping. Investigating that incident, he'd discovered that for some strange reason DCI Leggate had been given charge of the enquiry. For a long time it had puzzled as to why a Scottish-based senior detective should be involved in a North Yorkshire job, and tracking her down to resolve that had proved difficult and frustrating. She'd tried to fob him off with weak story once he had finally found her operating in his own back-yard at Barnwell. That had only made him dig his heels in further to get to the bottom of it - with devastating consequences. Almost nine weeks ago to the day, he had raced to his parents' home after receiving the frantic phone call from his mother and hearing her hair-raising cries on the other end of the line. By the time he had got there, DCI Leggate was already at the crime scene, along with his boss. In anger and frustration he had cornered her into giving him answers.

What she had told him had rocked his world to the core.

The last time he had seen her had been on the 26th September and he had prayed it was for the last time. Yet here she was again and in his face.

He reluctantly reached out and took hold of her soft, slender hand, but part of him was telling him that this wasn't happening.

"Hello Hunter, nice to meet you again. How are you?"

That soft Scottish voice broke Hunter out of his reverie. "I'm fine thanks." He couldn't think of anything more meaningful to say.

She held his hand for a few seconds. "Good. No hard feelings then?" It was a rhetorical question. She slipped her hand away and turned back to her escort. "I'd love a glass of red wine, thanks."

The Detective Superintendent ordered drinks for everyone, then one of the Indian waiters showed them to their table. They had all pre-ordered their meals during drinks and as they selected their places at the long table the first course of mixed pickle and chutney with popadoms was already waiting.

Fighting spoon against spoon with Barry Newstead, seated opposite, to scoop out the lime chillies from the small metal dish they were sharing, helped Hunter to relax slightly, though he couldn't help glancing towards the end of the table where Dawn Leggate was next to his boss.

It had crossed Hunter's mind, as he guessed it had crossed many others around the table, that Michael Robshaw and the Scottish DCI were now an item. There had been office gossip and several sightings of the pair at a local restaurant over the past few months.

It couldn't be easy carrying on a relationship with six hours' driving time between them, Hunter thought as he watched the pair chatting with DI Gerald Scaife and his wife. He just hoped it wouldn't be permanent. He felt uncomfortable in her presence; she knew too much about him and his family.

As they all finished the first course, two waiters glided in and cleared away the crockery. The table was ready for the next course; he had ordered Chicken Chat.

A sudden repetitive tinkling of metal against glass grabbed the table's attention. Michael Robshaw was tapping the side of his beer glass with his fork.

It brought the team to order.

"I just want to say a few words." He set down his fork but still held his pint glass. "This is not a night for speeches, but there are three celebrations tonight."

Hunter began searching faces around the table, but was met with a series of raised eyebrows and shrugs,

"First and foremost, to the team for another successful outcome. Your hard work during the past eight weeks has paid off. We got a good result last week, the guilty verdicts with a twenty-five year minimum life sentence was a good judgement. It was well deserved after all the hard work you all put in and I'd like you to raise your glasses"

There was a resounding response around the table. "To us!"

"And now secondly. This has not been an easy decision. I have thoroughly enjoyed my time with you lot. This is probably the best team I have ever worked with in my career, but I have decided that with three years to go before I can officially retire I'm going to take a back seat. Though you all know I dislike the politics of the job, sometimes in your career you have to run with the devil. What I want to say in a nutshell is that next month I am moving on to headquarters. I am being promoted to Detective Chief Super."

"And not a moment too soon," Barry Newstead shouted from his seat. "Well done. Congratulations." He raised his glass and drank.

The squad followed suit.

Barry kept his empty glass held up. "We'd thought we'd never get rid of you gaffer," he added with a mocking grin.

There was a ripple of laughter around the table.

"Thank you Barry, I'll take that as a compliment. From you those are heartfelt words. And do you know something deep down I'll even miss you! By the way your P45's in the post."

There was another flurry of chortling.

"Now for the last celebration. I invited Dawn tonight for a specific reason. Not just so you could all gossip about us and yes we are an item but I wanted you all to share and celebrate her success." Michael Robshaw glanced to his side and Dawn met his gaze. "Dawn has made a life-changing decision in the past few weeks. From today she is a member of South Yorkshire Police and more importantly she is here on promotion to Detective Superintendent." He thrust forward his half full glass of beer. "Dawn will be shadowing me on this case for the next month and then she will be taking over. Please raise your glasses to your new SIO."

Hunter's head snapped up. Those words struck him like a Tsunami.

He didn't join in the celebration - it wasn't a deliberate snub, but his thoughts were elsewhere.

When he turned his attention back to the table, the second course had been put in front of him. He picked at the spicy pieces of chicken in crispy pancake casing. Suddenly he wasn't hungry any more.

- ooOoo -

CHAPTER THREE

DAY TWO: 25th November.

The alarm woke Hunter at 6.45am and he slipped out of bed quietly and pulled on his training top and joggers. Beth and the boys were still slumbering as he locked the front door behind him. It would be at least another half an hour before they stirred.

The morning air was moist from overnight rain and the pale orange glow of dawn was rising above a grey blue horizon as he hit the streets to run the four miles into Barnwell station. At a slow jog, he slotted the small ear pieces of his i-Pod into place, selected 'The Platinum Album' by 30 Seconds to Mars, and clipped it onto the waistband of his jogging bottoms before picking up the pace. At the first corner he slipped up the hood of his top, there was a noticeable chill.

After four hundred yards his rhythm and breathing were in sync and he began to increase speed. He had always found that the harder he pushed himself when training, the easier it became to unwind. Hunter needed to clear his head before he got into work. It wasn't just the latest case which had disturbed his sleep, the shock announcement delivered by Detective Superintendent Michael Robshaw the previous evening was also preying on his mind. He had tossed and turned well into the early hours, and when he woke, everything was still tumbling around inside his head. He got up, determined to sort the muddle out so that he could be focused for the start of this new case. The last thing he wanted was to be out of kilter when there was so much to do.

Deep down, he was feeling vulnerable and he could kick himself for acting like a petulant teenager. After all, he didn't know Dawn Leggate, and that was why her presence had got to him. Even though other members of his team, including Detective Superintendent Robshaw, knew about his parents' past, he hated the fact that she knew all the secrets of his family and yet he knew nothing about her.

Grow up Hunter, he cursed inwardly, *get over yourself and move on. What's happened has happened and it's not her fault.*

Suddenly he realised his pace had slackened. He picked up his heels and turned his jog into a run.

In the female toilets of Barnwell Police station, Detective Superintendent Dawn Leggate checked her appearance in the mirror. She ran a finger around her lips, softening the edge of the gloss which she had applied just two minutes earlier.

Not too much make up, she told herself.

She straightened her dark blue jacket, flicked at the collar of her white blouse and stepped back a few paces to take in the overall image. Outwardly she looked calm, but inside her head and heart were racing like a clubber on speed.

Her first day of promotion, and a new team to manage.

Meeting the MIT squad last night had filled her with trepidation, particularly after what had gone on two months previously with DS Kerr. She had voiced her anxiety to Michael before they had left his place and he had tried to reassure her that everything would be okay. In some ways he had been right but meeting up again with Hunter had not proved easy. She had tried to catch his eye a few times through the evening and had sensed him staring at her, but whenever she had caught his attention, he had quickly looked away.

Standing before the elongated mirror above the hand basins, doing her best to hide her nervousness, her mind drifted to what lay ahead. She couldn't afford for things to be edgy between her and one of her team supervisors, not with an investigation in full flow.

She needed Hunter back on side. Michael rated him highly. Hunter Kerr reminded her so much of a detective sergeant she had left behind at Stirling. How she wished she had DS John Reed's support now. She knew he would help her build bridges, both with Hunter and the team.

First opportunity she would have a clear the air session with Hunter, especially given that on her very first day she was in at the deep end of a major enquiry and working with a team she knew very little about a team which Michael had moulded.

This had been a giant leap for her and the past couple of months had been a whirlwind. At the heart of it had been Michael, who had filled a void in her life. Until ten weeks ago, she had thought love would no longer be part of her life again until she met him. After an evening meal together she had done something which she had not done since university, she had jumped into bed with a first date. Michael's timing couldn't have been better. Her marriage had just ended and he offered her the kind of emotion and love she had craved for years.

The sudden chasm in her life had been partly her own fault. Since her teenage years, she had always thrown herself into everything she had done, love life and job as well. Recently, she had chosen the job; she had been promoted DCI into a very busy divisional CID. But she had thought she had done a pretty good job juggling both until four months ago. Getting home late from work that Friday evening, she found the note on the kitchen side from Jack, her husband of eight years, telling her that it was all over and that he had left her. He hadn't even had the guts to face it out. Over the following weekend, she discovered that he had moved in with a female colleague from his work, a liaison which had been going on for eighteen months.

She, one of Scotland's top detectives, hadn't even suspected.

For the best part of a week he had refused to take her calls or reply to her texts and then when she had finally tracked him down to his workplace he had told her during a stand-up row in the foyer that she only ever thought of herself and her job, and that their relationship had been a sham for years.

She'd slapped him across the face hard, and stormed out of the building and out of his life.

The only way she now communicated with Jack was through her solicitor.

Going for that promotion board a month ago had been the hardest decision she had ever made. She already had a distinguished career and worked with some pretty damn good colleagues who were also friends.

But at this stage in her life, a fresh start was required.

She took a final look back at her reflection, checked the hem of her skirt and moved towards the door. Taking a deep breath, she pulled it open and stepped out into the corridor.

* * * * *

Hunter showered and shaved at work, then, with his hair still damp, he made his way up to the office. That run into work had been a tonic - he felt refreshed. He was also glad he had refrained from drinking too much last night, because his head felt clear.

The rest of the squad were in and there was a buzz about the room. It was always like this the first day of an investigation, everyone was eager to get a quick result.

Buttoning up his collar and sliding the knot of his tie into place, Hunter eased himself into his chair, looking to the front of the room. The incident board had been set up, but there was very little written on it. The personal details of Jeffery Howson ran along the top of the white board, and below that the time-line sequence had begun. A head and shoulders shot of him was Blu-tacked in the top left hand corner.

Hunter checked the time-date sequences. The first was the sighting by Howson's daughter, who had visited him three days prior to his death. The second time-frame covered the phone call with Barry Newstead that same evening, and the third denoted the finding of Jeffery dead by his daughter.

"Okay guys, listen up." Detective Superintendent Michael Robshaw brushed past Hunter's desk and made his way to the front.

The incident room fell silent.

He grabbed the incident board. "Give me your eyes and ears for the next half an hour. We've got a lot to get through."

Out of the corner of his eye, Hunter caught Dawn Leggate settling herself down on the edge of DS Mark Gamble's desk. Mark was his counterpart and supervisor of the other team in the department.

Hunter turned and was met by her smile. He forced one back - it felt awkward. He looked away and concentrated on his SIO.

Det. Supt Robshaw opened up the briefing. "Victim is sixty-three year old Jeffery Howson, a retired detective. He was last seen by his daughter when she visited him on Saturday afternoon. She brought him some shopping, put it away, did a little bit of tidying up, made him a snack and left about quarter past four. She was with him just under an hour. Our victim had heart problems and had recently been diagnosed with terminal lung cancer. Because of that he had trouble getting around, but when she left him she says he was settled in his chair, watching football on television. Apparently he spent a lot of time in that chair, even taking to sleeping in it recently because he couldn't get comfortable in his bed. We also know that later that day, eighteen minutes past ten in the evening to be precise, he made a phone call to Barry Newstead here with a request to meet. Barry, will you give us the heads-up on your conversation with him?"

Barry ran a hand through his dark rumple of unruly hair and pushed himself back in his seat. In his broad South Yorkshire accent, he outlined the conversation he had had with the murder victim three days earlier. A precise recollection of the chat with Jeffery Howson clipped off his tongue as though it had happened only a few minutes ago. As background, he also repeated the version of the Lucy Blake-Hall murder story told to him by Sue in the pub.

Barry really knows how to grab an audience, Hunter thought to himself as he watched his former mentor fold his arms across his distended belly as he finished.

"Thanks for that Barry," said Robshaw. "We know from phone records that the call to Barry was made from Howson's land-line and at this stage we have no reason to believe that the caller was not our victim. What we do know is that Jeffery never made that meeting. In fact we know from the PM that he more than likely met his death shortly after the phone call with Barry. House-to-house has thrown up an interesting element which has come from his next door neighbour." He paused and surveyed the faces of his team. "Mr. Farmer, who has been Jeffery's neighbour for the past fifteen years, has told officers that just before eleven on Saturday evening his dog started barking and he noticed the outside security light, at the back of the house, had come on. He went out to do a quick check, but he says he didn't hear anything. He just assumed it was a cat or a fox, went back inside and then locked up for the night and went to bed. He was specifically asked if he heard the sound of breaking glass, as we know that the offenders got in via the side door, but he says he heard nothing like that and he definitely didn't hear any signs of a struggle or arguing coming from Jeffery Howson's place. So until anything more definite comes in regarding time frames, I am holding on to the fact that he was attacked some time between ten eighteen, when Barry spoke with Howson, and eleven pm when Mr Farmer, the neighbour, was disturbed by his barking dog." He darted his gaze between detectives. "What we don't have at the moment is a motive for his murder. We know about his phone call with Barry, the crux of which was his concern over the murder of Lucy Blake-Hall back in nineteen-eighty-three. To use his phrase to Barry, 'the wrong man was convicted of it and I know who really killed her.' And we know about the mysterious key found in his stomach contents, which he obviously swallowed for a reason. But what we don't know yet is that reason, or what that key opens up.

"I guess when we discover that, we will get our motive. But there is also another element we need to focus on. There are signs of a search, certainly in the lounge area, so we also have to ask ourselves if this is a burglary gone wrong." Robshaw faced the room again. "Guys, this was one of our own. We owe it to him and his family to get a quick result."

Letting go of the incident board, he rubbed his hands together.

"Forensics are at a very early stage. They will be returning this morning to do a thorough examination of the house. House-to-house has only been done with immediate neighbours. Besides Mr. Farmer's information, we have learned that Jeffery was a relatively quiet and private man who had very few visitors. So far, no one has seen anything out of the ordinary. We're casting the net a little bit wider this morning. Task Force will be continuing with the door-knocking and will also be doing a finger-tip search of the garden. That will be extended. Beyond his garden fence there is a footpath leading into the woods." The SIO paused. "Okay, actions." He opened his hands and tapped his thumb. "First. We re-interview the daughter, get a thorough background everything she knows about her father. I also want to know what that key fits. See if the daughter knows. He swallowed it for a reason, and as I have already mentioned, my guess is that reason got him killed. But we don't reveal to her or to anyone outside this room how we found it." He tapped the palm of one hand with an index finger. "Second, he made great stay about the murder of Lucy Blake-Hall back in nineteen-eighty-three. Barry has already given an insight into that but I want a copy of that file and I want to know everything about that case. Contact the Cold Case Review team." He progressed along his fingers. "Third, we trace Jeffery Howson's colleagues. I know he's been retired a good few years now, but a number of his ex-colleagues should be around. I want to know who he worked with at divisional CID who was his partner? I want to know everything about him. I want someone to speak with the Intelligence Unit. Has there been a spate of burglaries recently? Who is active in that area? And finally for today, we make a request for his telephone records. We know about his phone call to Barry, but I want to know if he made any other calls after that and anyone he spoke with in the week leading up to his murder. Given his state of health, the phone was his lifeline to the outside world and we need to know if the list throws up any suspects."

Michael Robshaw tucked his hands into his trouser pockets.

"That's it for now everyone. We meet back here at eight-pm for de-brief." He took a deep breath and steadily scanned the room. "Team, it would be nice to put this one to bed quickly. I want the bastards who did this nailed and pronto."

* * * * *

Hunter and Grace had only been waiting in the foyer of the newly built Maltby police station, which housed the Cold Case Review Team, for a little over five minutes before Detective Sergeant Jamie Parker, the officer in charge of the team, appeared through the door at the side of the glass fronted reception area. He greeted them, remaining in the doorway, propping it open with one foot; an invitation for them to enter.

The DS was tall and slim and smartly dressed in collar and tie. His short dark hair was giving way to grey and a neatly trimmed half-beard and moustache lined a cheery smile. He proffered his hand, announcing his name as they approached and shook Hunter's first in a firm grip. Then he took Grace's and eased open the side door a little further to allow them to slide past.

They found themselves in a carpeted, brightly lit corridor lined with numerous doors. Many were open and it was apparent from the noises within that there was lots of activity going on either side.

"We've got a murder running - just started this morning," Parker said, almost as if he had read Hunter's thoughts.

"They've drafted in detectives from other stations. It's a bit manic this morning."

"Always is at the start of a job," added Hunter thinking about his own team's new case.

Jamie nodded. "We're up on the first floor," he said, pointing them along the corridor to a set of double doors.

A metal stairwell took them up to the next floor. The Cold Case Review Team was housed in the first office along the corridor. It was a long oblong room, made cramped by metal filing cabinets, filling almost the length of the back wall, and six desks, which took up most of the floor space. Three detectives were at their desks. They cast Hunter and Grace a quick glance before returning to their work.

Jamie Parker took up his own seat at his desk and offered up two empty seats either side of him. "It's a good job the other two DCs are out on enquiries, otherwise it would have been standing room only," he said, leaning forward and pushing back the desk jotter to make room to rest his arms. "We drew the short straw when we moved in here. We were the last team in. I think they gave us the janitor's storeroom by mistake," he said. "Can we get you a cuppa?"

"I'd love a tea." Hunter said.

"Coffee, thanks," added Grace.

One of the detectives stepped over to the filing cabinets, shuffled together a load of cups amassed on the top and left the room carrying a laden tea tray.

"How long have you been here?" asked Hunter.

"It'll be two years in January. We were set up not long after the Major Investigation Units started."

The DS's comments jogged Hunter's memory. His own unit had been one of many set up by the Force in 2006 to investigate major crimes as a result of a Government review. One of the remits had been to pick up old rape and murder cases which still lie undetected in station vaults and would benefit from modern policing and scientific techniques, particularly using the advancement of DNA. Originally his team had cherry-picked a few cold cases but then along had come current major crime and those investigations had taken a back seat. He guessed this was why the Cold Case Review Team had been formed. He recollected that several months ago, this team had earned a great deal of publicity from local TV and newspapers. A serial rapist who had kept trophies from his victims after carrying out a series of brutal attacks on lone females during the late 1970s and early 1980s was captured twenty years after his last reported rape because a family member had committed a drink-drive offence and had their DNA taken. It was the first familial DNA case in the country.

"How many cases are you working on at the moment?"

"We usually pick up two or three each at a time and juggle around with them. Some of them are really fascinating and it's especially gratifying when we can go back to a complainant or a parent after all those years and tell them we have enough evidence to take their attacker to court."

"How many cases are there still outstanding?"

"Too many to mention. This Force has records stretching back to nineteen-seventy-four when it was formed and there are also records from when it was the West Riding. The oldest file I have seen is an undetected murder from nineteen-sixty-two."

Hunter pursed his lips in a silent whistle.

"The case you're after is the murder of Lucy Blake-Hall from nineteen-eighty-three is that right?"

"Yeah. Well before my time. I didn't join the job until nineteen-ninety-one."

"Well it's all there." Jamie Parker pointed to an array of cardboard file boxes stacked next to a metal cabinet.

Hunter guessed there must be at least a dozen stacked boxes. He hadn't expected that amount.

"You're in luck. We've had a quick scan through and it looks as though everything is there." Parker pushed himself up from his seat and moved to the pile. Giving a cursory glance at its label he prised open the lid of one box and lifted out a thick file with both hands. "This is the summary, main witnesses evidence, and suspect interview file which was presented at the trial. In the other boxes are the house to house forms, original witness statements, scene of crime photographs and the Home Office forensic forms for the science labs. Oh, and in your case quite a few of the boxes contain the original index cards for the job."

"You got this quick. We only rang about this case a couple of hours ago."

"There was a message left on my voice-mail this morning from a Detective Superintendent Dawn Leggate. I got in at half-seven, so I was able to arrange a driver to pick up the case box-files first thing." The DS handed Hunter the thick bound file.

Hunter weighed it in his hands, turned it and fanned apart some of the pages with a thumb and glanced at the top typewritten sheet. It had the patina of ageing but was easily readable. He glanced at the strap-line, reading it off inside his head; Regina v Daniel Weaver.

"You're very lucky. Many of the really old case files have been destroyed. Forces have had to be ruthless because of the lack of space, and I know from experience that huge swathes of paperwork have been binned. I've had a cursory look inside the boxes of your case. There's an inventory at the top of each one. And although all the paperwork appears to be there, I'm afraid there're no exhibits. I don't know yet if those have been destroyed or not."

Hunter pursed his lips and shot a quick glance at Grace.

"No need to look downhearted. I do have some good news. Since I've been doing this job we've discovered that the forensic science labs, unlike the police, have kept files and samples from every job ever submitted to them. So somewhere in their system will be samples taken during the Lucy Blake-Hall investigation. Once you sort through the paperwork, if you let me know, I can set things in motion with an e-mail and go up to forensics with you, if you'd like?"

Hunter mouthed "cheers" and returned the file. He cast his eyes along the pile of cardboard archive boxes.

There's certainly a lot of paperwork to go through, he thought. He set the lid back on the carton and heaved it up.

"We'll give you a hand to load it," offered Jamie. He picked up a box from the pile and hoisted it mid-chest. "Listen, we have loads of experience now of dealing with cold cases, especially tracking down witnesses. We have found it can be tricky tracking down female witnesses. Many women get married, change their surname and also move away, but we have tried and trusted ways of finding them. Once you've gone through the boxes and sorted everything out, if you get stuck with anything just give us a bell."

Hunter cast him an appreciative smile.

"Just a bit of advice as well. When the time comes for you to speak with the detectives who previously worked on the case, I know from experience that some of them get very nervous when you start going back over things, because methods that were used during their time were not always the right ones. Just remember that was then this is now! Your focus shouldn't be about how the case was detected."

Suddenly, Hunter got an image of Barry Newstead. He knew exactly what Jamie Parker was talking about. He'd been introduced to many unorthodox methods in his pursuit of villains during his early CID days; all of them instigated by Barry. He couldn't help but crack a grin as he turned towards the door.

* * * * *

Dressed in a black and grey D&G logo T-shirt and faded denim jeans, Katherine Edwards answered the front door with her mobile pressed to her ear. She pointed to it and mouthed the words 'My mum' back at DCs Tony Bullars and Carol Ragen, standing shoulder-to-shoulder inside her porch.

She waved for them to come in with her free hand, spun on her heels and sauntered off along the hallway towards the back of the house, still speaking on her phone as she went. She was finishing her conversation as the two detectives caught up with her in the kitchen.

"Yeah the police are just here now. I'll give you a ring later when I find out what's what, okay? Yeah love you too bye." She ended the call and placed the mobile onto the marble surface of the kitchen's central work island. It was a bright and airy L-shaped kitchen diner in a contemporary black and white theme. Italian design high gloss units lined soft cream walls. Most of the light came from a large set of French doors, which gave a view out to her well tended garden. Today, everything was in the grip of the first signs of winter. The clipped bushes and mature trees could just be made out in the morning's cold damp haze .

The expensive, well designed look of the kitchen reminded Tony that she had told him the previous day that as well as holding down a full time job as a sports injury therapist, she boosted her income with private consultations working from home.

"Sorry about that. That was my mum I've only just managed to get hold of her and break the news. She didn't get back from Gran Canaria until the early hours of this morning." She picked up the electric kettle and filled it from the tap. "Can I get you a drink? Tea? Coffee?"

Both agreed on tea.

"Sorry to burden you at a time like this, Katherine," opened Tony with a sympathetic look. "But as you can probably appreciate we need to move on this quite quickly in order to find your father's killer. I know I bombarded you with quite a number of questions yesterday, but I need to go back over things with you. We have a number of gaps that need filling, both in terms of his past history, as well as recent events in his life. We're hoping you will be able to fill those in?"

"I couldn't sleep last night. I can't believe what's happened. It's something you dream about isn't it, someone in your family being murdered I mean. And Dad as well. All those murders he's investigated in the past and now he himself has been murdered." She set the filled kettle back onto its electric base and switched it on. Then she plucked out three cups from a wall cupboard and arranged them around the kettle. Turning back to face Tony, she swept a hand through one side of her dark bob of hair, tucking it behind her ear. "You can't imagine it, can you?"

She fixed him with her grey/blue eyes. "This is such a shock. Thing is, I thought I'd done most of my grieving for him several months ago when I found out he had terminal cancer. I've been to hospital so many times with him these past few months that I'd thought I'd become hardened to the fact that he was going to die." Her voice trailed off on a brittle note. Dabbing a forefinger into the corner of one eye, she turned quickly back to face the boiling kettle. "But this...I mean Dad murdered. It's just so hard to imagine."

Tony got a whiff of her perfume. It reminded him of roses. He couldn't help but think that at 42 she was in really good shape. She was tall and slim, with a well toned physique, though today he noted how drained she looked. Dark rings circled her eyes, a clear sign she had endured a restless night. He wasn't surprised, given the previous day's shock.

Tony had spent several hours with her the day before, prising out of her as much background information as he needed for the present stage of the investigation. But she had repeatedly burst into tears. Today, he was here with the added support of the Family Liaison Officer Carol Ragen to squeeze out that bit more.

"Katherine, I want to introduce you to DC Carol Ragen." He swapped his gaze from Katherine to his colleague. "After today, Carol will be spending quite a lot of time with you and your Mother throughout the duration of this enquiry. She will be here to support you both, and give you everything you need. If there is anything you don't understand, just ask her. She will keep you up to date with the enquiry. Is that okay?"

Katherine Edwards nodded as she took the female detective's extended hand.

DC Ragen met her gaze. "As Tony says, if you want to know what is going on or anything you don't understand, I'm there for you and your Mother. The only thing I ask is that what I tell you is kept to yourself." Carol had a noticeable Lancashire accent which accentuated the 'o's' in her words. She removed her hand from Katherine's grip, then smoothed it through the soft curls of her shoulder length fair hair. At 45 years old, Carol Ragen had been appointed FLO because of her similar age to Katherine. She had been a cop for 22 years, the last ten of which she had served in Headquarter Public Protection Unit dealing with victims of domestic violence.

Tony continued. "It's a bit of a cliché Katherine, but do you know if your father had any enemies? Or if he'd fallen out, or he'd had an argument with anyone recently?"

"He was a detective for thirty-odd years, I guess he made loads of enemies over that time. If you mean did I know of anyone who hated him that much to do this to him, then the answer is no. However I do know something was troubling him of late."

Tony's eyebrows raised.

"What do you mean, troubling him?"

"Well, as you will have gathered, I've been spending quite a lot of time with him, especially over the past month. He'd deteriorated quite a lot in that time. He'd lost a lot of weight and he was in a lot of pain and had trouble sleeping. The nurses had increased his morphine dosage to help him and I found he was chatty more than normal when I went round to sort it out, you know, tidy round a little and get him some of his meals although his appetite had dropped off. I guess that was to do with the morphine." She handed them their hot drinks. "Sorry, I'm going off at a tangent. What I'm getting round to is that I switched off most of the time. I thought he was just rambling on because of the drugs, but some of his words stuck with me. I thought that some of what he said was a bit strange."

"Strange?" said Tony.

"Yes. He'd say things like I've done some bad things in my time Katherine. I've done things when I was detective that I shouldn't have done. He'd say other stuff like he'd not been a good husband or a good dad but he'd keep going back over the fact that he'd done something bad when he had been a detective."

"Did he mention exactly what that was?" Tony was asking the questions as Carol took notes.

"To be honest, I don't exactly know. The last month he was so high on the morphine they were giving him. Some of the time he didn't always make sense. He'd start with one thing and then start rambling on about something completely different, so I only half-listened to what he was saying. I do recall him saying that he was going to put things right." She paused for a second, deep in thought. Then she shook her head. "Sorry, I don't think he expanded on that." She pulled a face. "I feel awful now that I didn't listen properly or push him to tell me more."

"When you say he said he was going to put things right, did he say how he was going to do that?"

Katherine tightened her mouth and shrugged her shoulders. "Sorry. I feel terrible. I wish I'd have listened better to what he was saying."

"Don't worry about it. It's one of those things. You weren't to know this was going to happen. Would there be anyone else

60

he might have talked to about this? Any other visitors? Close friends?"

For a couple of seconds she stared at the ceiling, as if searching for the answer. Then she returned. "I'm not quite sure. I know he kept in contact with a couple of his ex-colleagues. I've turned up a couple of times with bits of shopping for him and he's been on the phone. I picked up on him reminiscing about jobs he'd been involved in and just guessed it was people he'd worked with. I know he was particularly close to someone from the old days. It's a good eighteen months ago now, but there were a couple of times when he'd mentioned he'd had a run out in his mate's car and they'd stopped off at a pub and had a couple of beers and lunch. I think he said his name was Alan, I've never met him. Other than that, he seemed to keep himself very much to himself. I've only really got to know him since I moved back here five years ago." She looked up, swallowed hard and returned her gaze. "He's been living alone since he and mum got divorced back in nineteen-eighty-four. I don't think there was anyone else in his life, but to be honest that's not something I would discuss with him. It's taken quite a lot of time getting to know him again. It's not been easy for him or me. I went with mum when she left him. We moved to Skegness. We had a caravan there and lived in it for a while. Mum wouldn't talk about why they'd split up and so I just shut myself off from it all. I was seventeen at the time. I swapped schools for a year, got my A levels, and then I went to uni, where I made a new life. While I was away mum met Derek, my stepfather, and moved in with him and they married. I went back to Mum's for a short while but it just didn't feel right. Not that I didn't get on with Derek or anything, but being away for three years you know I'd moved on. Then I got a job as a sports injury physio at Skegness hospital and moved out. I met Sean, he was a colleague in the same department. It was a bit of a whirlwind romance. We were married within eighteen months. Amy, our daughter, came along a few years later and that was it, I had my own family to focus on. Dad never seemed to feature. He never came to the wedding and never saw his granddaughter until five years ago. Quite sad really. It's taken a lot to get to know each other again. I only came back this way because Sean and I separated and I saw a job advertised at Barnwell General. It just seemed right to return to my roots." She stirred her tea, licked the spoon before setting it down and took a long sip of the hot drink. "We've never really picked up on the lost years. I had my new job and new house. Don't get me wrong, I did nip round a couple of times every week and he would have Amy quite a lot when I did my private work in the evenings. And he did my garden regularly. I returned the favour with some home cooking. But whenever I'd raise anything to do with mum or the divorce, he'd just say he'd rather leave that alone. After a while, I just stopped asking him questions." She switched her gaze between the two detectives. "Don't we all lead such complicated lives?" It was a rhetorical question. "If only we could go back eh? The sad thing is I was always going to ask why he never came to my wedding and why he never acknowledged the birth of Amy his granddaughter but it never seemed to be the right moment. Even when I knew he was going to die with cancer."

She took another sip of her tea.

"Sorry to push you Katherine. Just to take you back a little to where your dad mentioned about putting things right. You said that you had overheard some of his phone calls with his old colleagues, reminiscing about jobs. You mentioned one of those colleagues as being called Alan. Do you recall anything from those conversations?"

She shook her head. Her dark bob of hair released itself from behind her ear and fell to the side of her face. She stroked it back.

"I can't focus at the moment. I'll think all this over and if anything comes to mind I'll tell you. There's so much to take in you understand? It would be worth your time speaking with my mum. Like dad, she's never really discussed why they split up. I have broached it a few times but all she used to say is what's done is done. I'll give Mum her due, she never slagged him off when I was around. "

"We'll be doing that as part of our enquiries. And don't worry about not remembering, something might come to you later. Think about it in your own time. Now just to take you back to Saturday. What time did you last see him?"

"It would roughly be about quarter past four. I'd done a bit of shopping for him with Amy. I was chatting to him as we put it away. He was watching football on Sky."

"Can you recall anything of what was said?"

"Not exactly. I'm afraid I was going off on one. I told him off about the full ashtray again. Cigarettes are what caused his lung cancer." She took another sip of her tea, cupping her mug with both hands. "But I do remember the conversation we had on Saturday night when he rung me late on. I remember it because of what he said before he hung up."

Tony raised his eyebrows. "Tell me about that."

"When the phone rang, I'd only just poured myself a glass of wine and put my feet up. I let Amy stay up a little later on Saturdays, so it was just after half past ten. To be honest I'd not long tucked her up and got out of the bath myself so I was going to ignore it, until I saw Dad's name displayed and I thought he might have taken a turn for the worse. I was surprised when I answered because he seemed quite chirpy. He apologised for the time it was and then asked me if I could take him for a run out, the next day, to The George and Dragon pub in Wentworth, he had to meet up with someone Sunday lunchtime. I told him I couldn't, I had a couple of private work appointments. He said no worries and that he'd get a taxi. I asked him if it was anything important and he said no, that he felt a little better and wanted to sort something out with an old colleague. I feel a bit guilty about it now especially because of what's happened."

Tony guessed that when they checked the records, the timing of the phone call to Katherine would follow the one with Barry Newstead.

"He finished the call by saying something strange. I can remember now the exact words he used." She looked at Tony over the rim of her cup. "If anything happens to me Katherine I want you to look in the safe. That's what he said. Not 'when' anything happens, but 'if', as if he expected this to happen to him."

"Look in the safe?" Tony repeated.

"Yeah, the safe in the back room. He has a small safe hidden beneath a panel in the back bedroom's fitted wardrobes. It's covered by his shoes."

"Have you seen what's in the safe?"

"He showed me where it was not long after he was diagnosed. He said I would have to deal with everything in there and that he would leave me instructions inside it which he wanted me to follow. He said the house deeds, insurance policies and important papers were all in there. He opened it up and let me glance inside, but that's all. I never saw exactly what was in there. There were a few large brown envelopes, I can remember that."

Tony's eyes lit up. He reached into his suit jacket pocket and retrieved the clear plastic exhibit bag that contained the brass key, removed from Jeffery Howson's stomach. He held it up to Katherine. "Do you recognise this key, by any chance?"

She screwed up her eyes as she looked at the contents of the forensic exhibit bag. "Yes. That looks like my dad's safe key."

* * * * *

Despite the background heating being on inside 12 Woodland View, Detective Constable Mike Sampson shivered. Half an hour earlier he had discovered that the white forensic suit in the boot of the CID car was on the small size for his frame and no matter how hard he had tried he had not been able to squeeze it over his suit jacket. He'd had to leave his coat in the car, and now he was cursing, because the coldness of the early winter morning had finally crept through the thin fabric of the protective over-suit.

How he wished he could lose some weight.

He had tried to take his mind off the cold by busying himself around the crime scene. For the past half hour, using the forensic floor plates as stepping stones, he'd mooched around the house, upstairs as well as down, trying to fend off the chill in his bones. Now he was back in the lounge trying to get an insight into the life of Jeffery Howson. He'd checked out the reading material, including a small pile of various national newspapers many of which were folded open at the horse-racing section. The only magazines lying about were those with TV listings. In a low level bookcase he had cast his eye over the spine titles of various hardback and paperback novels. There was a mix of authors and genres. He spotted Ed McBain's 87th Precinct novels, mentally ticked off those he had read, and tried to recall their plots, but moved on when he found himself blurring one into the other. Picking past Harold Robbins, Clive Cussler and Wilbur Smith, he found the bottom two shelves contained a large selection of hardback Enid Blytons *The Famous Five*; *Secret Seven* and *Mallory Towers* adventure stories, which he guessed belonged to Howson's daughter Katherine.

Then he'd checked out the half dozen or so photographs on the walls. Most of them were black and white images of Jeffery as a young man, either hugging, or with an arm around a gangly, dark haired teenage girl. There were shots taken at the seaside and in the rear garden, and two, taken at different angles, were of the pair posing on the bonnet of a saloon car on the front drive of this house. These two were in colour, though yellowing drastically with age. He recognised that the car was a 1981 registered 3 Series BMW. Memories flooded back. That had been the first make and model of car he'd driven after passing his test. His dad had bought it for him. It was metallic blue and twelve years old. He didn't have it long. One Sunday morning, less than six weeks into owning it, while blasting along the A170 towards Scarborough, he blew the engine and damaged the cam shaft and the last he saw, it was being towed to the nearest scrap yard. He smiled as he pulled himself back to the present and focused again on the photos. Mike guessed from the resemblance that the girl with Jeffery was his daughter Katherine, the woman he had met and interviewed with Tony Bullars the previous day.

He couldn't see any of Jeffery with his ex-wife.

Moving away from the photos, he turned his attention to the back of Scenes of Crime Manager Duncan Wroe, who was overseeing the work of a pretty dark haired girl member of his team. She was running a light source along the surface of a mahogany writing bureau looking for fingerprints; Katherine had pointed out the previous day that she thought it showed signs of being searched. She said that before she had left on the Saturday afternoon she had tidied up the few bits of paper which had been left lying about and rolled down the bureau flap to secure it. After she had found her father dead, she noticed it open and papers and envelopes strewn around.

The sudden ringing of his mobile brought him back to the present. He fished through the gap in the forensic suit and pulled out his phone.

It was his buddy Tony Bullars. He hit the answer button, listened to him talking for the best part of a minute, not interrupting, nodding occasionally. Then he ended the call.

Mike turned to the Scenes of Crime Manager. "Duncan, has any of your team found a safe upstairs?"

Duncan Wroe straightened himself, shrugged his shoulders and pursed his lips.

"Seems as though Jeffery has a safe secreted inside one of the wardrobes in the back room."

The detective stepped onto the next light-weight plate and followed the route into the hallway and up the stairs. He knew the bathroom was the first on his right of the landing and next to that was the second largest bedroom, overlooking the rear garden.

He poked his head around the door. Another female member of the forensic team was pulling back the sheets of a three-quarter size bed.

"Have you been through the wardrobes yet?"

She shook her head.

"Mind if I take a quick look inside?" he asked pointing towards the dark wood floor-to-ceiling fitted wardrobes.

"Try to touch as little of the surface as you can," she replied.

Most of the bedroom floor was covered with plastic sheeting. It crackled as he stepped across the room. Opening the right hand door of the first set of double wardrobes with one finger through the handle, he spied a row of well polished shoes lined up in two rows along the floor space. He took them out carefully. There were six pairs in total and he laid them out along the plastic sheeting. Then he smoothed his latex gloved hand over the flat veneer surface, searching for a way to lift the board. Within seconds, he had found a hole drilled in one corner, just large enough to slot his forefinger inside. He gave a quick yank and the board shot up.

"Bingo!" He spotted the green metal safe tucked into the far corner. It wasn't large, roughly thirty centimetres square. He tested to see if it would move by prising his fingers into a gap at the back. It was set fast and he guessed it had been bolted into the floor joists beneath. It had been fitted so that the door was facing upwards. A chunky brass coloured handle was set off-centre and a key-hole was to one side. He gripped the handle and tried it. There was no movement. He took out his mobile and speed-dialled his partner.

* * * * *

Tony Bullars turned up ten minutes later. He had left DC Ragen with Katherine, working through the history and background details of her father.

Calling Mike from the hallway, he bounded up the stairs and joined him in the bedroom.

Mike pointed out the safe and Tony removed the small brass key from the sealed clear plastic exhibit bag. On bended knees, he leaned inside the wardrobe and tried it.

"Fits," he called back excitedly, turning the key. The door, though surprisingly heavy for its size, opened upwards smoothly. In the gloom, Tony could make out a number of packages and envelopes. He took each one out individually, using only finger and thumb, and passed them back.

Mike laid them out on the plastic sheeting.

Running a hand around the inside of the safe, satisfying himself it was empty, Tony pushed himself up and turned to his colleague. In better light he was able to see the contents from the safe more clearly. There were two small Jiffy bags and three envelopes, A4 size. Each was marked in neat copperplate handwriting. He scanned the packages, picking out the words 'last will and testament' and 'life insurance' on two of the envelopes.

"That's the one we want," said Mike, picking up a brown envelope. He handed it to his partner.

Tony Bullars read the words written across the front and felt at the package. It was apparent to him from its thickness and flexibility that it contained a small wad of paper. He turned the envelope over. It had been stuck down and additionally sealed with sticking tape. He turned it back and re-read the front sentence neatly written in black ink.

'For the attention of Barry Newstead'

* * * * *

Hunter stretched in his chair, hooked his hands behind his head and gazed around the incident room. It was the first time in over an hour that he had looked up from his desk. He and Grace had got back from the Cold Case Unit at midday, and over a sandwich and mug of tea he had immediately delved into the Lucy Blake-Hall murder prosecution file. Now he became conscious of the noise levels and activity going on around him and realised that he had immersed himself in the story of the 1984 trial of Daniel Weaver, who had been charged with his part in the killing of Lucy, and he'd been oblivious to the work going on in the room. He spotted his counterpart, DS Mark Gamble, leaning back in his chair, one leg propped upon the corner of his desk, a telephone handset clamped between his right shoulder and ear, doing more listening than talking.

Grace was at the front of the room leaning over a long table, moving postcard size buff coloured cards across the surface like a croupier in charge of a Black Jack table. In front of her were row upon row of similar cards and she appeared to be switching or adding to the piles she had created. He realised she was sorting out the old recording index system from one of the case boxes.

"Having fun?"

She looked up. "Having fun? This is a nightmare. It's like sorting out a thousand piece jigsaw with some of the bits missing. I can't make head nor tail of some of the cross-referencing or the information written on some of these cards."

"You can see how they made so many mistakes with the Ripper enquiry, can't you? That's why they introduced HOLMES.

She rolled her eyes and shook her head. "I'm hoping that when I start going through some of the paperwork it will all fall into place."

"I'm sure it will Grace." He unhooked his hands and pointed to the bound prosecution document he had just read. "Interesting story, and a well put together file. The summary is a lot more long-winded than some of today's files but it makes for good reading. In fact, having read it, I'm puzzled now why Jeffery Howson made that phone call to Barry, because on paper the job seems cut and dried. The evidence against Lucy Blake-Hall's killer is so strong."

Grace pushed herself up and stretched her spine. "Give me a quick run-down then and fill me in. It might help me make some sense of this lot that I've got to sort out."

"Okay, briefly, Lucy was just twenty-two years old when she disappeared back in August nineteen-eighty-three. At the time, she was married with a young daughter..." Hunter paused and glanced down at some notes he had made, "...Jessica," he added and continued with his narration. "It appears she'd been having an affair with a guy called Daniel Weaver for approximately six months and he'd made arrangements to rent a place in St. Neots, near Cambridge, where they were going to live together. On the night of her disappearance, he checked his notes again, "Friday the twenty-sixth - the start of the Bank Holiday weekend - witnesses saw her and Daniel together in a pub, and an hour later they were seen arguing in the market place. That's the last anyone saw of her. Husband reported her missing the Saturday morning and when Daniel was paid a visit a day later, on the Sunday, he had scratches to his face so he was arrested. Jeffery Howson and a Detective Sergeant Alan Darbyshire were the arresting officers and they had several interviews with him. Initially he denied the affair and denied meeting her on the Friday. On the second interview he changed his story. He admitted the affair and admitted seeing her that Friday. He also admitted that the marks to his face were caused by Lucy. He said they had rowed because she had changed her mind about running away together. His place was searched and they found Lucy's handbag hidden among some sacks in his garden shed. In a third interview Weaver confessed to killing her. That's it, in a nutshell."

Grace looked puzzled. "But didn't Sue tell Barry that while she was working as a reporter with the Barnwell Chronicle, they'd repeatedly covered the story because Lucy's body's never been found?"

"It hasn't."

"Well if Weaver admitted to killing her, why didn't he tell the interviewing officers where he had buried her?"

Hunter casually hunched his shoulders. "Well he did in a fashion. In his last interview he coughed to strangling her during a later row back at his place and then, when he realised she was dead, in a panic he took her up to Langsett Moor in his works van and buried her somewhere up there. He said he couldn't remember where because he was drunk at the time."

"But I thought he pleaded not guilty."

"Oh he did, but the ins and outs of that are not on the prosecution file. I know from Barry's conversation with Sue that Weaver alleged at his trial that he'd been fitted up, so I'm hoping to find the details of his defence among the paperwork in one of the other boxes I've yet to go through. But on this file all there is are the main witness statements and his interview notes."

The unexpected ringing of his desk telephone made Hunter jump. He reached across and snatched it up.

"DS Kerr, Major Investigation Team," he offered. Then he listened to the caller, reached for his pen and began scribbling notes onto scrap paper. Less than two minutes later he was dropping the handset onto its cradle.

"Come on Grace, get your coat on," he said pushing himself up from his seat. "That was Bully on the phone. The key found in Jeffery Howson's stomach was for a safe which they've found hidden in a set of wardrobes. He wants us to join him at the scene. He said he's found something of great interest."

* * * * *

Jockeying his way through heavy traffic, Hunter managed the journey to Woodlands View in less than twenty minutes and he tucked the CID car behind one of the SOCO vans parked at the head of the cul-de-sac.

69

A TV camera crew team had set up this side of the first taped cordon slung across the road, the backdrop of their focus being Number 12. A reporter appeared to be in the middle of a shoot.

He nudged Grace. "Make sure your lippy is on girl, you'll be on Look North tonight." He flashed a wink as he pushed his driver's door to and popped the locks.

Approaching the top of the drive of number twelve Hunter saw that a large blue canvas had been erected against the side door, protecting as well as hiding the entrance. He flashed his warrant card, gave his and Grace's names to the uniformed scene-logging officer and trooped off down the crumbling concrete drive, squeezing past Jeffery Howson's ten-year-old Volkswagen Polo, as he made for the way in.

They found Tony and Mike in the dining room at the back of the house, hunkered over an oval mahogany dining table. The well polished surface was littered with a raft of papers, many of which appeared to be official police forms covered in handwriting, all sealed within clear plastic forensic evidence bags.

Hunter noted that this room, although slightly musty, had none of the stale tobacco or urine smells which had disgusted him during his visit the day before. And it was a lot brighter. A double-glazed set of patio doors, overlooking the overgrown rear garden, took up half of one wall, allowing bleached light from the pale mid-afternoon sun to filter in.

"I thought you might want to see this little lot before Forensics take them away," said Tony Bullars, looking up. He pushed a couple of the bagged pages towards Hunter. "They've all been photographed and Duncan's promised me he will have the images e-mailed to me for tomorrow morning's briefing, but I wanted you to read this interview record and cast your eye over these documents we found." Tony tapped the manila envelope with its handwritten inscription. "They were inside this envelope addressed to Barry. It's pretty interesting stuff. If it's the real deal, then it certainly opens up our investigation!"

Hunter stared at the array of documents across the table. There must have been at least twenty pieces. Six of the clear plastic forensic bags contained newspaper cuttings, yellowed and pitted with age. Hunter saw that someone had taken the patience to cut out, organise and neatly paste a series of different tabloid articles onto separate sheets of paper. He took in a couple of the headlines 'DISAPPEARED WITHOUT

TRACE'; 'THE LAST PERSON TO SEE LUCY'; 'LUCY BLAKE-HALL MAN CHARGED WITH MURDER.'

Several black and white photographs were dotted throughout the articles. He recognised a shot of The Coach and Horses pub in Barnwell town centre, which he knew from reading the Daniel Weaver prosecution file earlier was one of the last places where witnesses saw Lucy Blake-Hall.

Another was a head and shoulders shot of a smiling young woman, blonde hair piled up and fashioned into a bunch at the crown. Dark mascara ringed glistening eyes and a thin slender nose complemented cherub-like features. The caption gave Lucy's name, with the addition of 'where is she?'

Very pretty woman, Hunter thought to himself. It was his first sighting of Lucy; previously she had just been a name on paper.

He would like to have read them further but out of the corner of his eye he could see Tony anxiously beating a tattoo over one particular piece of evidence.

Hunter slid the plastic bag from beneath Tony's forefinger. Spinning it around to its correct way up, he saw that the exhibit pouch contained the first sheet of a formal record of interview form identical to the ones he had seen in the murder file that morning. Reading his way down, he picked out that it was the contemporaneous account of an interview with Daniel Weaver, conducted by Detective Sergeant Alan Darbyshire and Detective Constable Jeffery Howson on Monday 29th August 1983. Questioning started at 2.20pm and was concluded at 3.25pm that same day. He began reading the script, penned in black biro and still very clear and legible after all this time. In fact, unlike the clipped out foxed newspaper articles, it looked as though it had never seen the light of day since it had been written.

As he inched his way down the text, he felt more and more confused. Why had such an important document been locked away in Howson's safe? It should have formed part of the prosecution file against Daniel Weaver.

For the next twenty minutes, Hunter meticulously read every handwritten sentence of the chronicled interview. As he put aside each separate sheet, Tony Bullars fed him another, until all the twelve pages had been digested.

Taking in the last sentence of the final page, Hunter, set it aside with the others. He let off a low whistle and pushed himself up. Supporting himself on his straight arms, he said,

"I think this is what got Jeffery Howson killed."

CHAPTER FOUR

DAY THREE: 26th November.

A gloomy early start to the day meant that the overhead fluorescent lighting in MIT had to be on for morning briefing. The bright lights bathed the room in a warm glow, masking the cold outside.

Detective Superintendent Dawn Leggate stood beside the incident whiteboard at the front, looking around and feeling uncomfortable. She took a deep breath and clenched her stomach muscles. Her insides were churning. It was at times like this she really could do with a cigarette. She had stopped smoking 10 months ago, yet there were still occasions when the craving came back and this was one of them.

She exhaled slowly.

"Good morning everyone," Dawn said in her soft Scottish voice, gratified when no nervous inflections came out.

Casting her eyes quickly around the room, she could see that everyone was seated at their desk, with the exception of Family Liaison Officer DC Carol Ragen, who was perched on one corner of Grace's desk nursing a steaming mug of coffee.

Most of the team had fresh hot drinks and some had even made themselves a slice of toast. It was such a familiar sight, she thought to herself as she gazed around. In spite of the faces being different and the Police Forces being hundreds of miles apart, this briefing scene could have mirrored the many that she had conducted with her old team back in her native Scotland.

"Mr Robshaw has had to start at Headquarters today, to sort out the budget for the investigation, so he's asked me to take briefing. We have quite a lot to go through this morning especially the revelation yesterday so we'll run this from the top."

She tapped the incident board with her pen.

"We all know that sixty-three year old retired detective Jeffery Howson was found murdered at his home on Monday and the likelihood is that he was killed late Saturday night. We also know that before his death he made a phone call to Barry here, stating he wanted to meet and tell him about the murder of Lucy Blake-Hall in nineteen-eighty-three. That the wrong person had been convicted of it and that he knew who had done it. Have I got that right?" She turned to the Civilian Investigator she'd heard so much about but had not had time to get to know yet. In fact, such had been her baptism, thrown immediately into this murder enquiry, that with the exception of Hunter she hadn't had the time to get to know any of her new team.

Barry nodded back.

"I can also see from the notes on the board that we now have the background to the Lucy Blake-Hall murder. Hunter, you and Grace had that enquiry. Can you expand on the information on the board?"

Dawn watched Hunter pick up his loose notes from his desk. She shot him a delicate smile.

"Yes Boss. We picked up the investigation in its entirety from the Cold Case Unit yesterday. We've haven't had time to go through everything, as you will appreciate, but I have read the prosecution file and the report on his appeal, and Grace is currently trying to organise the old card index system for inputting into HOLMES. She has also spoken with the Forensics lab at Wetherby. It would appear they still have the exhibit slides from the original investigation and they have their own set of comprehensive notes, which is a real plus."

The team listened as Hunter outlined the Lucy Blake-Hall case. He gave a brief resume of her family circumstances - married with a five year-old daughter, back in 1983, and then focused in detail on the last sightings of her on Friday 26th August when witnesses saw her with her lover, Daniel Weaver, firstly in the Coach and Horses pub, and then later that same evening arguing in the market place in Barnwell.

"Jeffery Howson and a Detective Sergeant Alan Darbyshire, whom, I've been informed by Barry, retired as a DCI in nineteen-ninety-two, arrested Daniel the day after she had been reported missing after visiting him at his home. He had scratches to his face and refused to say how he had got them. Weaver was known to the police. He has previous for a chemist break-in and also possession of a controlled drug with intent to supply. He did eighteen months in a young offenders' institution in nineteen-seventy-seven."

He outlined the interrogation of Daniel Weaver at the police station, in which, after initial denials, he admitted to his affair with Lucy and confessed that she had scratched him during an argument on the evening of her disappearance. Hunter revealed how Jeffery Howson and DS Alan Darbyshire had also discovered Lucy's handbag hidden under sacking during a search of Weaver's garden shed and that after making another initial denial he had gone on to give a full and frank admission as to how he had strangled Lucy and then buried her body up on Langsett Moor.

"A team of police officers spent a fortnight up on the moors searching for signs of her burial site, but at that stage Weaver had been appointed a solicitor and refused to cooperate with the investigation further, so her body was never found. The trial of Daniel Weaver took place in April nineteen-eighty-four. He did go in the box and give evidence. And I've got the next bits from the newspaper articles covering the trial." He paused before continuing. "He admitted to the affair and to the argument with Lucy in which she had scratched his face. He said they were caused while trying to reason with her and she had pulled away from him. He admitted making a number of statements during his interviews but he flatly denied making the one where he admitted to strangling her and burying her body up on Langsett Moor. And he accused the police of planting the handbag. After a three week trial, he was found guilty of Lucy's murder and given life. His defence submitted an appeal but it was turned down on the grounds that the trial was conducted fairly, and that without fresh evidence the conviction was deemed to be safe."

Hunter glanced up from his jottings. "To be honest, on my first reading of the file I thought everything was cut and dried. That was until we found that statement in Jeffery Howson's safe. Last night I re-examined the case file. All the interviews in it were written and recorded on the appropriate forms and witnessed by the defendant, Weaver. With the exception of the last set of notes in which he made his confession. On those, where he should have signed, the words 'refused to sign' have been penned."

"Sorry to steal your thunder Hunter," said Dawn, "If I can come in there now?" She again tapped her Biro against the sides of the incident board, where reduced digital images of the paperwork recovered from Jeffery Howson's safe were affixed in the top right hand corner.

"This find could change everything about the trial and conviction of Daniel Weaver. The originals of these are currently on their way to Forensics for chemical dating analysis and for fingerprint identification, but at the moment everything about them screams they are the genuine article. What we have here, team, is a set of recorded interview notes conducted with Weaver during the time he was in police custody on twenty-ninth August, nineteen-eighty-three. As we have heard, the interviewers were Jeffery Howson and Alan Darbyshire, and going by the handwriting, which matches that on the envelope they were found in, looks as though they have been completed by our murder victim Jeffery Howson. Prior to the introduction of PACE and taped recorded interviewing all interviews conducted in a police station had to be handwritten. The notes take the form of a question and answer session between the police officers and the defendant, known as contemporaneous notes, and had to be read and witnessed by the defendant. The paperwork found in the envelope, for the attention of Barry, has been witnessed by Daniel Weaver and bears no resemblance to any of the interviews on the original prosecution file. In fact they are a clear denial in the involvement of Lucy's disappearance and there is certainly no admission to her murder, in fact, quite the opposite. Daniel Weaver states that he last saw Lucy after their argument in the market place at about nine-thirty pm on the Friday evening. He says she told him she was going home; that her husband had found out about their relationship and was holding onto their daughter Jessica, threatening Lucy that she would never see her again. She told Daniel that she couldn't leave her daughter behind, so was calling it off. He did his best to make her change her mind and at one stage grabbed hold of her. And that's how he got his face scratched when she pulled away. He goes on to say that he went straight home to his flat, drank a few whiskies and watched some TV, and then went to bed where he remained until the next day when he went to his parents' house about eleven am, where his Mother made him some breakfast. When he was asked about the handbag being found hidden under sacking in his shed he stated and I quote 'someone must have planted it.'

Dawn looked around at the intense faces of her new team. "This could overturn the conviction against Daniel Weaver for Lucy's murder. If those notes are the real thing, and had been part of the original prosecution file then I am not convinced he would ever have gone to trial, in fact they would have opened up the entire investigation into Lucy's disappearance. It would have been nice if Jeffery Howson had left a note to explain all this, but I'm guessing that he didn't leave one because he was fully intending to explain everything to Barry when they met. And as we all know he was murdered before he could make that meeting. So, now, in the absence of any other information, we are left to speculate why they were never submitted. Their discovery certainly supports the comment he made to Barry in his telephone call on Saturday night that the wrong person was convicted and he knew who murdered Lucy."

She glanced at the incident board, where earlier that morning she had scribbled notes in red ink.

"There are only three people who can provide the answers to the validity of those notes. One is Jeffery Howson, who is now dead, the second is retired Detective Chief Inspector Alan Darbyshire and the third person is Daniel Weaver, who is currently serving life for Lucy's murder. Hunter has already told us that on the original file he found that the contemporaneous notes outlining Weaver's admission were not signed. The ones we have recovered from Jeffery Howson's safe are timed and dated, exactly the same as Weaver's admission interview notes. Only one of those sets can be the original notes and I know which ones I am inclined to go with."

Dawn studied the faces of the detectives.

"I don't want to even mention the unmentionable here, that two police officers perjured themselves to convict an innocent man of murder, but if the notes from Howson's safe are the originals of Daniel Weaver's final interview, then that is what we are looking at. And if that is the case, we have to ask ourselves why did Howson hold onto them? Why not destroy them? Because they clearly incriminate him and Alan Darbyshire. Were they some kind of insurance policy? Again, I am speculating. There are a lot of unanswered questions at the moment. But one thing is for sure— someone found out about the existence of those notes and wanted desperately to get their hands on them, even if it meant killing Jeffery Howson. And I guess that is also the reason why he swallowed his safe key to protect the evidence. Without doubt, the finding of this piece of evidence has opened up Pandora's box, and for now we need to keep a lid on it. The last thing we want is an out of control media frenzy interfering with our enquiry which is still at its early stages. If anyone gets a whiff that the press is onto, this, they report back to me immediately okay?"

She returned her gaze to her handwritten comments on the dry-wipe board.

"Okay everyone, new set of actions."

Turning to DC Bullars, she said, "Tony I want you to talk to Howson's ex-wife. I want to know everything about his life.

Who his friends and associates were during his CID days. I especially want you to see what you can learn about him during nineteen-eighty-three, when he was involved in the Lucy Blake-Hall case. We know from Katherine, his daughter, that he was separated and divorced a year later, so something had gone wrong in his marriage during this time. I want to know what that was."

She switched her look. "Hunter and Grace, I want you two to find out where retired DCI Alan Darbyshire is living now, and go and talk to him about his CID days, particularly his partnership with Howson. I do not want him to know he is under scrutiny at this stage and I especially don't want him to know about the discovery of the interview notes. See if you can sneak in about the Lucy Blake-Hall case without throwing up suspicions. I know that will be hard because he is ex-CID but I'm sure you'll come up with some way of doing that." She smirked at Hunter.

"We also have additional tasks, which DI Scaife will allocate after this briefing. The house-to-house forms have thrown up a number of enquiries, none earth-shattering, but they need to be bottomed and he has also drawn up a list of fresh actions from the Lucy Blake-Hall case. At this stage we have potential links, and although it doubles our workload they need to be established. I want all the main witnesses from the original investigation tracking down, and I want them interviewing as if it was a fresh enquiry. And find out which prison Daniel Weaver is serving time in. I know that the added enquiry is complicating matters. Lucy's disappearance was twenty five years ago, but do your best guys. That's it for now. Thank you all for giving me your fullest attention. There is a lot of work to do, but I know you will come up trumps."

As she watched her new team move into action she realised the earlier tightness in her stomach had completely gone.

That's a good thing she told herself. It was a sign she was back to her old self. *Back to being in control.*

* * * * *

"Push up girl, let me get in," Barry Newstead said, wheeling his chair next to Grace and pushing her aside with his elbow. He tucked his legs under her desk and glanced between her and Hunter before hunching over.

"Listen, I did a little bit of digging last night," he said, lowering his voice as if it was a private conversation between the three of them. "I contacted a few of my old colleagues to get the low-down on Jeffery and Alan Darbyshire after you told me about those interview notes. I'll just tell you what I found out before you go and see Alan."

Hunter's brow creased.

"Don't worry I didn't tell them anything about the investigation, especially about the Lucy Blake-Hall link. I made out I was just after background stuff about Jeffery and his work and was chasing up anyone he knew or worked with him. It wasn't easy getting stuff out of them. You know what the job was like back then. Nothing was ever straightforward and detectives took chances. Some are starting to distance themselves from Jeffery, not exactly clam up but they're not so forthcoming about what he got up to. And I'm afraid I'm not much of a help. You see, although I knew him and Alan Darbyshire, they were part of another team, the only time we ever got together was during major incidents, and even then we worked with our own partners, so except for seeing them round the office and hearing what collars they had brought in, I had very little to do with the pair. To be honest, Alan Darbyshire grated on me. He was a bit too flash for my liking. Used to come to work dressed like a tailor's dummy, three piece suit, matching tie and handkerchief, the works. And he always had to go one better. If you'd done a job well, he always let it be known that he'd done a similar one and better. And his villains were always more important than yours. I guess that's why he got promoted." He shook his head, cinched his lips together and huffed.

Hunter cut in. "Do I detect pangs of jealousy, Mr. Newstead?"

"Jealousy my arse! I could match him any day. It was the way he used to shout his mouth off in the office whenever he got a good collar. Don't get me wrong, he did get some good results. He must have had some damn good informants on the go. It was just the way he went about things, always running into the gaffer's office when he cleared a job up. It used to wind me up. I guess that's why he got promoted and I didn't." He pursed his lips again. "Anyway that's what I remember about him and I'm afraid I can't help you with the years we're focusing on because I transferred across to Headquarters Serious Crime Squad. So what I've done is track down who was in the office at that time to see what they could recall. I never mentioned Alan by name but a couple of my old colleagues actually dropped out his name during conversation and said that the pair were pretty thick with one another." His mouth set tight. "And by that comment I mean thick as thieves. They were partners not just in work but it appears that they were close socially as well. A couple of the lads have said to me that from what they remember Alan and Jeffery sailed pretty close to the wind at times."

"Didn't every detective, during the eighties?" said Hunter. "You've already acknowledged that detectives took chances. I remember some of the things I learned from you, and your stories."

"Not like that Hunter, not with the job, but outside of it. It appears the pair of them were regular visitors to a strip joint. Not just a strip club, it was also believed to be a knocking-shop. Back then, places of that ilk were well dodgy, and it was an absolute no-no to frequent them unless you were doing an operation. Well, talk in the office was that these two were regular visitors, and it was even hinted at that they were taking favours from the girls, and in exchange tipped off the owner every time it was due to be raided. Also one of my ex-colleagues mentioned that the pair were renowned for holidaying in Spain. Two, to three times a year, they'd go with their wives. Benidorm I've been told. In the same villa every time. Belonged to some businessman. No one's said anything about them being bent or anything, and to be honest they were renowned for working loads of overtime, so they could easily afford holidays abroad. Their arrest rate was very good, especially on the important jobs, and because they kept the detection figures high they were the gaffer's blue-eyed boys." Barry pushed himself back in his chair. "What would you do without a real detective being around eh?" he grinned. "Well that should give you two a little bit of a heads up when you start pumping him for background stuff."

* * * * *

Retired DCI Alan Darbyshire lived in a semi-detached refurbished police house nestled amid half a dozen others in a small cul-de-sac. He had been easy to find on the pension payroll computer.

Hunter and Grace didn't call ahead, they wanted to see his reaction when they turned up unannounced, flashing their warrant cards.

Recalling what Barry had told him earlier, Hunter knew that cops and guilty ones at that felt the pressure just as much as guilty villains especially when they were being interviewed by one of their own. What prevented Hunter from approaching this interview the way he would have desired was Alan Darbyshire's rank even though he was retired. Despite what Barry had told him, he knew that in some way Darbyshire would have earned his promotions and it had been instilled in him throughout his career that respect should be granted to those of seniority, regardless of what you thought of them.

As Hunter pulled up outside the retired DCI's home he glanced across at Grace, wondering if she could tell he was uneasy. He checked his watch as he alighted from the CID car. Just after 10.30am. He made a mental note of the time as he pushed open the front garden gate.

Double-glazed windows and a side extension had been added to the property in an attempt to differentiate it from the other police houses around it. Hunter knew that many other cops who had bought identical police houses during the Thatcher era had done the same.

The man who answered the door was the same height as Hunter but twice his build. He was vastly overweight, with a double chin that blended into a flabby neck. His hair was thinning and Brylcreemed back in a style which Hunter thought lent itself more to the early 1960s than today's fashion, and he had a neatly trimmed pencil-thin moustache.

Hunter pushed his warrant card in front of the man's face and introduced Grace and himself. "We're here about the murder of Jeffery Howson. I guess you saw it on the local news last night?" He watched for a reaction. There was none.

Casually, Darbyshire answered, "I got a phone call on Monday afternoon about it actually. You know what the police grapevine is like, even if you are retired. I guessed you'd be coming sooner or later to talk to his old colleagues." Then he checked with, "It is a social visit?"

Quick-off-the-mark, Hunter replied, "Course, why shouldn't it be?"

"Only kidding," he grinned. "You'd best come in then. Oh, and if you wouldn't mind taking your shoes off before you come in the lounge," he added, padding away in carpet slippers to an open door at the end of the hallway.

The room they entered was tastefully decorated and furnished, though a little too chintzy for Hunter's tastes. A plain cream carpet, allied with similar coloured painted walls, was complemented by a mocha coloured large two-seater Windsor style sofa and two matching armchairs. Swag-and-tail curtains framed the large lounge window. Above the replica Adam's fireplace, Hunter spotted one of Ashley Jackson's wild moorland scenes, and despite the fact that it was a print he knew it would have set Darbyshire back a few hundred pounds.

This was a different scene to the one he had taken in at Jeffery Howson's home.

Alan Darbyshire lowered his bulk into the armchair, nodding at Hunter and Grace, indicating them towards the sofa opposite. "Make yourselves comfortable," he said, then added, "Now what can I do for you?"

"We're trying to build up a picture of Jeffery. We know you were a colleague of his for quite a good few years."

"We started out as DCs together," Darbyshire said. "And then I was his DS when I got promoted. I was lucky, they kept me in the department and we carried on working together on the same team until I was promoted again. We always kept in touch though, before and after retirement."

Grace had already removed her notebook from her handbag and begun making notes.

"How did he die, if you don't mind me asking?"

"Course not Alan. He was suffocated." Hunter wasn't going to expand on the fact that a cushion was used to carry out the act, while another person held him down. Given the fact that Alan Darbyshire could also have been involved in the murder, he needed to be guarded about what he divulged.

The retired DCI inhaled sharply. "Good God. Poor Jeff."

Hunter watched his face. He looked genuinely shocked.

"When did you last see Jeffery?"

He took another deep breath and composed himself. "It'd be about two weeks ago now. I called in to see how he was. As I've already said, we still kept in touch, though visits dropped off over the years. You may have already gathered that Jeff was very much a recluse, kept himself to himself. I don't think he really got over his wife leaving him. She took his daughter as well, which made it even worse. And when she married again, well that really hit him hard. It's awful to say, especially with what's happened to him, but I thought at one stage he was going to top himself so I spent a lot of time with him. That's why I asked you how he died."

"It definitely wasn't suicide."

Alan nodded an acknowledgement. "So what else do you want to know?"

Hunter responded, "As much as you can tell us. You know the type of thing we're after. We've only spoken to his daughter so far."

"He thought the world of Katherine. Her being taken away was the hardest part for him, though they're back in touch with one another now, which I'm guessing you will already know. He rung me and told me when she moved back to work up at the hospital and said she'd found a house just round the corner from him. That made a world of difference to him, I can tell you."

"Why did he and his wife split up?"

Alan Darbyshire shrugged. "You know how it is. Being a copper's not easy. The unsociable hours and everything that comes with it. Being married to a detective is even harder for some wives. The long hours."

"When did things start to go downhill for him?" Hunter already knew from Jeffery Howson's daughter's background statement that his wife left him in 1984, the year following the Lucy Blake-Hall case, and he wanted to check how much Alan Darbyshire was prepared to reveal.

"Jenny, his wife, was always a bit of a funny bugger. In our early days me and my wife, and Jeff and Jenny, went out such a lot together, but to be honest I always got the impression she did it just for Jeff's sake. She could be a bit stuck-up. I know she used to give him some right earache when we went out on drinking sessions. I don't think she was happy with him being a detective. What I'm getting at is that things between them were always strained and they just deteriorated. I personally thought good riddance when she went, but Jeff was devastated. He did everything to try to get her back but she wasn't having any of it. In fact, to spite him she went off with someone else. If you ask me, I think she had a fancy man all along. I used to tell him he was better off without her."

At the periphery of his vision, Hunter caught Grace rolling her eyes. He could guess what her views were of Alan Darbyshire. He smiled to himself. No doubt when they got back in the car she would express them. Moving on he said, "Okay thanks for that. That gives us some picture of his life. Now when did you last see Jeffery or speak with him?"

Alan Darbyshire rubbed his flabby chin and looked up to the ceiling, then replied, "To be honest, once we both retired, things drifted away between us. I took on a part-time job doing some security work, while Jeff became a bit of a recluse. I think the only time he went out was to nip down to the bookies.

He used to like his horse racing. Then a good couple of months ago Jeff phoned me up after getting his bad news about the lung cancer, so I called round to see him. He was pretty down. I offered to take him for a beer but he didn't feel up to it. I nipped over at least once a week during the past few months. I watched the cancer eat him away. It wasn't a nice thing to see."

"So when was the last time you saw him?"

"The Monday or Tuesday of the week leading up to his murder. He was killed over the weekend, right?"

Hunter nodded. "Late Saturday night, we believe."

"I was at home with Pauline, my wife."

Hunter thought he caught an awkward look on the retired DCI's face, then noted how quickly he had retrieved his composure.

Alan said, "That's the ex-detective in me, answering like that. Everyone you interview is a suspect, right?"

Hunter masked his thoughts by returning a forced smile. He recalled what Barry had told him about the nights that Alan Darbyshire and Jeffery Howson had spent together in the strip club, and the holidays with their wives, courtesy of an unknown businessman and wondered if he should raise it as a series of questions. He also remembered what Detective Superintendent Leggate had said at the morning briefing. Keeping on track with what he had rehearsed inside his head he asked, "What was he like as a detective?"

"Brilliant. Good thief taker, good interviewer. Worked hard and played hard. Everything a good detective should be."

"Sorry to have to ask you this Alan, but you were his DS and his friend. Did he get up to anything dodgy?" *This was his opportunity to mention the strip club.*

"I don't mean to be funny, but where is this going?"

Hunter hadn't managed to throw him off guard. "I'm not trying to draw you into anything Alan. I'm trying to establish if you were aware of anything untoward in Jeff's past. We haven't got a clue at the moment as to why he was killed."

"Depends on what you're hinting at. We did things differently back then. We didn't have all that fancy forensic help that you lot have got today. We had to do things the hard way. We took more chances to get our results. Let's just leave it with the fact that Jeff was a good detective."

Hunter sensed an edge to his voice. "I'm not trying to accuse him of anything, or you for that matter. I know policing was different during your era. I know that from working with Barry

Newstead when I first went in CID. I'm working with him now. He's a civilian investigator with us and I have to listen to his ranting on about how the job's not what it used to be on almost a daily basis."

Alan Darbyshire's face creased into a smile. "I remember Barry as a fresh-faced detective. He was a good thief-taker himself, from what I remember. Not as good as me mind, but if you were taught by Barry then you can't be all that bad."

The retired DCI's response triggered what Barry had told him earlier about Darbyshire's boasting. Hunter continued. "Going back to that last question. Did he have any enemies, or do you know of anyone he'd come up against in the job who could have held such a grudge against him to do this."

Alan Darbyshire dipped his eyes down to the carpet. A split-second later he raised them again. That diversion of his gaze was enough for Hunter. He knew he had hit on something. Under different circumstances he would have gone for the jugular. But now wasn't the time to push. He'd store it for later and see first what Alan was prepared to tell them.

"I've been thinking about that since I found out about Jeff. You could say all the collars we felt became our enemies. It's like I said, we did things differently when he and I were around in CID. There were no custody suites like there are now. Just a couple of cold cells and if the villains didn't play ball they got banged up for the night without a blanket. They were so cold, the next morning they'd sell their grandmother for a cup of warm tea. And I know a couple of the lads in the office would give their prisoners a bit of a slap to make them confess. That's just how it was."

"Was that Jeffery's style?"

"Not giving anyone a slap. I never saw Jeff ever hit a prisoner. He could talk the hind leg off a donkey. His villains would cough just to shut him up." He gave off a short laugh.

"What about any cases he worked on?" *There.* He'd given him the opening. It was his ideal opportunity to introduce the Lucy Blake-Hall investigation. He watched him slowly shake his head, lips set tight.

"We worked on so many over the years and you always got the odd villain whingeing or threatening to make a complaint about you because they weren't happy with their treatment." His eyes danced between Hunter and Grace. "You know how it is?"

"Any high profile ones that spring to mind?"

"Well there was one I recall. The Terry Braithwaite arrest brought lots of publicity."

Hunter's brow creased. He couldn't bring that case to mind.

"The papers referred to him as The Beast of Barnwell."

Hunter remembered it now. The case was an old one and he had often heard Barry talking about the job. He nodded.

"It was before your time, probably before you were born in fact. There were a number of indecent assaults and rapes on women in the late sixties and early seventies. Always in late autumn and winter and during a full moon, that's how he got his nickname. For five years he ran amok, and then late one night in the woods he was disturbed by one of the night fishermen at Barnwell Lakes. The man heard screaming from inside a van parked in one of the car parking areas. It had always been a haunt for courting couples, but by good fortune such was the man's concern at the cries that he went to investigate. He disturbed Terry Braithwaite in the middle of carrying out a rape on a young girl and he started banging on his van. The fisherman ended up in a scuffle with Terry but he managed to get away, but not before the witness had banged his hand one final time on the roof as the van was taking off. The next day the body of seventeen year old Glynis Young was found in bushes at the edge of the wood." He lifted his arms, intertwined his fingers and rested them on his distended belly. "Terry Braithwaite had been one of our suspects for a couple of the assaults because he matched the descriptions of a couple of the e-fits the victims had given us, and he owned a van like the one described. The next day Jeff and I locked him up. He'd cleaned the inside of his van but he'd forgotten to do the outside as thoroughly as the inside and SOCO found the fisherman's handprint still on the roof. It was one of Jeff's first big jobs; he'd been in CID about a year. The upshot was that Braithwaite got life in nineteen-seventy-three with a minimum thirty year sentence. He sent word out from his cell that he was going to get us back for that. He said we had stitched him up even with the evidence from the witness. He had two appeals turned down. He did over thirty in the end and was released two years ago. You might recall there was a big splash about him in the local paper. The Chronicle got wind of his release and didn't know if he'd come back to Barnwell to live. I read that the Probation Service stated Braithwaite was in a bail hostel in another county." Alan Darbyshire diverted his eyes again to the floor then glanced back up at Hunter. "Terry Braithwaite would be a good start for your enquiries. He was a nasty piece of work and never forgave us. Jeffery and I visited him in prison on quite a few occasions over the years because we were always convinced he had done more rapes than he was convicted of, either in neighbouring forces, or because some of the women hadn't come forward; but he refused to talk to us. Yeah, if you can track him down he would be worth talking to. He'll be in his sixties himself now, but he looked after himself inside."

Hunter spent the next half an hour teasing out aspects of Jeffery Howson's career, and although he freely talked about Jeffery's working style and about their drinking sessions together Alan Darbyshire avoided mentioning the visits to the strip club and gave away no revelations which would take the enquiry forward. Bearing in mind what Detective Superintendent Dawn Leggate had said, he decided to bring the interview to an end.

"Well, thanks for that Alan," he said, pushing himself up from the sofa. "You've been a great help."

Grace shut her notebook and returned it to her handbag.

They shook hands and made for the door. The retired DCI opened it and as they were about to step out, Hunter turned.

"Oh, there was just one thing Alan. We've found some of Jeffery's old pocket note-books," Hunter lied.

"Pocket books?" he frowned. "They should have all been handed in when he retired. They destroy them after seven years."

"That's what we thought. Well it seems as if he hung on to a couple. We've got to go through them thoroughly but they seem to feature a case you haven't mentioned. What was it now Grace?"

"Oh, the Lucy Blake-Hall murder back in nineteen-eighty-three." Grace had quickly latched on to her partner's wavelength.

Hunter could have sworn the retired DCI gulped. Despite the pudgy neck, there was a clear movement.

"Lucy Blake-Hall," he seemed to stumble over the words. "Sorry, you caught me unawares. I had to think hard for a bit then. It was so long ago now. Jeff and I interviewed the man who killed Lucy. He confessed to her murder. Yes I remember now. He was found guilty at Crown and got life. It was such a long time ago that I've forgotten most of the details senior moment and all that"

Yes I bet you have! Your memory was pretty damn good when it came to recalling The Beast of Barnwell case, which was ten years earlier.

"It's strange he should have kept those. Did he leave anything else about that case?"

"Don't believe so." Hunter raised another fake smile and followed Grace out onto the path. "Well thank you for your time Alan. If anything else crops up we know where to find you now don't we?"

- ooOoo -

CHAPTER FIVE

DAY FOUR: 27th November.

Hunter dropped his right shoulder and exploded forward with a deft uppercut. He followed up with a left jab, and a swift right, before dancing away into the centre of the ring and setting up his guard again.

Sweat dribbled into the corner of his eyes. He experienced a momentary sharp stinging sensation before blinking and wiping the salty water away with his training mitts. He switched his footwork and took up a leading position in readiness for another onslaught.

"Come on son, last thirty seconds," barked his dad, Jock. "Then you're done."

Flexing his shoulders, he sprang forward again. Two hard and fast punches, right and left, smacked the leather training pads his father held. He dodged away and took in a great gulp of air. He had only been sparring with his dad for ten minutes, but he was drained.

It had been a long while since they'd done this. September had been the last time he had done any serious training with his dad. Of course he had visited his father's boxing gym since then, but he'd only had time to lift weights and work the training bag.

There was also another reason they had not trained together. Hunter still felt a certain awkwardness when in his father's company. He had tried to put the events of the past two months behind him, but in the background it had nibbled away. It wasn't the ordeal he had been put through, but the fact that his father had deceived him and then tried to hide his past even when that past had got people killed. And now it was like his father was pretending nothing had happened. Hunter had done his utmost to reconcile himself with things, but it was still jarring away inside. *'Your dad will talk about it when he's good and ready,'* Beth had said to him on more than one occasion during the past few weeks, but with one thing and another, especially his work, he'd not been able to grab any time for a clear the air session.

"Two more punches son, and we're done."

Hunter swung in a flourish of quick jabs and finished with a strong uppercut, lifting the pad his father held. As he dropped his arms with exhaustion, his dad sideswiped his head.

"Keep your guard up at all times son." His dad gave him a wink and cracked a grin as he gripped one pad under his armpit and tugged it off. "That's it, we're done."

Pulling off the other pad, he reached across to Hunter and grabbed his hands to help as he slipped off the training mitts.

"Good session that Hunter. Shower now, eh?" He dropped the gloves and pads against a ring post and ducked under the middle rope. "What time did you say you had to be in to work?" he asked, glancing back as he stepped out of the boxing ring. "Have you got time for a quick cuppa before I open up? Don't know about you but I'm parched."

Hunter nodded. He was still trying to catch his breath. He grabbed a towel off a corner post and wiped his face and the back of his neck as he made his way to the changing room. The adrenaline was still coursing through him. He felt energised despite the workout he'd just had.

He was glad now that he'd dragged himself out of bed early. He'd even had the time to take the boys to school that morning - something he'd not been able to do for ages. Now he felt set up for the day; he could take anything that was thrown at him.

"Put the kettle on, I'll be ten minutes," he shouted after his father, who was sloping off towards his office. "I don't have to be in until eleven this morning, I've got a funeral to go to, for that ex-detective. That case I'm on that I've told you about?"

* * * * *

Barry Newstead grabbed Hunter the moment he strolled into the department.

"I've been trying to get hold of you on your mobile most of the morning," he said excitedly.

Hunter pulled his phone from his pocket and examined it. His face creased.

"Sorry Barry, I've had it on silent. I've been down at my dad's gym."

"You'll never guess what I've discovered?" He thrust a sheet of paper at Hunter.

Hunter saw that it had a list of numbers, in time, day and date order. Barry stabbed a finger over one number highlighted with yellow fluorescent ink.

"That's the top copy of Jeffery Howson's itemised phone bill for his land-line. Guess who he rung on the afternoon of his death."

Hunter scrutinised the tinted telephone number. It didn't mean anything.

"Alan Darbyshire. He rung Alan Darbyshire just before five pm on that Saturday he was killed. It's one of the last numbers he called that day. The next one was mine and the last one was his daughter Katherine."

Hunter fixed Barry's glistening brown eyes.

"Good God Barry, this is a real turn up for the books. It completely contradicts what he told me and Grace yesterday. He told us that he had last spoken with Jeffery on the Monday or Tuesday prior to his death. Does the gaffer know about this?"

"Yeah, I fed it into this morning's briefing. He's chasing up forensics to prioritise examination of some of the exhibits, see if we can find something good enough to bring Alan in."

* * * * *

Hunter stamped his feet on the damp grass. The cold was beginning to get to him. A biting north westerly wind had picked up since he had emerged from the warm church and was disturbing the fallen autumn leaves around the headstones in Barnwell cemetery. The dry rustling noise disturbed an uncanny silence.

He flicked up the collar of his overcoat and buried his hands in his pockets as he scanned the faces of the mourners huddled graveside.

Ten minutes earlier, he had followed up at the rear of the slow procession as Jeffery Howson's casket had been carried from the church to his final resting place in the cemetery. The light wood coffin now rested upon two wooden posts above an open grave.

Hunter could smell the freshly turned soil and clammy earth.

Four of the coffin bearers, two either side of the grave, each grabbed hold of the end of a rope, and took the weight of the casket as the supporting props were slid away. The bearers began to lower the coffin.

Hunter watched the casket making its descent.

"We commit this body to the earth, ashes to ashes, dust to dust," said the vicar in sombre tones, his head bowed. He peppered the coffin lid with a handful of loose soil.

Hunter looked at the burial group, scanning their faces. It wasn't a large assembly, made up of mainly elderly men. Hunter guessed they were ex-colleagues.

Three women made up the burial party as well. Katherine and her daughter, Amy, were two of them. Katherine was sobbing uncontrollably. A slender, dark dyed-haired woman, who looked to be in her mid-sixties, had a comforting arm around her. Hunter guessed it was Katherine's Mother; Jeffery's ex-wife.

Hunter hated funerals.

He had been tasked with attending Jeffery Howson's service, and he knew nearby there would be a member of the Intelligence Unit covertly filming everything. It was standard procedure; it was not unknown for the killer to turn up at the funeral of his victim.

That thought made him lock onto Alan Darbyshire who was huddled amid the congregation. The man met his gaze, as if he had known he was being watched. He quickly turned away and dropped his head.

If that wasn't the actions of a guilty man, thought Hunter.

Hunter's concentration was disturbed by the machine-gun rattle of a solitary magpie somewhere to his left. He turned his head and fifty yards away, by the boundary hedge, he caught a sudden and unexpected movement. A broad, squat figure dressed in a black padded jacket and wearing a dark woollen hat, which covered most of his head and his ears, disguising his features, was standing close to a gap in the cropped line of holly.

Hunter eyeballed him for several seconds. The unknown guest was staring in the direction of the funeral party.

Hunter took a few steps back, pulling out his radio from inside his coat. He switched it into life. It had been pre-loaded onto the same frequency as that of his colleague's from the Intelligence Unit. Although he couldn't see him, he knew he would be somewhere nearby.

Turning away from the gathering, he pressed the handset close to his mouth and in a low tone requested the plain clothed officer's attention.

The radio crackled but there was no response.

He tried again, in a firmer tone this time, and began striding toward the stranger.

Hunter knew he was in the open but he had little option. Instinct was telling him that something wasn't right.

He'd only made a half a dozen steps before the incomer saw Hunter and began edging away towards the breach in the holly hedge.

Hunter picked up his pace and hissed into his radio as the stranger made the gap.

In a flash, the man had disappeared. Hunter smacked the radio against his thigh in frustration.

Damn it!

He knew that even if someone did respond in the next few seconds it would be too late - the dark-clad figure would be long gone.

- ooOoo –

CHAPTER SIX

DAY FIVE: 28th November.

"Hunter Kerr I'm surprised at you," scolded Grace, looking over the rim of her coffee cup. "It's not like you to be a nine-o'clock-critic."

"I'm just so frigging miffed. We could have caught that guy at the funeral. Instead he did a runner and we've no idea who he is."

Grace pushed herself forward. Leaning across the desk, she said, "It was a mistake. Anyone could have made it. The Intelligence Unit guy had simply switched his radio off for the church service and forgot to switch it back on...end of. He wasn't to know that the stranger was going to turn up in that part of the graveyard. His job was to film the congregation of Jeffery Howson's funeral and he did that."

Hunter held up his hands. "Yep, fair comment Grace. It just would have been nice to find out what he was doing there."

"Course it would, but we didn't, and so we have to live with it. He'll come again. We'll find out who he is, don't you worry." She took a sip at her drink and set it down, hands still wrapped around her warm mug. "Anyway, he did manage to get some good footage of Alan Darbyshire. Did you see the look on his face as you were chasing after the guy?"

Hunter nodded.

"Picture wasn't it? You could tell from his reaction that he knew who that man was."

"There's no doubt Alan Darbyshire is up to his neck in this. I'd love to bring the slimy lying toad in, but you heard the gaffer at this morning's briefing. He wants us to hold off for the time being, see if we get something concrete that will link him physically with Jeffery Howson's death."

"It'll happen. We know he told us one lie about the last time he spoke with Jeffery because of the telephone records, and don't forget his signature on those notes we found in Howson's safe. If they are the originals, then we've at least got him for perjury in the Weaver trial. That will be enough to arrest him and get enough of a lever on him to quiz him about the murder."

Hunter nodded again. "I can see where the gaffer is coming from. Because Darbyshire's ex-job, especially an ex-DCI, he wants us to get enough evidence so that when we do finally give him a tug we can make it stick, but it's so frustrating."

"It'll come good in the end." Grace pushed herself upright and took a last sip of her coffee. "Anyway, we have enough work to handle just now. You weren't here for this morning's briefing, but the Super wants us to speak with Daniel Weaver before he hears it from the press that we've re-opened the Lucy Blake-Hall case, especially as he's already had one appeal turned down. I've already set things in motion. He's currently in Wakefield Prison, and I've also managed to track down his barrister from the trial back in nineteen-eighty-four. He's defending a stabbing case at Sheffield Crown Court which is listed for three days, so I've left a message with his secretary for him to get back to me."

"Good job Grace. Once you sort out a time and date with him to meet, I'll contact the prison and fix up a visit. This will not be an easy one, you know. If those notes from Howson's safe prove to be original, he's going to be more than a little pissed off. He's served twenty-four years for a murder he might not have done."

"And we're going to come in for some flak from the media. They just love a miscarriage of justice story like this."

"That's why it would be nice to have Alan Darbyshire in a cell before we go and speak with Daniel Weaver."

"Trouble is we need the evidence, and we haven't got enough."

"Talking about evidence, how've you gone on with the old card index?"

"Don't ask. That has been a nightmare. I've managed to get it in some semblance of order, but only thanks to Isobel from the HOLMES team. She's worked on the old card system on quite a few murders in the past, so she helped me piece it all together. It's currently laid out over two desks in their office, and the team are slowly inputting it into the computers. She's estimated that in roughly a fortnight's time, we'll be up to speed and be able to run the Lucy Blake-Hall enquiry from HOLMES. But it's going to make for a fair bit of leg-work. And I can see we're going to need some help from the Cold Case Team"

"How do you mean?"

"Well, Isobel's already identified that quite a few of the witnesses are dead. Added to that, some of the addresses no longer exist. Some of the old terraced streets have been knocked down, and to complicate matters further, some of the female witnesses have changed their names. Got married and moved. This is not going to be an easy investigation."

"And let me throw something else into the mix."

Grace set aside her mug, looking puzzled.

"You might wonder where this has come from, but it was something that came into my head yesterday. I tried to dismiss it, but it's still niggling away." He paused and met his partner's gaze. "Lucy might not be dead."

They stared at each other for a moment.

"I know Grace. I can see by your reaction what you're thinking. And if I try to rationalise things, that suggestion doesn't make sense. After all no one has seen her for twenty-five years. Everything says Lucy is dead. However, you and I know that stranger things have happened. Especially after finding those contemporaneous notes in Jeffery Howson's safe. It means Daniel Weaver's confession is false, so all we have is the last sighting of her in Barnwell market place."

Hunter tented his fingers and looked across at Grace. "I've gone back over the prosecution file. The original murder investigation never found an attack site. And though we have witnesses who saw and heard Daniel Weaver and Lucy arguing, we have no one who actually witnessed any assault upon her. And there was never any blood found on Weaver's clothes, or at his flat. All we have is that the confession made by Weaver is probably false, and if that is proved to be the case, we are left with the puzzle of finding out where Lucy disappeared to on twenty-sixth August nineteen-eighty-three."

* * * * *

Tony Bullars and Family Liaison Officer Carol Ragen rang the front door bell of Katherine Edwards' home and waited. From deep inside, they heard a shout to 'Come in' and so let themselves into the hallway. Carol called out again and a woman's voice answered from the back room. As the two detectives entered the kitchen they found Jeffery Howson's ex-wife, Jennifer West, standing half in, half out, of the open French doors. She was taking a long draw on her cigarette. She acknowledged them with a raised hand, and then flicked the smouldering remains out onto the paved patio.

Tony and Carol watched her shiver as she took a last look out across the rain-sodden garden before stepping back into the warmth and closing the doors.

"Gosh, it's brass-monkeys out there today," she said as she stepped towards the sink, filled a glass with water and took a mouthful. "You won't tell Katherine you caught me smoking, will you? I'll not hear the last of it if you do. I've told her I've quit since Jeffery was diagnosed with lung cancer." She took another sip of water and then set the glass down on the drainer. "It's easier to tell a white lie than to argue with her. I've been smoking since I was fourteen and it's hard to break a fifty year habit."

"Cross my heart," Tony replied, drawing a sign over the left side of his chest.

She smiled, fixing him with twinkling grey eyes.

As she leaned back against the work surface, Tony couldn't help but notice the striking similarity to her daughter. She was tall and slim with dark collar length hair, though unlike her daughter's natural colour, Jennifer's hair was dyed. And also unlike her daughter's fresh complexion, her features were heavily lined and creased. Despite the newly acquired tan from her recent holiday, she looked somewhat older than her sixty-four years. Tony guessed that was down to her half-century of smoking, yet he could definitely see where Katherine got her looks from

"Katherine's already filled me in. You want to know about Jeffery?" she said.

"If you don't mind. We've obviously got some recent stuff from Katherine, and we've talked to some of his ex-colleagues, but as his parents are now dead you're the person who probably knew him the best during his younger years."

"Only until nineteen-eighty-four. That's when I left him."

"Yes we know, and that's the period I want to focus on, if you don't mind?"

Jennifer looked puzzled.

Tony continued. "You appreciate that I can't go into things in any detail, because the investigation is still in its infancy, and we haven't arrested anyone yet for Jeffery's murder, but a few things have cropped up since we started this enquiry which makes us want to look into his past, and the nineteen-eighties are a period of his life we are interested in."

"Oh I see. I realise you have your reasons why can't say too much but it's during that time that he and I had our differences."

"Yes we know. That's why I want to ask you a few questions about that period of his life."

"Yeah okay, I can understand that. But you'll have to appreciate this is not going to be easy. I don't want to paint Jeffery in a bad light, especially for Katherine. I've never really told her anything about why me and her dad split up. She's only really just got to know him."

"Don't worry Jennifer, we'll treat what you tell us with confidence. We're only interested in anything which may point us in the direction of his killer. Having said that, it is also important that we have the right picture painted of him. Especially his background."

"This is going to be awkward. Do you know, I've never sat down and discussed with anyone what went on in Jeff's and my life before I left him? Don't get me wrong, when I first left, I told snippets of it to a couple of close friends, and I have mentioned the odd thing here and there to Derek, he's the man I'm married to now, but I didn't even tell my solicitor some of the stuff Jeff had done, because I knew it would lose him his job." Jennifer West wrung her hands.

Tony could see threads of broken veins close to the skin. Suddenly she appeared frail. "All I can say, Jennifer, is that we'll do our best with what you tell us. But it is important that we get to know everything about Jeffery. It might give us our best clue as to who killed him."

She nodded. "Yes I know. Do you know this is so weird? So many times in the past I have listened to Jeffery's stories of some of the enquiries he has been involved in and how he has interviewed witnesses. Never did I think I would be one of those witnesses myself."

"Strange world we live in eh, Jennifer?" Tony exchanged a quick glance with Carol. He could see she had her pen poised over her journal. "Tell me a bit about yourself and Jeffery, when you married et cetera, just for background. Speak freely. I'll interrupt if I want something different okay?"

She nodded again, switching eye-contact between Tony and Carol. "I first met Jeffery in nineteen-sixty-four, not long after he'd joined the job. He was nineteen and I was twenty. I worked at Woolworth's and I'd caught a young lad shoplifting. Jeffery came to arrest him, and he actually asked me out while he was taking a statement from me. It was so spontaneous and he was so handsome. A man in uniform and all that." Her solemn look suddenly transformed into a smile. "He took me to the cinema to see Goldfinger. I know it's corny and all that but I saw a resemblance in Jeffery to Sean Connery. And that was it, I was smitten." For a second her gaze was distant, as if lost in her thought. Then she blinked and said, "We went out together for just over a year and I got caught with Katherine. It was a real blow for both of us. We had talked so much about what we wanted to do before we settled down, but that put paid to both our dreams." She glanced between Tony and Carol. "Don't take that the wrong way. Once we got our head around things we were both overjoyed, and Katherine's made my world perfect, but it was just at the time you understand?"

Never having had a child, Tony didn't understand. Nevertheless he nodded.

"We had to get married before she was born, because the job frowned on it. But they gave us a police house to live in. A three-bedroom semi. It was better than what both our parents had. Those early years were good times. Short of money, but we had such happy times as a family. And then he went in CID." She glanced at Tony. "Sorry. I didn't mean that to sound like it did, because we still had some good times even in his early CID days. The extra money he brought in from his overtime was more than welcome. It helped us get together the deposit for the house at Woodlands View. But it also meant he was spending a lot of time at work. Sometimes I didn't see him from one day to the next, especially if he was on a murder. And especially when he got in with that Alan Darbyshire."

Tony straightened up from his slouch at the mention of that name. "What about Alan Darbyshire?"

"Oh don't read too much into that comment, he was just a bad influence. Jeffery was never one for drinking, but when he got in with Alan they seemed to be never away from the pub. It was putting a strain on our marriage and I told him so. And I told him that he had a daughter to think about."

"Can you remember roughly when this was?"

She glanced away momentarily, a look of concentration on her face. For a couple of seconds she started worrying her bottom lip, then said softly, "He went in CID in the summer of nineteen-seventy-two, and he was probably three or four years in, when he started with the regular late drinking sessions with Alan. He didn't come in rolling drunk, or anything like that, it was just that it'd be the early hours of the morning before he got home. He always used to say he'd been working late. It caused quite a few rows, I can tell you."

"Did you get to know Alan Darbyshire well?"

"Oh yes. I saw a lot of Alan. We used to go out as a couple, me and Jeffery and him and his wife Pauline. She was nice, and he was quite a character."

"It's been mentioned that you used to go on holiday together?"

"Oh yes, that was in the early eighties. Alan knew someone who had a place in Benidorm, and so it only cost us for the flights and our spending money. We'd go there a couple of times a year. It worked out cheaper than a holiday in England."

"What kind of place are we talking about in Benidorm?"

"It was a two bedroom villa with its own pool, lovely place."

"Do you know who it belonged to?"

"To be honest, at first I didn't think anything about this. As cops, and you'll know what I mean when I say this, you get to know a lot of people, from all walks of life, and Jeffery used to tell me it was a case of 'you scratch my back and I'll scratch yours'. He told me that he and Alan had done a businessman a favour and in return he was letting them use his holiday home when he didn't need it." She fixed on Tony's expression. "And before you ask, no I don't know what that favour was. But I don't believe it was anything underhand. Jeffery wasn't the kind of man to do anything wrong. He loved his job. I have to say though, I was never too sure about Alan. I always used to say to Jeffery that I thought he was a flash git. You see he got promoted and he had a bit more money and used to throw it around a bit."

"What do you mean by that comment Jennifer throw it around?"

"Well, things were a bit tight for us even with the overtime. I didn't work and we had Katherine. Alan and Pauline didn't have children, and she worked, so it always seemed as if he had a lot of money, and he liked to show off by flashing it around."

Tony swung his gaze towards his FLO colleague. He could see Carol feverishly scribbling away in her journal.

"Did you ever get the impression Alan would do anything dodgy?"

Jennifer rolled her head from side to side. "Not to my knowledge, but Alan always acted the Jack the Lad, and after a while it grated on me. I felt as if Jeffery was a bit of a lap-dog around him, both at work and when we were out, and I didn't like it. I told Jeffery my thoughts on quite a few occasions and we'd end up rowing over it. It wore me down in the end and I deliberately forced some space between us when it came to going out as couples. I used to make excuses about not feeling well, or say we couldn't get a baby-sitter, and then I told Jeffery I couldn't face going on holiday with them. I guess that's when I realised our marriage was in a mess. I did try to make a go of it but I could tell Jeffery wasn't happy and that's when he and Alan started boozing regularly together. We started to drift apart. And I started to re-evaluate my life. The final straw was when he came home with the new car. A brand new BMW, I ask you. I went spare because money was tight enough as it was, but he told me that the businessman Alan and he had done a favour for brought them over from Germany, because he fiddled the VAT, and he'd got the car on a nought per cent interest deal. It was at that stage I felt something wasn't quite right. I know the police are sticklers when it comes to accepting gifts, or even credit, and I wanted him to give it back. I told him he could lose his job if anyone found out. All he kept saying was that it was all above board and he was paying for it but without the added interest, and that Alan had got a similar deal as well."

"Is that what caused your marriage to break up?"

"Not exactly. It was well on its way by then, in my eyes. I started to get suspicious about Jeffery's late night jaunts. I've already mentioned about his drinking sessions. Well, on a couple of occasions when he came home I could swear I smelt women's perfume on him, and I fronted him up about it, but he just told me it was because of this night club he and Alan went to. I got a friend of mine to follow him one night and I discovered he was visiting a private club in Wakefield, which I found out was a strip club. That was it. I dolled myself up one night and turned up at the club. I found Jeffery and Alan entertaining a couple of women at the bar. They were dressed like whores, and for me that was the last straw. I came straight back home, packed two suitcases, got my dad to pick me up, and I left with Katherine and stayed at my parents' caravan in Skegness until I could fix myself up with a place for us both. Then I filed for divorce. I never came back. Jeffery came to the van and pleaded on bended knees, but by then I'd really had enough. I knew I'd be better out of it. Jeffery had changed so much as a person."

"When was this, Jennifer?"

"Nineteen-eighty-three. And I got divorced the following year on the grounds of his unreasonable behaviour."

"That year's important to our enquiry Jennifer. You've mentioned earlier that Jeffery used to tell you about some of the jobs he was involved in. Can you recall him ever mentioning the name Lucy Blake-Hall?"

Jennifer West nodded. "I certainly do. It was splashed all over the local papers as well. He and Alan played a big part in that job. Jeffery told me that they had arrested the man who had murdered her." She pushed herself upright from the work surface she had been leaning on. "In fact, that was the night I caught him and Alan with those women. He tried to tell me, once I'd caught him out that he was celebrating because they had charged Lucy's killer with her murder. You see, the strip club belonged to Lucy's husband."

- ooOoo –

CHAPTER SEVEN

DAY SIX: 29th November.

The only sound in the house came from the crackling logs burning in the grate. Hunter had lit the fire the moment he had got downstairs, having seen the state of the weather when he opened the bedroom curtains that morning.

Taking a spell out from his paperwork he stared into the dancing flames and day-dreamed for a brief moment. It reminded him of his and Beth's very first viewing of this house; the image before him prompted the recall every time. Passing by after a shopping trip, they had spotted the owner's home-made sign and he had stopped the car and reversed to get a better look. They had lingered at the top of the drive for a good five minutes, Hunter taking in the well appointed three-bedroom semi. He could remember thinking that this was too good to be true. They knew the location well from walks they had taken together in the fields at the rear of the property when they were younger, and both of them, at one time or another, had talked and dreamed about living in such a house. They decided to knock on the owner's door - it was too good an opportunity to let slip. By sheer chance they were the first viewing, the sign had only gone up that morning, and the minute they had entered the brightly lit hallway they knew this was a house with potential. Once they had been shown into the richly furnished lounge and had been greeted by the roaring fire, Hunter had looked into Beth's eyes and knew this was the place for them. That was ten years ago and since then it had become a family home with the births of Jonathan and Daniel.

Hunter returned his gaze to the documents spread out over the large oak coffee table. The previous evening, he had brought home the Daniel Weaver prosecution file and photograph exhibits. At work he had already read through all of its 500 pages twice but he wanted to fully ingrain the important elements of it to memory before he and Grace visited Daniel Weaver later that day: Grace had earmarked a visitors' slot for 4pm at Wakefield Prison where Daniel had been held for most of the twenty five years inside.

He pawed at the bound file, searching for the first statement he wanted. He had four hours to plough his way through the file before Beth came home from work to join him for lunch; it was her half day today, and she had dropped the boys off at school on her way to the surgery, leaving him to get on with his task.

Jeffery Howson's witness statement was the first he had earmarked, and he pinched together the dozen or so typed sheets and settled back against the tan leather upholstery of the sofa to read through it again, slowly. This was one piece of evidence he couldn't afford to rush through - this, and the testimony of Alan Darbyshire were the crucial accounts which had condemned Daniel all those years ago and he concentrated on the facts and comments they had recorded. The forensic results had come back on the notes found in Jeffery Howson's safe - the tests on the paper and the ink had confirmed that they dated back to 1983. Daniel Weaver's conviction was now unsafe and he knew that Detective Superintendents Robshaw and Leggate had a meeting scheduled that morning with CPS to discuss the latest developments. The likelihood was that Daniel Weaver's case would be presented before the High Court inside the next seven days and he would be released on bail pending a re-trial. Hunter knew that this afternoon's interview was not going to be easy. Weaver's solicitor had already started asking pointed questions.

Next to him was a pile of foolscap papers, each one covered by a series of boxed grids, Hunter's own personal index system to record and summarise the evidence in each individual witness statement. On one side of the A4 sheets were the names of all thirty-two witnesses within the file; on the opposite side was a section for noting a summary of their evidence. Some had very little to say, but others had played a crucial role in Daniel Weaver's prosecution. The evidence was in two parts - independent witnesses, who had seen Daniel and Lucy together on the night of her disappearance, and police witnesses, including forensics. Hunter knew some of the detectives who had been involved in the investigation. They were all retired now and he wondered what their reaction would be when he broke the news that the case was being re-opened. Given the new nature of the investigation, he wondered if they would be willing to talk. This was going to be a very uncomfortable case to examine, he told himself.

From time to time, as he read through Jeffery Howson's statement, he paused and made notes on important points. When he got to the part detailing the first visit to Daniel

Weaver's flat, two days after her disappearance, he turned to the folders of bound black and white crime scene photographs, picked up the booklet which contained the interior shots of Weaver's flat and slowly thumbed through the images. The ones he was especially interested in were those of the garden shed where Lucy's handbag had been discovered. There were two close-up shots of a small, fake leather bag, which Jeffery Howson's statement, told him was cream coloured, poking out of a pile of hemp sacking beneath a bench. The discovery had been crucial to the prosecution's case and was now one of the pieces of evidence being put under his spotlight. The other photos of interest to him were of Daniel Weaver himself, particularly the close-up head shots of the left-hand side of his face and the three diagonal scratch marks on his cheek. Unlike the allegations of the 'planting' of evidence, which surrounded the finding of Lucy's handbag, there was no such question mark over how Daniel Weaver had obtained his injuries. He had already admitted they had been caused by Lucy. He had stated both in his statement and at his trial that they had been caused when she had pulled away from him during their argument in the market place.

Hunter sighed as he finished reading Jeffery Howson's statement. The evidence appeared so precise, yet most of Howson's testimony was in doubt because of the contemporaneous notes found in his bedroom safe. If only he had left a note explaining matters, Hunter thought. As he set aside Howson's statement and picked up Alan Darbyshire's, he let out another sigh. He knew this was going to mirror exactly what he had just read, but nevertheless he had to scrutinise it thoroughly before the interview with Daniel Weaver that afternoon.

* * * * *

Hunter steered the MIT car into HMP Wakefield car park and aimed it, nose first, into an empty visitors' parking space. He killed the engine.

"What do think the reception's going to be like?" Grace asked, pulling down the passenger side mirror, wetting the tip of her right index finger and smoothing it across her right eyebrow.

"I think Daniel Weaver's going to be pretty pissed off," said Hunter as he gazed at the fortified entrance gates of the Victorian prison. "And I guess he's every right to be. Although, if you had asked me that same question before we found those contemporaneous notes in Howson's safe I would have given you a different answer. I've read the prosecution file three times now and know it back to front. At the time of his trial, you can see why the jury returned a guilty verdict. Several witnesses saw him and Lucy arguing that night and no one saw her again after that. And there is no one who can alibi Daniel Weaver after he left the market place. He told police he went home, got drunk and then the next morning went to his mother's house for breakfast. Weaver lived alone and no one saw him come or go. His only comments in his defence is that he had no idea where Lucy had gone once she left him and that the police planted the handbag in the shed and then fabricated his confession. We now know the last part of that could be true."

"I spoke with Prison Intelligence yesterday to get a bit of background on Weaver. It appears he's kept himself to himself at every prison he's been in. There are times when he has been a pain in the arse, as the prison officer put it, because he regularly challenged officers when he felt he was being badly treated. For that he served some time in the punishment block. Added to that, he also refused to engage in any prisoner therapy; one of the main reasons why he hasn't been considered for parole or early release." Flipping the mirror back up in place, Grace added, "Do you know what you're going to say to him?"

Hunter shook his head, "Not exactly. I've got an idea of where I want it to go." Hunter reached behind and pulled a bulging folder from the back seat. "I've made notes and I'd like to lead him back through that night, but it all depends on what his brief has advised him to say."

Tucking the folder beneath his arm, Hunter locked the car and strode towards the prison gates. Grace trotted beside him.

At reception, Hunter produced his warrant card and appointment letter, after which he and Grace passed through metal sliding doors into the search area, where they emptied their pockets into trays and stepped through the airport style electronic security portal. Then they were taken to the main hall, where the wives, girlfriends and families of prisoners had all congregated to meet their loved ones and children were chasing around screaming at one another.

They were shown into a small room just off the main hall which mirrored one of their own interview rooms back at the police station. As the door closed behind them, most of the noise muted. In the centre of the room was a table, the surface of which had been well-graffitied and gouged, together with four chairs, all secured to the floor. Hunter and Grace each took a seat.

They had been waiting in silence for less than ten minutes when the door opened and Daniel Weaver appeared. He was dressed in a sweatshirt and jeans. Behind him was a well groomed man in a suit, who Hunter guessed was his solicitor. A prison officer stood behind the pair.

Daniel entered the room first. He had his hands in his pockets and as he took a seat opposite, lifted them out, and folded them in defiant pose.

Hunter remembered the head and shoulders black-and-white shots he had seen of Daniel. He still had his curly hair, though it was showing distinct signs of thinning and much of it was greying. They were roughly the same size, with well-developed shoulders and arms, but unlike himself, Daniel was carrying a paunch.

Hunter asked him if he wanted a drink. Daniel Weaver shook his head.

"Daniel, do you know why we are here?"

"Yeah, my brief's told me. You're here to apologise for fitting me up and negotiate the amount of compensation I'm due."

The reply threw Hunter for a second. He fixed his gaze and forced a smile. "That's not my job Daniel. That's something for your solicitor and the Home Secretary. I'm here to tell you that we're re-opening your case and I want to ask you some questions."

Daniel leant forward and rested his folded arms upon the table. "You've got a nerve. The last time I was asked questions by your lot, I got thirty years."

"That wasn't me, Daniel."

"No, but you're all the same."

"Believe me, we're not all the same," said Grace.

Daniel Weaver pushed himself back in his chair, pursed his lips and shrugged. "Whatever."

"Daniel I have read your prosecution file from nineteen-eighty-four and I went to go back over the events of what happened between you and Lucy."

"No offence like, but if you think you're gonna get any help from me you've got another think coming. You lot got it so wrong back then and I was fitted up. Now you're trying to make amends. I've done twenty-five years for something I didn't do and you come here with your false smiles and expect me to help you. You can take your questions and shove them up your arse."

"I realise there's a lot of things going through your mind right now Daniel. And you've every right to feel bitter towards the police, but I can assure you this time things will be different and I hope you will be willing to co-operate."

"Co-operate! You have got to be joking. Look what happened the last time I co-operated."

"Okay Daniel let me try a different approach. Are you aware the reason why we have re-opened the investigation into Lucy's disappearance back in nineteen-eighty-three?" He watched his face a second. There was no reaction. "Okay I'll tell you. A detective involved in that case has been murdered and has left behind some evidence which raises questions about one of the interviews with you when you were arrested."

"Is it Darbyshire or Howson?"

"All that will become clearer to you in the next few days. At the moment that's not an issue. What is, however, is the new piece of evidence we have discovered which casts doubt over one of your initial interviews."

"But knowing which one of the bent bastards is dead is important to me," he answered determinedly. "It's so gratifying to know that one of them has finally got their just deserts. The other one will get his payback as well, once I'm out of here."

The solicitor, who until Daniel's outburst, had been making notes with a poker-face, quickly looked up. He reached across and grasped Weaver's wrist, then turned to Hunter.

"As you can appreciate detective, my client is a little frustrated. This news has been a complete shock."

Daniel shook off the solicitor's grip. "Frustrated! Fucking frustrated! That is an understatement! I'm fucking furious. You have the audacity to come here after twenty-five years and ask me to help you out with your enquiries into a murder which I was stitched up with and you expect me to be nicey-nicey about it all? That's a fucking joke." He pushed himself up. "I'll find out soon enough which one of those cops is dead and I'll tell you now the only tears you'll find me shedding, are those of joy. And I want you to pass on a message to the one who's still around. You tell him he'd better keep looking over his shoulder."

"Is that a threat?"

Daniel made for the door. As he grabbed the handle he turned to face Hunter. "You bet it is." Then he stormed out of the room.

The solicitor quickly scooped up his papers and made to follow his client. "Mr Weaver doesn't mean anything by that detective. I'll have a word with him once he calms down.

He almost skipped out of the room. Hunter could hear him shouting after his client, his voice drifting away into the distance.

Hunter pulled together his own loose papers, tapped the edges level and slipped them into his folder. Snapping shut the cover he said, "Well Grace, that didn't turn out the way I had planned."

"Yes. I wouldn't say it was one of your best interviews, would you?"

* * * * *

Barry Newstead still had a flush on from his evening bath and had just got to the bottom of the stairs, tucking his shirt into his trousers, when the doorbell went. He got a view of the top half of a silhouetted figure through the frosted glazing of the front door. He opened it. Standing in the porch was a man, the same size and shape as himself, with close-cut, salt-and-pepper, greying hair. His hands were thrust deep into a long, camel-hair coat.

"Sue Siddons?" the man enquired, his voice nasal and high-pitched.

"You are?" Barry replied, sucking in his belly as he pulled the leather belt through its buckle to secure his shirt into his waistband.

"Guy Armstrong," said the man, holding out his hand to shake. "I used to work with Sue on the Barnwell Chronicle many years ago."

Barry didn't take the hand. He fastened up his shirt cuffs.

"She has mentioned you." He looked a lot older than Sue had described, but then she had been drawing on memories from over twenty years ago and a lot had gone on in her life since then.

"You must be Barry. She's told me about you as well."

Barry's face set tight.

"Can I speak to her?"

"She doesn't want to see you."

"She didn't say that on the phone when I spoke with her yesterday afternoon."

"Well she's decided that now, since she's spoken to me."

A sly grin crept across his mouth. "Typical cop."

"Ex-cop."

"But you still have a fear of reporters?"

"Not a fear. Just don't like them."

"Sue's mentioned that you're working on the murder of a retired detective who was involved with the Lucy Blake-Hall case back in ninety-eighty-three. I worked on that case and I have a source who believes they know who killed her all those years ago; I only want a quick chat – a bit of background about this detective's murder. I won't reveal my source."

"Mr Armstrong, you managed to catch Sue off guard yesterday afternoon. She's already told you more than she should have done. Now you may have been colleagues all those years back, but she is no longer a reporter, and I would prefer it if you left her alone. She has nothing else to say to you about either the Lucy Blake-Hall case or about the death of one of my former colleagues."

"Are those her words, or yours?"

Barry could feel the frustration welling up inside him. "Mr. Armstrong, this conversation has finished. I now want you to leave. Do I make myself clear?"

"Look Barry. If you've spoken with Sue you know I worked on the original story when Lucy went missing back in nineteen-eighty-three. I know there are links between the murder of the detective and Lucy, because my source has told me, and I've also made a phone call to Daniel Weaver's barrister and he's told me that detectives interviewed him earlier today in Wakefield Prison. The story is going to come out soon; you know how it is. I'm just wanting to be ahead of the game - put the police's side of the story first."

"Then you're talking to the wrong person. If you want a quote, contact the press office."

"Is this a miscarriage of justice?"

"I said conversation over."

Guy Armstrong shook his head. "I can help you with your investigation? I spoke with the witnesses back then. I dealt with Lucy's family and I also know Daniel Weaver's family. I scratch your back and you scratch mine."

Barry slowly started to close the front door. "Goodbye Mr Armstrong."

The reporter placed his foot over the threshold.

Barry glanced down at the reporter's black scuffed shoes and then fixed him with one of his meanest, hardest, looks. "You take that foot away now or I'll break it. Then I'll put my own foot up the crack of your arse and boot you all the way back up the drive. Do I make myself clear?"

Armstrong withdrew his foot, looking sheepish. "Is that a quote?"

"No, but this one is...fuck off!" Barry slammed the front door shut and kept his huge hand tight on the handle, watching as the blood drained from his knuckles. He waited until he saw the silhouette of Guy Armstrong fade away. After this, other reporters would be in on the chase. He turned to the phone. He needed to let the gaffer know.

- ooOoo –

CHAPTER EIGHT

DAY SEVEN: 30th November.

Hunter got into work just before seven am, brewed himself a cup of tea and immediately attacked his pending work. Opening his e-mails, he found three relating to the suspicious death of the girl found in the cellar of the derelict pub ten days earlier. He still had a number of gaps waiting to be filled, and with the recent murder case he hadn't had time to conduct his own enquiries into identifying the victim, discovering where she lived or finding any witnesses; a big ask, given the circumstances of her death. Nevertheless, he wanted to make sure he had tied up every loose end. Several days ago he had made a series of phone calls to uniform officers he knew from his beat days and also sent out a global e-mail to duty groups posing those questions.

His first e-mail was from the Coroner's Officer. He prayed this was going to provide him with a name for the victim and the cause of her death. The opening paragraph read: 'The girl has been identified as 23 year-old Jodie Marie Jenkinson, goes by her nickname 'JJ'.' His prayers had been answered. At the post-mortem he had seen those initials tattooed on the back of her neck. He read on. They had managed to identify her by fingerprints, despite the damage caused by the rats. She had a previous conviction for drunkenness, and an assault and she was currently on probation for shoplifting. As a bonus, the Coroner's Officer had listed her Probation Officer and his telephone number. Hunter scribbled down the details onto his blotting pad. That was tomorrow morning's first job after briefing. He skimmed through the remainder of the e-mail and saw that cause of death was drug related. The syringe found beside her contained heroin of a purer concentration than that normally found on the streets. He guessed that she had been so used to the cut-down stuff that her body hadn't been able to cope with the good gear. That information took his enquiry a giant leap forward and he rattled off a thank you back to the officer, adding that he owed him a drink.

His luck continued with the second e-mail. It was from an old uniformed colleague, now attached to one of the Community Beat Teams, whose patrol area took in the derelict pub. He made regular checks of the place because nearby residents had complained that it had become a haunt for drunken teenagers. He hadn't found any teenagers but he had come across a local tramp, nicknamed 'Chicken George', who was using the place to doss down. The officer had last spoken with him two months ago and was now trying to track him down to ask if he had seen the girl or anyone else in the premises. Hunter responded with another thank you and requested an update once he had caught up with the tramp.

The last e-mail was from Duncan Wroe, the Scenes of Crime manager, which stated that he had forwarded on an album of photographs relating to his suspicious death.

Hunter looked at his pending tray and lifted off a couple of reports from the top. Tucked between the paperwork, he found a blue coloured A5 bound photograph album. He opened it to reveal the first colour print - a front view of the derelict pub. Its sign was missing, as was the lettering above the front windows and door, though he knew it used to be called the Barnwell Inn. Once white plaster was heavily stained, and large clumps had fallen away from the walls to reveal crumbling red brickwork beneath. It looked a mess, thought Hunter, though he knew from the builders that it was about to get a new lease of life as a pub-cum-diner. The next picture showed the view from the entrance door, along a narrow strip of corridor, towards the beer cellar. He could make out the absence of the bottom door panel of the cellar door, the result of one of the builders having put his boot through to get access. The next view took in most of the cellar itself. Jodie Marie Jenkinson was slumped face down on the concrete floor, arms by her side, legs tucked beneath her in a child-like sprawl. He concentrated on this photo. It was a stark reminder of what he had encountered when he had been called out that day. The combination of the fetid stench of stagnant beer, stale faeces, animal and human, and damp, mixed with the decay of someone long dead, had greeted him. As he stared at this photograph the images and smells returned. The last remaining shots were close-ups of the girl. The images were vivid. It wasn't just the decomposition, but the damage caused by the vermin attacks. As well as her fingers, the tip of her nose was missing and part of her right ear had also been chewed. Mournfully, he shook his head. Two of the remaining photographs were close-ups of her heavily blanched bare arms, which bore multiple healed criss-crossed scars, the tell-tale signs of self-harm. The next couple focused on the drugs paraphernalia surrounding her, the used syringes, strips of burnt foil, and two spoons which showed signs of being heated. He closed the album and thumbed his way back through the pages again. Something about those images was disturbing him, though taking another look was not resolving the doubts. He tried to conjure up visions from previous drug-related deaths he had investigated during his time on the Drug Squad, but that wasn't helping either. He went over the shots a third time, a little slower, but he still couldn't put his finger on what was troubling him. *It might just be me*, he told himself, he might be reading something which wasn't there. For now, he decided to fill in the gaps with this recent information, speak to her Probation Officer over the next few days and then re-visit the photographs when he had a little more time.

Footsteps coming along the corridor outside snatched him back to the present. He checked his watch as the office double doors swung open.

Barry Newstead barrelled in like someone entering a Wild West saloon. "Now then me old mucker, touch of insomnia have we?"

"Got in early to try and sort out some paperwork. No rest for the wicked."

"Talking about the wicked. I had a visitor last night I want to tell you about. But first, the most important job of the day. I'll stick the kettle on." Barry said with a broad grin.

Hunter watched Barry slip his jacket off and sling it across his desk before heading for the kettle. The tail of his shirt was hanging out of his waistband again. Hunter smiled. Sartorial elegance was certainly not one of Barry's strong points.

Barry made two drinks, dunking tea bags into mugs of hot water, adding milk and sugar to both before sidling back to Hunter's desk. He dropped down into Grace's empty chair opposite and slid across a mug.

Hunter looked at the weak contents, decided it was the best he was going to get and picked up the steaming brew, muttering his thanks.

"What about this visitor of yours then?"

Barry pretended to spit. "Time to circle the wagons! The press have got wind."

"Who's that then? Local or national?"

"I think the guy's a freelance, but to be honest I'm not sure, I never gave him much chance. I threatened to put my boot up his arse."

"Good to see the old Barry Newstead is still alive and kicking."

Barry took a sip on his tea. "Well, they get on your bloody nerves don't they? And the cheeky bastard had managed to get to Sue before she could speak to me."

"Has she said anything?"

"She's told him a little. He knows about Howson and how we've re-opened the Blake-Hall case. He knows the link between them because he told me he worked on the case years ago, but he doesn't know about the notes we found."

Hunter watched Barry's eyebrows knit together.

"He caught her on the hop. He knows her. They were colleagues when she worked for the Chronicle."

"Barry there's no need to apologise on Sue's behalf. I guessed it wouldn't be long before someone would sniff out our investigation."

"Yeah, I guess so. Anyway, just in case you come across the leech, his name's Guy Armstrong. He was the crime reporter at the Chronicle when the Lucy Blake-Hall story broke. Sue tells me that he made his name from the case, and got a staff job with the Mail as a result. He became one of their northern crime reporters. There is, however, a bit of a black cloud hanging over him. Sue told me that she's certain that a few years ago he was involved in an accident in which a cop got killed and she's almost sure he went to prison because of it. I'm going to follow that up and see what's behind it."

Hunter's concentration was broken by the sound of clicking heels, followed by female voices, coming from outside the department. The office doors opened and in stepped his partner Grace, along with DC Carol Ragen. He glanced at his watch 7:45am - fifteen minutes to briefing.

He switched his gaze back to Barry. "Okay, thanks for the heads up. Keep me posted once you find out something, will you? And let me know if he contacts you again."

"Somehow I don't think he will. My size tens are a fearsome weapon." Barry winked, picked up his mug, scraped back Grace's chair and drifted to his own desk.

* * * * * *

Morning briefing was short. Detective Superintendent Michael Robshaw took it, with Dawn Leggate looking on.

It was Hunter's first opportunity to feed in the results of his follow-up enquiries from his interview with Alan Darbyshire. "As you know, when I asked him about anyone who might have a grudge against Jeffery, especially from high profile cases that he and Jeffery had been involved in, instead of him mentioning Lucy's case he referred to the Beast of Barnwell investigation from the seventies. He told me that he thought the offender, Terry Braithwaite, had been released to a bail hostel two years ago. I've made a couple of phone calls and found that Terry Braithwaite is in a care home in Bridlington. He's seventy-two years old now and in very poor health. He suffered a stroke shortly after his release and lost the complete use of his left side. He needs a wheelchair to get around. I think we can definitely rule him out of the enquiry."

He then reported on his and Grace's visit to Daniel Weaver. The SIO sympathised and responded with an update from his meeting with the Head of the Crown Prosecution Service. An appeal had already been lodged with the Home Secretary by Weaver's Barrister and had been listed for the following Friday. He added that, given the new evidence, The Appeal Court Judges would not hesitate to grant bail; Daniel Weaver would be out before the next weekend. The news was met by silence.

Det Supt Robshaw asked Barry to give an update about which of the original witnesses from the Lucy Blake-Hall case were still around. Barry had been working with the HOLMES team who had been transferring information from the old card index system from the 1983 investigation onto the computers. He was the ideal choice for this work. Not only did he have experience with the previous recording method but was also familiar with the current protocol for capturing information.

He said, "The girls on HOLMES have been working round the clock, and they're not far away now from listing all the witnesses and summarising what's in their statements. I've been doing the electoral register checks against the names and made a number of phone calls. What I've learned is that Weaver's mum is no longer around. She died of a heart attack six years ago. And the landlady of The Coach and Horses, where Weaver and Lucy had their last drinks together, has also died. The three witnesses who saw the pair arguing in the market place - a man and two women - lived on a street which was knocked down fifteen years ago. I've got the council going back through their records to see if they were re-housed locally. We're having difficulty tracing the women because they were just young girls at the time, eighteen and twenty, so the likelihood is they've got married and changed their surnames. We're also having trouble finding Lucy's best friend, Amanda Smith. Once again, we're guessing she's got married."

Hunter remembered his earlier conversation with DS Jamie Parker of the Cold Case Unit. It looked as though they would have to bring in someone from his team to help with the tracing.

"On the plus side, we've tracked down Lucy's husband, her parents are still around, and living at the same address in Bakewell, Derbyshire, and we think we know where Lucy's daughter, Jessica, is now living. She's now married and has a daughter of her own. With regards the detectives who worked on the case, we know where they all are from the Forces pensions records. That's it, boss."

"Okay, good work Barry. Right, actions everyone," said Robshaw. "We've got our work cut out on two fronts. Firstly, the murder of retired detective Jeffery Howson, and secondly the re-opening of the Lucy Blake-Hall murder from nineteen-eighty-three. The links between the two enquiries rest with the finding of those interview notes in Howson's safe. With regards the murder of Jeffery Howson. Sad as I have to say this, but as we all know, our major suspect to date is a retired DCI. He told Hunter and Grace that he last saw and spoke with Howson two weeks prior to his murder. We now know that is a lie. Phone records clearly show that Alan Darbyshire rang Howson on the Saturday evening, twenty-second November, prior to his body being discovered on Monday the twenty-fourth. Given the circumstances, it is not something he would forget, and therefore we have to assume that he's covering for himself, and, or, for someone else. As we know from the pathologist's examination of Howson's body, two people were involved in his killing. Plus, the finding of the contemporaneous notes in Howson's safe, now indicates he perjured himself in the Lucy Blake-Hall murder trial. We know from Barry here that Howson was about to spill the beans on the whole affair, so it gives Darbyshire the motive for wanting Howson dead." The SIO tapped the top of the incident board. There was now a photograph of Alan Darbyshire stuck alongside those of Jeffery Howson. It was an enlarged, very formal shot of him in a collar and tie, from Force archives. He looked in his early to mid-forties.

Robshaw continued. "Because of who he is, I want to make sure we have as much solid information as we can possibly get before we bring him in for interview. Therefore, I want as many of the witnesses as possible from the Lucy Blake-Hall enquiry tracing and re-interviewing. If we are still struggling to track down people by the middle of the week, I'm going to make an appeal through the media. Sooner or later the press are going to learn of our enquiries, and I'd rather have them with us than against us, especially now that we know Daniel Weaver is going to be released." The Detective Superintendent clapped his hands together. "Okay guys, that's it, unless anyone has any questions or anything to say?"

Hunter exchanged a quick look with Barry, wondering whether he was going to mention Armstrong. Barry never flinched.

The teams broke up, clambering around DI Scaife's desk for their next set of assignments. The office was buzzing again.

* * * * *

Hunter and Grace had the job of speaking to Lucy's husband, Peter. They had been told he was living in a renovated farm complex, in the picturesque village of Hooton Roberts. Hunter knew the area well; he had painted there in the past. He also knew that it was a village of two halves. The handful of sandstone cottages and small farms were separated by the main A630 Rotherham to Doncaster road and because of that, Blake-Hall's home took a bit of finding. Hunter had driven past twice before Grace spotted it at the top of a rise, along a narrow lane and in between cottages.

As Hunter swung the unmarked CID car in through a wide opening onto a gravel chipped driveway, he saw that Peter Blake-Hall's home was a converted barn. It looked a lavish conversion. A central gabled area set with large glazed doors was its entranceway. It had low walls and a steep tiled roof, in which was set a number of window-lights. Today, the grey tiles glistened, because a light rain was falling from a grey, damp, heavy-clouded sky.

"This must have set him back a bob or two," Hunter said to Grace, as he slowed the car to a halt. For a few seconds he left the engine idling and stared out through the windscreen. Slowly the image of the Grade II listed barn became distorted as droplets of rain spattered the screen.

He said, "I want to play this just the same way as we did with Alan Darbyshire. No pushing. Try and let him do most of the talking and see what he gives."

Grace nodded in agreement.

"I'm not going to mention the re-opening of his wife's case unless he asks about it. I'm going to come at him from the angle of being someone Howson was closely linked to in the past and see where that leads to. I'm only going to let on that we've spoken to Howson's ex if he's not forthcoming. I want to see what he is prepared to offer without encouragement."

"I'm sure we will get around to his wife's case, so if that happens I'll try and divert him with a few questions about his relationship with her prior to her going missing. See what he'll also tell us about Daniel Weaver."

"Good idea Grace. I've noticed that file has very little in the way of background. It doesn't say in Peter Blake-Hall's statement whether or not he knew about her affair with Weaver. It would be interesting to know."

Hunter turned off the engine and opened his door slowly. The cold and the damp hit him and he shivered. Checking for puddles, he alighted. Immediately, he heard raised voices. He could see from Grace's expression that she had heard them too.

The voices were coming from around the side of the house. It sounded like two men, and the conversation was heated. One of them was swearing profusely.

Hunter threw a quizzical look at Grace. "Someone's venting their spleen. We'll take a shufty, shall we?"

Locking the car, Hunter skirted past the front entrance and edged around the side of the building where the two voices had reduced to one. Behind him, Grace's low-heeled shoes scrunched over the loose gravel chippings. There would be no element of surprise.

He turned the corner in time to witness a man in a camel-hair coat being pushed from a doorway, his arms windmilling, as he fought to keep his balance, and in doing so a small hand-held tape recorder flew up in the air and landed behind him. Hunter recalled what Barry had told him about being door-stepped by a reporter the previous evening. The description Barry had given fitted this man to a tee.

In the doorframe a tall, beefy man was spearing a finger in the direction of the journalist.

He shouted, "Now for the last time, piss off."

Hunter stepped into view. "Having a spot of trouble?"

Both men turned his way.

"And who the fuck are you?" said the stocky one.

Hunter dug into his jacket and found his warrant card. "CID," he announced, flashing his badge.

"Well, you're just in time to witness me kick this man's arse off my premises for trespass." The thickset man moved from the doorway and onto the drive.

Grace quickly stepped forward, putting herself in front of the reporter. He was scrabbling in the wet gravel, attempting to recover his tape recorder and the batteries which had spilt from it.

"There's no need for that, now we're here. I'm sure this gentleman was just leaving." Hunter turned to the reporter. "Weren't you sir?"

The man huffed, snapped the batteries back in place, made a quick visual check of his tape-recorder, wiped the wetness from it on his coat sleeve, slipped it into his pocket and turned on his heels without saying a word.

Hunter's gaze followed him as he tramped away down the driveway. As he neared the gate, Hunter turned back to the well-made man. "I'm guessing that was a reporter?"

"Yes, fucking leeches." He turned to Grace. "Pardon my French miss." Then he turned back at Hunter. "He says you're re-opening the case into my wife's murder. Is that right?"

Best laid plans... Hunter reflected. Quickly gathering his thoughts, he replied, "Well Mr Blake-Hall, we're investigating the murder of a detective who worked on your wife's murder. That's what we're here for. Can we come in and have a word?"

Hunter studied the man for a few seconds, never breaking eye contact. Then he smiled, though Hunter could tell it was strained.

"Yeah, sure." Peter Blake-Hall stepped to one side and invited them into the house.

From a short hallway Hunter and Grace stepped into a large, airy, open-plan house. The lounge and dining room were one, and at the far end, through a set of open glazed doors was a bespoke fitted kitchen of cream painted units and light oak work surfaces.

Hunter found himself staring around the room. He was in awe. Without doubt, this was a conversion which had money and time spent on it. The interior had so much space, with a timbered roof structure in full view. A galleried landing ran most of the way around the walls, with light oak doors leading off. Hunter guessed that was where the bedrooms and bathroom were. The majestic stone fireplace before them contained a roaring log fire burning in a large dog-grate, throwing out welcoming warmth. Although the place looked sumptuous, its design managed to maintain a rustic appeal.

"This is a beautiful home, Mr Blake-Hall. The nightclub business is obviously doing well." Hunter eyed the man carefully. Peter Hall-Blake looked to be in his middle to late fifties. He still had most of his light brown hair. However, it was beginning to grey and the front had thinned to a widow's peak. This morning he had a layer of stubble. At some stage he had used weights regularly but now the muscle-tone was giving way to fat. Though, viewing the bulk of his upper arms straining the sleeves of his casual striped shirt, Hunter thought that he still looked as though he could handle himself given the situation. It had been a good thing that Grace had got between him and the reporter, or they would likely now be interviewing him under caution for assault, rather than chatting with him as a possible witness in their murder enquiry.

"I see you've done your homework on me." Peter sank down onto a large mushroom coloured sofa close to the stone fireplace, and gesticulated for them to sit in another large sofa opposite. "Be my guest." As Hunter and Grace sat, he said "I'd prefer it if you wouldn't refer to my place as a nightclub. It's licensed as a private lap-dancing club. I offer something totally different to one of those vulgar places. Maybe in the old days my place was viewed as being somewhat lascivious, but thankfully the world has moved on. And yes, in answer to your question, it has allowed me a good lifestyle over the years." He crossed his legs. "You'll have to pay us a visit. And I don't mean in the official sense. Come socially one night on me. Bring a couple of colleagues." Peter Blake-Hall turned to Grace. "My offer extends to you, but it might not be to your tastes dear."

Hunter could sense Grace, shuffling beside him, seething. He knew the remark would have wound her up. Before she had chance to bite, he replied, "Thanks for the offer, but that might not be a wise thing, what with the investigation and everything."

Blake-Hall looked perplexed again. "Everything?"

"A throwaway comment sorry. I just meant under the circumstances."

"My, things have changed. I guess this is what I've heard your retired colleagues moan about. Political correctness and all that. The detectives I knew in the past would have jumped at my offer."

"Well, I wouldn't say it's political correctness, but yes, things have changed." Hunter flipped open his folder. "If I can just tell you why we are here."

"To be honest I've been expecting you. I believe you want to ask me about Jeffery Howson."

Hunter was caught off guard again. He asked, "Did that reporter tell you that?"

"No, Alan Darbyshire rang me and told me what's happened. Terrible shock."

"Oh? When was that?"

"A couple of days..." He paused, stroked his un-shaven jaw-line and then continued. "Yeah, it was either Thursday or Friday when he told me." He shook his head and smiled. "You detectives I don't know. There's nothing sinister about Alan ringing me up and telling me what happened. We go back a long way. But then you know that, otherwise why would you be coming to see me about Jeffery Howson? Let me just say on record that I'm indebted to those two guys. If it hadn't been for them, my wife's killer would never have been caught. Since then, we've kept in touch. In fact, when Alan retired from the Force I gave him a job."

This was news to Hunter. He dearly wanted to look at Grace. Out of the corner of his eye, he could see her making notes. "He never told us that when we spoke with him the other day."

Peter Blake-Hall shrugged his shoulders. "It's no big secret. I took him on to manage the staff in my club. He'd interview and vet the staff for me, and to be honest it made good business sense when it came to getting the licence when we changed across to an official lap-dancing club. He was with me until about eighteen months ago."

"Did Jeffery used to work for you as well then?" said Grace.

"Jeffery? Good God no. Jeffery kept himself to himself when he retired, although I'm guessing Alan would have told you that. No, Jeffery changed after he got divorced. To be honest I'm partially to blame for that. I don't know if you know, but Alan and Jeffery used to come to my club regularly, more-so after they arrested Danny Weaver. I treated them to a few beers and the entertainment. I know officially it was frowned upon, especially the type of premises they were back then, but it was my way of saying thank you. One night, Jeffery's wife turned up at the club and caught him chatting with a couple of the girls. There was a right to-do between them. She accused him of carrying on with one of them, slapped him across the face and stormed out and that was the end of their marriage. I learned from Alan that she had left him. He did come in a couple of times after she left, but it wasn't for long. To be honest, I had to politely ask him to stop coming, he was so bloody morbid and miserable around the punters. I kept in touch with Alan though, and as I say he worked for me once he retired."

"So when did you last see or speak with Jeffery?" asked Hunter.

"Crikey, that is a question." Peter Blake-Hall stroked his chin and gazed up into the roof space. A few seconds later he said. "It wasn't that long after Danny Weaver's trial. That's when I had to have a quiet word with him. As I said, he became a miserable sod. He came in just to prop the bar up and drown his sorrows. He took the request well though. There was no animosity between us about it. You can check that back with Alan." Blake-Hall uncrossed his legs, and hunched forward, planting his hands onto the top of his thighs. "Can I ask you something?"

"Sure."

"That reporter I threw off my doorstep said you were re-opening my wife's case. Is that right? And do you think Jeffery's murder has something to do with that?"

Inwardly, Hunter was cursing. He'd make sure that sooner, rather than later, he'd track down that journalist and give him a piece of his mind. He said, "You have to appreciate, Peter, there are some things we can't discuss. It would be fair to say that as a result of Jeffery's murder we are looking into the possibilities of why he was killed. That includes looking at some of the previous cases he was involved in. Your wife's case is one of those. Does that answer your question?"

"I guess so." He leaned back against several large cushions. "Does that mean you're looking at Danny Weaver? I thought he was still inside?"

Hunter didn't want to mention the previous day's interview, or the likelihood that he would be shortly released. He'd prefer to deal with that when it happened.

Before he had time to magic up a response, Grace rescued him. "Mentioning Daniel Weaver, did you know him prior to his arrest? I have noticed that on a couple of occasions you have referred to him more personally as Danny rather than Daniel."

Blake-Hall switched his gaze. "Nothing gets past that pretty little head does it? The answer to your question is that I did know Daniel Weaver before his arrest for Lucy's murder. Danny worked for me. I used to import cars from Germany, Mercedes and BMWs. It was very lucrative. Before the nineties you could get away with bringing in cars, and so long as you registered an individual, and not a business, as the owner you'd get away with not paying any VAT. It was a loophole in customs. I'd have a circle of people, including Danny, who'd bring the cars in and register them in their names. I'd keep them garaged for six months and then move them on. I made a nice tidy profit." His mouth suddenly tightened. "I looked after Danny and that's how he repaid me."

"So when did you find out about him having an affair with Lucy?"

"I didn't. Not until after he'd been arrested. It was a complete surprise. Apparently they'd been carrying on under my nose for over six months."

"So the news was broken to you by Alan Darbyshire and Jeffery Howson?"

"I think it was Alan who told me."

Hunter said. "Now my colleague has raised the case of Lucy, I'd like to just clarify one or two things from your original statement made back in nineteen-eighty-three, if that's okay?"

Peter Blake-Hall turned back to Hunter. "You're asking something there. That was such a long time ago."

"Don't worry about that, I'll prompt you as we go along." Although Hunter hadn't got the statement to hand he had read the case file so many times that much of it was locked inside his head. "You said in your statement that the last time you saw Lucy was on Friday tea-time, twenty-sixth of August. Can you remember that?"

"Yes, that's something I'll never forget. It was August Bank Holiday and I went in early to the club because Bank Holidays were our busiest times. I can remember that."

"And you stated that when you got back in the early hours Lucy wasn't in the house?"

Peter nodded.

"Yet you didn't report her missing straight away. In your statement you reported her missing late the next morning. Is that correct?"

"No that's wrong. I actually reported her missing in the early hours of Saturday. As you say, when I got back from the club, about one am, Lucy was nowhere to be found, so I telephoned the police station then, but the guy in the control room said that as she was an adult they wouldn't make any enquiries until she had been missing for twenty-four hours and that I should ring back then if she hadn't returned home. I then rang around a couple of her friends I knew. I got them out of bed in fact, and the next morning I couldn't wait any longer and so I contacted Alan Darbyshire. I told them it was unusual for Lucy to disappear like that, and he took it seriously. He and Jeffery came round to see me straight away. The rest is history."

"So they instigated a search and everything?"

"Yeah. Alan rang his boss and the next thing the whole place was swarming with cops. Later on that day in fact, it was early the Saturday evening Alan rang and told me that Lucy had been seen arguing with a man in the market place on the Friday evening and gave me a description of him. I told him I thought it fitted Danny and mentioned that he worked for me."

"And the next day the Sunday they arrested Daniel?"

"Yeah that's right. Alan told me that Danny and Lucy had been seen having a fight, or something like that, in the market place and he had scratch marks to his face. They had also found her handbag hidden beneath some sacks in his shed."

"Did you see the handbag they found?"

"Yeah. Alan and Jeffery brought it round. It was definitely Lucy's. Her purse and other stuff with her name on it was still inside. Later on that night, Alan and Jeffery turned up at the club and told me that Danny had confessed to killing her."

"Can you remember roughly what they said to you about the confession?"

Blake-Hall's eyebrows knitted together. "I'm intrigued now. Why would you ask me about Danny's confession like that? Surely a confession's a confession?"

"Humour me Peter. It's just an angle in a number of enquiries we're following up."

He shrugged. "Fair enough. I suppose you'll tell me at some point." He pursed his lips. "Well as I say they came to the club to tell me that Danny had given them a statement and he would be charged with her murder." He paused and scanned the room. After a couple of seconds, he looked back at Hunter. "This was such a long time ago now, you appreciate. I was so delighted at the time, I just wanted to treat them to a drink." He paused again and cleared his throat. "I may have used the wrong word there, detectives. I think the word I should have used was relieved. Relieved that I knew what had happened to Lucy, and yet also sad of course."

"Of course."

"Anyway, we had a couple of drinks together and they told me that Danny had told them that he had strangled Lucy during an argument at his flat and then put her in the back of his van and taken her up on Langsett Moors and buried her. And she's still up there somewhere. They searched but they never found her body."

"Just to clarify. You said they told you Danny had confessed. Was it both Alan and Jeffery, or was it one of them?"

He screwed up his face in deep concentration. Then he answered, "It was Alan who told me."

"I know it's a long time ago now Peter, but can you remember what Jeffery Howson was like that night when they came to your club and gave you the news?"

"Not really. You have to appreciate it all came as a surprise. All kinds of things were going around inside my head." He paused again. "Although now I come to think about it, Jeffery was a little subdued about it all. Usually if they'd had a good result and came into my club, the pair were buzzing. That night Jeffery was a lot quieter than normal. Why? Is that significant?"

It was Hunter's turn to shrug. "Honest answer Peter don't know yet. As I say, our enquiries are really in the early stages."

"Do you have any clues as to who killed Jeffery then?"

Hunter gave him a smile. "I'm not going to tell you that, am I? Let's just say we have a number of leads we're following up, and leave it at that." He pushed himself up from the sofa. "Well Mr Blake-Hall, you've been most helpful. We'll leave you in peace now, but we may be back with some other questions before the investigation is over."

Pushing himself up from the sofa, Peter Blake-Hall proffered an outstretched hand. "Well, you know where to find me."

Hunter shook his hand.

Peter then offered his hand to Grace. After the shake, he didn't let go. Looking deeply into her eyes he said. "Forgive me, I didn't get your name."

"DC Marshall," Grace replied, peeling away her hand.

"And does DC Marshall have a first name?"

"She does, but I'd rather keep things formal if you don't mind."

Blake-Hall pulled a face. "Well, that's told me."

Hunter stepped in. "My colleague's right, Mr Blake-Hall. We have to distance ourselves at all times during an ongoing enquiry."

He smirked. "Things have really changed, haven't they?"

Peter Blake-Hall showed them out through the large glazed entranceway. It was still raining and Hunter made a dash for the car, popping the locks as he jogged.

Jumping into the driver's seat, he quickly slid the key into the ignition. Grace bounced into the passenger seat beside him, flipped down the visor mirror and flicked a comb of fingers through her damp curls.

"A little feisty there, Miss Marshall," said Hunter.

"What a tosser," Grace replied, snapping up the visor.

"Now now, don't let Mr Blake-Hall get inside that pretty little head of yours."

Grace glanced sideways. "And don't you start with that Hunter Kerr, you're not too big to get a slap."

He laughed as he started the engine.

* * * * *

Most of the day's jobs were completed before 6pm. Except for Hunter's and Grace's feedback from the meeting with Peter Blake-Hall, there was very little in the way of de-briefing and Detective Superintendent Michael Robshaw wound things up early. En masse, the MIT team decamped to the George and Dragon, in Wentworth village, for a swift drink before heading off home.

Hunter didn't immediately go into the pub. He sat in his car and phoned Beth on his mobile, telling her would be home within the hour. He had just disconnected the call when his passenger door swung open and in jumped Barry Newstead. Barry kept the door open, leaving one leg dangling outside. He leaned in towards Hunter.

"I'm glad I've caught you. I couldn't make the briefing because I was tied up with the HOLMES team, but I wanted to have a quick word with you about your visit to Peter Blake-Hall this afternoon."

"Oh yeah. Well actually I've got something to tell you, because guess who was at the house when we got there?"

A frown creased Barry's forehead.

"None other than that journalist friend of yours."

"You mean Guy Armstrong?"

"We didn't get his name, but from your description of him it certainly fitted. We just turned up in the nick of time. Blake-Hall was giving him the same reception as you. In fact Grace had to protect him. It looked as though Peter was about to hit him."

"You should have let it happen."

"Now, now Barry. This is the modern police service." Hunter smirked. "Anyway, what's so important it can't wait 'til we get in the pub?"

"I got a phone call today from an old friend of mine from my CID days about Alan Darbyshire." Barry lowered his voice.

"You remember what I told you before about Alan and Jeffery Howson being thick as thieves and using a strip club et cetera. Well surprise, surprise, guess who he's linked with?"

"Peter Blake-Hall?"

Barry shot Hunter a bewildered look. "How did you know that?"

Hunter tapped his temple. "I'm psychic." His mouth creased into a smile. "No I'm not. Peter actually mentioned that he knew Alan, and I put two-and-two together from what you already told us. In fact, he told us that Alan worked for him for a good few years at the lap-dancing club after he retired, hiring and firing staff and generally making sure the place kept a clean licence."

"Ah, but did Blake-Hall tell you how he originally got to know Alan Darbyshire."

Hunter shook his head. "No."

"He was a snout for Alan for years. You know how I said about how good his arrest rate was?"

Hunter nodded.

"Well it seems that most of it was down to Peter. And I'll tell you what else my friend mentioned on the q.t. You know how I told you about the holidays Alan and Jeffery had in a businessman's villa in Benidorm?"

Hunter nodded again.

"Well that businessman was none other than Peter Blake-Hall. It seems as though Alan and Jeffery had a right old thing going on with Blake-Hall. It's my guess he was giving them the info and everything, to keep the pair sweet and in return they'd tip him off if any raids or other stuff was coming his way."

Hunter cupped his chin and said "Hmm." Then he added, "Have you told anyone about this?"

"Not yet. I only got the phone call an hour ago. This old mate of mine doesn't want to get involved if he can help it. He used to work on the same team as Alan and Jeffery and had a lot of time for them. He said that deep down he respects Alan and that he was a very good gaffer to work for."

"Yeah, but it looks now as though he's not only bent but he may have murdered Jeffery."

"I know, and mentioned that to my old friend, but he'd rather stay in the background for now. I've promised him that I'll try and keep him out of it if I can. He's given us some good stuff to start doing some digging. Just keep it under your hat for now, I'll make some more calls, and see what I can come up with, and then if we can confirm everything from other sources, then we'll use those people instead."

"Look Barry, you know how important this is. I'll give you a couple of days to do your digging and if you don't get anywhere then I'm afraid this friend of yours is going to have to stand up and be counted."

Barry gave Hunter's wrist a gentle squeeze. "Give me until Thursday." Then, using the passenger door as support, he launched himself out of the passenger seat and pulled himself upright. "I'll get the first beers," he said, striding towards the back door of the pub, never looking back.

* * * * *

Just after 7pm Hunter left the pub feeling hungry and tired but relaxed. The wind had picked up, and rain which had dominated the sky for most of the day was now being whipped across the car park in angled sheets. For a second he stood in the doorway, cursing the weather. Then, hitching up the collar of his quilted outdoor coat and hunching low, he sprinted through the squall to his car.

He wiped the dampness from his face and waited for the windscreen demister to kick in. Two minutes later, with a clear view before him, he flicked on the wipers and swung his Audi out of the pub car park, onto Wentworth High Street and began his wend home. The opening chords of Genesis' 'Invisible Touch' played out through his six speaker system. He turned the stereo up several notches until he could feel the bass vibrate.

Picking up speed, he'd only travelled half a mile, when he spotted a dark coloured saloon car tucked next to the stone wall of the small village brewery on his right-hand side. He was sure there was someone in the driver's seat, and although he had seen cars parked there frequently during the day, at night, when the brewery was closed, the place was usually deserted. He eased off the accelerator and looked in the driver's side mirror.

Less than a hundred yards on, in his mirror, he saw the car's headlights suddenly blaze. Then he watched it pull onto the road and follow.

Suspicions aroused, Hunter hit the accelerator. The Audi's diesel turbo injection system kicked in, and within seconds he had reached sixty mph, the car's low profile tyres hugging the wet tarmac as it thundered along the stretch of unlit road in the direction of home. The winding roads ahead were in total darkness, but he knew this area of the countryside like the back of his hand and although he could still make out the headlights of the car behind in his rear-view mirror, he saw that they were slowly diminishing as he left it behind. Taking a sharp left, without indicating, he tore up a switch-back climb of road and then, two hundred yards along, he hit the brakes, wrenched the steering hard left and skidded into a side lane. As his car rocked to a halt, he turned off its lights.

Fifteen seconds later, the saloon flew past. He had enough time to get a fleeting look at the driver. He was sure it was the reporter, Guy Armstrong alone.

Hunter banged into first gear and booted the accelerator. The wheels spun, churning up the track below and fish-tailing momentarily as he whipped the Audi back onto the glistening road. Snapping through the gears, he could hear the engine roar, but in less than thirty seconds he was only twenty yards from the back of Guy Armstrong's car. He turned on his headlights and hit high beam. The rear of the reporter's car was hit by a blaze of white light. Hunter saw the saloon's brake lights flash on and the rear end of the car wobbled. Then it began to angle sideways and slide. He hit his brakes as Armstrong's car scythed sideways for several seconds before bouncing against the grassed verge and coming to a stop.

Hunter flung open his door, whipped off his seat belt and dashed towards the driver's side of the still-rocking saloon. He yanked open the door and was met by a pale-faced and shocked looking Guy Armstrong.

Hunter composed himself. "Mr Armstrong, if I'm not mistaken. And I thought I was the one with the certificate in surveillance."

"You bloody idiot," he spluttered. "You could have got me killed."

"That'll teach you for trying to sneak up on me. Now why are you following me?" Hunter wanted to swear. In fact he really wanted to drag him out of the car by the scruff of his neck, but he didn't know if Armstrong had his tape recorder switched on.

The reporter took a deep breath and sank back in his seat. He exhaled loudly. "I wasn't sneaking up on you. I just wanted a quick word with you about Peter Blake-Hall."

"Well I don't want to have a word with you. Especially to do with Peter Blake-Hall. This is a murder investigation and you know that."

"This is off the record. Hence the reason why I followed you."

"Off the record. How many times have I heard a journalist say that?"

"But this is. Believe me. I think I can help you. I have a source who "

Hunter held up his hand. He choked back the words he wanted to use and forced a tolerant smile. "Thank you very much Mr Armstrong for your kind offer, but I don't need your help."

"No, I really can help you."

He could feel a rage building up. "Mr Armstrong. This conversation is over. Good night."

With a mighty fling, he slammed the door shut. The car rocked.

As he made his way back to the Audi, Hunter realised how wet his face and hair had become. And his ears were stinging with the cold. He shook off some of the wetness.

As he slid into the driver's seat he felt a dampness creeping into his trousers and realised the seat was soaking. He cussed loudly and slammed the palm of his hand on the steering wheel. The car horn blared.

In a fit of temper he snapped the gear stick into first and stamped on the accelerator, flinging up a blanket of spray as he sped away from the scene.

- ooOoo –

CHAPTER NINE

DAY EIGHT: 1st December.

At morning briefing, Hunter gave details of his encounter with Guy Armstrong, warning the team to be on their guard.

Barry Newstead followed up by relaying his success at tracking down Lucy's best friend Amanda Smith. He had spoken with her briefly over the phone. Amanda had indeed changed her surname. "She got married in nineteen-eighty-five, the year following Lucy's murder trial. Her husband, back then, was a serving soldier, a member of the Military Police and they moved to his base in Germany. They came back to this country in nineteen-eighty-eight when he left the army and the pair are now living in Cumbria. In fact, both she and her husband have joined the police up there. She's now called Rawlinson - Amanda Rawlinson and she's a uniform sergeant stationed at Kendal," he said. "I spent ten minutes chatting with her on the phone late yesterday afternoon and told her about our re-opening of Lucy's case. She didn't sound too surprised. I've told her someone will be going up to interview her within the next few days." Barry added that had also found contact numbers for Lucy's parents and her daughter Jessica. He had spoken to them on the phone and warned them to expect a visit later in the week.

SIO Michael Robshaw finalised briefing by telling everyone there was a press conference that afternoon and that they should expect a lot of interest in the days ahead. He told them that he was already fending off calls regarding Friday's High Court Appeal following the request for his immediate release from Daniel Weaver's barrister. "We're up against the clock now on this," he concluded.

* * * * *

Following morning briefing Hunter made toast, poured himself a fresh drink of tea and made Grace a coffee. Then, while she chronicled the previous day's meeting with Peter Blake-Hall, he put in a phone call to the local Probation Service. He caught up with Jodie Marie Jenkinson's Probation Officer, a man called Ray Austin, as he was about to leave the office for his first court appearance of the day. He could tell from the man's reaction that the news of her death had come as a surprise. He told Hunter he would be back in the office for eleven o'clock and they arranged to meet then.

Hunter settled down to catch up with his own paperwork, and at 10.40am he picked up the folder containing Jodie Marie Jenkinson's sudden death report and headed off out for his meeting.

Barnwell Probation Service was housed in a large double-fronted Victorian building in a cul-de-sac of similar style dwellings. It had once been an area where the well-to-do business people of the locale lived, but over the years, as people's lifestyles and status had changed, the place had altered. Some of the houses had been sold on to developers, who had divided them into flats, and the two buildings either side of the Probation Service housed a firm of accountants and a private dental practice.

Hunter entered the reception area, gave the woman behind the reinforced glass screen his name, and told her he had an appointment.

There were a couple of young men in the reception area taking up seats flanking one side of the wall. Hunter immediately clocked one of them. He'd had dealings with him before over drug offences. They stared at each other for several seconds before the young man looked away sheepishly.

Hunter had only been waiting for a couple of minutes when a door next to the reception counter opened. The man framed in the doorway threw Hunter for a second, because he bore a striking resemblance to the torn photograph recovered from Jodie Marie Jenkinson's jeans pocket. Hunter realised he had seen this man in and around the magistrate's courts building. He quickly recovered his composure, hoping the man hadn't spotted the startled look. When the probation officer gave him a faint smile, Hunter realised his reaction hadn't drawn attention.

The man said, "DS Kerr?"

Hunter nodded.

"We spoke earlier. I'm Ray Austin. Would you like to come through?" He opened the door fully and stepped to one side.

As Hunter brushed past, out of the corner of one eye he glanced at Ray Austin again. This revelation meant that he had to change his approach and the line of questioning he had originally planned, until he got to the bottom of why Jodie had a photograph of her Probation Officer.

He led Hunter up a switch-back staircase to the first floor landing. There, a security door prevented them going any further. Ray Austin punched a four digit code into a key-pad and the door clicked open. He directed Hunter down a dimly lit corridor and then showed him into an office, the heavy four-panelled door of which bore a plate with his name. Hunter saw that Ray Austin's title was Senior Probation Officer.

Austin slipped past Hunter and dropped down into a high-back chair behind a cluttered desk. He offered Hunter a seat, then parted some of the paperwork and rested his forearms.

"Can I get you a drink?"

Hunter shook his head. "No thanks. To be honest I'm in the middle of a murder enquiry at the moment and I've a tight schedule today. I'm fitting in this in between my other enquiries.

"You've confused me Sergeant Kerr. You said on the phone you were investigating Jodie's death and now you've just said you're involved in a murder enquiry. Are the two not the same thing?"

"Sorry. My apologies. I explained myself badly there. Yes I am investigating Jodie's death and I am also involved in a murder enquiry, but the two are not related."

"So how can I help?"

"Well I'm led to believe you're her Probation Officer."

"Yes, for my sins. Jodie came to me after her last court appearance six months ago." He leaned further forward. "When I say for my sins, I don't mean that in a derogative way. Jodie had her faults, but like a lot of our clients, once you got past the veneer there was a different person under the surface. You might find that difficult to believe, I guess, from your dealings. But they come to us having received their punishment and the majority just get their heads down. Jodie wasn't like that though. I realised long ago that her probation sentence actually put some structure and purpose into her life, and it was a pleasure to work with her. She always did everything we asked and was always on time for her appointments, unlike many of our other clients. Hearing of her death this morning has come as a real shock, I can tell you." He paused and licked his lips. "To be honest I was about to write her up for breaching her sentence. She missed her last two appointments. That was unusual and I did cut her a bit of slack because of how good she had been in the past and so rang her mobile on several occasions. When she didn't return my calls and didn't turn up for the second appointment, I thought she'd done a runner." He shook his head. "I know why now. When did Jodie die?"

The comment about him trying to contact Jodie on her mobile jolted Hunter's brain. Where was her mobile? It hadn't been in her possession or at the scene where she had been found. He stored that thought away and then asked, "Can I ask when those appointments were?"

Ray Austin grabbed hold of the computer mouse for his desktop system and tapped it. Switching his eyes to the computer monitor, he made a series of swipes and clicks with the mouse and then returned his gaze to Hunter.

"The first one she missed was on Tuesday eighteenth November. She was booked in for three-thirty. The second one was last Tuesday, the twenty-fifth at two o'clock. We had another scheduled for tomorrow afternoon. I had just reduced them to weekly appointments because she was doing so well."

"Jodie's body was found on the twenty-first, but we believe she had been dead for the best part of a week."

"That's terrible."

"So if her appointments with you were weekly, the last time you saw her then was the Tuesday before, the eighteenth?"

The Senior Probation Officer gazed back to his monitor.

"Yes, the eleventh. Three o'clock. For the past couple of months they were always mid-afternoon because it fitted in with her job."

"She was working, then?"

"Yes, she'd got herself some work in a bar, though I don't know where that was."

"Do you know where she was living?"

"Yeah. I actually fixed her up with a place before she went for sentence. I did her pre-sentence report, and when she told me who she was dossing around with I told her if she wanted any chance of keeping out of prison then she needed to dump them soon as. She said she had nowhere else to go and as we have a list of landlords who are prepared to take our clients, I made a few phone calls and got her a place. I thought that if I could get her a more permanent residence then there was a fair chance of her getting probation, and so I fixed her up with a flat in one of the houses at the top of this road. I also sorted out her benefits, so she had enough money and didn't need to go out shoplifting again. You might find this strange but I had a bit of a soft spot for Jodie."

"When you say a bit of a soft spot?"

"In the strictest professional sense, of course. I've known Jodie a long time, in fact almost nine years. She did her first probation sentence when she was sixteen. Don't get me wrong, Jodie could be a pain in the backside at times, but she also had a heart of gold once you got to know her."

"And how well did you know her?"

"Probably better than any of others in the office. In fact, she could cause some of the girls here a bit of grief at times. Jodie had a bit of a temper on her, you see. Especially when she'd had a drink. And so I used to get her every time you lot had charged her. Everyone else wanted to avoid her, but I got on well with her."

"Why was that?"

"I don't know, to be honest. I suppose I didn't give up on her like others had done. She had a pretty shitty life you know."

"Were you fond of her?"

Ray Austin's brow creased into a frown and his mouth tightened. "Fond of her. I don't get what you mean?"

"Mr Austin Ray, I won't beat about the bush. When we found Jodie's body, in her jeans pocket she had a photograph of you."

"A photo of me?"

Hunter flipped open the cover of Jodie's file, withdrew the clear plastic evidence bag containing the torn photograph, and turned it so that it was facing him. "That is you?"

"Wow. Now I know where that photograph went."

Hunter had expected the Senior Probation Officer to look embarrassed or surprised, but he did neither. It was Hunter's turn to frown.

"That photo went missing from my desk well over six months ago. In fact, it'll have been longer than that. It was the start of the year when I noticed it had gone from my frame. I wondered where it had gone to." He reached out to a wooden photo frame next to his desktop computer and turned it around to face Hunter. "This is another copy of the same photo. I replaced it."

Hunter studied the framed photograph. He saw that the image contained not only Ray Austin's head and shoulder pose but he had his arm around the shoulders of a tanned, dark haired, good-looking woman, in her mid to late thirties. There was no doubt that the torn section of photograph they had recovered from Jodie's jean pocket was in part an identical copy of this one he was looking at.

"That's my wife, Sarah, with me. We've been married almost ten years." He returned the framed photograph to his desk top, nudging it into roughly the same position it had been before. A smile creased his face. "Now I realise why you were asking me the type of questions you were. You thought something was going on between Jodie and me."

Still guarded, Hunter said, "Was there?"

For a second Austin's smile grew wider, then just as quickly it was gone and his face straightened. "You're being serious aren't you? Look, when I say I was fond of Jodie it was nothing like you think. It was strictly probation officer and client when we met. But like I said, I did have a soft-spot for her. You didn't know Jodie like I did. She had a shit life and it wasn't getting any better."

"Tell me about it."

"As I say, I first came across Jodie when she was sixteen. She'd got drunk and badly assaulted a younger girl at the care home she was in. I'm afraid Jodie was yet another failure in our care system. She had suffered a life of neglect and abuse by parents who drank heavily, and went into care when she was twelve as a result. She was fostered out a few times but caused havoc with every family she was placed with and so in the end no one would have her. She started drinking heavily when she was fourteen, and by the time she was fifteen had been cautioned three times. The assault was her first court conviction and I was given her file. After that, I got her paperwork every time she went to court. Don't ask me how, but I just seemed to be able to get on with her. In fact, even when she wasn't on our books she'd pop in to see me and have a chat. She did say to me once that I was the only person who listened to her and understood what she was going through. I don't know if that's true or not, but she obviously could relate to me."

"Obviously. After all, she took your photo and kept the part of it with you on."

He shook his head. "I never realised I had that impression on her life." Momentarily, he drifted his gaze up to the ceiling. Returning his look back to Hunter he said, "Can I ask you now how she met her death? Was it to do with drink?"

"No. Drugs actually."

"Drugs?"

"Heroin."

He looked startled. "Heroin?"

"Yeah. An overdose. She was found in the cellar of a derelict pub. The place had been used as a shooting den. You sound surprised?"

"That's because I am. As far as I was aware, Jodie never touched drugs. Maybe the odd spliff now and then, but not the hard stuff. In fact, you know when I said earlier that at times she had a heart of gold?"

Hunter acknowledged with a nod.

"Well, that was to do with drugs. A couple of the care staff from the home where she lived told me that Jodie used to come back there from time to time, and if she found any of the kids using gear she'd end up preaching to them about the dangers of the stuff. She had some success as well. Helped get a few of the kids clean. She was actually a role model for some of them, in a strange way." He paused, stroking his bottom lip. Then he said "Are you sure it was heroin? You're not mistaken?"

"Absolutely. A really pure concentrate as well. Not the normal street smack."

"I really find this difficult to believe. If you'd said she'd died as a result of choking on her own vomit from drink, then yes, I'd believe that, but not drugs."

Hunter pushed himself back into his seat. There was something in Ray Austin's response which was setting alarm bells ringing. He thought back to the crime scene photographs, especially those relating to Jodie's post-mortem. And then it hit him. When he had viewed Jodie's photographs yesterday, he had missed vital evidence. The scarring on her arms from her years of self-harm had distracted his investigative eye. Everything was suddenly a whirl. He shook his head in an attempt to dismiss the chaos in his brain.

Ray Austin eased himself back. "You look a little concerned, DS Kerr?"

"That's because I am. I think I've been walking down a blind alley over this. What you've just said has completely changed my thoughts about Jodie's death. I thought she'd overdosed. Now I'm going to have to go back and re-look at things." He glanced at Jodie's file. "Just another couple of things to sort out before I leave you in peace?"

"Oh yes?"

"First thing, her address?"

"Sure, no problem." He picked up a bunch of bright yellow Post-its, scribbled on the top one, tore it off and slapped it fast to the inside cover of Hunter's folder. He pointed at his note.

"Her flat's on the top floor. It's only a one bedroom place, but she never had many possessions, so it was just right for her. She shared a bathroom with two other flatmates on the same floor. There're ten flats in that place, mainly DHSS clients."

Hunter glanced at the address on the note. "Thanks. We found a key on Jodie so I'm hoping it's for this place. I'm going to nip up there next. Just one more thing Ray, we also found a Christmas card in her possession. It's signed Mr X. You wouldn't know anything about that, would you?"

His face creased into a smile. "Goodness me, has she still got that? I sent her that donkey's years ago. It was sent as a bit of a joke type thing but I know she appreciated it. I've already mentioned that she used to pop in the office from time to time for a chat, even when she wasn't on probation?"

Hunter acknowledged Ray's comments with a brief nod.

"Well, one Christmas time when she was about eighteen or nineteen, she called in for a chat after she'd done some Christmas shopping." His eyes sparkled. "I know what you're thinking. No, she hadn't been shoplifting, it was genuine Christmas shopping. Anyway, she saw all the cards on my desk that everyone had sent and she just said that she'd never ever been sent a Christmas card. I found that comment so sad and so I sent her one and signed it as Mr X as a bit of a joke. She knew I'd sent it, because she turned up at my office waving it around and thanked me. I thought she was going to cry." He pursed his lips and rolled his head from side to side. "That's quite sad, don't you think? The only person to ever send her a Christmas card was her probation officer."

Hunter flipped Jodie Marie Jenkinson's file shut. "It obviously brought comfort to her, because she'd held on to it after all these years."

Ray Austin's eyes suddenly glistened, then he exclaimed, "Do you know the mention of Christmas has just triggered something Jodie said to me the last time we met."

Hunter was intrigued. "Oh? What's that then?"

"Well I don't know if it's relevant to your enquiries or not, but after she'd told me this I can remember warning her to be careful."

"What did she say?"

"I can't remember the exact words, but I said something about Christmas to her. I think I asked her what she was doing for Christmas, and she said, with a bit of luck going on holiday. It wasn't the reply I expected so asked her if she'd won the lottery, as a joke, and she said: 'Just as good as. I know a secret that's going to make me a lot of money.'"

Hunter repeated, "A secret?"

"I'm afraid she wouldn't tell me what the secret was. She just said I'd read about it in the papers."

"You're sure she said that?"

"It wasn't word for word, but it was certainly something close to that. I looked her straight in the eyes after she'd said it and I could tell by her face that she was serious. That's when I told her to be careful, that she couldn't afford to get into any more trouble. She just laughed at me and told me not to worry, she could look after herself." Ray Austin slowly stroked his chin and exchanged looks with Hunter. "Are you thinking what I'm thinking? That, secret could have just got her killed."

Hunters brain went into full spin. What Ray Austin had said meant that closing Jodie's death report was certainly not going to happen today. There were too many unanswered questions.

He replied, "That is just what I need to find out, but it's looking like a distinct possibility." Then he pushed himself up out of the chair and extended his hand for a thank you shake.

* * * * *

Glancing at the address scribbled on the Post-it note stuck to the dashboard, Hunter slowed the unmarked police car, swung it in towards the kerb, braked and switched off the engine. Looking out through the driver's door window, he saw that he was parked outside a large and majestic looking detached, soot-stained, sandstone Victorian dwelling. Staring beyond its low perimeter wall and mature garden of overgrown, lifeless bushes he could see that, outwardly, the front of it still retained all the elegance and splendour of its Gothic architecture. At first he marvelled at the sight before him. Then he let out a sigh of despair, for he knew that this majesty was not going to be mirrored within its interior, given what he had been told about the place housing DHSS tenants. Over the years he'd been in so many flats where single people on housing benefit lived, and he had always left them feeling that many of their residents either knew no better, or actually couldn't give a damn about, the conditions they were living in.

Before he left the car he got hold of Grace on his mobile and told her what he had just uncovered. "I'm just going to do a quick visit to her flat. If it looks okay I'm going to make sure it's secure, contact the landlord and then pay a visit with SOCO tomorrow." He was about to tell her to inform the Office Manager, DI Scaife, what he was up to, when she interrupted him. She had submitted the account of their visit to Peter Blake-Hall, and they had been allocated the job of visiting and speaking with Lucy's parents. She'd already spoken with them on the phone and fixed up a meeting for two o'clock that afternoon.

Hunter looked at his watch. It was 12.15pm.

"Grace there's no way I'll get back to the office in time. And I'm sorry, but this can't wait. I don't think Jodie's death is an accident after what her Probation Officer has just told me and I urgently need to do some follow-up enquiries." He apologised again and suggested that she either took someone else from the team with her to interview Lucy's parents, or re-scheduled the meeting. He could sense her frustration as she told him she would catch up with him later and ended their call.

With a pang of guilt he pocketed his phone. He didn't like to let his partner down, but he knew he needed to visit Jodie's place.

Twisting the brass doorknob of the wide Victorian glass patterned entrance door, he pushed. It was unlocked and he stepped into the hallway. He had guessed right about the interior. It was dingy. Many of the original black and white floor tiles were chipped and scuffed. A couple were missing and concrete patches replaced them. Torn, woodchip wallpaper covered the walls.

Trying not to make too much noise, he climbed the hairpin staircase up to the second floor, where Ray Austin had told him he would find Jodie's bed-sit. At the head of the second stairway the landing split left and right with a door at either end. He spotted the door number he was seeking to his right.

Still treading carefully, he made his approach to Jodie's room. Three steps along the landing, he faltered. He could hear sounds from inside. He saw the panelled door was cracked open a fraction and clocked that the jamb around the door hasp had splinter marks. It had been forced.

Senses heightened in a sudden rush of adrenaline, he clenched his fists and edged forward. Inches from the door he paused and listened. The earlier noise had stopped, and the only sound now seemed to be from a television set in one of the flats below.

Using his foot, slowly, he inched the door open. It creaked on its hinges, reminding him of a horror movie. As the gap widened he tried to get a better view inside but the gloom made it difficult. The curtains were drawn, but enough light pierced through the gaps at either side for him to pick out the outline of various pieces of furniture in the dimness. He was about to step inside when a dark shape shot into view, rocketing towards him and taking him by surprise. Instinctively he threw up his hands into boxing stance, but it was an instant too late. He never saw the blow. It caught him full in the mouth, knocking him sideways and sending him crashing against the wall. He banged the back of his head and instantly a display of fireworks detonated inside his brain, blanking out his sight. Before he had time to react, a second blow to the midriff sent the air exploding from his lungs. His legs buckled and he only just managed to throw out his hands in time to stop himself from fully hitting the deck.

He felt the figure brushing past but couldn't do a thing about it, he was still scrambling around, trying to recover. There was a distinct sound of someone bounding heavily down the stairs. Using the handrail as support, Hunter yanked himself upright and looked downwards just in time to see a squat, stocky man, in dark padded jacket, a woollen hat pulled low over his ears and hiding his features, disappearing through the front door. His assailant looked to be of the same build and shape, as well as wearing clothing of a similar style and colour as the man he had chased three days earlier at Jeffery Howson's funeral.

For a second his head was in turmoil. There was no reason in this world why this should be the same person. There was no link between Jeffery Howson and Jodie. He took a deep breath, closed his eyes, committing the description to memory and then let out a heavy sigh. If it was the same man, then that was the second time he had let him slip. There wouldn't be a third, he told himself as he thumped the handrail in frustration.

Taking another deep breath, he felt his strength returning and delved into his jacket pocket for his mobile. He needed to call this in. Back-up would be too late to capture the fugitive, but he needed to preserve the scene and get forensic support here quickly. He was confident now that Jodie's death was no accident, that he may have just missed her killer, and that this was as fresh as a crime scene as he could possibly have.

As he speed-dialled the communications room, he realised he was bleeding at the mouth - he could taste and smell the coppery tang of blood upon his lips. He was running his tongue around them as an operator came on the line.

* * * * *

The marked Response Car got to Hunter inside five minutes. He quickly briefed the driver and his partner as to what had happened and gave them the offender's description, such as it was, and left them to get on with coordinating a search, while he began to fathom out how best to secure the premises. He knew this wasn't going to go down too well, given the nature of some of the residents. Already, one of the male tenants had stuck his head around his door and demanded to know what the fuck was going on.

Still angry about losing his attacker, Hunter was in no mood to appease him, and had thrust his warrant card in his face and told him to "Get back in his room and shut the fuck up." The young man had obliged without argument. Next to arrive was Grace and Mike Sampson. They had been about to set off to Bakewell, to interview Lucy's parents, when they'd picked up his distress call and had immediately diverted.

"Which way did he run?" said Grace.

Hunter shrugged. "Don't know. Best guess is he made a left into the side streets. There're quite a few alleyways he could've shot down and from there he could have made the town centre or out towards the hospital. I don't even know if he had a car or not. I didn't hear one. But to be honest it took me a good couple of minutes to get my breath back and get down the stairs." He could feel the blood again on his lips. "He caught me off guard and packed a hell of a punch." He dabbed at his mouth with the side of a hand. A small circle of red covered the area around his thumb and forefinger. "I'll punch his fucking lights out when I get hold of him."

Grace shook her head.

He said "What?"

She pointed to his mouth and said, "Don't worry, it's not made any difference to your looks. You're still as ugly." Then she smiled. "Come on then Sergeant Kerr, start dishing out the orders, tell us what you want us to do."

"Uniform are covering a lot of the ground, and CCTV are looking in and around the town centre, so there's not a lot to do about him at the moment. I could do with finding out who lives in these flats and who's in at the moment. I've spoken to one of the tenants already." He pointed back down the hall. "I'm going to secure the area between the first floor and second floor, I've got SOCO on their way."

Within ten minutes Hunter had donned a white forensic over-suit from the boot of his car and sealed off the staircase between the first and second floors. He had listened to the sounds of Grace and Mike knocking on doors below and knew that the pair were currently in the flat belonging to the resident he had encountered immediately after his assault. He wondered if the guy would make a complaint about him swearing. Then he dismissed the thought from his head he could trust his team mates to talk him out of it.

He heard the front entrance door click open below, then slowly close, followed by the clipped sound of heels on the tiled hall floor. Hunter peered over the banister and caught sight of Detective Superintendent Dawn Leggate coming up the staircase towards him. He recognised her distinct auburn tinged bob of ginger hair.

In her Scottish brogue she called out, "Hello. DS Kerr?"

"Up here ma'am."

She craned her neck, swapping glances, as she continued climbing the stairs. "Please don't call me ma'am Hunter, I bloody hate that word. Makes me sound like the Queen. Just call me boss or guv." She paused on the last step before the landing and faced Hunter. She was wearing a brown checked duffel coat. With a leather gloved hand she began un-pegging it.

"I'm afraid you're going to have to put up with me, DS Kerr. Mr Robshaw's going to run the Howson enquiry and I'm running this one. I hope you're okay with that?"

Hunter licked his bottom lip and nodded. He felt a sharp tinge from the cut at the side of his mouth and winced.

"Bloody good job, 'cos I wasn't giving you an option." The Detective Superintendent flashed him a mischievous smile, reached up and tapped his shoulder, "Anyway, it will give me the chance to work closely with someone on my new team." She removed her gloved hand. "Getting my teeth into my own investigation is just what I needed. Right Hunter, tell me what you've got? I've heard over the radio that they're still searching for the guy who slugged you, though it looks as though he's gone to ground."

Hunter felt his face flush. He was still smarting. Not just from letting someone thump him without any form of retaliation, but also knowing that he let his quarry get away. He gave his SIO a resume of the background to the case, explaining how he had initially thought that Jodie's death was the result of a drugs overdose. "I have to confess I took my eye off the case because of the Howson enquiry. The information given to me by her Probation Officer this morning made me want to check out her flat." He relayed the earlier conversation with Ray Austin. "Especially that bit about the secret she said she had about someone, which was going to make her lots of money."

"And so, like me, you're thinking that this guy who you've disturbed had something to do with that secret and her death."

Hunter nodded. "It's a fair bet, yes, although she didn't tell her probation officer what the secret was, or who it was about."

"And you got the impression that this guy was the same one you chased at Jeffery Howson's funeral?"

He tightened his mouth again and rolled his head. "I couldn't swear on it. Not exactly a hundred per cent and it doesn't make sense why the same guy at Jeffery Howson's funeral should turn up here. But it was just the way he was dressed. It looked as though he was still wearing the same gear. And I know I only got a fleeting glance of him at the churchyard, and my view of him today was from up here, but there were so many similarities to his shape and build that makes me think it's the same man."

"Just hold onto those thoughts for now. We've got a lot of enquiries ahead and you say that uniform are still out there searching for him, as well as the camera boys in the CCTV suite, so we might be able to rule him either in or out later on, okay?"

Hunter agreed with a nod.

"Okay, now show me what you've got so far."

Earlier, he had removed Jodie's file from the MIT car. It was now tucked beneath his arm. He slipped it out, flipped open the folder and half-turned it toward the Detective Superintendent for her to view. "This is what I've got in terms of evidence." He balanced the folder across an open palm and picked out the Scenes of Crime photograph booklet within it. "These are shots of the pub and the cellar where Jodie's body was found and also of her PM."

Hunter showed Dawn Leggate Jodie's post-mortem photos, selecting those which focused on her arms. "I'd looked at them a couple of times and there was something I wasn't happy with, but I couldn't put my finger on it. Since learning everything this morning, especially her stance on drug abuse, I gave them the once-over again and I've realised that there are no track-marks on her arms, or anywhere else on her body. The self-harm scars completely threw me."

Then he flicked back to the sequence of images SOCO had taken of the premises. "Also there was something else bugging me, but I couldn't quite put my finger on it. Twenty minutes ago that came to me as well when I looked back over the scene photos again." He pointed out the shot depicting the long stretch of corridor which led towards the cellar. He gave her enough time to study it and then flipped to the next photograph, a close-up shot of the door to the cellar with its broken panel. "The foreman told me that they had to kick this in to get access. This door was fitted with a mortise lock. And I remembered that they told me that it was locked." He scrutinised his boss's face. She was hanging on to his every word. "The only key we found on Jodie was for this flat, and that's a Yale make. While I've been waiting, I've managed to get hold of Duncan Wroe, he's our Scenes of Crime manager, who went to the scene. He's on his way here as we speak. He's told me that they didn't find any other key during their search. Also, the cellar where she was found was too clean to be a shooting den. Just look at the photograph which shows her slumped along the floor." He thumbed to the next shot in the album. "All that's around her is a couple of syringes, a couple of spoons and a few silver wraps. That's it. I've been to a few of these dens in the past and there's usually discarded drugs paraphernalia all over the place. That's not all, there was no cigarette lighter or matches, either on her possession, or in the cellar. This was staged for our benefit." He closed the evidence album. "She was never alone in that cellar. Someone else was there to heat up the heroin on the spoon before it was injected. And with that in mind, I've got back onto the builders at the site and spoken to the foreman. I've told them to stop what they're doing so we can do a thorough forensics job and extend the search area. Thankfully, he says they've not touched the cellar since Jodie's body was found."

"Well, you seem to have got most bases covered. What about witnesses here?"

Hunter told her what Grace and Mike Sampson were doing.

"As I said, you seem to have got everything covered." She checked her watch. "It's just gone one o'clock. My guess is it will take SOCO a good hour or so to get sorted and a good few hours for Grace and Mike to get round the residents here to see if any of them witnessed anything, so I'm going to leave everything in your capable hands while I sort us out an incident suite. I'll need to get onto the Coroner as well and fix up a second PM. I also need to bring in more resources.

We've got a couple of detectives joining us from the Cold Case Team to help out with the Howson enquiry, so I'll leave Grace and Mike with you doing the door-to-door, and I'll get back and speak with Mr Robshaw and see who else I can purloin." She glanced down at Jodie's file and said. "Can I take this back with me so I'm up-to-date with everything and can get the incident board set-up?"

Sliding it from his grasp, she slapped the folder shut and tapped his chest with it. Then fixing him with her hazel eyes, she smiled and said, "Good job, Hunter," before setting off back down the stairs.

Hunter was leaning over the balcony with his eyes glued to the front door. He was cold. He had been here almost two hours and the single radiator below him, in the hallway, appeared not to be working. It certainly wasn't throwing out enough heat to reach him up here on the second floor. He cursed to himself as he shivered uncontrollably.

Then the front door opened with a jerk and Hunter jumped. He was confronted by the sight of Duncan Wroe, Scene of Crime Manager, struggling to get through the gap in the door. Using the side of one hip, he was doing his best to force the opening wider, while trying to squeeze through. He dragged through an aluminium equipment case, clipboard and his forensic clothing in laden hands and arms.

Stumbling into the hallway, he called out, "Where is everyone?"

"Up here Duncan," Hunter responded, checking his watch, noting the time for his log: it was 1:55pm.

By the time Duncan had reached Hunter he was out of breath. He dropped his aluminium case onto the landing and pushed his free hand through his unruly mop of straw coloured hair.

Hunter greeted him. "You ought to exercise more."

"I would if I got time. Some of us have real work to do, Detective Sergeant Kerr."

Hunter laughed. "The same old Duncan. Never beaten for words."

Duncan straightened his back. "What have you got for me then?"

Hunter reminded the SOCO Manager about his attendance and examination of the scene where Jodie Marie Jenkinson's body had been discovered. Then he repeated what he had already told Detective Superintendent Dawn Leggate. "This is

JJ's bed-sit, Duncan. The only person I'm aware of who's visited the place since her death is that guy who socked me one. No one's stepped a foot inside the place since that happened."

"Good." The SOCO manager climbed into his white suit and picked up his case. "I noticed you've kept a sterile area down to the first landing. That's good as well. Did you notice if the guy was wearing gloves or not?"

Hunter shook his head. "It all happened so fast. He was wearing a woollen hat and padded jacket. That's all I had time to clock."

"No problem. We'll soon see once we start sprinkling the magic dust around."

Duncan Wroe made towards Jodie's door. Hunter fell in behind.

The SOCO Manager halted the landing side of the bed-sit and scanned the splintered lock area. "That wouldn't have offered much resistance." He glanced over his shoulder. "Who's the exhibits officer?"

"Everything's down to you and me at the moment Duncan. We're a bit thin on the ground, what with the retired detective murder case that's running, and we've also re-opened a cold case murder from nineteen-eighty-three that's linked."

"Yeah, I heard that." Thrusting his case before him and using its front edge as leverage Duncan pushed the door open wider.

On tip-toes, Hunter looked over the Scenes of Crime Manager's shoulder. It was his first opportunity to get a proper view inside Jodie's room. It didn't take him long - the space where Jodie had lived prior to her death was no bigger than ten-feet square.

It was a mess.

Not the type of mess one would associate with untidiness, Hunter thought, as he scanned the space. No, this place looked like a hurricane had ripped through it. The mattress from the single bed had been flipped over onto the floor, its duvet and pillow shredded. A set of double cupboards above a small sink and draining board were open, and judging by the debris over the floor its contents had been emptied. A single wardrobe had its doors wide open and various items of clothing littered the floor. A portable TV had been upended, and a large number of photographs, DVDs and CDs covered the threadbare carpet.

Duncan glanced back. "I think you're onto something here Hunter. I would say this is no ordinary burglary. Someone was looking for something in particular."

"Well I hope he didn't find it."

"We shall see, we shall see." He turned and handed Hunter his clipboard. "I'm going to make a call back to the office. I'm going to need a hand here."

* * * * *

It was ten past six in the evening before Hunter, Grace and Mike got back to the office.

Mentally running through the day's events, Hunter made for his desk. He'd left Scenes of Crime still examining the scene, and managed to get the duty Inspector to provide a uniformed officer to stand guard and preserve the scene.

So far the door-to-door enquiries by Grace and Mike had not revealed anything startling about Jodie. A couple of the tenants had spoken with her on most days, but none of them were friends. However, the young man he had exchanged insults with earlier in the day had been surprisingly helpful. He had seen a skinny girl, with dyed blonde hair, roughly the same age as Jodie, going up to her bed-sit on several occasions and he had heard them partying together quite a few times. After one such party, about a month ago, he told Grace that he'd got so pissed off with the pair of them making so much noise, that he'd marched upstairs and banged on Jodie's door. The skinny blonde one had answered, and when he'd complained, she'd just laughed in his face and told him to 'fuck off, you're only jealous, freak.' He'd collared Jodie the next day on the stairs and she'd apologised. He told Grace that he had seen this girl twice in the past week going up to Jodie's room. Realising the significance, because Jodie had been dead for well over a week, Grace had pushed him for a description, but he hadn't been able to offer any further help. Grace had fixed up for him to do a digital e-fit in a hope that it would help identify the girl.

It's been a good start.

The only person in the office was DI Gerald Scaife. He was sat at his desk, head buried in a large amount of paperwork.

Hunter said, "Only you in boss?"

The DI looked up. "There are a few of the HOLMES team next door, the rest have gone. The Detective Super sacked it early. He's had to go over to Sheffield, to the BBC studios, to do a piece for Look North, for tonight's news. Not much has happened here today so everyone is back in tomorrow for eight am briefing. I'm just trying to clear some of the backlog." He laid down his pen and pushed himself back from his desk. "Your day's been quite eventful, I understand."

For the third time that day, Hunter told Jodie's story, quickly brushing over the part where he had been assaulted. He was still embarrassed that he had come off second best. "The place had been well and truly turned over by that guy, and it's now looking likely that she's been murdered. Someone injected her with a lethal dose of heroin to make it look as though it was an accident." He looked serious. "What for yet, we don't know. When I left, half an hour ago, SOCO had not turned up anything, and we've still got to track down this blonde girl who's been a regular visitor in the past few months. With a bit of luck, she might know the secret Jodie was keeping. Until we find that out, we're struggling to come up with any answers. The Super, Dawn Leggate, was going to arrange a second PM for tomorrow to see if that will turn anything up. Jodie had bruising to her cheek and I have to confess I initially thought it was where she had fallen, but it now could be evidence of an assault. It's something the pathologist can check." Out of the corner of his eye he saw Grace picking up items from her desk and returning them to drawers. She was ready for home. He asked. "Do you know where Detective Superintending Leggate is? Has she said anything about what she wants us to do?"

"Yes, she told me to tell you to call it a day. She went off to headquarters a couple of hours ago to see if she could sort out an incident suite and see what other resources were available. She'll ring you later at home and let you know where you need to be for briefing tomorrow."

Hunter turned to his own desk to tidy things away.

The DI said, "There's a couple of messages on your desk. That reporter Guy Armstrong has been trying to get hold of you most of the afternoon. He's left his mobile number and home number and asked if you'd call him the minute you got in. I think he's also left a message on your voicemail."

Hunter viewed several scrap pieces of paper on his desk blotter. There were four notes in all, two of them with phone numbers. He bundled them together and dropped them into his pending tray.

Turning toward the doors, he called back, "He's a determined man if nothing else. He'll have to wait until tomorrow now. I've got a glass of whisky with my name on it waiting for me back home.

- ooOoo -

CHAPTER TEN

DAY NINE: 2nd December.

Closing the garden gate behind him, Hunter stood for a moment admiring the landscape. A hoar frost blanketed as far as he could see. Taking in a long, deep breath, expanding his chest, Hunter held it a few seconds and then exhaled slowly. The breath left his mouth as a wisp of freezing air.

After speaking with Det. Supt. Leggate late last night, he knew he had the time this morning to have a lengthy run into work; she had earmarked an incident suite for the Jodie Marie Jenkinson investigation, but it wouldn't be up and running until later in the day and so she told him to turn up at the MIT department as usual.

Jogging on the spot to warm up his leg muscles, he gazed at the sky. A milky light from a pale winter sun was just beginning to bleach through a thin veil of light grey. The day ahead looked promising, he thought, as he set off on his run.

Within a couple of seconds he had pushed his way through frozen waist-high ferns and joined the track of the old racecourse which abutted his garden. Adjusting his breathing, and fixing his gaze to where the straight hit the first bend on his route, he kicked his heels up a pace and headed off in the direction of work.

Showered and changed into his suit, feeling buoyant and fresh, Hunter entered an office bustling with activity. A couple more detectives swelled their ranks this morning; two members of the Cold Case Unit had joined the team.

Despite the new arrivals, he knew they were still going to be stretched, especially now there was his investigation to add to the mix.

Putting a Windsor knot in his tie, he settled into his seat, glancing across his desk to where Grace was blowing into a well-filled cup. He saw that his own mug, resting on its coaster, had been filled. The contents were still steaming. He picked it up firmly between two hands and took a gulp.

"Mmm, that tea's like nectar. Just what I needed after my run," he said, then asked, "Been in long?"

"Ten minutes, that's all."

"Much happening? I see a couple of lads from the cold case unit have joined us."

"Yeah, they came in apparently after everyone had gone home to help the HOLMES crew man the phones following Mr Robshaw's appeal yesterday."

"I saw that on the late evening news. Did anything positive came out of it?"

"I had ten minutes with Isobel this morning and she tells me that they only got a dozen or so calls all night. She said a few of those were helpful. One of them was from a friend of one of the girls who was a witness at Daniel Weaver's trial. She says her friend saw Weaver and Lucy arguing in the market place. She told me that the girl's now married and lives near Yarmouth. Isobel's expecting to get a call from the woman this morning. That'll be a good run out for someone. And one has given us a lead in the Jeffery Howson case. A couple coming back from the pub on the Saturday night saw a car parked up close to the bottom of the path which leads up to the back of Jeffery's garden. That looks promising. Other than that, the usual crank calls - a couple from mediums who say they know where she's buried. That sums it up, I think. I've had a quick chat with one of the new lads as well. He told me that their brief is to help with tracing the remaining witnesses from the Lucy Blake-Hall case." Grace set down her cup. "By the way, have you heard the other news?"

"News? You mean TV/radio news, or police gossip news?"

"Guy Armstrong's dead!"

"Guy Armstrong, as in nosy, pain in the arse reporter, Guy Armstrong?"

Grace nodded. "Killed in a road accident last night."

"You are kidding me?"

"No. Isobel told me that she bumped into the duty Inspector last night, before she went off. He was just turning out to the accident. I don't know all of the details - Traffic are dealing - but it looks as though he's missed a bend on his way home from the pub last night and crashed into a tree. His car went up in flames."

"Jesus, poor guy s'cuse the pun. I know I said he was a pain in the arse, but I wouldn't wish that on him." Then Hunter remembered his conversation with DI Scaife. He set down his mug and rifled through his pending tray, pulling out the four scribbled notes on scrap paper he had tidied away. He spread them out on his blotter and studied each one. None contained any specific details, other than to state that Armstrong wanted to speak with him. Two contained a mobile and landline telephone number.

Suddenly he felt guilty about not calling. Hunter started to collect together the notes, and then recalled something else DI Scaife had said just before he left the office. He snatched up the handset of his desk phone and punched in his voicemail number and code. Gripping the receiver between ear and shoulder, he grabbed several blank sheets of scrap paper from a pile and picked up his pen, ready to make notes. Then he hit the number one key to retrieve his recorded calls. He had six messages on his list - five of them were old ones he had stored. Guy Armstrong's was the only fresh one. He tapped the star key to play it. The message lasted twenty seconds. Although he had his pen poised over paper, Hunter never made a note. While listening to Guy Armstrong's recording, his eyes wandered blankly around the office as he took it in.

When it had finished, he said excitedly, "Bloody hell Grace, just listen to this message Armstrong left me."

He punched the play key again and engaged the speakerphone. Despite sounding a little bit mechanical, there was no doubt that it was Guy Armstrong's voice.

"Detective Sergeant Kerr, this is Guy Armstrong. It's important that I speak with you. I've just learned that Jodie Jenkinson is dead and that you are investigating it. The reason why I am ringing you is because Jodie was the source I mentioned to you the other night. It was her who tipped me off about the Lucy Blake-Hall case. A couple of weeks ago, she overheard a conversation between two people which leaves me to believe that Daniel Weaver really is innocent of her murder. I could do with seeing you. I've left you my mobile and home phone number and I'm going to call into the George and Dragon at Wentworth tonight to hopefully catch you. As soon as you get this message, please call me."

Hunter struck the store key on his desk phone and slowly set down the handset.

To Grace, he said, "Talk about a voice from the grave."

* * * * *

It was almost ten-thirty before morning briefing started.

Following Hunter's phone call, Detective Superintendent Dawn Leggate hot-footed it back from District Headquarters, and with the help of Hunter and a member of the HOLMES team set up an incident board displaying all the latest information associated with the death of Jodie Marie Jenkinson.

Grace had printed off the computerised incident log, relating to the previous evening's incident involving Guy Armstrong, which was still categorised as a fatal road traffic collision. The print-out was lengthy and had taken her a good quarter of an hour to read and digest. She had underlined wherever a police officer's, or fire officer's name appeared and had made a note of which Scenes of Crime Officer had turned out - all were potential witnesses. She had also been given the job of locating Armstrong's address as well as finding out who he worked for.

The two Cold Case Unit detectives seconded onto the team were already hard at it, working alongside Barry Newstead, following up the previous evening's phone calls from the Detective Superintendent's TV broadcast, and tracking down the last few remaining witnesses from the Lucy Blake-Hall file, who had not been traced because they had either moved, changed their details, or both, since the court proceedings. Other members of the team were making phone calls relating to the tasks they had been given, or writing up the results to feed back into the system.

The sudden call of, "Okay folks, listen up," grabbed everyone's attention and a sea of eyes followed Detective Superintendents Michael Robshaw and Dawn Leggate as they made their way to the front of the incident room.

There were now three separate incident boards. The two SIOs stopped either side of the latest addition; the one which displayed information relating to Jodie's death.

Michael Robshaw opened the briefing. "First things first. Last night's TV appeal. I'm guessing you all saw it? We've got a couple of good calls. One of them, giving us the new details and address of a previous witness in the Daniel Weaver trial, which we'll be following up. But one I'm especially excited about relates to Jeffery Howson's murder. A couple who live three streets away from Jeffery were on their way back from the pub just before half-past-ten on the Saturday evening, when we believe he was killed, when they noticed a dark coloured four-by-four parked very close to the entranceway of the path which leads into the woods. And as we all know that path runs past the bottom of Jeffery Howson's garden. I want that call following up as a priority this morning. See if we can identify that vehicle, and more importantly, if they saw anyone with it. That's our first positive lead." He paused and looked around the team. "We don't happen to know what vehicle Alan Darbyshire drives do we?" The SIO's eyes levelled on Hunter.

"To be honest boss, I never questioned him about what car he drove, because I didn't want to arouse suspicions," Hunter responded, "but there was a gold coloured Toyota Avensis parked in front of his house."

"I can make a discreet phone call regarding that," piped up Barry Newstead.

The Detective Superintendent turned to Barry. "Okay I'll leave that one with you." Then his attention returned to the room. He slapped a hand, palm-flat, against the incident board he was standing beside. "Okay, fresh focus everyone! Jodie Marie Jenkinson, twenty-three year old single girl, who lived at flat ten, Westville House, Victoria Road, Barnwell. She was last seen alive by her probation officer on the afternoon of Tuesday eleventh of November." He pointed to the scenes of crime photograph which depicted her crumpled form, slumped across the concrete floor. "She was found in this state by builders, in the cellar of the old Barnwell Inn, on the morning of Friday twenty-first of November. We know from the post-mortem that her body had lain there at least a week, and that her blood results indicate that she had a high concentration of pure heroin in her system. Until yesterday, it was believed that her death was an accidental overdose. The information Hunter gained from her Probation Officer yesterday afternoon, the discovery of the burglary at her bed-sit, and the message left by reporter Guy Armstrong, who incidentally was found dead in his crashed car last night, has changed all that." Michael Robshaw slapped the board again. "Ladies and gents, we have another post-mortem being carried out on Jodie's body later today, but it's my firm belief, given everything we have learned in the past twenty-four hours, that she has been murdered. Someone has gone to a lot of trouble to make Jodie's death look like an accident. And I also believe we have the reason behind her murder. Her probation officer states that she had a secret, which was going to make her a lot of money and he would read about it in the papers. Guy Armstrong's recorded message on Hunter's voicemail states that Jodie was his source for the Lucy Blake-Hall case, and I quote, 'a couple of weeks ago she overheard a conversation between two people' which led him to believe that Daniel Weaver was innocent of her murder." The Detective Superintendent then pointed beyond Jodie's incident board to the wipe board containing the timeline sequence and information relating to the killing of Jeffery Howson. "We also have tenuous links to Jeffery's murder, in as much as the man Hunter disturbed burgling Jodie's bed-sit, and who assaulted him, fits the same description as the man he chased at Jeffery's funeral." Michael Robshaw's eyes moved from one detective to another. "This may be just a coincidence, but I don't like coincidences, especially when that person is linked with two murders, so until anyone brings me anything different I am linking Jodie's death to our current investigation. And it may not end there. Traffic are bringing me the report on Guy Armstrong's accident last night and I have specialist forensic officers joining our scenes of crime at the location to carry out a thorough examination. His accident is also just too much of a coincidence. So with that in mind I'm also organising tasks this morning relating to Guy Armstrong." He dipped his hands into his trouser pockets, his face earnest. "In the past year we have had our fair measure of harrowing and complicated cases, but never have I known one with as many twists and turns as this. We have our work cut out."

* * * * *

Over another mug of tea Hunter caught up with his journal, putting in the details of his conversation with Ray Austin and also logging the incident at Jodie's bed-sit. He re-visited the scene in his head, trying to magic up a better image of the man he had encountered, but no matter how hard he concentrated he was stuck with the mental picture of a faceless, squat, stocky man in dark clothing and woolly hat.

He realised there were still a number of gaps about Jodie's personal life and he put in a call to the Probation Service.

Ray Austin had not yet gone off to court and the receptionist put Hunter through.

The second he answered Hunter said, "Ray, DS Kerr here. Did you manage to find out the name of the bar where Jodie worked?" Down the line he heard the Senior Probation Officer clear his throat.

He replied, "I'm afraid I've not had much luck Sergeant. I've wracked my brains since you left yesterday, but I can't remember what she told me. I spent most of yesterday afternoon checking back over her file and I trawled through the notes of my recent meetings with her, but I don't appear to have written it down. I've spoken to a few people here who knew Jodie, just on the off chance, but as I told you yesterday I was the only one in the office she'd confide in. I've asked the receptionists to check with a couple of clients who knew her, when they come in for their appointments, to see if they might know which bar she worked at. Other than that I can't help, I'm afraid. If I do get anything, I've got your number."

"When you say clients, do you mean friends of hers?"

"Not as such Sergeant Kerr. Jodie didn't have many close friends. She knew a lot of people, but I wouldn't class any of them as friends. We have one associate on file, who I remember she was close with, but I checked her status out this morning and she's currently in Newhall Prison, serving eighteen months for shoplifting." He gave Hunter the woman's details.

Hunter shared the information they had gleaned from door-to-door inside Westville House. He relayed what the tenant living below Jodie had told them about the skinny, blonde woman who had been seen in Jodie's bed-sit.

After what seemed like an interminably long period of silence, Ray Austin answered, "Sorry again, Sergeant Kerr, that description doesn't ring any bells. I've made a few notes and I'll ask my colleagues here and go back through Jodie's paperwork again and see if I can come up with the name of anyone that might fit."

Hunter thanked him, passed on his mobile number, with instructions to ring the minute he came up with anything and then hung up. Next he dialled Duncan Wroe's office phone, to check if he had recovered anything from his examination of Jodie's room. His call went straight through to Duncan's voicemail. He inwardly cursed with frustration and left him a message, then dropped the receiver onto its cradle as if it were a hot potato.

Finishing his notes with a flourish, he returned his journal to his top drawer and locked it. Then, draining the remnants of his lukewarm tea he dragged his coat from off the back of his chair. Looking across desks, he saw Grace's eyes were glued to her desk-top computer screen.

"You good to go?" he asked.

She lifted her gaze. "Just clearing my e-mails."

"I want to pay a visit to Jodie's place and see if SOCO have come up with anything, then I want to go out to where Armstrong had his crash last night. You okay with that?"

For the next five minutes Hunter fidgeted in his seat, forced to wait while Grace skimmed through her e-mails, closed down her computer and returned unfinished paperwork to her pending tray. Impatiently, he drummed his fingers on the desk while mentally ticking off the things he needed to do.

Finally catching her gaze, he pounced out of his chair and snatched up his folder.

Pushing herself up, Grace slid open her top drawer, took out a lipstick and applied a fresh layer of gloss. She met his look. "I'm going as fast as I can."

Shaking his head in exasperation, Hunter steered her out of the office and jockeyed her down the stairs, into the backyard and then tossed her the keys to one of the team's unmarked cars. "You drive Grace. We'll go to Jodie's flat first, see if there's any SOCO there, and then we'll go to the crash site."

"Aye, aye, Captain," she said, pointing the electronic fob towards the blue Vauxhall Astra and popping the door locks.

He caught her playful smile as he jumped into the passenger side. As she climbed in beside him and belted up he said, "Sorry Grace. I've got a million and one things on my mind this morning."

"So have I, and not all of it's police work," she responded, slotting the key into the ignition, "I was reminded by the girls this morning there's no cereals left and we've almost run out of bread. And David has asked me if there's any chance of us sitting down as a family and having an evening meal together any time in the near future." She started the car.

Hunter tried to catch her gaze. "Point made Grace."

"I forgive you Sergeant." She blew him a kiss out of the side of her mouth and then engaged gear. "Anyway, don't you want to know how I've gone on this morning?"

He gave her an inquisitive look.

"I was given the job of tracking down who Guy Armstrong worked for." Grace swung the car out of the police station yard and onto the main thoroughfare. "Well, he wasn't freelance at all. For the last five years he's been employed at The Star in Sheffield. I've spoken with one of the newsroom editors and he tells me that he was one of their investigative reporters. And a good one at that, by all accounts. He told me that when he got in this morning there was a message on his desk, which had been left by one of the evening staff, stating that Armstrong had rung in last night and said that he was onto a hot lead with regards to the Lucy Blake-Hall murder and would file copy this morning for this lunchtime's deadline. You can imagine he was in a bit of shock when I told him what had happened. He asked me if the accident was being investigated as suspicious. I tried to give him the usual bullshit about it being a fatal and as such would be investigated thoroughly. As soon as he asked why a detective was ringing him up with these questions I could sense he was having none of it, so don't be surprised if a few reporters start following us around."

Hunter blew out a soft whistle. "So Guy Armstrong really was on to something."

* * * * *

An empty liveried police car parked in front of Westville House was the only sign of any police presence at Jodie's bed-sit.

Hunter told Grace that he'd only be a couple of minutes and to keep the engine running. Less than five minutes later he was back.

"There's only one uniform around and Jodie's room's been sealed off. He was told during hand-over that SOCO had finished processing the scene in the early hours and we would be back later today to carry out a search. He's a bit miffed off now I've told him it might not be until this afternoon before we can get there. He's also told me that the landlord came this morning, saw it and is not best pleased. He wants to know how long we're gonna need the place 'cos he's got a list of people who want to rent it." Fastening up his seat belt, he added, "I've told him if the landlord turns up again just get a contact number and we'll get back as soon as we can. Right, let's see what we've got on Guy Armstrong."

Grace had to double-back until she had picked up the stretch of road which led out towards Wentworth. The crash site was on a sharp bend outside the village on the road to Harley.

Hunter knew the location fairly well from previous drives out there and was aware that it featured a notorious stretch of road where a number of deaths had occurred down the years. This would be yet one more to add to the statistics, he thought without emotion.

Ten minutes later, as they were nearing the junction, which gave them access to the crash site, they spotted a Road Policing Unit Range Rover blocking their way.

Hunter nudged Grace and nodded.

A small posse of journalists, huddled on the pavement beside the Range Rover, gawped as they approached.

"You were spot-on about reporters," he said.

Pulling alongside the Traffic car, Grace hurriedly dug into her handbag, pulled out her warrant card, pointed it towards the attendant officer's face and then zipped through a gap without a backward glance.

Less than two minutes later they were forced to pull up again. The small country lane was littered with all manner of marked and unmarked cars - there was even a Fire Service Forensics van abandoned half-on-half-off the road.

It looks bloody manic, thought Hunter, as he got out and gazed around, though he knew that it was anything but. It was a preserved and controlled crime scene, where everything being done was in strict accordance with the manual on Crime Scene Investigation.

Over the hedgerow to his right, where the field dipped down from the road and met a line of trees, was a large white tent. Hunter spotted his SIO Dawn Leggate and SOCO Manager Duncan Wroe. The Detective Superintendent was just disappearing inside the tent.

He went around to the hatchback, opened it up, slipped off his overcoat and quickly donned a protective suit. Grace followed, and the pair picked their way through a break in the hedgerow and down the embankment to join their colleagues.

Duncan Wroe had his head down, scribbling on papers attached to a clipboard.

Hunter approached him. As usual Duncan's hair looked unkempt but this morning at least a good day's growth sprouted from his jaw-line and his eyes were red rimmed.

Hunter said, "You look bleary-eyed Duncan."

"You would be as well if you'd only had four hours' sleep. Do you know what time I finished your job last night?"

Hunter shrugged and shot Duncan a 'don't know' expression.

"Ten o'clock, that's what time! And then I'd just got back to the office when they called me out to this. By the time I'd wrote everything up it was four am before I crawled into bed, and then your gaffer dragged me back out an hour ago and told me they wanted me to go over this scene again."

Hunter said, "Just think of the overtime Duncan."

"Pah! They don't pay me enough for this."

Hunter blew into his hands. He was beginning to feel the cold. "Anyway Duncan, to digress, did you find anything at Jodie's place?"

"Lifted a few different sets of prints, you'll be pleased to learn. I'll try and get them off later today. Though I don't think they belong to the bloke you disturbed. Around the door lock and hasp, on one of the wardrobe handles and on a section of the handrail of the banister I've recovered some fibres. Looks like he might have been wearing gloves. I'll process them all the same."

"Okay Duncan, thanks. Dare I ask you about The Barnwell Inn, where Jodie's body was found?"

Duncan pulled back the cuff of his Tyvek make protective suit, revealing a bare wrist. "Here, take my blood won't you?"

Hunter couldn't help but grin. He tried to hide it. "Sorry Duncan, I was only asking."

"The answer is no. It's on my to do list. With a hundred-and-one other jobs. It might even have to go out to another team elsewhere in the force, depending on how long and how much I have to do here."

With that the SOCO Manager made an exaggerated stab with his pen onto paperwork, as if signifying he had finished whatever he had been writing, and turned on his heels back towards the tent.

Grace nudged Hunter and mouthed the word 'Tetchy.'

Now he couldn't help but break into a broad smile. In a whisper he retorted, "Just like someone else I know."

She dug him hard with her elbow as they followed Duncan.

The forensic tent Hunter entered had trapped the smell of the burning. A nauseating mixture of rubber, petrol and cooked meats clogged in the back of his throat. He swallowed hard.

His eyes took in the scene. Guy Armstrong's Citroen C5 was a heap of charred metal, even the interior had been destroyed. Wire framework was all that remained of the seats and Guy's body was still in the driver's seat, slumped forward over the remnants of the steering wheel, his chargrilled head welded into the framework. Guy Armstrong was no longer recognisable. Lumps of barbecued flesh clung to his scorched bones.

The concertinaed front end of the saloon was wedged into the trunk of a mature Chestnut tree. The bark nearest the car had also succumbed to the flames, and the ground around the base of the car was blackened and oily.

Hunter said, "It must have been one hell of a fire."

Looking up, Detective Superintendent Leggate said, "A fire-ball is how the first fire officer on scene described it."

"The petrol tank had already gone up before the Fire Service got here. Guy Armstrong had no chance. Traffic didn't get here until the fire was almost out."

"Any witnesses?" Hunter asked.

"Not to the accident. A couple driving back from the restaurant in the village called 999. They said it was well ablaze when they came across it and there was nothing, or no one else around. They hung on for the Fire Service and Traffic. Their call was logged at eleven-o-nine. Fire Service got here at eleven-twenty-one. Traffic about ten minutes after that. They got Armstrong's details from the VIN number on the car."

The Vehicle Identification Number etched into the chassis and engine block of the car linked to the registration plate allocated to the car.

She continued, "One of the Traffic Officers has already been to his address. Went at just after two, this morning, but no one answered. They've given it another knock a couple of hours ago, but no reply. One of the next-door-neighbours says he's lived on his own for as long as she's known him. We'll check on his personal status when we speak with his employers at The Star again."

"Do we know if he'd been drinking? The message he left me on my voicemail said he was going to wait for me at The George and Dragon last night."

"I got one of the Traffic lads to nip up there. The landlord confirms he was in there late on. He remembers him because it was a quiet night, but he says he wasn't drunk when he left. He had a couple of pints and finished off with a couple of Cokes. Left just before eleven, which, given the distance between here and the pub, ties in nicely with the timing of when his car was found by that couple."

"And was it an accident?"

The Detective Superintendent turned towards Duncan Wroe.

He slipped his clipboard under his arm, nipping it next to his chest. "Oh the car was certainly involved in an accident. It has a dent to its rear offside and I've found remnants of its back light cluster up there on the carriageway." He pointed a finger up towards the road and then slowly traced it back. "You can see the ruts the wheels have made, where it's come through the hedge, before colliding with this tree. As to the fire, however, that was definitely not caused by the accident. The petrol cap had been removed and I've found burnt remnants of cloth which had been pushed down inside the inlet pipe to the tank." Duncan exchanged glances with the SIO, Hunter and Grace. "Someone's fired this deliberately." He slipped his clipboard out from beneath his arm. "In terms of evidence, I'm afraid that so far we have very little. The entire surface of the car has been burned. We have the petrol cap, but all I've found on that so far is a couple of partial prints, which could be Guy Armstrong's, and some fibres, which indicate to me that someone has also handled it with gloves. There're quite a number of footprints around here, so I've photographed them and I'm going to take a number of casts. We might get lucky, but don't hold your breath, this place was swamped with Fire Service and Uniform last night. When I got here everyone and their grandmother was trampling around the scene. Your best bet is if you can track down the vehicle which rear-ended Armstrong's car. At least we should be able to match paint samples."

There was silence as Duncan's words sunk in. The magnitude of the task ahead to catch the culprit who had done this, was daunting.

The Detective Superintendent's head was bowed, as if in prayer.

Suddenly she clapped her hands, making everyone jump. She announced, "Okay, no time for hanging around, we've got a murderer, or murderers, to catch." She turned to Hunter and Grace. "I want you two to go straight across to Guy Armstrong's place and see what you can find. If you can't find a key lying around, and he hasn't left one with neighbours, force entry. Get someone else to help you search. See what Mike and Tony are doing. I'll clear it with DI Scaife to release them from their immediate tasks."

"What about Jodie's PM this afternoon?"

"It's not going ahead today, Hunter. The Coroner rang Mr Robshaw this morning. He only got the message first thing, so we can't get hold of another pathologist to carry it out until tomorrow. To be honest it' will give us a bit of breathing space, especially as headquarters have told us there are no more resources. There was a double-fatal shooting yesterday evening in Sheffield, so we've got to make do with what we've got."

"What about Task Force?"

"I've managed to snaffle one search team, the bulk of the team have been drafted in to Sheffield for the shootings. It's believed to be gang related. I'm meeting with them here..." she paused and took a quick glance of her watch, "...in the next half hour or so. They're gonna do a search here first, and then I've earmarked them to go over to the Barnwell Inn to carry out an extensive search of the building and grounds, once Duncan and his team have finished doing a second sweep."

Out of the corner of his eye Hunter caught Duncan's expression. He'd never seen the man look so stressed. He looked as though he had the weight of the world on his shoulders, thought Hunter. *This enquiry is certainly testing people's limits of endurance.* He grabbed Grace's arm to get her attention, nodded back towards the car and mouthed, 'it's time to go.'

As they trudged back to the car Grace mumbled, "That's me in the bad books again when I get home tonight." She turned to Hunter. "Correction, change that to if I get home tonight!"

* * * * *

DCs Mike Sampson and Tony Bullars were already waiting outside Guy Armstrong's 1970s semi, by the time Hunter and Grace showed up.

Mike jokingly mentioned that they'd left a DI back at the office very displeased after having his instructions usurped by an 'incomer'. Mike wiggled his index fingers in the air as he mouthed the word.

"We've just left her at the crash site," Grace said.

"What do you make of her?" asked Tony.

They were close to the front of the house.

"I'm having difficulty understanding what she's saying," said Mike. "I'm having to watch back-to-back episodes of Taggart so that I can get to grips with her accent." He paused then said "There's been a murder," exaggerating the rolling of his 'r's.'

The team burst out laughing.

"You'd better not let her hear you say that," said Grace. "Anyway, I think she's lovely. It's just what you men need, a strong woman to put you in your places."

The four of them enthusiastically set about door knocking in the hope that one of Guy Armstrong's immediate neighbours might hold a spare key to his house. No one did. They followed up by ferreting around the perimeter of his home, but despite a thorough search of all the usual hiding-places they didn't turn anything up and checked if any of the ground floor windows were insecure. No luck.

Disappointed, Hunter said, "No other option but to kick the door in." He nodded to Tony. "The back door looks the best bet, Bully."

"You want me to do it?" he said.

"Who's the one with the stripes? Stop whingeing and get your shoulder against it. It's not as though you've never done this before. What about that time you nicked those two muggers you chased to someone else's flat? You told the neighbours you thought you could smell gas."

Tony tried to suppress a smile. "I could!"

"Well pretend you can smell it now and get that door in."

Using the heel of his foot, it took Tony Bullars half-a-dozen attempts before the mortise lock finally gave way. With a resounding crack, the solid-wood door crashed against the kitchen wall, its metal security hasp shooting across the laminate floor.

"Right everyone," said Hunter, stepping into the kitchen and slipping on a pair of latex gloves, "We take a room each. I'll take the lounge."

Unpleasant smells greeted him as he stepped further into the house. As he passed through the kitchen into the hallway, his nose picked up the stench of old cooking fat. The untidy work surfaces were spilling over with various plates and cups, stained by remnants of food, and a frying pan, which contained globules of furred fat floating on top of an oily surface.

Then he pushed open the door into the loung and the sight which met him was not pleasant. The pattern of the carpet was barely visible, every inch covered by a sea of paper. Some was torn handwritten sheets from notebooks, but the majority was from newspapers. The room also contained a sofa and two armchairs. Only the seat cushion of one chair was visible the other two pieces of furniture were piled high with books and more newspapers.

Hunter sighed. This lot was going to take an eternity to sift through, he thought.

As he bent down to scoop up the first batch of handwritten notes, a cry came from upstairs. It was Mike Sampson.

"Get up here you lot and just have a butcher's at this!"

Hunter took the stairs two at a time and met Mike on the landing.

Grace and Tony were not far behind.

Their colleague's outstretched arm pointed into one of the rear bedrooms.

Hunter poked his head inside. What he saw took him completely by surprise. The room had been kitted out as an office-cum-study. It contained a desk and chair and a bookcase crammed with books. The desk overflowed with pile upon pile of handwritten notes and like the lounge below, every inch of floor space was taken up by handwritten notes on different types of paper. However, it was the stuff on the walls that grabbed his attention. Pasted, Sellotaped, stuck, and pinned, to every conceivable inch of space on three walls was an array of photographs, newspaper cuttings, hand-drawn diagrams, and copious Post-it notes containing scribbled information. Some of it was new, but the majority of the items had the patina signs of ageing.

Hunter turned to his colleagues. "You know what this is, don't you?" He didn't wait for a response. "This is everything relating to the Lucy Blake-Hall case. This is Guy Armstrong's very own incident room."

- ooOoo -

CHAPTER ELEVEN

DAY TEN: 3RD DECEMBER.

Barnwell MIT incident room was crammed to capacity for morning briefing. More members of the Cold Case Unit had been drafted in, together with another Family Liaison Officer. An Inspector and Sergeant from Task Force were also present. For some it was standing room only, and the office was uncomfortably warm despite the biting wind and rain battering against the windows.

SIOs Michael Robshaw and Dawn Leggate held court together at the front of the room. Another incident board had joined those of Jeffery Howson's, Lucy Blake-Hall's and Jodie Marie Jenkinson's. This one was full of information and photographs from their most recent murder case Guy Armstrong.

It was seven pm the previous evening before Hunter, Grace, Mike and Tony had left Armstrong's house. What they had uncovered in his study had been a revelation. Newspaper cuttings and original black-and-white photographs from The Barnwell Chronicle, together with other national and regional tabloid newspaper articles, covered every conceivable bit of space around his small upstairs room. Additionally, blanketing the floor, were dozens of other discarded black-and-white photographs, together with smaller colour shots, as well as hundreds of handwritten notes, chronicling every event, from Lucy being reported as missing, the arrest of Daniel Weaver and the subsequent search of Langsett Moor for Lucy's body, up to the eventual trial and guilty verdict of Weaver during 1983 and 1984.

The team stayed at the house, going through Armstrong's collection, for almost seven hours, but had only scratched the surface. They planned to continue sorting and cataloguing that morning.

Hunter highlighted all this when he addressed the room, following Detective Superintendent Michael Robshaw's request for an update.

"It looks like his laptop and his Dictaphone are missing." Hunter said. "It was his editor who brought it to our attention. Apparently he should have filed a story yesterday morning, via e-mail from his laptop, regarding the lead he had from Jodie.

As we know it never happened because he was killed before he could do it." He looked around the room. "The editor assures me that he took them everywhere with him. I can confirm that about his Dictaphone, because I saw him drop it when he had his run-in with Peter Blake-Hall witnessed by Grace and I three days ago. We've not found them at his place and they're not in his burned-out car."

"So that's one of the priorities," said SIO Michael Robshaw. "Sorry to interrupt." He aimed a quick glance at Hunter. "Find that laptop and his Dictaphone and we should find out who our killer is. We already know from his editor and from the message stored on Hunter's voicemail that he had a lead on a story which was going to prove Daniel Weaver's innocence in the murder of Lucy Blake-Hall." He stared into the room. "Someone has gone to great pains to silence three people who all had stories to tell about the murder of Lucy, and the sooner we can bring them in the better. Everything seems to centre on that case from nineteen-eighty-three. And so that's where we are going back to. We strip everything back to that original investigation. I know some of the witnesses have died but we still have quite a number around. You've done a sterling job in tracking them down, and now I want them all visiting and sitting down with the original statements they made back then. See if it's still relevant, or if there's anything's different, or was missed when they made it. We already know, because of the forensic examination of Weaver's contemporaneous notes found in Howson's safe, that his confession is unsafe. That may well be corroborated by something which was missed out in one or more of the witness statements." The Detective Superintendent's look changed. "I don't need to emphasise to you how serious the implications are in this and how sensitive the case is. We have two suspects at the moment, one is as yet a mystery, but he has turned up twice in this enquiry and already assaulted one of the team in order to escape. Our other suspect is a retired DCI and we cannot afford for that to be leaked outside of this room." Pausing for a few seconds, he continued. "Resources wise, this is it ladies and gents. Sheffield have a double shooting, involving rival gangs and so their job takes priority. The only other help I've managed to get is from forensics. Guy Armstrong's car has been removed to the drying room for further examination and SOCO are going to finish off with the crash site today. Road Policing Unit and Air Support are going to complete a GPS survey of the location. The forensics team

I've brought in are going to the old Barnwell Inn and doing another sweep of the cellar. Task Force will follow up with a search in and around the perimeter of the place and there will be another post-mortem carried out on Jodie's body this afternoon. Finally, I want everything on Guy Armstrong. Not just recently, but what he was up to back in nineteen-eighty-three, when he originally covered the Lucy Blake-Hall investigation." He paused again and held up one hand. "I've said this before and I'll say it again we are up against the clock on this. Daniel Weaver's appeal court hearing is this Friday and I have no doubts he will be freed. In a few days' time we are going to be under the spotlight. Every aspect of this current enquiry, as well as the original case into Lucy's murder, will be scrutinised. I don't need to emphasise the pressure this places on us all."

* * * * *

Hunter, Grace, and Mike Sampson pulled up at Guy Armstrong's house shortly before 10am and trooped down his drive, each holding an armful of exhibit bags.

Hunter opened up the back door with the new key the locksmith had supplied to him the previous evening. He was anticipating a long day. Ahead lay the task of cataloguing and collating the things they had discovered in the study, the lounge and the dining room. It didn't help that they were a team member down; Tony Bullars had been given the job of speaking with Lucy's parents.

The stale and musty smell greeted him once more, though, as he pushed open the door into the kitchen, Hunter thought that it wasn't as strong as yesterday. As he made for the stairs he decided to leave it slightly ajar and let some fresh air blow through.

Before leaving the previous day the team had already gathered up much of the paperwork from the floor and desk in the study, and stacked them into organised piles, and today's mission was to sift through and record the items, notably to collate and bag anything relevant to the Lucy Blake-Hall investigation.

As Hunter entered the small room and looked around, he knew that this was going to be a laborious task.

Picking up one of the piles from the desk, he set it to one side, creating himself some room and dropped down his stack of clear plastic exhibit bags into the space.

"Okay, let's get this organised. Mike you record and log, and Grace and I will gather and bag." He reached up to the wall and removed the first exhibit, a newspaper article Guy Armstrong had written when he had been the Crime Correspondent with The Barnwell Chronicle in 1983. It was a front page piece, reporting the disappearance of Lucy Blake-Hall and the discovery of the damning evidence at Weaver's flat. There was a subsequent quote from a Force press officer 'that a man was in police custody and had been charged with the murder of a twenty-two year old woman.' The story contained the same black-and-white photograph of the smiling Lucy, which Hunter had found in the original prosecution file. Looking along the wall, he identified the follow up edition, which focused on the search for Lucy's body up on Langsett Moor. He was interested in this story, because precise details had not been given in the file; only short reference had been made of it in the documents' summary. He skip-read the opening couple of paragraphs and looked at the accompanying photograph. It depicted a single line of uniformed officers tramping across moorland heather. The picture made a powerful statement, given the fact that Lucy's body had never been found, and it gave him goose-bumps. He carefully peeled back the tape fastening the article to the wall and slipped it inside an exhibit bag. As he scoured the gallery of newspaper cuttings, notes, maps and photographs and studied the content Hunter realised he was looking at Guy Armstrong's storyboard, chronicling, in date order, every event relating to Lucy's disappearance and Daniel Weaver's trial. There were even articles about his appeal. The reporter had covered it all, and for him to leave it up here as a permanent reminder meant that he always had a suspicion or belief that something wasn't right about the investigation. Hunter hoped that by the end of the day they would find the answer in this lot.

The team missed lunch, deciding to work through because they were making such significant inroads, though they had taken timeout, munching through a packet of biscuits they had found in Armstrong's kitchen cupboards, and Grace had busied herself scouring out three mugs so that they could have a warm drink.

Hunter had almost cleared two of the room walls when a cry from Grace broke his concentration.

"Bloody hell, just look at what I've found!"

Hunter turned.

170

Grace was waving in the air a wad of yellowing newspaper cuttings.

* * * * *

By the time DCs Tony Bullars and Carol Ragen left the police station, the wind and the rain had subsided. Tony chose to drive the slightly longer route, across the Strines, to Bakewell, and he made good time because he met very little traffic and was able to put his foot down. As he approached Bakewell, Tony was forced to ease off the accelerator as he joined the line of slow moving traffic negotiating the narrow bridge over the River Wye into the bustling market town.

At the first roundabout, following Carol's instructions, he aimed the car in the direction of where they needed to be. Less than quarter of an hour later, Tony turned into the lane where Lucy's parents lived.

Richard and Margaret Hall's home was a pretty cottage built of Derbyshire stone and slate with rolling hillsides as a backdrop. Today, the tops of the hills couldn't be seen. A thick bank of low cloud covered them, and the damp atmosphere which pervaded made everything look grey and cold.

Richard Hall had the front door open before they had stepped through the garden gate.

Tony saw that he was a big man who carried some weight, especially round the middle.

He greeted them with a warm smile and a soft handshake and then stepped to one side to let them enter.

"Nice place," said Tony, lowering his head to pass beneath the low-lintel front door and into the sitting room.

"It is now," Richard Hall replied, shutting the door behind them. "But it wasn't always like this. We've had to do a fair bit of work to get it like it is now."

Tony studied the room. *This is what a cottage should be like*, he thought, as he admired the log burning fire set inside a stone inglenook fireplace. A low beamed ceiling, cream painted walls and soft furnishings completed the warm and inviting look.

Two small sofas, arranged in a broken L shape were the only seats in the room. Margaret Hall was already sat in one. Slightly hunched forward, she had her hands clasped loosely together, resting in her lap. She had a bob of soft greying hair, which framed a well rounded, cheery face.

Richard offered Tony and Carol the other sofa and then lowered himself into the space beside his wife.

"Can I get you a drink?" Margaret offered.

Tony declined. "I'm awash with tea, thank you," he said. "I'll be going to the toilet for the rest of the day if I have any more," he smiled.

Carol shook her head, "Me too."

"You said on the phone that you're re-investigating Lucy's murder?" Richard said, shuffling into a more comfortable position, leaning into the arm of the sofa.

"Yes, that's right." Tony flipped open his folder, revealing photocopies of the original witness statements made by the Halls back in 1983, together with a bundle of blank witness forms in case they provided new information. "Our boss went on TV last night and made an appeal. Did you see it?"

"No sorry, we don't get Yorkshire's news down here."

"Does that mean Danny Weaver is innocent after all?" Margaret asked.

"I don't want to use those words, Mrs Hall. And not wishing to be impolite but I don't want to elaborate or give anything away about the investigation at this stage. But it would be fair to say that we do have evidence which casts doubt on what was presented at Weaver's original trial."

Richard glanced sideways at his wife. They exchanged searching looks. Then he returned his gaze to Tony. "Have you found Lucy's body?"

"I'm sorry to say but no, we haven't. It is one of our lines of enquiry - carrying out another search. We're going back over every part of the original investigation to see if anything was missed first time round. And of course forensics, and search techniques have moved on so much since then, so hopefully that's something we can resolve this time around. What will happen from now on is that every time something new comes in you will be kept up-to-date. You will be the first to know if we find Lucy. I promise you that."

Carol met Margaret's eyes. "I picked up on the question you asked about Danny Weaver. It was the way you said it which intrigued me. It was as if you were expecting this. Do you know something about Weaver that you didn't tell the police during the original enquiry?"

"Ooh no. It's just after all these years of thinking about what happened and dwelling on things. To be honest, I was really surprised all those years ago when those detectives told me that Danny had confessed to killing her and that they'd charged him. You see, I told those two detectives at the time that Lucy seemed to be so happy, especially those few days before she disappeared."

Tony had been separating their witness statements for them to read. At this comment, he looked up from his folder. "Did you see and talk with her regularly then before she went missing?"

"Oh yes. I saw Lucy and Jessica, that's our granddaughter, at least three times a week. She'd come up to the house or we'd go into Barnwell shopping."

"What, she'd come all this way?"

"No, no. We haven't always lived here. We used to live in Wortley. That's where Lucy was brought up. We lived on Constable Row, just behind the church. We came here a couple of years after the trial. We couldn't bear staying in the same village any more. We came here with Jessica."

"Tell them the truth Margaret!" Richard butted in. "We couldn't abide to be anywhere near that supercilious husband of hers." He switched his look between Tony and Carol. "We found stuff out about him that never came out in the trial. It was no wonder she was unhappy."

Tony said, "Now you've lost me. Margaret, you said Lucy was happy just before she disappeared and Richard, you've just said she was unhappy."

"Lucy never told us anything," Richard replied. "We've found out stuff about Peter from Amanda, Lucy's best friend from school. We never realised the half of it." He shot a quick sideways glance at his wife again. "It was heartbreaking for us." He shook his head as if attempting to dislodge his unhappy thoughts. Then he said, "Have you spoken to Amanda? She's in your job. She's a Sergeant up in Cumbria. Married with a daughter herself now. She's still kept in touch with us over the years. I mean it's not as much now. The calls have dropped off, but her and Margaret still have the odd chat from time to time. In fact, we rang her last night when we knew you were coming."

"I wished we'd have known you were still in touch with her. It could have saved us a lot of time. You wouldn't believe the effort we've put in to track everyone down from the original enquiry. Someone has spoken to her on the phone and we've made arrangements to see her in the next day or so."

"Well, she'll be able to tell you a lot more about Lucy and what went off. We've found out little bits from her over the years that have shocked us, I can tell you, but we don't think she's told us everything, because she didn't want to upset us any further."

"We've still got to speak with Amanda, but if you could just tell us what you know that's relevant about Lucy's disappearance, it would help us immensely."

"Where do you want me to begin?" He dabbed at the corner of his eyes with the knuckle of a thumb.

Tony opened up his notebook ready to scribble down notes. "Shall we start where she met Peter, and I'll nudge you from time to time if I need you to elaborate on anything."

Richard stroked his chin and narrowed his eyes before he began. Clearing his throat, he said, "Lucy met Peter just before her seventeenth birthday. He was older than her, early twenties, but to be honest that didn't bother us, especially when we first met him. He was well turned out, polite and acted a lot more mature than some of the other boys Lucy was friends with. We'd never met him before, he lived at Thurgoland with his gran, but used to come to The Wortley Arms drinking. That's where he met Lucy. She was under-age to drink but it's such a small village, as you know, so the landlord used to let her and a few mates go in there and just have soft drinks. When she first introduced him to us he was working as a mechanic, but as a sideline he bought and sold his own cars. He was a good worker and always seemed to have plenty of money. Lucy was certainly happy with him back then. Then we heard one or two whispers about him."

Tony glanced up, "Whispers?"

"The landlord at the Wortley Arms and a couple of regulars in there just said to keep an eye on him. We wondered what they meant and then we were told that his dad was a rum 'un. That he was in prison because he'd killed someone. We tried to find out what he'd done, but no one was quite sure. They thought it was some kind of robbery he'd done. We never got to the bottom of it and we decided not to say anything to our Lucy. We just hoped the relationship would run its course and they'd finish, but it didn't. Lucy got caught with Jessica and then Peter asked if he could marry her. What could we say? We mentioned to Lucy what we'd heard about Peter's dad and she said he'd told her all about it. He'd told her that his dad had broken into a shop in Sheffield and had got caught by the owner and that he'd killed him in a fight." Richard paused and continued, "He's dead himself now. Apparently he was killed about ten years ago. Stabbed in prison, I think. Peter and Lucy went to his funeral."

Tony made a few quick notes. "So just going back, Peter and Lucy got married?"

"Yes. It was a rushed job, a registry office wedding, three months before Jessica was born. It was against our wishes, we wanted her to have a proper wedding after Jessica was born but Lucy would have none of it. She said she was happy with that. I have to say back then Peter was good to her. He'd even got together enough money for a deposit for an old cottage in the next village at Tankersley. For the first year of their marriage Lucy was in her element. Jessica was born and Lucy spent all her time putting together a home. Peter worked really hard and long hours. In fact, he also began making quite a bit of money importing cars from Germany, BMWs and Mercedes if I recall. Then in the second year of the marriage he bought a big old nightclub near Wakefield, spent thousands doing it up and changed it into a private members' club. That's when we noticed the cracks beginning to appear in the marriage. Peter seemed to be out all hours. Then we found out the club Peter owned was in fact a strip club. We were mortified. We tried hard not to interfere, but felt we needed to talk with her about it. When we did, we could see that Lucy wasn't happy about it herself, but she stuck up for him. She just kept saying that Peter was working very hard because he wanted to make lots of money for them. Sure enough, he did that, and he bought an old farmhouse, just outside the village, which he had done up for Lucy and Jessica, but we could see things weren't right. Then a few months before Lucy disappeared we noticed a difference in her. For about a year, her regular visits had dropped off. Then, around June time in nineteen-eighty-three, she started turning up the two and three times a week again like she used to and was just like her old self again, so bubbly. Of course, what we didn't know at the time was that she was having an affair with Danny Weaver, and that was the reason for her happiness.

"And that's why I was so surprised when those two detectives came to our house that Sunday evening and told us he had confessed to killing Lucy," added Margaret. "She was so happy, the months and weeks leading up to her disappearance. It was such a shock when they said she was missing, and then especially when they came back and broke that awful news to us. We went every day to the trial. It was such a shock when we learned how long things had been going on between her and Danny. Although Amanda did cushion us from some of it."

"Did Amanda know about it all then?"

"Oh yes. Lucy and Amanda were like that." Margaret crossed over her fingers to form an X. "Lucy told Amanda everything. Even why she'd had the affair. Amanda told us that Peter had started knocking Lucy about. Though she never said that in the witness box." She looked hard at Tony. "Apparently it wasn't relevant!"

Tony held her look. "What do you mean, not relevant?"

"I don't know. Those two detectives, who were in charge of the case, just told Amanda to talk about Lucy's affair with Danny. Supposedly, that was all the Judge wanted to hear. I've spoken with her many times since then and she says now that she wished she'd mentioned Peter had beaten Lucy. Since the trial, we don't have anything to do with Peter. It isn't just because of what went off with Lucy but what he has done to our Jessica. We looked after Jessica once Danny was charged. Peter just said it would be for the best while he got his head around everything. Then after the trial he asked us if we would adopt Jessica, because she reminded him too much of Lucy and he wanted to just forget it all and start a new life." Margaret shook her head. "How can a father do that to his daughter? For years we had all sorts of problems with her." She tapped at her temple. "Psychological problems. She's had some terrible nightmares. In the end we had to take her to a psychologist. She doesn't have anything to with her father now. Good riddance, that's what I say."

Tony shrugged and offered her a sympathetic look. "Just one more question. Peter's name, Blake-Hall? Is the Hall part of his name a coincidence?"

"No that was Peter's idea before they got married. He was called Blake. He thought changing it to a double-barrelled one would be good for his business."

Tony snapped shut his notebook and gathered together his paperwork. He wet his thumb and started to separate the photocopied witness statements. "Margaret, Richard, you've told us a lot more than what was put down in your original statements here. I'd like you to go through them again and then we'll take some fresh ones, adding everything you've just told us."

* * * * *

SIO Michael Robshaw had called an early evening de-brief. By 7pm, everyone on the team, including the newcomers, had drifted back into the incident room. Once again it was standing room only. The Detective Superintendent opened up discussions by announcing that lines of enquiry had borne fruit which he wanted to share with the team as a matter of importance.

"I'm going to bring in Detective Superintendent Leggate first. She went to Jodie Jenkinson's second post-mortem this afternoon."

Dawn Leggate was standing alongside Michael Robshaw, elbows crooked and hands tucked into the pockets of her short, tailored jacket. She brushed the sides of her skirt lightly as if removing something, then said in her Scottish burr, "The second PM has uncovered something which was not picked up the first time around. Chiefly because of the state of the body, and not because of the slackness of the first pathologist's examination, might I say. Under different lighting conditions, the pathologist has discovered bruising beneath the skin of both wrists, consistent with her being restrained. Her skin has been swabbed for DNA. Secondly I can confirm she was not a smackhead. There are only two needle puncture sites over her entire body, and those are on her left arm. One of those missed the vein, the other of course didn't. Again, we've taken DNA swabs. Finally, the injury to her face." She met Hunter's look. "I'm afraid that's still inconclusive." She returned her focus to the team. "So it looks as though someone restrained her, either by gripping, or by using something, and then killed her. In this case, by injecting her with a lethal dose of purer than normal street heroin." She slotted her hands back into her jacket pockets and shared a sideways look with Michael Robshaw, mouthing the word "Done."

"So that's where we are with Jodie." Robshaw said, taking a step forward. "Hunter, I want to bring you in now. Tell everyone what you and Grace found at Armstrong's place today."

The room fell silent as Hunter pushed himself up from his desk. In dramatic fashion he snatched up a yellowing newspaper broadsheet from a pile on his desk, and holding it aloft, slowly ranged it left to right so that everyone got a good look at it. The large headline made for a powerful statement. The word 'BUTCHERED' was only slightly smaller than the newspaper masthead.

"This edition of the Sheffield Telegraph and Star is dated fifth October nineteen-seventy-four, and outlines the story of the murders of Frank and Cynthia Pendlebury. They ran their own small family jewellery business in Attercliffe. On the morning of the fifth they were found dead by an officer, doing his rounds, checking premises on the High Street. He found the front door open. Frank's body was found just behind the counter, in the front of the shop, and his wife Cynthia was found at the top of the stairs just inside the entrance to their flat. Both had been stabbed several times. At the bottom of the article there is a quote from a DCI Burrows, who was leading the enquiry, to the effect that the case was being treated as murder, and that it was believed that Frank and Cynthia had disturbed robbers at their premises." Hunter tapped a hand across the top of the pile of papers where the broadsheet had come from. "These papers here all contain follow-up articles relating to the murders. They contain articles which reveal that the safe in the Pendlebury's shop had been blown open and a large quantity of jewellery had been stolen. A few of them describe the search for the robbers and have the usual stuff the papers put out about any manhunt. But this one," he said, putting down the broadsheet he was holding and then picking up another from the top of the pile, "Contains the story of the arrest of three men for the murders." He showed to the team another copy of the same named newspaper. It bore the headline 'MURDER SUSPECTS DETAINED.' "This edition is dated a week later, and describes the raids on two homes, the discovery of items of jewellery and the arrest of three men. The names of the suspect are not revealed as per protocol. However, down the side of the article, written in pen, are three names." Hunter tapped the edge of the newssheet. "From other samples of handwriting we have found in Guy Armstrong's house, I believe this is his writing. He has entered the names of George Blake, Peter Blake and Ronald Bishop." He tapped down on the pile of papers again. "Later editions outline that a George Blake, thirty-nine years old, from Sheffield, was charged with the murders of Frank and Cynthia Pendlebury, and on twentieth January nineteen-seventy-five, he pleaded guilty at Sheffield Crown Court and was given a life sentence."

Detective Superintendent Robshaw interrupted Hunter's speech with a loud clearing of his throat. He held up his hand. "I'll just stop you there for now Hunter, because I want to bring in Tony." He switched his gaze to DC Bullars. "Tony, I think you know why I've brought you in at this point. You went to see Lucy's parents, over in Bakewell this afternoon. Tell the team what you found out."

Tony Bullars, pushed back his chair and met his colleagues' stares. He explained what Richard and Margaret Hall had told Carol Ragen and himself earlier that day and finished by saying "They told us that Peter Blake-Hall is in fact plain old Peter Blake. He changed his name by deed poll after his marriage to Lucy."

The SIO said."'I'm going to stop you there as well Tony, because I think everyone has got the message." His eyes travelled around the room. "Today's enquiries have turned up some very interesting information. It doesn't solve who murdered Jeffery Howson, Jodie Jenkinson, Guy Armstrong and Lucy Blake-Hall, but I think it takes us down another avenue regarding the suspects. And for me it also provides the answers as to why Guy Armstrong had so much of a fixation with the Lucy Blake-Hall enquiry, and why he'd given so much of his time carrying out his own investigation into her disappearance and Daniel Weaver's trial. He knew from the outset that something wasn't right. And we now know that as well. The finding of that statement in Jeffery Howson's safe confirms it. Now all we've got to do is determine who actually killed these four. And although we now have Lucy's husband in the frame, for the first time, we mustn't lose sight of who our prime suspect still is - Alan Darbyshire."

* * * * *

The evening briefing ran out of steam at 9pm. It had taken two hours. Detective Superintendent Robshaw had rattled off a long list of enquiries for the next day, drawn them up on each of the dry-wipe boards and then checked back with everyone.

One of the key tasks identified was to see if DCI Burrows, who was in charge of the Pendlebury murders, was still around, so that they could get the police version of the case. Barry Newstead had volunteered for that job. He told the room that 'Ted' Burrows had been his DCI when he had been attached to Headquarters Serious Crime Squad in the 1980s and that although he knew he had retired in the early nineties, he believed he was still living somewhere in Sheffield.

The personal backgrounds of Jodie Marie Jenkinson and Guy Armstrong still needed doing. And there was the forensic evidence to chase up.

Detective Superintendent Robshaw closed the session by saying "Team, we have two new names now, which although not suspects at this stage, we need to know a lot more about. Especially Peter Blake. We know Peter has links with our main suspect Alan Darbyshire, and as Lucy's husband he has to be looked at more carefully now, especially given this latest information about him beating her. Although let's be guarded by this. It's come from Lucy's parents and it's not corroborated so far. We also have the name of Peter Blake listed by Guy Armstrong on the newspaper article in relation to the Pendlebury murders. Is this the same Peter Blake? If it is, then I also want to know who Ronald Fisher is." The SIO pursed his lips. "I don't think I need to remind everyone about the pressure we are under to get a result. We have three fresh murders and one old one, which could bring about an enquiry regarding a miscarriage of justice, and so far we have very little evidence to bring anyone in. We need to change all that, and soon."

* * * * *

Hunter sat in his car with the engine running. He turned down the music and fished out his mobile. Scrolling down his contacts list, he tapped 'Home'. Beth picked up on the fourth ring.

"Hi Love. Just got done. Everything okay?"

Jonathan and Daniel were in bed. "Daniel's got the face on," she said, "They had a penalty shoot-out competition at football training tonight and Jonathan won it. He's got a baseball cap and wanted to show it you. On the other hand Daniel, because he didn't win anything, has a face as long as a fiddle, so don't forget to praise him will you?"

A pang of guilt stung him. "Sorry I wasn't there. It's been one of those days, loads happening. Are they still awake?"

"No they were shattered. Went straight off. You can see them tomorrow morning."

"Everyone's just finishing off with a drink. Do you mind if I have a swift one before I come home?"

"No, you go. To be honest Hunter, I'm whacked myself. I'm going to make a warm drink and go up. See you later."

Hunter ended the call with a smile. He was so blessed to have met Beth. She was one in a million, he thought to himself, as he engaged gear. She understood the pressures he was under when a job was running and was always there to offer support, even if that was letting him wind down with a beer and without complaint, despite the fact that he had hardly given her or the boys any attention for days.

* * * * *

Hunter got in a few minutes before eleven pm. The house was in darkness. He toe-heeled off his shoes, kicked them under the hallway radiator and tip-toed upstairs. He sneaked into the boys' room. In the darkness he could just make out their forms, tucked up beneath their duvets in their single beds. He leant in and kissed each of their foreheads, mouthed silently, 'good night, sleep tight,' and crept back out onto the landing where he began to undress, lazily draping his clothing over the balcony rail. He felt drained.

He showered quickly, and, feeling cold as he stepped out of the shower, dried himself even quicker, before jumping into bed.

He pushed himself close to Beth. Instantly he felt the welcoming warmth of her body and he nestled closer, taking in the fragrance of her body lotion. "You smell good," he said quietly.

Beth moaned. "Hunter, you're freezing and I was asleep." She reached back and started to push him away. "Turn over and I'll cuddle you."

"Spoilsport," he chuckled before flipping himself over. She turned with him, and draped an arm and a leg across him.

"I was asleep," she said, her words trailing away.

Within minutes, warmth had returned to his body. He closed his eyes and willed himself to sleep, and though he was tired, he knew it would be quite a while before he drifted off. His head was awash with thoughts about the case. In the darkness, he listened to the sounds of the house settling around him.

* * * * *

Someone was crying, or was it a moan? It was coming from one of the rooms below. She shuffled along the corridor, towards the light which drifted up the stairwell. It was a dull, warm glow that broke up the scary shadows and the coldness of the floor boards beneath her bare feet. Slowly, she moved nearer the brightness and the sound; a strange gutteral noise, like someone was in pain. Pushing open the door, she glanced

181

down at her feet. Something squelched between her toes. She stared down at her bare feet. Small bunchy toes peeked beneath the hem of her nightdress. A red liquid seeped and bubbled between the cracks in the flagstones and enveloped her tiny feet. She wiggled her toes in the redness. Then everything changed. She was slipping in the red stuff, falling backwards, trying to pull herself away. Then she was running scared. Running into the abyss...

Jessica awoke with a start. Darkness engulfed her and she was drenched in sweat. For a second she wondered where she was, and then it came to her she was in her bed. More importantly she was safely in the sanctuary of her bedroom.

Sitting up quickly, she blinked, then closed her eyes, trying to recapture the visions. It was a long time since she'd had this dream. And she guessed she knew the cause. It had to be the phone call from her grandma Hall, earlier that day, telling her that the police were re-investigating her mum's disappearance. There was no other explanation why, after all this time, she should have the dream again. If only she could make sense of it all.

Beside her, her husband stirred. He rolled over onto his back.

"Something up?" he said.

Jessica tried to reply, tell him everything was all right, now that she was awake, but a lump stuck in her throat.

"That dream again?"

She nodded, dislodging the lump and blurted out, "Nightmare."

Her husband looped his arm across her, drew her close and comforted her.

- ooOoo -

182

CHAPTER TWELVE

DAY ELEVEN: 4th December.

Hunter got into the office shortly after 7am and was surprised to find the place bustling and teeming with officers. It had been a while since he'd seen it this full; generally he was first in, with a good quarter of an hour at least to himself.

He slipped off his jacket, slung it over the back of his chair and made for the kettle, ready for his first caffeine hit of the day. With the heavy workload ahead, this could be his last strong cup of tea for a while. As he waited for it to boil, he scanned the room. Although he couldn't pick up on any individual conversations, snippets he gleaned were about the status of the investigation. As he poured hot water over a tea bag in his mug, he told himself that today was going to be a good day.

Returning to his desk, he took a first sip of tea while booting up the computer. Settling back in his chair, he checked through his e-mails. Among them was an up-date regarding 'Chicken' George. There had been a sighting of him around Barnsley town centre and that a message had been left for the night shift team to get a fix on him. Hunter replied with a note of thanks. The next one was from Duncan Wroe. He checked the time it had been sent - 22.27 last night. Duncan had obviously had another long day, he thought. He scanned the few lines. It was simple and to the point and outlined that the samples from Jodie's flat, together with the few he had processed from Guy Armstrong's crash scene, had been sent by carrier to the Forensics lab, marked as priority, as had the fingerprints found at Jodie's bed-sit. Those should be fed into the National Automated Fingerprint Identification System within the next couple of days. Finally, Duncan and his team were returning to The Barnwell Inn to re-examine the cellar. Things were beginning to come together, he thought excitedly, as he composed another thank you response. The rest of his on-screen list was in-force spam, which could be dealt with later. He closed down his computer.

As Hunter drained the last of his tea, he felt a tap on his shoulder. He looked up as Grace slid past him, dumped her handbag and coat onto her desk and slumped into her chair.

"Cutting it a bit fine," Hunter said, looking at his watch. "Domestic issues?"

"Domestic issues!" she checked back. "Nightmare of a morning. I'd forgotten it was the school Christmas party and disco tomorrow. Both girls needed clothes ironing. I ended up losing my rag with them, telling them it was about time they learnt how to use an iron. And then to cap it all David wanted me to iron him a shirt for work. I tell you, I'm up to here this morning," she tapped her forehead with the side of her hand. "The sooner this enquiry is put to bed, the better. If it goes on much longer, I can see me heading for the divorce courts."

Hunter smiled and stood up from his desk. "Deep breaths Grace. Deep breaths. You get yourself sorted and I'll get you a coffee." As he made his way to the kettle again, he turned and said, "Tell you what, the only job we've got today is to finish off at Guy Armstrong's house. We've lost Mike and Tony because they've got other jobs, but you and I should break the back of it by mid-afternoon and then you take a flyer. I'll finish off here and do de-brief."

"Are you sure about that? I would really appreciate it."

Looking back over his shoulder he said, "Sure I'm sure. That's what kind-hearted sergeants are here for."

* * * * * *

Morning briefing was short. Detective Superintendent Michael Robshaw summarised the previous evening's discussions and then the team received their designated chores. One of the main issues resolved was the supervisory roles both SIOs were taking to overseeing the investigations. It was determined that Detective Superintendent Robshaw took the Lucy Blake-Hall and Jeffery Howson murders, while Detective Superintendent Leggate focused on Jodie's and Guy's killings.

* * * * * *

By 10am Hunter and Grace had entered Guy Armstrong's house, ready to finish off the search of the one remaining room the lounge.

Hunter had given the room a fleeting look over during their first visit, but as he pushed open the lounge door and got his second view, it became apparent that the task was bigger than he'd thought. Volumes of stacked papers filled every nook and cranny and there was barely an inch of floor space showing.

Hunter and Grace exchanged looks.

Hunter sighed. "This is going to take ages."

Grace smiled. "It's a good job then you've got someone as organised as me on your team."

As Hunter began sorting and collating his pile of papers, he realised he was dealing with very different pieces of information in this room. The upstairs study, contained specific articles and notes relating to the Lucy Hall-Blake investigation, with possible links to the husband Peter Blake, whereas, this room, contained a mismatch of things. A lot of the newspapers featured articles that Guy Armstrong had written for the Barnwell Chronicle, when he had been their Crime Correspondent, or for The Daily Mail, when he had been one of their Northern reporters. There were also a few recent pieces he had written for The Star. Skip-reading his way through the opening paragraphs, none appeared relevant to their investigations and so he made a makeshift pile of them in the hall. The scribbled notes he picked through appeared to be the original jottings in a mix of both longhand and shorthand that Guy had put together prior to writing those articles. After an hour-and-a-half and getting bored, he spotted a pile of A4 colour photographs, and decided to check these out. It was an inspired decision. As he picked up and looked at the fifth photo, he called out.

"Bloody hell! Just look at this I've found Grace." He held up the photograph at chest height. The next one in the pile caught his eye as well. He selected it. There was another of interest below that. The three photographs seemed to be a sequence of shots taken only seconds apart. They depicted three men standing close together on the top of some steps, at the front of what appeared to be a club entrance. The clarity was exceptional and there was no mistaking who two of the men were - Alan Darbyshire and Peter Blake-Hall. And the third man in the group especially caught his eye. Hunter couldn't be certain, but he was a similar height and build to the fellow he'd chased at Jeffery Howson's funeral and who had recently assaulted him. This was a golden nugget, he told himself, scooping up the remainder of the photographs.

* * * * *

It was another early de-briefing session. SIO Michael Robshaw bounced on the balls of his feet as he made his way to the front of the incident room.

He said in an elated voice, "Eyes and ears guys, important things to discuss." Excitedly, he rubbed his hands together. "Not one, but two breakthroughs today. Firstly, Road Policing Unit took a call from a man who lives in Wentworth. He's told them that about eleven o'clock on Monday night, he'd just let his dog out, and was standing on his doorstep, when a dark coloured four-by-four went speeding past on the High Street, travelling towards Harley. He describes the vehicle as going like the clappers, and said it was not displaying any lights. Although he wasn't able to clock its number, he's been able to identify the make and model of the vehicle because he's got a similar one. It's a Mitsubishi Shogun Sport and he says it's got blacked out windows. That's the second time a four-by-four has featured in this enquiry. If you'll recall I mentioned the day before yesterday, that a couple had seen a dark coloured one parked near to the entranceway of a footpath, which leads up to the bottom of Jeffery Howson's garden, on the evening of the night we believe he was murdered. Now, as I've said before, this may just be a coincidence, but I don't like coincidences, especially where murder is involved, and so I've sent someone round to his house straight away to get a statement from him and see if he can tell us any more than what he's already told Traffic. And for the second piece of good news, I'm going to hand over to Hunter."

Hunter sprang from his seat, holding aloft two of the photographs he had found in Guy Armstrong's house. "These were among a dozen-or-so similar shots we found in his lounge and I've picked out these two for a reason." He separated the photos, placing one in each hand. Raising them before his audience, he continued, "I think you can all make out that it features our main suspect Alan Darbyshire, and the person who is poking him in the chest is Peter Blake-Hall. I recognise him from our interview the other day. And, although I can't be one-hundred-per-cent sure, the third person, who has his back towards us, looks a lot like the man I disturbed at Jodie's. These photographs are all timed and dated digital shots and were taken at eleven-oh-four on the morning of tenth November. Now to me, looking at the actions of Peter Blake-Hall, and by his facial expressions, this looks as if he and Alan Darbyshire are in a heated discussion. On the back of the photos, the names of Alan Darbyshire and Peter Blake-Hall have been penned, plus one other, Ronald Fisher."

As he sat down, he could see, from the faces of the team, that the significance of all this was starting to sink in.

"I know what you're all thinking," said Detective Superintendent Robshaw, holding up his hand. "But there's just one more person I want to bring in before I outline what the next lines of enquiry are." He turned to Barry Newstead, "Barry, you've spoken with retired DCI Burrows today."

Until the SIO's invitation to speak, Barry had been hunched over his desk, listening intently. He now jerked back in his seat, tugged a finger at the collar of his shirt and cleared his throat.

He responded, "Yeah boss, I caught up with Ted Burrows earlier today, he's living over in Ecclesfield. He's seventy-four now, but his mind is still sharp as a knife and he can certainly remember the Pendlebury case." He shuffled forward. "You've heard most of the story already, from what Hunter read out in the papers, and judging by what Mr Burrows told me, the headline of the first article we saw yesterday adequately sums up what was discovered that morning. Ted Burrows says it really was a vicious attack - blood everywhere. He described the place as like a slaughterhouse. The couple had over fifty stab wounds between them and in old man Pendlebury's case his head had almost been severed." Barry stretched his neck from his loose shirt collar and cleared his throat again. "The robbers had got away with quite a bit of gear. As well as some of the jewellery from the displays, the safe had been expertly blown and virtually emptied. The Pendleburys, however, had kept good records. The couple had written and described all their stock in a ledger upstairs, which meant that the investigation team were able to compile a list of what had been stolen and get it circulated quite quickly. Within a couple of days they were given a name of someone who was trying to sell on some of the stuff - Ronnie Fisher." He paused and wiped his mouth. "Ronnie, back then, was known to Sheffield police, but only as a car thief. He'd been pulled a few times but led a bit of a charmed life. Even as a youngster he was known as a 'no comment' merchant. When he was first mentioned for the Pendlebury job, despite him being twenty years old he'd already had one spell in borstal. He'd got twelve months for nicking a couple of cars when he was fourteen. However, Ted says that once they started doing some digging about him, they learned that a few months before the Pendleburys' job, there was a rumour circulating that he'd stabbed a man during a pub fight. The man he'd supposedly stabbed was himself a well-known villain, with a bit of a hard-man reputation. But there hadn't been a complaint, so as part of the enquiry, they visited him. The villain's name was Shaun Brown - he's dead now - died of cancer a couple of years back. He was more than happy to grass on Ronnie Fisher, not only confirmed that Ronnie had stabbed him in the shoulder, and in the leg, after an argument over a girl, but he also told the team that it was common knowledge that Ronnie carried a knife and it was all round the grapevine that Ronnie had been involved in the Pendlebury robbery and was desperate to get rid of the gear. He not only dropped Ronnie's name but also George Blake and his son Peter. In George's case, everything fitted together. They had lots of intelligence about him. He'd done time in his early twenties for house and shop burglary and had apparently learned how to blow safes during his first prison spell. In the early seventies, there'd been a spate of safe jobs at working men's clubs up and down the country and George's name had been put forward on quite a few occasions. Unfortunately, despite him being pulled in, the evidence hadn't been there to convict and so he'd got away Scot-free. There was also a rumour that he was doing jobs down in London for some of the gangs there, but again they couldn't get enough evidence against him to convict. The Flying Squad had even given him a tug, but he was clean as a whistle and so never did any time. That was until the Pendlebury job." He wiped his mouth again. "The team raided George's house in High Green and Ronnie Fisher's mum's house at Ecclesfield. Peter Blake lived with his dad back then. He was an apprentice mechanic working for a local garage. Although they didn't find any of the stolen jewellery at their homes, they also had info about a lock-up garage which Ronnie used and they searched that as well. It was there they found most of the gear from the Pendlebury job. All three were arrested and the upshot was that George confessed. To be fair, they did find a pair of boots belonging to George, which perfectly matched a shoe print they found in old man Pendlebury's dried blood, so it was obvious he had been at the scene, but Ted Burrows tells me it took the team completely by surprise as to how quickly George had rolled over and admitted everything. There were a lot of inconsistencies about George's story, but no matter how hard they pushed him, he stuck to his confession. Even when they charged him, they believed he was only admitting it to protect his son, Peter, and Ronnie. In fact the more digging around they did into Ronnie and Peter's background, the more they realised that was the case. They pulled Peter and Ronnie in on several occasions throughout the enquiry, however, they couldn't get a cough out of the pair - both alibied one another and George indicated he was happy to plead guilty to the Pendlebury murders. In nineteen-seventy-five he got life. Ted Burrows told me that the sad thing about the case was that he knew they had not got to the bottom of the job. They were convinced that Ronnie and Peter had been involved in it and that they believed it had been Ronnie who'd murdered the Pendleburys. They did a couple of prison visits to George, but he stuck to his story and that was it. Then, in September ninety-ninety-eight, he was found dead in his cell. Someone had cut his throat. It's believed a razor was used on him. They never found who'd done it." Once more he wiped his mouth this time with the cuff of his jacket sleeve. "That's it regarding those murders, but I'll tell you what else I've found, and I've been able to check some of it out with the Intelligence Unit." Barry glanced down at his jotter. It was full of his scrawling handwriting. He put on his glasses, focused on a section of it for a few seconds, then looked up and removed his reading spectacles. "In nineteen-eighty-six there are several entries in the system linking Peter and Ronnie to drugs. It's low-grade intelligence from a couple of users, and it's not supported by hard information, but they all state the same thing, and that is that they were bringing in amphetamine from Holland and banging it out in Wigan and Leeds at soul night venues. Now we've already been told that Peter was importing cars from Germany during the nineteen eighties. The suggestion was that he was bringing in the drugs hidden inside those cars. As I say, none of the intelligence is corroborated by any of the agencies and there's nothing on the system indicating if it was acted upon or not. There was a marker on the intelligence though. It would appear that the pair had been flagged up by the Crime Squad, at that time, who operated out of the Wakefield office. As you're aware, it no longer exists now, The Serious and Organised Crime Agency has been set up in the place of Crime Squads, so I've spoken to someone from the Intelligence Unit there and they've told me that, sadly, Ronnie and Peter are not on the new system. When the new organisation was formed there was a trawl through the old intelligence and if it wasn't current and hadn't been updated for three years then it was discarded. So I'm trying to track down those members who were part of number three crime squad back in the eighties, to see if I can get the full sp on Peter and Ronnie."

"Until now we haven't listed them as suspects," interjected Detective Superintendent Robshaw. "From now on, all that changes."

Everyone's attention turned to the SIO.

"Thanks Barry, you've done some good digging there, and we've also Hunter and Grace to thank for the thorough search of Armstrong's place. What's been found at his home has really turned things around. It's just a shame he wasn't here to tell us in person. But I think we can all see now why he had to be silenced." Michael Robshaw rubbed his hands together. "Okay everyone, time to draw up fresh lines of enquiry."

- ooOoo -

CHAPTER THIRTEEN

DAY TWELVE: 5th December.

The moment Grace entered the office, Hunter said, "Don't take your coat off." He snatched up the folder from his desk, marched towards her, grabbed her by the elbow and guided her back the way she had just come.

"Full day for us today partner. Loads to do."

"What, not even time for a cuppa?"

"Nope," he shook his head and released her arm as they set off down the stairwell to the rear car park.

"Not even time to put on my lippy?"

He glanced back at her, rolled his eyes and then continued his descent. "By the way, how did your evening go? Back in the good books again?"

"Oh yeah, great thanks. The family thing didn't work out exactly as I'd planned - the girls went round to their mates but it did give me and Dave some time to catch up. We even cooked together - that's the first time we've done that, for what seems ages. And I got to wrap up some of the girls' presents."

Hunter pushed open the back door and stepped into the rear yard. "Crikey Grace, I hadn't even thought of Christmas," he called back over his shoulder while striding across the yard. He aimed his car fob at a line of parked cars. Spotting the flash of orange from the indicator lights of a silver coloured Astra, he deviated towards it.

"Anyway," said Grace, pulling open the passenger door and adjusting her top coat to make it easier to climb in, "How did briefing go last night?"

Hunter dropped into the driver's seat and started the engine. He told her what Barry had revealed. He watched her face light up and said, "Good stuff eh? It's certainly opened up the enquiry now. Everyone's buzzing this morning." He dropped his folder onto Grace's lap and tapped it. "The DI was dishing out a load of new actions and I've managed to snaffle us a nice trip out for the day. We've been given the job of speaking to Amanda Rawlinson, Lucy's old school friend. Remember her? She's now a Sergeant with the Cumbria Force."

Grace nodded.

"I spoke with her first thing and she's day off today so the timing's perfect." He drove out of the rear yard and headed

191

towards the motorway. "But before that we've got a deviation to make into Sheffield. They've tracked down 'Chicken George' to a homeless place run by a charity. It's a place he's used regularly in the past. A guy on the desk rang in last night. He knew we were looking for him and George apparently booked in late yesterday afternoon, so he gave us a call. I've managed to get two PCSOs down there and they're babysitting him so he doesn't do a runner. Also, we've confirmed that George had been staying at the old inn where Jodie was found, because Task Force found a couple of carrier bags containing some of his stuff in the loft during their search yesterday. There was an old mattress up there and some other bits of furniture as well, so it looks as though he was using the place as his regular doss-hole. The sergeant says that judging by what they found up there, it looks as though George has made a quick exit, so I've got my fingers crossed it's because he saw something which scared him off."

"That'd be good if he has. Anyway, why's he called Chicken George?"

Hunter smiled. "I asked my old mate that. He walks the beat where George used to live. He tells me that it was because of his lifestyle. Apparently he was a bit of a character. In fact during the early eighties he earned a name for himself when he had a stand-off with bailiffs and the police at his home for the best part of a week. He held them off with a shotgun. Apparently he used to own this big sprawling house, with quite a bit of land, which he ran as a smallholding, breeding chickens, and the council took out a possession order against him, because it was slap bang in the middle of where they needed to run through a section of new bypass. He was headline news for the best part of a week. Some of the locals held a demonstration around his property in support. The upshot was that eventually they managed to talk him around and he gave himself up. He was compensated and the council re-housed him but he wasn't allowed to breed his chickens any more and ended up becoming a bit of a drinker and a recluse. In the early nineties he was found regularly in and around the town centre worse the wear in drink and caused quite a few problems for shopkeepers and stallholders in the market. In the end he got locked up a couple of times and did a short spell in prison. He lost his home and when he came out he just started dossing around anywhere he could get his head down."

"Aw, that's really sad."

Hunter shrugged. "C'est la vie Grace, c'est la vie."

They had reached the southbound intersection of the motorway. Hunter turned the unmarked car onto it and headed towards Sheffield.

The charity-run homeless building was a concrete structure of 1960s architecture on the edge of Sheffield city centre, close to the University. Hunter managed to find a spare parking place on an old cobbled street at its rear.

Pushing through the double entrance doors, they came upon an office-cum-reception point to their right. Hunter and Grace were greeted by a thin, wiry man with wavy ginger hair. Hunter showed him his warrant card and before he had time to tell the man why they were here, he said.

"You're here for George."

"Yeah, someone called us last night. I sent a couple of PCSOs just to make sure he hung around."

The man, lifted up onto his tip-toes, reached over the counter and pointed down along a poorly lit corridor. "I've put them in a room down there. They're having a cuppa with him." The man lifted a hatch and opened a half-stable door and stepped out from behind reception. "It must be pretty important," he said setting the hatch back in place. "Can I ask what you want to see him about? Has he done something wrong? Not that I'm nosy, but we have responsibility for him while he's here. "

"I can understand that," said Hunter, slipping his warrant card back into the inside pocket. "As far as we know he's not done anything wrong, but we think he might have witnessed an incident at a place he was dossing down in."

"I'll show you where they are," answered the ginger-haired man, setting off down the dim corridor. "He's not too good is George," he said, without looking back. "He's been sleeping rough under the railway arches, and the drink's got hold of him now. He's in a bit of a sorry state since I last saw him here."

The man paused by a door at the bottom of the corridor and opened it. "They're all in here," he said and stood to one side to allow Hunter and Grace through.

As Hunter stepped into the room, two things greeted him. The first was the smell - a dirty, unclean, and unpleasant stench of decay and stale body odour and the second was the heat, which emphasised the pong. He crinkled his nose.

Hunched forward in a vinyl covered seat, hands clasping a mug of steaming contents, was the saddest looking human he had set his eyes on in a long time. It was obvious where the smell was coming from.

George glanced up.

His face was sallow and waxen, and Hunter couldn't help but notice the yellowing of his eyes which were sunken in dark sockets. His collar-length unruly hair was a mix of greys and he had a thin, wispy beard. His clothes had seen better days and the trousers were heavily stained, especially around the crotch area. It looked as though he had wet himself, thought Hunter. On his feet was a pair of new looking fawn coloured slippers. Hunter guessed the centre had given them to him since his arrival.

Hunter nodded to two male PCSOs who were standing by a window. It was wide open. He smiled to himself. The smell had obviously overwhelmed them. He acknowledged the pair with a raised hand and mouthed 'thanks'. It was their cue to go and they seemed only too happy to leave Hunter and Grace to it.

Hunter took a deep breath, pulled another vinyl covered chair from the side of the room and dropped it a metre away in front of the tramp. Grace remained standing by the door.

"George, do you know who I am?"

"A detective I'm guessing. Those two young coppers said CID wanted a word with me."

"In a way that's right, but we're not exactly CID as such. We're from the Major Investigation Team at Barnwell. We're making enquiries into a murder."

"Oh aye, and what's that to do with me? I ain't killed no one." He raised his mug to his mouth and took a long slurp.

"I'm sure you didn't George, but I think you know why I'm here, don't you?"

Hunter was watching him carefully. The tramp's yellowish eyes darted a glance towards him and then just as quickly returned to looking inside the rim of his mug. That exchange was enough. Hunter said, "George, you've been sleeping rough at the old Barnwell Inn recently, haven't you?"

George made a grunting noise.

"You've been sleeping in the loft. I know that because we found some of your stuff up there."

He shrugged and had another swig of his drink. "No harm in that."

"No of course not George, but I'm interested in why you left so quickly." Hunter searched his face again. He remained looking inside his mug. "Shall I tell you what I think George? I think you left so sharpish, because you saw something which scared you."

The yellow eyes met Hunter's.

"I'm right, aren't I George? I know I am. Come on, tell us."

"Din't see nothing."

"You see, just saying that in reply is one reason why I don't believe you. I've been in this job a long time and I know when someone is not telling me the truth."

George bent his head lower so that Hunter could no longer see his face.

"Come on George, stop hiding from me. You saw a girl get hurt there, didn't you?"

Shaking his head, he never looked up.

"Look George, we really need your help. A young girl was murdered in the cellar of that old pub and I believe you witnessed what happened."

"Din't see nothing."

"Well maybe you didn't see, but you heard something."

George glanced. The sunken eyes were slits.

"Please George, we really need your help." Hunter waited for a few seconds. When he didn't reply, he added. "What if I tell you that we know what went off and we have a fair idea who killed her but we just need confirmation. Come on George, you can do that, can't you? What if I show you some pictures of the people who we think killed the girl there." Hunter reached inside his folder and pulled out one of Guy Armstrong's A4 photographs of Alan Darbyshire, Peter Blake-Hall and Ronald Fisher. He leaned forward, thrusting it in front of George's face.

It made him jump.

Keeping it there, Hunter said, "George, please help me. This is really important. A young girl lost her life in that pub and this is a photograph we have of the three people who we think killed her."

George studied the photograph carefully.

Hunter said, "What if I say what you tell us stays in this room? No one will know what you've told us. This is just between us three."

George lifted his head and eyed Hunter suspiciously.

"Promise, George. Just help me out and we'll leave you in peace."

The tramp shook his head then answered, "Just two."

Hunter tapped the photo. "Two people in this photo? Is that what you mean?"

George nodded. "Yeah just two, not three."

"Can you point out which two for me George."

A grubby hand with dirt beneath the fingernails hovered over the photograph for a couple of seconds. Then he stabbed an index finger at two of the images.

"Those two. They carried the young lass in. I heard them pull up in their big car and then I heard her screaming. I looked out of the window. They were carrying and dragging her. Then they disappeared inside with her. I heard screaming some more and then everything went quiet. I hid upstairs. I was shit-scared. Then they left without her. I didn't see what they had done to her but I guessed it must have been something bad, 'cos they took off so quickly."

"When you say they had a big car George, what do you mean by that?"

"One of them big four-by-four things. A big black 'un with blacked-out windows."

Hunter tapped the photograph. "And you're quite sure it was these two you saw dragging the girl into the pub."

George nodded. "I was shit-scared I tell you, but I honestly din't see what they'd done to her."

"I believe you George."

Ten minutes later, Hunter and Grace were shown out by the same man who had let them in. Hunter stood on the damp pavement for a second looking up into the murky grey sky. He started smiling.

Grace said, "I don't why you're looking so smug. We can't use any of that you know?"

"Course I realise that Grace, but what other way were we going to get out of him what we did? You can see the life he leads. How is he going to make a good witness? Do you think he'd stick around if we told him we wanted him to be a witness at Jodie's murder trial? In fact, you heard what the man on reception said about George. About the drink thing? Didn't you notice his eyes? They were yellow. That's a sign his liver's packing in. Even if we were to get him as a witness, he'd probably never live long enough for the trial. He's probably looking at another few months at best." Hunter shook his head and tapped the folder, tucked beneath his arm. "No, that was the best way of doing it. Now we know who killed her. We've just got to get the evidence, that's all." He winked at her and set off back to the car.

* * * * *

Despite the long journey ahead, Hunter felt jubilant as he left South Yorkshire. He couldn't wait to get back for the evening de-briefing session to report what he and Grace had learned.

He enjoyed the lengthy drive through the Dales, particularly when he caught up again with long-forgotten views, prompting memories of the many holidays that he, Beth and the boys had shared there in the past. And the roads were surprisingly quiet as was the weather. Until they entered Cumbria, where the skies turned. As they cleared the town of Kendal, a dull orange glow replaced the previous pale blue colour of the horizon and the light grey clouds became thick and dark, turning day almost into night. By the time they had reached Keswick a howling wind had picked up, buffeting the car, and sleet and light snow fell, raking the windscreen so hard that it sounded as though they were being hit by grit stone.

Thankfully, Hunter didn't have to endure the changed conditions for long, because just a mile outside Keswick he spotted the signpost for Portinscale, the village where Amanda Rawlinson lived with her husband and two daughters, and he swung off the A66 trunk road onto the sweeping lane, which dropped down to the narrow main thoroughfare leading to Derwentwater.

Within minutes of entering the village, following Grace's directions, he found the address they were looking for. Drifting towards the kerb, he stopped the car in front of an Edwardian three bedroom house and turned off the engine.

Lethargic after the three hour drive, Hunter yanked himself out of the car and indulged in a wide stretch. A cold snap of wind whipped past his cheeks and ears, bringing about an instant freshness, though it made him shudder. He leaned back into the car, retrieving his clip-folder from the back seat and turned towards the house.

A pebbled path led to a porch covered front door. Hunter pressed the bell.

Amanda Rawlinson received them with a warm smile and words of, "I bet you two could do with a warm cuppa." She beckoned them inside, into a patterned tiled hallway.

Hunter noted that she had not lost any of her Yorkshire accent.

"It's DS Kerr and DC Marshall isn't it?" she said turning away. "Come on in, we'll go into the kitchen, its warmer in there –the range is on, I've been baking."

It was a well-proportioned kitchen that Hunter and Grace followed her into, fitted out in typical country style fashion and dominated by a large pale green Aga set into a feature fireplace. A solid oak table with four chairs sat in the middle of the room.

Amanda pulled out one of the chairs. It scraped along the tiled flooring. "Please take a seat," she offered. "I'll just put the kettle on." She filled a kettle and set it on one of the Aga hotplates. "I'm so glad to hear you've re-opened Lucy's case." She dropped some teabags into a Cornish blue teapot. "It's just been on the one o'clock news by the way," she continued, as she brought three cups together and poured a drop of milk in each. "There wasn't much about it on, just the fact that Daniel Weaver had been granted leave to appeal and was being allowed out on bail. I guess there'll be a longer piece about it on tonight's news."

It didn't take long for the water to boil and Amanda soon brought three steaming cups to the table. She pointed to the sugar bowl in the middle. "Help yourselves," she said.

Hunter slipped off his padded coat and hung it on the back of the chair. Then he sprang open his folder to reveal a photocopy of Amanda's witness statement, made twenty-five years earlier.

"Is that my statement?" she asked, pointing and dropping down into a seat, opposite Hunter and Grace. She pulled one of the mugs towards her.

Hunter nodded. "I'm not going to show it you just yet Amanda, because as you'll appreciate we are speaking with every witness as though it was the first time. I know it was a long time ago now, but I'm sure once we get into it there'll be a lot you still remember, without me needing to show you your statement."

"That suits me fine, because if I remember rightly those two detectives who took my statement never put in everything I told them anyway." She glanced between Hunter and Grace. "There were quite a few times when I'd tell them something, and the sergeant I don't recall his name now just kept saying that wasn't relevant because they'd got somebody locked up for it and he'd confessed. Of course, knowing what I know now, with the job and everything, I realise it should have gone in and that I should have said a lot more than I did do in the witness box. But I was so naïve back then - I was only twenty-two. And I've thought about this a lot just lately, especially when I heard you were re-opening the case. I can't make my mind up whether those two detectives were just being lazy or there was more to it. I mean, I was really surprised when they

198

first told me that it was Danny Weaver they'd got for Lucy's murder."

"Why do you say that?" asked Grace.

"Well, for the last few months before Lucy disappeared, all she ever talked about was Danny and he didn't sound like someone who wanted to harm her. Now if it had been Peter well that would be different."

"Peter her husband?" said Grace.

Amanda nodded and took a sip of her tea.

Hunter made notes. He knew his partner was on a roll with the questioning.

"Mandy, I know I'm not structuring this interview right but that comment you just made about Peter, what do you mean by that?"

"He used to bash her about, didn't he?" She returned her comment as if it was something they already knew. Amanda's hazel eyes searched out Grace's.

Grace gave her a blank look.

"What? Do you mean no one's told you this before?"

"Lucy's parents hinted at it."

"God, he was a right bully towards Lucy. She showed me some of the bruises he used to leave her with. He used to punch her at the top of her arm or in the back near to her kidneys, where it didn't show. He was a right bastard. In fact, when she told me about Danny I told her to go for it. 'Good for you girl,' I said. She seemed so happy."

Grace held up a finger. "Amanda, I want to stop you there and take you back to your relationship with Lucy when did you meet?"

Amanda seemed to ponder on the question for a few seconds, then answered, "We were school friends. We went to Barnwell Comprehensive together. We hit it off in the first year - sat next to each other. Went through school together. In fact, we went everywhere together."

"And you were around when she met Peter?"

"Yeah. A gang of us would go up to the Wortley Arms on a Thursday and Friday to meet up once we'd finished school. We were only sixteen, too young to drink but the landlord allowed us in and we'd just have a few Cokes, that's all. Peter used to be in there with a couple of his mates and after a few weeks he just got round to chatting Lucy up. Next thing, she'd started going out with him. Don't get me wrong, he was different back then. Or at least seemed it. There were the rumours of course, about his dad, being in prison for killing someone, but that was his dad, not Peter. Anyway, when we first met him, Peter was really nice. And to us it seemed as though he always had lots of money, and he was quite generous with it, 'cos we were always skint. He was a mechanic at a local garage and he told us he made some extra money by buying cars and doing them up."

"When was this?"

"We were just seventeen. He was slightly older - he'd be about twenty-one, twenty-two."

"So that would be late seventies?"

Amanda momentarily gazed up to the ceiling, then answered, "Nineteen-seventy-eight it was. Next thing, Lucy told me she was late, you know, thought she was pregnant - she was of course. Then they got married at Barnsley Register Office. I was her chief bridesmaid. Peter had bought them a place in the village. It was a lovely cottage. Lucy was in her element sorting it all out. Then Jessica was born."

"And everything was okay between her and Peter?"

"Oh yes, really good for a couple of years. I was working for the local council back then, but I'd see her at least three times a week and we'd catch up." She broke into a smile, revealing beautiful white teeth. "She used to look forward to me going because I knew all the gossip. She'd dropped out of things you see, with having Jessica." She took another sip at her drink and then licked her lips. "Peter was working really hard and seemed to be making loads of money for them. He'd bought a bigger house - an old farmhouse which required some renovation and she was overseeing the work. He'd also bought an old working man's club out near Wakefield - the one he still has - though I didn't know at the time he was turning it into a strip club. When Lucy told me about it and she learned what it was, I could tell from the look on her face she wasn't happy. I think that was when things started to go wrong with the marriage. Although I can't remember the date even the year now but it was probably about six months after him opening the club when she first told me he'd hit her."

"How did she tell you?"

"I can't remember exactly how she told me, but she said that she'd suspected he was seeing someone and thought it was one of the girls. She said that they'd rowed one night and that's when he'd hit her. I didn't see the marks but she told me he'd blacked her eye and she'd had to stay indoors for almost a week. I think that was the start of it. I wanted her to go to the police but she wouldn't. She said she daren't. She told me that even if he was locked up she still wouldn't be safe 'cos he would set Ronnie on to her."

"Ronnie?"

"Ronnie Fisher. He was Peter's best mate. They went everywhere together. I never liked Ronnie. There was just something about him. Have you not come across him?"

"He's just featured in our enquiry," said Hunter. He rubbed his bottom lip with the side of his hand. It bought back a painful memory.

"Now if they'd have told me Ronnie had killed Lucy, and not Danny, then I could have believed that."

"Why do you say that?"

"I can't put my finger on it, just intuition I guess, but there was just something about him. The way he acted. The way he looked." She shuddered.

Grace continued, "But you never saw Ronnie being violent?"

"No. I didn't, to be honest. But someone did tell me that he had stabbed someone once. Over a girl I think. I was always wary of him. We all were."

"Okay, just moving on. When did you first learn about her seeing Danny Weaver?"

"Again I can't remember an exact date or anything. It was roughly six months before the night she disappeared, so I suppose it would be around March time of nineteen-eighty-three. I suddenly saw a change in Lucy's mood - really upbeat, the way she used to be. She didn't tell me at first, but a woman's intuition an' all that and she spilled the beans. I did know of Daniel, had met him before, because he had been doing some of the work on Peter and Lucy's house and I think he did a bit of driving work for Peter. Peter used to bring cars in from Germany, some tax fiddle and Danny was one of the drivers." Amanda stopped and gave them both an enquiring look.

"We didn't know about where Danny fitted into all this, but we did know about Peter importing the cars," said Grace.

Registering Grace's response with a nod, she continued. "I think that's when I said 'Go for it girl,' after all, there was no doubt she was happier in herself and Danny was a real good looker. And a nice personality. If I'm honest I was a bit jealous at the time. Now I look back and feel a bit sad about things. I mean I used to think she was so lucky. She had the big house, loads of money, but I now know I was the lucky one. I was the one never covered in bruises."

Grace gave her an understanding look and continued with her questioning. "Did Lucy tell you any details of her relationship with Danny?"

"Not as such. I did know that when she met up with Danny she was leaving Jessica with her mum and dad on the pretence of doing some shopping. And I have to confess that a couple of times I looked after Jessica for her."

"Did she ever mention if she thought Peter knew about the relationship?"

Amanda shook her head. "Nope, though she did once tell me that Danny had asked her to run away with him. Start afresh."

"When was that? Can you remember?"

"You mean date wise?" she shook her head again. "Sorry. Though it was pretty close to the time she disappeared."

Hunter looked up from his notes. "Amanda, a couple of times now you've used the word disappeared instead of murdered or killed. Is there something you know about Lucy going missing?"

She returned a thoughtful look. "No. I guess I've said it subconsciously, that's all. I'm not hiding anything, if that's what you mean. It's only because I guess they've never found her, have they? I mean, she was last seen at the market place that Friday night and I know people saw her arguing with Danny. But that was it. She just simply disappeared off the face of the earth that night. Those detectives back then told me that Danny had confessed to killing her, but now there's a question-mark over his guilt and it's just got me to thinking what really has happened to her."

"Do you think she's dead?" Hunter continued.

She bit down on her bottom lip. "I think deep down, I do. Especially after all this time. We were such close friends that if she were still alive I'm convinced she would have contacted me before now. And she absolutely doted on Jessica. Jessica was her world. No, I'm sure she's dead."

"And who would you put money on killing her?"

"I don't want to point the finger, and I don't know what you've found out already, or what evidence you've got but knowing what I know now, I think I'd be looking at Peter and his mate Ronnie." She switched her gaze between Hunter and Grace again. "And that's what I told those two detectives all those years back, especially after she told me that she was going to tell Peter about the pregnancy."

"About the pregnancy?"

202

She frowned. "Yes, isn't that down anywhere?

Hunter returned the frown.

"Lucy was pregnant with Danny's baby. That's why she went into town to meet him on that Bank Holiday Friday. She was going to tell him."

- ooOoo -

CHAPTER FOURTEEN

DAY THIRTEEN: 6th December.

Hunter stifled a yawn and stared out across the MIT office. Although he hadn't slept well overnight - his head filled with everything they had learned the previous day - he felt in buoyant mood and was eagerly awaiting the 8am conference.

He and Grace had not managed to get back for the previous evening's de-brief. Driving conditions on the roads home had been atrocious, especially on the trail across Cumbria and into North Yorkshire. They had encountered gale-force winds and sheets of snow right up until the border with South Yorkshire, and then, surprisingly, the weather had eased up - the snow had given way to a mix of rain and sleet. It had been nine-thirty before they had got back to Barnwell. A three hour journey had taken almost five hours of driving time, and knowing that the incident room had been shut down for the night, Hunter decided not to bother driving to the station. Instead, he dropped Grace off at her place and then had taken the unmarked car home and parked it up on the drive.

Beth was on the phone to one of her friends when he got in, and he knew from the way she had greeted him, with a waggle of her fingers and a flash of her sparkling blue eyes, before returning to her conversation, that she was in for the long haul with her chat. So he had poured himself a whisky and ran a hot bath. Then, mulling over the day's events, he had languished until the water had got too cold to lie any longer, before drifting back downstairs to join Beth, where he had poured himself another dram and watched the news before re-climbing the stairs to bed. He hadn't dropped off immediately he had found himself replaying the day's findings over and over again, until he had finally drifted to sleep. At six am, he had awoken with a start, realised he wasn't going to get any more sleep, thrown aside the duvet, had a quick shower, made tea and toast and then driven into work. As usual, he was first in, and he used the quiet time to write-up his daily journal, and prepare himself for the morning's briefing. By seven-thirty the team were beginning to drift in. He greeted them swiftly, but chose not to engage in conversation as he still had overdue paperwork and e-mails to attend to.

He caught sight of Grace coming into the office and he watched her make a path to the kettle. He acknowledged her with a raised hand as he clicked open his e-mail list. He had one waiting for him from Duncan Wroe, with the bold title of 'Prints identified.' Hurriedly he opened it up and scanned the short text. His face lit up as Grace was delivering his Sheffield United mug full of tea. "They've identified some of the prints found at Jodie's flat."

She raised her eyebrows.

"Kerri-Ann Bairstow!" He looked for a reaction. Grace's eyes lit up. "Remember her?"

She nodded.

"What's the betting that Kerri-Ann is the girl the downstairs neighbour saw in Jodie's room on several occasions? The one who gave him a bit of a slagging."

"It would certainly fit in with her character."

Hunter nodded in agreement. They had come across Kerri-Ann Bairstow a few months ago, in August. She was a sex-worker, feisty and loud-mouthed, who had reluctantly become a witness for them in the 'Lady in the Lake' case.

"Well, if that's not a turn up for the books. I'll feed that in this morning, as well as what we learned yesterday, and then you and I will see if we can track madam down and have a little chat. Fancy her cropping up in two murders in such a short space of time. She's certainly going to be pleased when she sees us two again - not!" A smile creased his face. "I'm betting she can tell us something."

"Aye, and it'll be like drawing teeth."

"Oh I'm sure with your powers of persuasion you'll get her to talk. You did last time, remember?"

Morning briefing took over an hour. Both Detective Superintendents were present and Michael Robshaw led the session.

Tony Bullars and Mike Sampson were first to speak. They had completed the search of Jodie Marie Jenkinson's bed-sit but hadn't found any significant evidence. Her mobile was still missing, and she hadn't been the type of girl who kept a diary, so they were struggling to build up a recent picture of her day-to-day life.

That was when Hunter broke the news about the identification of the prints found in Jodie's room. As expected, he and Grace were handed the job of tracking down Kerri-Ann Bairstow. Then he told everyone what he and Grace had learned the previous day. First, he reported on the interview with Amanda Rawlinson. He saw the looks around the room when he revealed Lucy's pregnancy. "She was meeting Danny Weaver that night to tell him she was carrying his child."

"So that could be the reason behind the flare-up in the market place," interjected Det. Supt. Robshaw. "But why didn't Danny Weaver explain when he was interviewed?"

"He might have boss, and Alan Darbyshire and Jeffery Howson chose to suppress it. Especially after what they had done to him with the confession," said Hunter. "We now know that Danny wanted Lucy to run away with him and the pregnancy would certainly complicate matters. It could well have been the trigger behind the argument that night. I guess the only other person who'll be able to answer that question is Danny Weaver himself, and he certainly wasn't forthcoming in prison. There is also the added element of her husband, Peter. We don't really know if he knew of all this and that's the reason why she and Danny were arguing. Let's not forget that when Lucy went out that night to meet up with Danny, we seemed to have overlooked the fact she went out alone. Amanda said that Lucy doted on her daughter, so why should she go out and leave Jessica? And there is nothing in the file which tells us who was looking after Lucy's daughter that night. Someone had to be. What if that person was Peter, and he was telling Lucy to end it, or something to that effect? We know he threatened her and used violence towards her." Hunter leaned forward on his desk and folded his arms. "I know, when we spoke with him the other day, he said he didn't know about Lucy and Danny's affair, but we only have his word for that. And after what Amanda told us yesterday, I wouldn't believe anything he said. She certainly paints Peter Blake-Hall in a bad light. And she was also extremely critical of Alan Darbyshire and Jeffery Howson. They persuaded her what to put in her original statement, and then primed her about what to say in court. Weaver never stood a chance." Hunter glanced across the room, his mouth set tight. "I got something else as well yesterday." He related his meeting with the tramp 'Chicken George'. When he got to the part about the photograph identification, he flushed, especially when he saw the look on Detective Superintendent Robshaw's face.

He said, "I know I didn't go about it right gaffer, but it was the only way I was going to get anything out of him. And to be honest I don't think he's got that long to live. You ought to see him. He's in a real mess. He has all the tell-tale signs of liver disease. But he has given us something really positive to work with. He definitely pointed out Peter Blake-Hall and Ronnie Fisher as being the two he saw carrying Jodie into the Barnwell Inn. She was kicking and screaming, he said. Under the circumstances, I don't think I could have got any better result."

The SIO's face changed. "Okay Hunter. I guess I would have preferred if the identification had been carried out according to procedure, but needs must in the circumstances. And it does give us something concrete to work with, but are you confident he told you everything? You're happy that he definitely didn't see what they did to her?"

"He said not, Boss. And to be honest I believe him." Hunter turned to Grace, who acknowledged his words with a nod. He continued, "There was no hesitation whatsoever when he said that as soon as he saw them drive away he left by the back stairs and that he didn't go anywhere near the cellar. We know from the layout of the pub that could be right and from the stuff he left behind in the loft, he certainly left in a hurry."

"And he told you they had a black four-by-four?"

"Yeah, with blacked out windows. No prompting."

"Okay, that's good." Michael Robshaw's eyes swept the room. "This is our first real break-through. The link to the three recent murders now is the black four-by-four and so one of the main priorities is to find that car. The witness at Wentworth seems to think it could be a Mitsubishi Shogun. I want to know if Peter or Ronnie own one, and if they do, where it's garaged." He switched his gaze to Detective Superintendent Dawn Leggate, standing beside him. "Dawn, what do you have for the team?"

She didn't have much to say. Scenes of Crime had completed processing the derelict inn and no significant evidence had been found. Task Force were scheduled to finish their search of its perimeter grounds that day, but she wasn't hopeful of finding evidence, she added. "Much of the scene had been heavily contaminated by the contractors and their vehicles before we got called there." She had managed to persuade the head of the forensic science team at Wetherby to fast-track all their submitted samples.

Detective Superintendent Robshaw brought in Barry Newstead. "You've managed to follow-up on the Crime Squad thing, I understand?"

Barry, seated at his desk, slipped on his reading glasses, quickly skimmed several sheets of paper in front of him, then removed his spectacles and addressed the room. "I mentioned that there was some intelligence about Peter and Ronnie bringing in amphetamine from Holland and it was believed they were using imported cars from Germany to carry the stuff. I told you that they had been flagged up by number three crime squad as targets. Well I managed to track down the DI who was in charge of the team doing surveillance on Peter and Ronnie. He's called Tom Stone, who's now retired and living in Devon. As soon as I mentioned the pair's names I couldn't shut him up. He'd every reason to as well, because the operation he ran went belly-up." He put on his glasses again and referred to his notes. A few seconds later he took them off again. "They took the job from drug squad when intelligence indicated they were bringing in the stuff direct from Holland. They started following Peter and Ronnie around in March of nineteen-eighty-six. It wasn't anything earth-shattering at first. All they had was evidence from a couple of users that Ronnie was the one who was knocking out the gear. And they had nothing on Peter, other than a whisper that it was his money being put up. The fact that he was using the imported car business to bring in the gear came from a significant source six months into the surveillance. In fact, that intelligence highlighted where the collection point was in Holland and some of the distribution outlets in Sheffield and Leeds. Tom says that the job was running really smoothly, and that they were putting together the evidence, slowly but surely, and then nine months into it things started happening which made the team suspicious that Ronnie and Peter were on to them, especially Ronnie, who was the one doing the running around. It was nothing concrete, but occasionally during the surveillance he'd suddenly deviate, double-back, or just put his foot down and lose them in a side street. Then they had regular sightings of two detectives at Peter's club." Barry paused and looked around the office. "Yes, you've guessed it, Alan Darbyshire and Jeffery Howson. There was nothing to say they were tipping off Peter or Ronnie, but their visits to Peter's club were too frequent for the Crime Squad's liking and so they decided to introduce an undercover officer." He paused again and narrowed his eyes. With mouth set tight, he continued, "And that's where it went belly-up. He momentarily stroked the line of his jaw with the edge of his reading glasses. "Just to digress a little, when I became aware that Guy Armstrong was sniffing around at the beginning of this enquiry, Sue, my partner, told me that she used to work with him, when he was a reporter with The Chronicle, and when he went on to work for The Daily Mail, that he was involved in a road accident in which a cop was killed. Well this is where it gets very interesting. That cop was the undercover Crime Squad Detective. Tom Stone said he has no idea how Guy Armstrong got involved or if he actually knew the UC man or not. He only became aware of the reporter after the fatal crash late one night on the road between Wakefield and Barnwell. The UC man had already established himself with Ronnie and had just gained enough trust to set up a sting deal. He had ordered a couple of kilos of amphetamine and was arranging a delivery. The detective had gone to Peter's club the night of the accident to put down a deposit for the gear. The next thing was that at around midnight on tenth July nineteen-eighty-eight, Tom Stone got a phone call about the accident. Apparently, the UC man was a passenger in Guy Armstrong's car, and was dead, and Armstrong had been taken to hospital seriously injured. Guy had been drinking he was two-and-a-half times over the drink-drive limit and his car had left the road on a bend near Millhouse Dam and had hit a dry stone wall. When they interviewed Guy in hospital, a couple of days later, he insisted they had been run off the road." Barry paused and stared around the room. He had a captivated audience. "Sounds familiar, doesn't it? Especially with recent events. The bottom line, however, was that they could find no evidence to substantiate his story and so he was charged with causing death by careless driving. He offered the same story at court but he was found guilty and given an eighteen month prison sentence suspended for two years. Because of Guy's job as a reporter, and because of the sensitive nature of everything, especially with Crime Squad being involved, they decided not to speak to him. And so they never knew what connection Guy had with the undercover detective, or if in fact he ever knew he was working undercover. The guess was that he was just following his nose for the story and the UC man was a source for him to tap into." Barry shook his head. "We shall never know." He glanced down at his notes again. "Anyway, there was an internal enquiry, and it was decided to hush the whole thing up and to shelve the ongoing operation against Peter Blake-Hall and Ronnie Fisher. But there is one interesting snippet arising out of this." He smirked. "I mentioned earlier that Crime Squad got significant information which changed the course of their investigation. Well that source was none other than Daniel Weaver. He apparently wrote to them from his prison cell."

* * * * *

After learning from a neighbour that Kerri-Ann Bairstow hadn't been seen at her own flat for the past fortnight, Hunter and Grace spent the morning driving around several of the council estates in Barnwell, banging on doors. Every time, they'd missed her by days - she had crashed down for a couple of nights before moving on. Finally, after two-and-half-hours of what seemed like a cat-and-mouse chase, they got lucky. At one address the female occupant told them that Kerri-Ann had left the previous evening and that she was in a bit of a mess - drinking heavily and not eating properly. In a drunken stupor, two nights ago, Kerri-Ann had rambled on about someone wanting to kill her, and the friend was really worried about her. She gave the detectives another address to try.

The bungalow at Oak Drive was registered to a pensioner. The front curtains were closed, but as Hunter neared the door he could hear signs of life inside - well, the TV was on, and he took that as a sign of occupancy.

Grace slipped around the back as Hunter banged on the front door.

He saw the curtains of the room window to the left twitch. A few seconds later, he heard raised voices coming from the rear before his partner shouted, "She's round here Hunter."

He found Grace grappling with Kerri-Ann Bairstow, trying to pin her against the wall. The girl was doing her best to squirm out of her black leather jacket in an attempt to get free.

Hunter grabbed hold of her arm and made sure she was going nowhere. Kerri-Ann's bleary blue eyes burned with a mixture of fear and hate.

"Get off me, you bitch," she screamed.

Her breath reeked of stale booze.

Hunter tightened his grip. "Kerri-Ann, calm down."

After a couple more failed attempts to break free, she stopped struggling. "I ain't done nothing. What're you fucking 'arassing me for?"

"We're not harassing you Kerri-Ann. All we want is a chat," said Grace. "Now I'm going to let go of you. If you kick-off again, or try to do a runner, then you will be arrested."

Grace and Hunter both released their grip. Kerri-Ann shook herself.

"I'm going to make a complaint. You can't do this when I ain't done nothink."

"Fine Kerri-Ann, absolutely fine," said Grace, "Come on. We'll take you to the police station, and introduce you to a nice inspector, if that's what you want."

She scanned the two detectives' faces. "Pair of fucking smart-arses." She exaggerated the re-arranging of her jacket. "Anyway, what do you two want again?"

"How do you know it's you we want to speak to? It might be Mr Thompson, who lives here," said Grace.

Hunter stayed quiet. On their last meeting, it had been Grace who had broken down Kerri-Ann's defences and persuaded her to be a witness in a recent murder trial. He was there in case she kicked-off again, or tried to escape.

"You ain't here for Len, because he ain't done nothing. I'm not stupid. I know you're looking for me 'cos I've been texted by people."

"Well then, you'll know what it's about, won't you?"

She gave a long drawn out "No," and attempted to look innocent.

"Yes you do Kerri-Ann, because for the past two weeks you've not been at your flat. In fact, we know you have been dossing around with whoever will put you up. Now if that's not the actions of someone who's scared or got something to hide, then I don't know what is."

Her face flushed.

Grace pointed at her bright red face, "You see Kerri-Ann, that tells me that you do know something. And I'll tell you why I know that, shall I, because we've found your prints all over a friend of your's bed-sit. A friend who has been murdered."

Kerri-Ann stared at the floor.

Grace put her fingers under the girl's chin and raised her face. She stared into Kerri-Ann's eyes. "I think you and I need to have a little chat."

Grace took hold of Kerri-Ann's arm. She shook it away.

"I'm coming. No need for the rough stuff."

Grace and Hunter exchanged glances. Then they followed Kerri-Ann to their car. She got into the back without any prompting.

Grace and Hunter jumped into the front seats.

Grace continued. "Look Kerri-Ann, please don't make this hard for us. We know you've been a regular visitor to Jodie because for one you had a bit of a spat with one of the tenants. And we also know that you know something about Jodie's murder."

"I don't," she said sharply.

Grace leaned her head over the back of her seat. "Stop right there, young lady. This is not a game. For the past two weeks you have been avoiding someone and we know from talking to the people where you've been staying that you've been scared witless. In fact you told one of them that someone was out to kill you."

"Big mouth," she said.

"Maybe, but that's because they care about you. Now I know you don't see eye-to-eye with us, but you know from last time that we looked after you when you were our witness and we can do the same again. Your friend Jodie has been murdered. And the people who did it tried to make it look as though she'd overdosed. Jodie didn't deserve to die and we know she died because she knew something, that she was hiding something. You don't need me to tell you, because you already know what I'm going to say, those same people will find you and you could suffer the same fate unless you let us help you."

"I don't need no help."

"Yes you do Kerri-Ann, because these people will stop at nothing until we put them away. And the only way we can put them away is with evidence." Grace paused and let her words sink in. Then she said, "We need to know what Jodie told you - what secret she was keeping."

"You don't know what these people are like."

"Oh, I think we do Kerri-Ann. And believe me, if you help us, I promise they won't harm you."

Kerri-Ann nervously picked at her fingers. She studied her hands for several seconds and then she looked up at Grace.

"Can you promise me?"

"Promise."

She searched out both Hunter and Grace's eyes. "It involves a cop you know...well an ex-cop. Well at least that's what Jodie told me."

"Go on."

She lowered her chin and muttered, "She overheard something where she worked."

"You'll have to speak up Kerri-Ann, I can't hear you properly." said Grace. She reached over the front seat and tapped Kerri-Ann's head. "Lift up and look at me please."

Kerri-Ann raised her head. Tears had collected in the corners of her eyes. "Jodie didn't do anything wrong. She was the bestest mate you could wish for. She got me off heroin you know."

"That's what friends are for, Kerri-Ann, there to look after you. Now it's your turn to return the favour."

"But I'm shit-scared about these guys. They don't mess about, you know. And what's to say, 'cos it's one of your own, you won't protect him?"

"Do you think if we wanted to protect him we'd be going to all this trouble to find you and offer to look after you?"

She shrugged.

"Think about it, Kerri-Ann. We want to put the people who killed Jodie away. I can assure you of that."

Kerri-Ann first looked at Grace, then at Hunter.

He nodded his head in assurance.

She said, "I only know what Jodie has told me. I didn't hear or see anything myself. In fact, now I wish she hadn't told me. If she'd have just kept her mouth shut, she might not be dead."

"When you say if she'd have kept her mouth shut, do you mean her telling that journalist?"

Kerri-Ann's mouth dropped open in astonishment. "You know about that?"

Grace nodded back. "I told you Kerri-Ann, we know a lot. We know she told her secret to a journalist, but we don't know what that secret was."

"She just wanted to make some money to start a new life, she said. To be honest, I told her to be careful."

"It's too late though now Kerri-Ann, isn't it? But you can help us get those responsible. We really need to know what Jodie told you."

She fiddled with her hands again, this time rolling a couple of gold rings around her fingers. She chewed her bottom lip, then responded. "I want screens at court, you know. I don't want these guys to see me."

"We can arrange that."

Kerri-Ann studied their faces for a few moments, then replied, "She heard an argument at the club where she was working."

"The club?"

"Yeah, Jodie had a job working behind the bar of a strip club near Wakefield."

"Owned by Peter Blake-Hall?"

"I don't know who owned it, but she did mention a guy called Peter and another one called Ronnie. She didn't tell me the

213

name of the ex-cop involved. She just told me she knew it was an ex-cop she'd heard them arguing with."

"Do you recall when this argument took place?"

She shook her head. "No, she told me all this about three weeks ago."

"And what did Jodie say about what she heard?"

She seemed to study the question and then she answered. "I can't remember what she told me word for word, 'cos she told me one night when we'd had a drink." She sniggered, "Well it was more than one drink, the pair of us were half-pissed."

"But you do remember what she told you?"

"Oh God, yes, I can't forget what she said."

"Go on then Kerri-Ann, tell us what you recall."

"Well she didn't know they were in the club. She'd gone in with the bar manager to help stock up. She was in the cellar and came up 'cos she heard arguing. She thought it was the manager at first. That someone had come in while they were shut and was trying to get a drink. When she got to the door, she realised it was the owner, that Peter guy, and his mate Ronnie. She's told me about Ronnie before. He tried to tap her up once and she told him to back off. She didn't like him at all. Anyway, she didn't like to go into the bar with the owner being there and so just stood waiting behind the door until they'd finished. She said that there was this other guy there - an older guy and he was shouting something about his mate wanting to go to the cops or something. And Ronnie was telling this older guy that he needed to keep him in order and tell him what's good for him. That if he grasses, then he as an ex-cop had a lot more to lose. That's when Jodie picked up on the older guy being one of your lot."

"Did she manage to get this man's name - this ex-cop?"

"She never told me that. The only names she mentioned were Peter and Ronnie."

"What else did she hear?"

"The ex-cop apparently said something about the other man having some evidence which could send them all down for a long time. Ronnie just went off on one after he said that - shouting at the ex-cop, saying that he needed to sort it or he would sort it for him. And Peter said if there really was some evidence then they needed to make sure it disappeared."

"Do you know what evidence this was all related to? Did she tell you that?"

"Jodie said that she'd found out later what it was all about, because she mentioned it to this reporter she knew, and he'd given her a hundred quid and was going to give her more if she could find out some more. He told her that what she had overheard related to the murder of a woman from a long time ago."

"Did the reporter tell Jodie the name of the woman?"

"Jodie didn't tell me any name, but the reporter told her it was Peter's wife. That's when I told her she needed to be really careful." Kerri-Ann looked solemn. "And I was right wasn't I? This got her killed. You can see now why I'm scared, can't you?"

- ooOoo -

CHAPTER FIFTEEN

DAY FOURTEEN: 7th December.

It was exactly seven-thirty-two am when the convoy of unmarked police cars, and Scenes of Crime vans, turned off the main trunk road and coasted into St. Margaret's Avenue. Twenty seconds later all seven vehicles fell neatly into line, parking up one after another, nose-to-tail along the cul-de-sac.

Hunter and Grace were first to step out onto the street, followed by Tony Bullars and Mike Sampson.

They closed their car doors with as little noise as possible and tiptoed across the road to Alan Darbyshire's semi-detached home.

As Hunter neared the gate, he glanced back over his shoulder and signalled to the search team and forensic teams to hang back. Then, followed by Grace, he trotted down the drive to the front door. Tony and Mike slipped around the side and secured the rear.

Hunter checked his watch, noted the time in his head and banged sharply on the front door. Then he took a step back and glanced up at the bedroom window. He saw the light come on and ducked back out of sight.

Less than a minute later the hallway light came on and he heard heavy footfalls coming down the stairs towards them. As the key turned in the lock, Alan Darbyshire called out, "Who is it?"

"Police," Hunter shouted back.

For a few seconds there was no movement, then Hunter heard a security chain being released and the door opened.

A blast of warm air greeted Hunter, as did a bleary-eyed Alan Darbyshire, wearing his dressing gown. He was fastening the belt around his oversized stomach.

Alan asked "What do you two want at this godforsaken hour?" but Hunter could tell from the look of resignation that he knew why they were there. When any cop called at this time of the morning it was only for two reasons - to be the bearer of bad news, or to arrest. Alan Darbyshire's face paled as he stared over Hunter's shoulder and spotted the line of cars parked opposite.

He said, "What on earth's this?"

216

Hunter wanted to say so many things, but he composed himself and stepping into the hallway announced, matter-of-factly, "Alan Darbyshire, I am arresting you on suspicion of perjury." Then he cautioned him. The retired DCI was forced to take a step backwards.

Grace followed Hunter into the carpeted, well-lit hallway, speaking softly over her radio set, telling everyone they were in.

She left the front door open and out in the street they heard the sound of cars doors banging, followed by the chattering of voices. The teams were getting ready to do their respective jobs.

Still drained of colour, Alan said loudly, "You'd better have something bloody good on me, because you're not going to hear the last of this."

"Believe me, we have," said Hunter. "I think you'd better get dressed, because we've got a nice warm cell waiting for you."

Darbyshire coloured and his eyes widened, "You need to be very careful about what you say to me young man. Do you understand?"

Hunter was about to react when he felt a tap on his shoulder, and turned sharply to see Detective Superintendent Dawn Leggate behind him. She had travelled in the convoy with DS Mark Gamble, to oversee the operation and offer the team support, given the fact that their target was a retired DCI.

She said, "Mr Darbyshire, I am Detective Superintendent Leggate. I am in overall charge of this operation. I am here to make sure this job runs professionally." She paused and then said. "After all, there can be no room for error, can there? We don't want anyone accusing us of a miscarriage of justice, do we?"

Hunter could have sworn there was a twinkle in her eye. He returned his gaze to Alan Darbyshire, whose face was the colour of beetroot. Hunter said, "I want you to get dressed now Alan and then we're taking you down to the station for questioning. You'll already know this, but you'll be able to contact a solicitor once we get there."

"Meanwhile, I'll be overseeing a search of your home," added SIO Dawn Leggate. "Is there anyone else in the house we need to be aware of?"

He gulped, "My wife, Pauline, but she's not very well. She's made up with flu. She's sleeping in the back bedroom."

"Well, we'll inconvenience her as little as possible, and we'll try our best not to damage anything. Now if you'd get dressed please and my officers will escort you back to the station. I will see you later and update you." The SIO beamed a broad smile at him. "After all, we want to make sure you have no grounds for complaint."

Hunter thought he heard Alan Darbyshire swear beneath his breath as he trudged his way upstairs to dress.

* * * * *

Once they had left Darbyshire's house, Hunter wanted as little contact as possible with their prisoner before his interview. He arranged for the retired DCI to be escorted back to the station by Tony Bullars and Mike Sampson, and for them to book him in at the custody suite. He knew that what lay ahead would challenge everything he had learned over the years, and so when he returned to the office he drafted an outline plan of how he intended to approach the interview. Twenty minutes later his pre-interview notes were ready. He cast his eye back over them, double-checking, matching times and dates against the evidence and information which had been recorded on the incident white boards. Finally he selected the exhibits he required, checked they were all labelled correctly, and that they corresponded with his notes. He slipped everything into a folder.

"Ready?" he asked, looking across his desk to Grace. She was resting her head in her hands.

"This is a first," she said getting up, "You making notes prior to an interview. After all these years, you're finally going to conduct an interview according to the rules."

He smiled. "You're know what they say about wit?"

"Anyway while you were preparing your stuff, I nipped next door to the HOLMES team and had a chat with Isobel. Things are really stepping up a gear."

"Oh yeah?"

"She tells me that they've done quite a few checks on Peter Blake-Hall and Ronnie Fisher. Associates, vehicle ownership and premises checks mainly. They've got an address for Ronnie and guess what?"

Hunter raised an eyebrow.

"Swansea have confirmed a black Mitsubushi Shogun Sport listed to that address. Ronnie is right in the doo-dah now. The boss has asked Tony and Mike to do some discreet enquiries to confirm if he's still living there and see if they can spot the vehicle. The gaffer's apparently trying to get hold of

Headquarters Surveillance Team to target him and Peter, especially now that we've pulled in Alan Darbyshire."

"Well, we'd better make sure we can sign, seal and deliver everything at our end then." He picked up his folder and a pen and made for the door.

In the interview room Alan Darbyshire was already seated at a table with the duty solicitor Miles Harper. As solicitors went, Hunter knew that Miles was one of the more amenable ones, who, providing the rules of PACE were adhered to, would allow the interview to flow without interruption.

Hunter had already decided he was going to play it straight down the line.

From chest height Hunter dropped his folder on the table and let some of the papers and exhibits spill out. The file was bulging, and his actions were deliberate. He wanted Alan Darbyshire to see exactly how much evidence they had against him. Hunter was determined to take a psychological advantage. He lowered himself into a seat opposite his adversary and tried to fix him with a stare. The retired DCI immediately dropped his gaze. Hunter loosened his shirt collar and slackened the knot in his tie. Then slowly he unfastened his shirt cuffs and rolled them back over his forearms. He clasped his hands in front of him, resting on the table.

Grace dropped into the seat next to him and switched on the tape recorder. A buzzing noise filled the room for several seconds.

When it stopped, Hunter said, "This interview is being tape recorded." He then went into the starting preamble to any police tape recorded interview, strengthening the tone of his voice as he reminded Alan Darbyshire that he was still under caution,

"You understand why you have been arrested this morning?" he asked across the table. Darbyshire was beginning to sweat. Droplets of sweat teased his Brylcreemed hairline.

"Yes, and all I want to ask is when this is supposed to have occurred?"

"Nineteen-eighty-four. The trial of Daniel Weaver ring any bells?"

"A long time ago now, but yes I remember it."

Hunter opened his folder and picked up his pre-interview notes. He scanned them, then looked up at Alan Darbyshire. This time he held Hunter's stare.

"Mr Darbyshire, in nineteen-eighty-three you were a detective Sergeant in headquarters CID, is that right?"

"Yes."

"And in August of that year, the twenty-seventh to be precise, you received a phone call from Peter Blake-Hall to the effect that his wife was missing. Is that correct?"

"It is."

"Can you lead me through what you did regarding that missing person enquiry."

Alan Darbyshire licked this lips, then answered, "Peter rang me early that Saturday morning and told me that his wife hadn't come home, and that he was worried because he had rung her parents, and round her friends and no one had seen or heard from her. I went to his house with Jeff Howson, made the decision that this was not a usual missing from home, and therefore took a few details and got a recent photo from him of his wife Lucy, then went back to the nick and began making enquiries." He paused, but he still held eye contact with Hunter across the table.

"Go on, tell me exactly what you did."

"You know what happened after that, because I'm guessing that since we last spoke you will have read the file, otherwise why would you be asking these questions?"

"Please Alan, just go through what you did regarding your enquiries."

He shook his head. "Well, as you know we found out that Lucy had been seen arguing with a man the night before in Barnwell Market place - the Friday, it was a Bank Holiday and there were quite a few folks about who had witnessed it. Anyway we found out that the person she had been seen arguing with was a Daniel Weaver. That was the last anyone had seen of her and so, early Sunday morning, me and Jeff went around to his flat and had a chat with him, hoping that Lucy was there. She wasn't, of course. He admitted he'd been having an affair with her, and that he'd asked her to come and live with him, but she'd told him it was over and they'd ended up rowing about it. We noticed scratches to his face and when we asked him how they'd come about he said that Lucy had done them when he'd grabbed hold of her and she'd pulled away. When we asked him what had happened after the argument, he told us she had left to go home. We weren't happy with that story and so we arrested him and carried out a search of his flat."

"And did you find anything?"

"Not in his flat we didn't. Later, Scenes of Crime found her prints there, but we knew from what he'd told us that she had spent some time there, so they were valueless. But we did find her handbag in a shed in the garden at the back of the flats, which was his. It was hidden in some sacking. He couldn't account for it being there."

"And it was definitely Lucy's handbag?"

"Definitely. Peter identified it."

"So you then interviewed him back at the station?"

"Yes."

"And what form did that interview take?"

"I interviewed him and Jeff wrote down everything."

"You made contemporaneous notes?"

"Yes, that was how interviews were conducted in those days."

"These notes?" Hunter opened up his folder and removed three clear plastic exhibit bags each containing a set of interview notes from the original prosecution file. "I am showing the prisoner exhibit numbers HK one, HK two and HK three."

Alan Darbyshire separated the bags, lined them up straight in front of him and scrutinised their contents. Then he replied, "Yes these are the original notes of those interviews with Daniel Weaver."

"And they are all signed and dated by yourself and Jeffery Howson."

Alan Darbyshire nodded. "Yes as I've already said, that is what we did in those days. Once the notes were completed, Daniel would be invited to read them and if he agreed with their contents he signed them and then we signed them."

"I just want you to look carefully at the notes Alan and confirm that numbers HK one and HK two were signed by Daniel, but in the case of the set of contemporaneous notes HK three, instead of Daniel's signature there are the words 'refused to sign' at the bottom of each page." Alan Darbyshire's face started to flush pink. "Why is that Alan? Especially given the fact that in those notes he has admitted to killing Lucy and burying her on Langsett Moor."

The retired DCI gulped. "I can't answer the reason why he didn't want to sign them. He just didn't. But what's in them is almost word for word of what he said. "

"Okay, fair enough Alan, I will come back to that later, but for now we'll move on." He put the three exhibit bags to one side. "So, based on his admission and the evidence of the handbag found in the shed, Daniel Weaver was charged with Lucy's murder and remanded to prison?"

"And of course the witness evidence of him and Lucy arguing in the market place yes."

"And in May the following year he went for trial, and you stood in the witness box and gave evidence regarding everything you have just said."

"Yes, you know all that. It's in the file."

"Okay, thanks Alan. I want to move it on a bit now. You know we are investigating the murder of your old colleague Jeffery Howson, because we told you that when we came to see you on twenty-sixth November.

"Yes, terrible thing that. Have you found out who killed him?"

"We have some leads." Hunter paused and watched for a reaction as he let the words sink in. Alan Darbyshire's look remained steadfast. "Putting those to one side, while we have been investigating his murder we have come across some disturbing evidence which impacts on the Daniel Weaver trial." He caught a reaction in Darbyshire's face. The retired DCI blinked several times, and gulped, but managed to re-compose himself. Hunter sifted through his exhibits and pulled out the plastic bag containing the contemporaneous notes from Jeffery Howson's safe. "In his house we found these. I want you to look at them carefully and see if you recognise them?" Hunter turned the clear plastic bag towards him and pushed it across the table. He watched as a trickle of sweat fell from Alan Darbyshire's hairline and down the side of his face until it collected at his jaw line.

The retired DCI spent the best part of a minute scrutinising the evidence inside the clear plastic bag and then looked up. He shrugged.

Hunter asked again, "Do you recognise them?"

"Should I?"

"Is that your signature at the top and bottom of the notes?"

He glanced at the exhibit again for a few seconds, then looked at Hunter. "Looks like mine."

"Well those notes are timed and dated exactly the same as the ones I have previously shown you, exhibit HK three, but they are signed by Daniel Weaver and what is interesting Alan, is that in those notes, just like as in exhibits HK one and HK two, he denies his involvement in the murder of Lucy Blake-Hall. What if I also tell you that those have been analysed by forensic scientists and they can be dated back to nineteen-eighty-three. You'll know what I mean when I say they've been analysed, won't you Alan? The grading of papers and the watermarks have been compared, as well as the chemical compositions of the inks. They were also ESDA tested. For the tape that is Electro Static Detection Apparatus testing, where graphite is poured onto paper and it fills in any indentations. You understand that process, don't you Alan?"

He nodded.

"The tape can't pick up nodding."

"Yes," he said.

"Testing found indentations of lettering transferred through from exhibit number HK two. You know what that means, don't you Alan?"

"Enlighten me."

"These notes from Jeffery Howson's house must have been at some stage been beneath the contemporaneous notes, exhibit HK two, for the handwriting impressions to have indented through. I therefore put it to you that these notes are the original ones Daniel made during your interview with him, and that notes HK three are a fabrication you and Jeffery Howson put together after interview to convict Daniel Weaver."

Alan Darbyshire stared hard at Hunter. The corners of his mouth set tight and then he answered, "No comment."

"You went into the witness box at Crown Court and told lies, didn't you?"

"No comment."

Hunter sat back in his seat and grinned. After several seconds of silence, he leant forward. "I want to now ask you questions about the murder of Jeffery Howson."

"What?"

"When we spoke with you at your home, one of the questions we asked you was, when did you last speak with Jeffery? If I remember rightly, your response was 'It'd be about two weeks ago now.' In fact, we know from phone records that Jeffery rang your home on the evening of twenty-second November, the day he was murdered."

Alan Darbyshire bit down on his lower lip, pondered on the question for a good ten seconds, then the look on his face lightened. "Now now, detective sergeant, I think you need to check your notes there. If I remember rightly you asked me when I had last seen Jeff, not when I last spoke with him." He threw his own smug grin back at Hunter.

Hunter glanced at Grace for support. She shrugged. He quickly gathered his thoughts.

"Okay Alan, my mistake. Moving on regarding that call he made to you, what did he say."

Darbyshire looked to the ceiling momentarily then answered, "Nothing much, just passing the time of day, this and that. I think he just wanted to talk to someone."

"It wasn't to tell you then that he was going to the police and tell us about the miscarriage of justice he and you had been involved in regarding Daniel Weaver."

The retired DCI coloured up. "No, definitely not."

"DS Kerr, that is out of order." It was the first time the solicitor had intervened.

Although Hunter knew he had struck a raw nerve, he also knew he needed to back off. He held up his hands in surrender, then said, "Changing tack Alan, how well do you know Peter Blake-Hall?"

He seemed to think about the question, then answered, "Long time. You'll probably be aware, if you've done your homework, that Jeff and I used to pay him a visit at his club in the early eighties. Used to drink there occasionally."

"And you used to work for him."

"Yep, no secret. I needed a job once I retired, and he had the ideal position of a club manager going vacant. I used to make sure everything ran smoothly at the club regarding his licence and the hiring of staff, et cetera."

"And when did you last see him?" Hunter paused, then added, "Or last spoke with him?" He put on a fake smile. "I don't want to get my questions misinterpreted."

"It'd be a good year or so. I don't have anything to do with Peter any more. I don't need to."

"Or Ronnie Fisher?"

The colour in Alan Darbyshire's face had just returned to some normality. His cheeks flushed again. "Look, where is this going?"

"What if I tell you we have a witness, who overheard a conversation between you, and Peter Blake-Hall, and Ronnie Fisher, discussing the murder of Lucy, as recently as early November this year, when you made a mention of evidence which could get you all sent down."

"I'd say she was wrong."

"I never said the witness was a she."

Alan Darbyshire's eyes widened.

"We, as you have already stated, have been doing our homework and we are building up a case which is not putting you in a very good light. We have a lot of unanswered questions, especially regarding Lucy's disappearance all those years ago, and now the murder of your ex-colleague Jeffery Howson. This is your chance to redeem yourself."

"I would prefer not to say anything further."

"If you're certain about that?"

"Yes."

"Well, I'll give you one last opportunity." Hunter shuffled out several more exhibits from his folder and laid them out in front of the retired DCI. "You have just said that the last time you saw Peter Blake-Hall was about a year ago. How do you account for these photographs, taken just over three weeks ago on tenth November? It looks to me as though you, Peter and Ronnie are having a heated exchange of words. What was that about Alan?"

Alan Darbyshire's chair almost fell over as he jumped up, face filled with fear. He smashed a fist hard down on the table and screamed. "You think you're fucking smart, don't you? You've no fucking idea who you're dealing with here"

* * * * *

Two phones rang at the same time at opposite ends of the office, breaking Carol Ragen's concentration. She looked up from her journal and glanced around the room. The place was empty and that surprised her, because twenty minutes earlier, when she had got back from her task of updating Jeffery Howson's daughter and ex-wife about the latest stages of the investigation, she had walked into a scrum-down between Detective Superintendent Michael Robshaw, Detective Inspector Scaife and Civilian Investigator Barry Newstead. She'd gathered that the three of them were working through the next lines of the enquiry. She had been so immersed in writing up her journal that she hadn't even noticed them leaving the department.

One of the phones stopped ringing and she waited for the other one on the Detective Inspector's desk to switch across to his voicemail. After thirty seconds of continuous ringing she realised that wasn't going to happen and giving out a long sigh she scraped back her chair and strode across.

"DC Ragen," she said, snatching the phone off its cradle.

The downstairs receptionist was on the other end. She explained that a woman had come in asking for someone from MIT - that she had information about the Lucy Blake-Hall case.

Carol was about to tell her to take down details, and that someone would go out and see her later, when she changed her mind. "Tell the lady I'll be down in a couple of minutes." Hanging up, she tramped back to her desk, picked up her notepad, and swept out of the office, down the back staircase to the rear of reception. When Carol sprung open the door into the foyer, she saw that the only person in there was a slim, dark haired woman in a bright red duffel coat, who, despite wearing too much make-up, appeared to be in her mid to late forties. The lady met Carol's gaze.

Carol said "Mrs?" and waited for a response.

"Aldridge. Lisa Aldridge." She took a step forward and removed a newspaper from beneath her arm. "I've come about this." She held up the paper.

It was the latest edition of The Barnwell Chronicle, with 'Innocent' emblazoned in large print across its front page. Carol had already read the article and knew that it featured Daniel Weaver's release on bail, pending the possibility of his appeal and the re-investigation into the Lucy Blake-Hall case.

"Would you like to come through?" she said, pushing the door open for the woman to pass.

Carol led the way down the corridor and showed her into a small ante-room, used mainly by uniform for taking complaints or statements. As such, it had very little in the way of comfort - just a table and four chairs.

Carol pulled out one of the chairs and gestured for the woman to sit opposite. Carol sat and watched the woman unbutton her bright red coat before taking up the offer. As she flopped into the chair she slid across the newspaper.

She appeared agitated.

Carol gave a reassuring smile. "I'm detective Carol Ragen, she said.

"As in Jack Regan, 'The Sweeney'?" the woman gave a short, throaty laugh.

Carol wished she had a pound for every time someone had said that.

Lisa Aldridge stabbed at the bottom portion of the paper, and a sub-headline relating to the re-opening of the Lucy Blake-Hall case. "I've come because I think I saw what happened to Lucy that night." There was a nervous inflection in the woman's voice.

Carol felt the hairs on the back of her neck prickle. She said "Oh yes?"

"I think I may have been one of the last people to have seen her, and I saw what happened to her after that argument in the market place."

Carol flipped open her notepad and thumbed through to a blank sheet. She wrote down the woman's name quickly. "Did you not make a statement back in nineteen-eighty-three, during the original investigation?" In spite of the heavy foundation masking Lisa Aldridge's face, Carol detected the woman's cheeks flushing.

There was an awkward silence and then the woman answered, "No. I'm sorry. I realise now I should have, but my mother told me you had arrested someone for Lucy's murder, and so I never did. It's only seeing this in the paper that's made me realise I should have done."

"What do you mean?"

"Sorry I'm not explaining myself very well am I?" Lisa held Carol's gaze for a second and then continued. "I was in the market place on that Bank Holiday Friday. I'd been out with some mates in town. We were celebrating me getting a job in Canada." She broke into a smile as if remembering the moment again. "I'd got a job as a nanny with a family in Medicine Hat and I was flying there the next day. I was having one last drink with my closest college friends. I left early. They wanted to go into Rotherham to a night club, but I didn't want to be rough for the long flight, so I told them I was catching the bus home. So after saying our goodbyes, I went to the bus stop in the market place. I'd forgotten it was Bank Holiday and there was a limited service, so I had to hang around there for a bit and that's when I saw Lucy arguing with him." Lisa stabbed at the newspaper again, directly over the photograph of Daniel Weaver. "It was a right old ding-dong between the pair of them. I was a bit nervous about it because it was going off just across the street from where I was and so I hid by the side of the shelter. I could still see and hear a bit of what was going on though."

"And what was going on?"

"I can still see it as if it was yesterday. He had hold of Lucy by the arms, shaking her and shouting something about 'It didn't matter. He still wanted her and he'd sorted out a place for them to go.' Well, words to that effect anyway. And she said that she couldn't go. She had Jessica to think of and something about 'You don't know him. You don't know what he's capable of' and that she couldn't go with him. She also said 'and if you know what's best you'll forget me'. Then she pulled away from him. He pulled her back and said something like 'I can't let you go like this' and that's when she pushed him away again. I think she caught his face, 'cos I saw him put a hand to his cheek and then look at it - you know as if there was blood on it. Then she just screamed at him 'Danny it's over. I'm not leaving Jessica. Now just go away'. And that was the end of it. He just stormed off."

"So Daniel Weaver walked away from Lucy. He didn't take her with him or anything?"

"No, no, she didn't go after him or anything like that. He went off on his own and she just stayed there on the pavement, watching him go. I still stayed where I was hiding 'cos I was a bit embarrassed. I didn't want her to see that I'd been watching them argue in case she turned on me - you know what I mean?"

Carol nodded. "And then what happened. Did Lucy walk away as well?"

"Oh, no. I saw her staring after Daniel, you know watching which way he went, and at first I thought she was going to run after him, but then this car comes screaming up to her. It came from nowhere, made me jump it did, and it pulled up right in front of her. That's when she got scared."

"Scared?"

"Well it was more like terrified. You ought to have seen her face, she looked scared to death! Especially when the bloke got out of the car."

Carol's eyes widened. She knew that she was on to something. She prompted, "Then what happened?"

"Well, he just grabbed hold of her by the arms, virtually picked her up off her feet. She tried to wrestle him off but he was just too strong. He shouted at her. Told her to get in the effing car. Yes that's what he said 'Get in the effing car Lucy,' but he swore properly. He was really mad with her."

"Did you know who this man was?"

She shook her head. "No but you could tell by Lucy's reaction that she knew him. She was struggling, like she did with Daniel Weaver, you know resisting like, but not really trying to get away if that makes sense."

Carol nodded "And then what happened?"

"Well, he flung open the passenger door, and just pushed Lucy in and then he took off. Wheels were spinning and everything. He was in a right strop with her."

"If you didn't know him, did you get a good look at him? I know it's a long time now, but can you describe what he looked like?"

"I can remember at the time thinking that he was a pretty big guy. By that, I mean tall and muscular like. He'd be a bit older than Lucy, late twenties, maybe early thirties, and he had dark brown hair. I think he had a centre parting. It was collar length." Lisa shrugged her shoulders, "I mean he'll have changed since then so I don't know if I'd recognise him now, but if you showed me a photo of him back then I'd maybe be able to recognise him - I'm not too sure though."

"What about the car he was driving?"

"Big red thing. A posh car. I think it was a Mercedes. It was one of those cars with a big silver badge on its grille. A three pointed star inside a ring. That's a Mercedes badge isn't it?"

"This is a wild shot Lisa, but did you get the number?"

Her mouth set tight. She replied apologetically," I didn't, but only because it confused me."

Carol's brow creased. "How do you mean?"

"Well it wasn't a British number plate. It was foreign." She held up a hand, "And sorry, but no I don't know which country. I only remember thinking it was foreign."

"Don't apologise Lisa, that's good. Just another couple of questions. Was he alone in the car, or was there anyone else with him?"

"He was alone."

"After all this time, why have you decided to tell us this? Why didn't you tell us this back in nineteen-eighty-three?"

Lisa Aldridge coloured up again. "Well, because of my mum."

"What do you mean?"

"As I've already said, I'd got this job in Canada and I was going down to Heathrow on the Saturday to fly off there. I told my mum when I got home what I'd seen and asked her if she thought I should go to the police. She said that it might not be anything and that if I went to the police I'd miss my flight and maybe lose my job, so she said she'd keep an eye on the news and if it was anything important she'd let me know and I could report it to the Canadian police if it was serious. A couple of days later when I'd settled in and phoned her, she told me that the woman had disappeared but that the police had arrested someone and he'd confessed to her murder. Then she later told me about the trial and him being found guilty, so I never gave things a second thought. I've been back in England for over five years and until I saw this in the papers I always thought that Daniel Weaver fellow had murdered Lucy that night. It's only now reading about it that I realise they're saying he didn't do it. So what I saw that night might have been to do with Lucy's murder, don't you think?"

"I think you may just have seen who killed Lucy. It's a shame you didn't know who it was who took her away in the car though."

"I didn't know him but I heard his name if that's any help."

Carol's face lit up. "You heard his name?"

"Well not his full name, but when the guy was tussling with Lucy and trying to get her into the car I heard her shout at him 'I'm getting in the bloody car. Just let go of me Peter, will you.'"

"And she definitely said the name Peter?"

"Definitely."

* * * * *

"It just has to be Lucy's husband," said Carol Ragen as she looked around the MIT office. Finally. she fixed her gaze on Detective Superintendent Michael Robshaw, standing by the incident boards at the front of the room. "I mean, which other Peter has featured in our investigation?"

"I agree Carol," the SIO said. "Did you ask this Lisa Aldridge if she would be able to give us an e-fit. It's a long shot, and I know it's so long ago now, and Peter Blake-Hall will have changed considerably, but maybe we can do a comparison with old photographs Lucy's parents have of him."

"I considered it, but I didn't ask because of the time lapse thing. What I have started on is trying to determine if Peter owned a red Mercedes back in nineteen-eighty-three. We know he was shipping them in from Germany during the early eighties, and that would certainly tie in with the foreign number plate Lisa recognised. So, I've faxed the DVLA at Swansea this afternoon to see if they can do a search of his records and find out the cars registered to him."

"Good job Carol." Michael Robshaw leant against the Lucy Blake-Hall incident board, crossing one ankle over the other, taking the weight on his standing leg. "I've already passed out this information to Tony and Mike who have been trying to locate Ronnie Fisher and track down the black four-by-four registered to him. I've got them parked up near to Peter Blake-Hall's club and I've asked them to update me if he or Ronnie turns up there. So far the pair have gone off the radar, I don't know if Alan Darbyshire's arrest has spooked them." He turned to Hunter. "Can I ask you to update everyone regarding your interview with Alan?"

From his desk Hunter addressed the group. "It went well at the start. He was unaware of the contemporaneous notes from Jeffery Howson's safe. Unfortunately, once we showed our hand, he clammed up. We let him have another long chat with his brief but that didn't help. Except for him telling us that he was with his wife Pauline on the night of Jeffery's murder, he gave us a 'No comment' second interview. He's refused to comment on the photos which Guy Armstrong took of him apparently arguing with Peter Blake-Hall and Ronnie Fisher and I didn't want to push him about Jodie's murder just yet. We've given him enough to think about for now."

"So you and Grace will have another crack at him tomorrow morning?" said Detective Superintendent Robshaw.

"Yeah. His face was a picture when I told him that. I think he thought we were going to bail him. We'll see what a night in the cells will do."

"Good, let's hope that'll loosen him up." He uncrossed his ankles and straightened up. Turning to his deputy SIO Dawn Leggate, he said, "And I gather the search of Alan's home hasn't turned up anything?"

She swept one side of her hair behind an ear and shook her head. "I'm afraid not. Though, if truth be known, I wasn't expecting us to find anything. He's had enough time to get rid of anything incriminating. Even his mobile has disappeared, so we can't track who he's phoned or where he's been. And, not surprisingly, his wife does alibi him for the night of Jeffery's murder."

"Never mind, a fresh day tomorrow and who knows what that will bring? Except for Hunter and Grace, who are going to continue their interview of Alan Darbyshire, I want the rest of you in here for six thirty am. We've put packages together for Peter Blake-Hall and Ronnie Fisher and we're going to do an early morning knock on the pair. Task Force will be with us and I've managed to borrow a few officers from the Community Beat team to help with the searches." Michael Robshaw tapped a hand on the photographs taken by Guy Armstrong. "If we include the murder of Lucy, these three are the prime suspects in four murders now and hopefully tomorrow we will have them in custody, answering for their crimes. Good hunting everyone."

* * * * *

Detective Mike Sampson tapped the wiper stick on the steering column and swept the back of his hand across the inside of the windscreen of the unmarked MIT car. It wasn't just the foul weather outside of the car, a mixture of drizzle and sleet, which was fogging his view, but a thin film of moisture had also collected on the inside of the front screen. He re-directed the heater to demist and cracked the driver's side window a fraction. The coldness of the night air took him by surprise and he shivered.

The blast of cold air also reminded him that he needed the toilet. He had felt it creep up on him half an hour ago but had tried to will it away. Now the feeling had returned and this time it hurt. He flicked the electric window shut.

After a few seconds the screen began to clear and in an attempt to divert his mind away from the uncomfortable feeling in his groin he focused outside. He had a good view of the front aspect of 'Le Chambre Rose' - Peter Blake-Hall's private club, fifty yards in front, on the opposite side of the road.

Straining his eyes in the dimness of the car's interior, he took a look at his watch. He struggled at first, but eventually managed to make out that it was just after ten pm. He and his partner, Tony Bullars, had been here for the best part of two hours.

Mike sighed and yawned. He was bored and desperate for a pee. It had been a long day and there was still over an hour before they could call off the observations.

Initially the pair had been directed to find the black Mitsubishi Shogun Sport, and since early that morning they had driven around every conceivable location. Unfortunately, they had found neither the 4x4 or its owner, Ronnie Fisher. It had been a tedious and frustrating day. To make things worse, as they were about to head back in for evening de-brief, they had been given new instructions directly from Detective Superintendent Robshaw himself. He wanted them to drive straight over to Peter Blake-Hall's club, park nearby until midnight, and report on any sightings, either of Peter or Ronnie! If either of them appeared, they were to call it in and await back-up.

The new command had puzzled them both at first. However, on the drive to Blake-Hall's club, they had both come to the same conclusion the enquiry had taken on a whole new direction.

More rain and sleet splattered the windscreen, once more blurring Mike's view of the street. He cleared the screen again and took another glance at his watch. *Bully's been gone a long time,* he said to himself.

Fifteen minutes earlier, Mike had announced that he was famished. Tony had responded by saying he had earlier spotted a fish and chip shop a couple of streets away and volunteered to go. It had been a good idea at the time but he hadn't realised he'd be away for this long. Especially as he was busting for a piss. Mike stared out across the street. In the past two hours they had only counted half a dozen punters going inside the club. Going for a piss would only take a couple of minutes, he told himself - he wouldn't miss anything, and he'd hear if a car pulled up.

He eased open the door, activating the car's interior light. Reaching up, he switched it off and swung his legs out onto the footpath.

It was fucking freezing, he muttered under his breath, pulling his jacket around him.

For a few seconds he stood by the car, watching and listening. The only sounds he picked up were those of the rain and sleet peppering the roof. He quietly closed the door. There was an unlit alleyway to his left and he strode towards it.

For a good twenty seconds he stood in the dark, listening to his stream of urine cascading against the crumbling brickwork, sighing with relief as the pain in his bladder eased. Then the sloshing sounds of tyres splashing through puddles fractured the silence. He heard a vehicle stop nearby, followed by the opening of a car door.

He tried to finish urinating but he was still in full flow. Fuck!

It took another ten seconds for him to stop. Thankfully, he could still hear the purring of an engine as he zipped up his fly.

He edged towards the entrance of the alleyway. It sounded as if the vehicle wasn't too far away. He wanted to see who it was, but he didn't want to reveal himself.

Craning his neck around the wall, he scanned the street. Parked in front of their MIT car was a dark coloured 4x4. It was the black Mitsubishi Shogun they had been looking for. A dark figure crouched down by the front offside tyre of their car. It looked as though he was letting the air out. Mike stepped into the street, shouting "Oi!"

A face, partially covered by a dark woollen hat, glanced his way.

Mike thought it looked like Ronnie Fisher. He darted out of the shadows.

In the couple of seconds it took Mike to get from the alleyway back to his car, the short, squat man was standing in a defensive posture. As Mike steamed towards him, balling his fists into a punch, he saw a face contorted with frenzy. The man's eyes were bulging and menacing.

Mike swung an almighty arcing punch, but the man ducked away and he found himself hitting thin air. The momentum spun him sideways and he banged against the side of the car just as a retaliatory thump found his unguarded ribs and knocked the wind clean out of him. A second punch found Mike's head and his vision shattered into a thousand pieces. His legs buckled and he slumped forward, throwing up an arm in an attempt to fend of another blow, but everything was a blur. He felt a searing sting in his groin and stumbled onto his knees. Then he felt a thump to the middle of his back. Then another and another. A sudden weakness overcame him. There was a sensation of a cold trickle of fluid washing around the sides of his waist and he realised he was having difficulty breathing. A veil of clouds swilled into his brain. The last thing he heard, as his face hit the wet tarmac, was his partner, Tony Bullars, calling out his name.

* * * * *

Hunter's eyes were closed but he wasn't asleep. For the past half hour he had been mentally rehearsing the lines of questions he was going to put to Alan Darbyshire the following morning. The ringing of the bedside telephone made him jump. Beside him, he felt Beth stir. He snatched the phone from its handset and propped himself up on one elbow.

"Hello."

"Hunter, sorry to disturb you."

It was Detective Superintendent Leggate. He pushed himself up further and used the bed head to support his back.

"This is just a courtesy call. I'm currently down at the District General." There was a pause, then she continued, "Mike's been stabbed."

It took a couple of seconds to sink in. Then he said. "Mike? Mike Sampson?"

"Aye."

"When? Who?"

"About three-quarters of an hour ago. You know he and Tony were carrying out observations on Peter Blake-Hall's club? Well it was there. We think it was Ronnie Fisher, but we ain't sure."

"And what about Bully? Is he okay?"

"Tony's fine." There was a little hesitation before she replied, "He found him."

"Found him?"

"Long story Hunter. I'll explain tomorrow."

"Tomorrow?"

"Yeah. As I said, this is a courtesy call because they're your team. I've called out Mark Gamble and his team to process the scene, and Tony and I are at the hospital with Mike. Uniform and CID are searching for Ronnie, and we're bringing the job forward on Peter Blake-Hall. We're doing it in the next couple of hours."

"Give me twenty minutes boss, and I'll get dressed and join you."

"No Hunter. Everything's sorted. I'm looking after things at the hospital and Detective Superintendent Robshaw's turning out to coordinate the search for Ronnie Fisher and oversee the raid on Peter Blake-Hall." There was another pause down the line, then she said, "It's not that I don't want you here, Hunter, or need your help, but you've got Alan Darbyshire to sort out tomorrow and I want you interviewing him with a clear head. I want what he's got coming to him to stick, okay?"

Frustrated though he was at not being able to do anything, Hunter knew that what she was saying made sense. He nodded in the dark, then asked, "How is he?"

"To be honest Hunter, I don't know. He's lost a lot of blood, though the ambulance crew stabilised him at the scene. He's in theatre and we'll not know anything for the next couple of hours, at least."

Hunter heard her sigh. With a heavy heart, he said, "So you want me and Grace in at the normal time?"

"Aye. There's no morning briefing. I'll leave a note for you about what's happening, or get someone to give you a message when you get in. Detective Superintendent Robshaw will more than likely be around anyway to update you." There was another long pause, and then she finished, "Hunter, I'm sure everything is going to be fine. You know Mike, he's made of good old Yorkshire grit." Then the line went dead.

Hunter hung on to the handset. The thoughts inside his head were undulating like a Mexican wave.

CHAPTER SIXTEEN

DAY FIFTEEN: 8th December.

Grace was already at her desk when Hunter got in at 7.30 am. He hadn't even closed the door behind him before she said.

"You could have rung me!"

He slipped his arms out of his coat. "It was late, Grace. I didn't want to disturb you." He draped his coat over the back of his chair and glanced at his desk jotter, looking for a note.

"But it's Mike."

He held up his hands in surrender. "Sorry Grace. I know it's Mike. But I couldn't afford for both of us to be worried and knackered this morning. We've got a big job ahead of us today and I wanted one of us functioning properly." He rummaged around his desk top, searching for a note. He turned his attention to his in-tray. There was nothing. At last, he focused on Grace. "Has anyone said anything about Mike? Do we know how he is?"

"Apparently Bully and Miss Jean Brodie are still at the hospital. He was in theatre for four hours. They're saying he's not out of the woods yet but he should pull through."

Hunter smirked. "Miss Jean Brodie. Where's that come from?"

Grace joined him in a smile. "That's what Mike's nicknamed the new gaffer."

Typical of Mike, thought Hunter. Shaking, his head he made for the kettle and cups. "I'll make us a drink before we get started on Alan Darbyshire." He added, "Has anyone said anything else about the attack?"

"Isobel got me first thing. She said that Bully had gone for fish and chips while they were doing obs on Blake-Hall's club, and that when he got back he found Mike collapsed and Ronnie Fisher's four-by-four fleeing the scene."

"Did he see Ronnie carrying out the attack?"

Grace shrugged. "I don't think so. Isobel didn't say, so I'm guessing he didn't. Bully found Mike unconscious and he still hasn't come round. Isobel says they're keeping him sedated for at least twenty-four-hours."

"Have they got Ronnie?"

"No, not yet. Apparently they turned out everyone and their grandmother last night, but it looks as though Ronnie's done a runner. They've got Blake-Hall though. They knocked him up in the early hours. He's downstairs in the trap."

"Have they locked him up for the stabbing as well?"

"No, for the murder of Lucy. Apparently, Swansea e-mailed back Peter's vehicle records. He owned a red Mercedes at the time of Lucy's disappearance and it still carried foreign plates. He didn't re-register it until October nineteen-eighty-three. How good is that?"

"Not good enough for a conviction."

"Ooh, you pessimist. It's a start though."

Hunter shook the kettle, listened to the sound of the water sloshing around inside and then switched it on. "Anyway, do we know how badly Mike was stabbed?"

Grace's eyes widened, "Hunter! Any stabbing is bad."

"You know what I mean," he said sharply, gathering together two mugs.

"Well, these are not my words, and I don't think Mike would be too pleased if he heard, but Isobel said that he'd received four stab wounds - one to the back and three to his right side - but because of his size none of them penetrated any vital organs." She emphasized the word 'size' by crooking her fingers in the air.

If it had been anyone other than a colleague, that comment would have drawn at least a smirk between them.

"So they think he's gonna pull through?"

"That's the latest, yes."

Hunter swept a finger around the room. "And everyone else is out?"

"Yeah, Mark and his team are at Blake-Hall's place with forensics and Mr Robshaw and the DI are across at District HQ in the Intelligence office. They're running the operation from there. I think CID are helping with the search of Ronnie's place and he and his vehicle have been circulated."

"Well, that leaves us to do our business." He made a tea for himself and a coffee for Grace. "We'll have these and then crack on."

Hunter pressed the bell by the entrance to the custody suite and when he heard the buzz of the electronic lock release, pushed open the door, stepping aside to let Grace enter first. He waited as a second inner security door opened and then made his way into the detention area.

It was pandemonium.

The Custody Sergeant was on the telephone, his back towards them. Another two phones were ringing behind the reception point. From the cell area, he could hear metal doors being repeatedly banged and a medley of raised voices drifted up towards him from the corridor. He tried to work out what was going on.

The stressed out Custody Sergeant glanced over his shoulder and greeted them. Mimicking the boy scout promise the officer stuck up two fingers, and silently mouthed the words 'two minutes', then returned to his phone call.

Hunter gazed at his partner. He nodded towards the cell area corridor and gave her a 'wonder what's going on?' look"

She shrugged.

It was well over two minutes before the Custody Sergeant slammed down the phone. The other two phones were still ringing but he chose to ignore them.

"Ha, the dynamic duo!" He said. "You two have caused me some right grief."

Hunter raised his eyebrows and pointed in the direction of the noise. "Am I missing something here? Are the prisoners a tad unhappy this morning?"

"Alan Darbyshire's collapsed!"

Hunter's looked from Grace to the Custody Sergeant. "What?"

The Sergeant nodded. "The custody officer found him semi-conscious in his cell half an hour ago. The paramedics are down there with him now. They think he's had a heart attack. They're just getting ready to take him to the hospital."

"He's bullshitting. He's pulling a fast one."

Stony-faced, the Custody Sergeant slowly shook his head. "Sorry Hunter, it's genuine. They've put the monitors on him. They're just sorting him out to take him up to the District General. I'm trying to fix up an escort to go with him."

"Shit."

"My sentiments exactly Hunter, but there you go. You won't be interviewing him today."

An agitated Hunter stormed back to the office, leaving Grace to catch up. He slammed his folder down hard on his desk and snatched up the phone, punched in a number and waited as it rang out. A female voice answered at the other end. He cut in the second she finished announcing who she was, though he didn't take in her name. He asked curtly, "Is Detective Superintendent Robshaw or DI Scaife there?"

"Just a second," the girl replied and then he heard the phone being put aside.

For a good thirty seconds Hunter listened to a distant humming down the line and then he heard the phone being picked up. His DI's voice came on.

He explained what had happened to Alan Darbyshire. "We're not going to get to him today, boss. We don't even know how bad he is until he's checked out up at the hospital. They're bound to keep him in him for a couple of days, at the least."

With a "Just a minute Hunter," DI Scaife went off the line. For the best part of a minute he listened to distant voices, trying to pick out what was being said, but it sounded as if the DI had covered the mouthpiece with his hand.

Then the line opened and the DI was back on. "Hunter, the boss is still co-ordinating the search for Ronnie Fisher who's done a disappearing act. We're turning over his house now. Some of his clothes have gone and there's no sign of his passport. We're currently trying to find where his relatives and associates live. His four-by-four's been found burned out on wasteland near the canal. We're in the thick of it here, so he's suggesting you speak with Superintendent Leggate. She's left the hospital and is overseeing the search of Peter Blake-Hall's place." With that, he hung up.

Hunter clicked down to end the call and then punched in Dawn Leggate's mobile number. She answered on the third ring. He repeated what he had told the DI. When he had finished he heard the word "Shit" explode down the line.

"My feelings exactly, boss."

There were a few seconds of silence. Hunter knew she would be running through a back-up plan inside her head.

"Okay, Hunter all is not lost. Peter's in the cell down there. You and Grace can have an interim chat with him. We haven't found anything here, I'm afraid. SOCO are still going through the house but they're not hopeful. And with regards to Mike's stabbing we don't think he was involved. When we knocked him up in the early hours he was in bed with a woman and she's said they'd both stayed there last night. He didn't turn out to his club. I'm afraid you're going to have to run with what we've got from Lisa Aldridge for now." There was a pause, and then she said, "I'm going to be here for another couple of hours, and then I'll join you back at the station and we'll have a scrum-down and see what we've got okay?"

"Okay, boss." He heard the line go dead, and hung up.

Taking a mouthful of tea, Hunter swallowed, set down his mug and picked up the phone again. He stared across at his partner. "I'm just going to let custody know we're coming down to interview Blake-Hall. I'm guessing he'll want a solicitor. Get us a copy of Lisa Aldridge's statement, will you?"

* * * * *

The excitement had subsided in the detention suite. Hunter could see that normality - if one could call it that - had returned. The Custody Sergeant certainly looked less stressed.

Peter Blake-Hall had requested the services of a solicitor and they weren't surprised when they heard it was Thomas Wilkinson, a partner with a firm who frequently represented clients who had grievances against the police.

As he entered the interview room Hunter stretched his neck, just like he did before entering the ring. He felt wired.

"Mr Blake-Hall, we meet again," he said, dragging out a plastic chair opposite the prisoner and sitting down. Pulling the seat forward he slid his knees beneath the fixed table and then placed his folder down on its surface. Shifting his gaze to the solicitor he asked, "And you are?" even though he knew the answer.

"Mr Thomas Wilkinson, of Grant, Harding and Wilkinson," he said.

The solicitor looked to be in his late forties. He was slightly overweight, with a good head of wavy brown hair, beginning to grey. He wore a dark pin-striped suit, white shirt and a blue and pink striped tie. Hunter said, "I presume you have fully briefed your client and he understands why he's here?"

"Two o'clock this fucking morning when I was banged up. For the murder of my wife, they said. You have to be kidding."

Hunter edged forward slightly, pointing at his own head. "Does this face look like I'm kidding?"

The solicitor made an exaggerated attempt at clearing his throat. "No need for sarcasm, officer."

Grace quickly intervened. "Peter, we're going to tape record an interview with you." She switched on the equipment and began the open preamble and formally cautioned him.

Hunter reached across the table, interlaced his fingers and fixed Peter Blake-Hall with a determined look. He took a deep breath and composed himself. His partner's well-timed intervention reminded him not to lose it. "As you rightly say, you have been arrested on suspicion of the murder of your wife Lucy back in nineteen-eighty-three. I say murder Peter, because although we never found your wife's body, someone else was charged, tried and convicted of her murder. However, recently, evidence has come to light which throws that conviction into doubt. So we have begun a new investigation and as a result of our enquiries you have been put into the frame for her disappearance." Hunter never took his eyes off Blake-Hall, though he could see that his opening sentence had no effect. Blake-Hall's arms remained locked in their folded position and he stared back straight-faced.

Hunter opened up his folder and slipped out several witness statement forms which he carefully laid out across the table.

"Peter, I have here a photocopy of the original statement you made to Detective Sergeant Alan Darbyshire and Detective Constable Jeffery Howson, who came to see you after you had reported Lucy going missing on the morning of Saturday twenty-seventh August, nineteen-eighty-three. Can you recall making that statement to those detectives?"

"Yeah, though I can't remember what I put in. It's so long ago."

"That's understandable, but don't worry because I'm going to take you through it." Hunter picked up the first page. "According to this, you told those detectives that you last saw Lucy at about seven pm on Friday twenty-sixth August, when she left the house, telling you that she was meeting up with a couple of friends."

"Yeah, Amanda Smith was one of them. I think she's called Rawlinson now. She was a friend of hers from school. She was a bridesmaid at our wedding. I can't remember the others though. It's such a long time ago now."

"No problem Peter. And you say you think she caught the bus into town. Well at least that was her intention."

Peter nodded, "Yeah. She did as well because I can remember they tracked down the bus driver who dropped her off near the market place."

"Did she tell you what her arrangements were that night?"

"You mean regarding her meeting up with Danny?"

"Well, I'm after what she said to you."

"She didn't mention that slime-ball, if that's what you're getting at. She said she was just meeting up with a few friends. She said she'd be back about ten. I was looking after Jessica and she knew I normally went to the club about that time. I expected her to be back. When she didn't come back I rung round some of her mates, Amanda first, and that's when I realised she hadn't gone out to meet them. I waited 'til midnight and then when she still hadn't come in I rang the police. I told you the rest the other day."

"Yes you did Peter." Hunter scanned down the witness statement. "You've put in this statement a description of the clothing she was wearing when she went out. Can you remember that still?"

Peter Blake-Hall stared up to the ceiling. He appeared to be deep in thought. Then he replied, "She had on a yellow dress and a fawn cardigan. That had some kind of design around the neck and cuffs. She had her handbag with her as well. The one you lot found in Danny Weaver's shed."

"The one Alan Darbyshire and Jeffery Howson found, you mean?"

"Yeah."

"They showed you that bag on the Sunday, according to your statement?"

"Yeah, that's right. They brought it to my house. Asked me if I recognised it. It was Lucy's, I told them and that's when they told me they had Danny locked up. And that's when they also told me she'd been carrying on with him for six months."

"So until Alan and Jeffery told you Lucy was having an affair with Danny Weaver, you had no idea."

"None at all. It was a complete shock."

"Can I just take you back to that Friday night when Lucy went out?"

Blake-Hall tipped his head.

"You said, both in your statement, and just now on tape, that when Lucy had not come home you first phoned round her friends and then just after midnight you rang the police?"

"Yeah."

"Did you go out looking for her?" Hunter thought he caught a flicker of unease in Peter's eyes. The man tightened the lock in his folded arms.

"No." A split-second later he added, "I was looking after Jessica, wasn't I. How could I go out?"

"Yes, of course you were." Hunter looked down at the last page of Peter's statement. He moved his head to make it look

242

as though he was reading what was recorded, then he raised his eyes. "Peter, just one thing. Can you remember what car you were driving at that time?"

Blake-Hall frowned. "What's the relevance of that?"

"It's just that it's cropped up in our enquiries."

Blake-Hall shrugged, "No idea."

"What if I give you a bit of a help?" Hunter leafed through his folder again and picked out the recent witness statement supplied by Lisa Aldridge. Instead of laying it out over the table in full view, he tantalizingly held it at an angle. In the periphery of his vision he caught Peter Blake-Hall making a slight movement, craning his neck, though doing his best not to appear curious. Hunter inwardly smiled.

"What about a red Mercedes Benz on German plates?" He knew the first bit and guessed the second. "I am right in thinking that around that time you were importing cars from Germany, Mercedes and BMWs?"

"No secret. They were cheaper from there. You didn't have to pay VAT on them. I wasn't doing anything illegal."

"I'm not accusing you of anything. I'm just trying to help you recall if you owned a red Mercedes saloon on the night of Lucy's disappearance."

"Can't remember. Might have done. I've owned one in the past."

"What if I help you out further by telling you that we have checked your records at the DVLA and they show that in ninety-eighty-three you owned a red Mercedes-Benz 380SL on German plates, which you re-registered in October of that year."

Before Peter Blake-Hall had time to reply his solicitor intervened with, "Detective Sergeant, what is the relevance to this line of questioning?"

Although Hunter was replying to the solicitor, he looked squarely into the eyes of Peter Blake-Hall, "The relevance is that this statement here," Hunter began shaking Lisa's witness statement, "Puts your client in Barnwell market place at around ten-forty-five pm, on Friday twenty-sixth August, nineteen-eighty-three, firstly he was seen driving his red Mercedes, and then seen dragging his wife, Lucy, into the front passenger seat, before driving away. Unlike his own original statement, which states nothing of the sort. According to this statement, your client, Mr Wilkinson, is the last person to have seen Lucy and in my book, that puts him clearly in the frame as a suspect." Hunter watched Peter Blake-Hall's face turn ashen. He was waiting for him to respond when the solicitor laid a hand on one of his tightly folded arms.

"In the light of this recent evidence, I would like to confer with my client."

They'd had no option but to bring the interview to an end. Hunter grinned at Peter Blake-Hall as they formally wrapped up the session. As he and Grace left the room, they knew they had their prisoner rattled. They also knew that upon their return there was the likelihood of him saying 'no comment' to any future questions. That proved to be the case twenty minutes later when they entered into a second bout of questioning.

Peter Blake-Hall sat back in his chair, arms again folded, displaying an air of arrogance, while Hunter read through the statement Amanda Rawlinson had given them. He deliberately broke off at the end of every paragraph, to check back with a question. Especially, he halted the readings when he came to the part where Amanda stated that Lucy had been assaulted by him. Each time Peter issued back 'no comment.' Thirty five minutes into the second interview, Hunter called it a day and handed Peter Blake-Hall over to the Custody sergeant to be put back in his cell.

Hunter left the custody suite with a disappointed frown creasing his face. He left Grace at the ground floor ladies toilets, and trudged his way up the stairs with a head full of dark thoughts. He shouldered the doors, almost falling into the room.

Detective Superintendent Dawn Leggate, sitting at his desk, took him by surprise.

"Oh, hello boss, I wasn't expecting to see you."

"I've just called the custody suite and they said you were on your way up here. How did it go?"

Hunter dropped down into Grace's chair opposite and outlined the interview he and Grace had just concluded with Blake-Hall.

When he finished, she said, "Bollocks."

It drew a smile from Hunter. "Couldn't have put it any finer boss. Anyway, how's it gone at his place?"

"Absolutely zilch. The house is spotless. And I'm sure he wasn't involved in Mike's stabbing. He was in bed when we went round there at one-thirty this morning. A woman was there as well. She says they've been together for the past ten years and that last night they both stayed at home and had a meal. Apparently he doesn't go to the club every night now. He has a manager to look after things. In the kitchen there was an empty bottle of wine and the dishwasher was full, so it appears he does have a good alibi for that one. We tried to draw him out about Ronnie but he was having none of it. Said he wasn't saying anything until his solicitor was present. I've seized his phone though - if he's had it a while, it'll give us some info. One of the team has whisked that across to Headquarters and the techies have promised to fast-track it." She rang her hands together. "So where does that leave us?"

Hunter watched the Detective Superintendent's expression turn studious. He knew she was saying it more to herself than him.

A couple of seconds later she said, "You didn't show him the photographs, taken by Guy Armstrong yet, did you?"

Hunter shook his head.

"Good. And you didn't drop out what the tramp saw?"

"For what that evidence is worth, no."

"I know it's not worth much, but we have to put it to him and see what answer or reaction he gives to it."

"You want me and Grace to do another interview with him then?"

"Not today Hunter, no. We'll let Mark's team and SOCO finish off completely at his house and have another go at him tomorrow. We'll bed him down for the night and start afresh. I'll authorise the extension to his detention. We can't have him disappearing like his mate Ronnie. In the meantime, check on how Alan Darbyshire is getting on. The last I was told was that it definitely was a heart-attack, and that he's now comfortable on a ward, but they're not going to release him for a couple of days at least. I've already given instructions for them to release his guard. He's not going anywhere." She yawned and clamped a hand across her mouth. "God, I'm knackered. I need my bed." She rested her elbows on the desk and supported her chin in her hands. "Mr Robshaw's going to give a de-briefing at seven tonight. I'm going to call it a day before I collapse. Is there anything you and Grace can pick up?"

Her question triggered a thought from his nighttime musings over the investigation. "There is something I'd like to run past you."

"Go on then. As Dumbo says, I'm all ears."

He cracked a grin, then said, "No one's talked to Jessica. Yes, we've spoken with Lucy's parents but we've not spoken with her daughter ever. Her grandparents said she'd seen a psychiatrist in the past because of nightmares and problems she had suffered as a child, but we never asked if their sessions had revealed anything. Why don't we speak to her? It's not going to harm anything is it? You never know, there might be something. She was five when her mum disappeared and I know that's young, but I think of what my own kids were like at five years old and it's surprising just how much they're aware of at that age."

He waited for a response. After a good fifteen seconds of silence, she replied. "I agree Hunter. What harm will it do? We've absolutely nothing to lose. You and Grace see if you can fix it up, and feed it back in at briefing." With that, she pushed herself out of Hunter's chair and headed for the door. She waved a hand without looking back. "See you in the morning."

Following Dawn Leggate's departure, Hunter updated Grace, and as he completed the day's paperwork she tried to contact Jessica. They hadn't a phone number for her but they had her grandmother, Margaret Hall's telephone number on file.

Grace's call to Lucy's parents was picked up and the first few minutes of the conversation were a barrage of questions about the latest developments in the investigation. Grace happily provided the answers, then moved on to the real purpose of her call. She explained that they had Peter in custody and needed to speak with Jessica. She was met with a good twenty seconds of silence, so she explained in detail about how they wanted to see if her granddaughter could recollect anything from her past. Grace could sense the anxiety in her voice when Margaret came back on the line. "She's very vulnerable you know," she repeatedly said, and added "She's gone through such a lot in her life, losing her mum and not having a father who loved her." After ten minutes, Grace managed to convince her that it was necessary, assuring her that they would tread sensitively. She invited Margaret to come along with her granddaughter and arranged to meet them the next day. Before she hung up she gave them directions to the police station and fixed the time for ten am.

As expected, the evening briefing was short. Nothing incriminating had been found at Peter Blake-Hall's home and the search teams were going to start on his club the next day. Ronnie Fisher had gone to ground. Task Force and CID had turned over a number of homes belonging to family members and close associates but they hadn't been able to find him. A nationwide manhunt was now in place.

Detective Superintendent Robshaw concluded the session by telling everyone that he wanted them all in for seven am the following morning.

Hunter squared up the edges of his loose papers and dropped them into his pending tray. They could wait for the next day. He grabbed his padded coat off the back of his seat and threw it over his shoulder.

He watched Grace tidy up her desk. As she dropped a couple of pens into her desk holder he said, "I'm just going to call in and see how Mike is on my way home, what about you?"

She glanced at her watch. "I'd love to be able to say yes Hunter, but I promised everyone a cooked meal tonight. I daren't be in the bad books again."

"No probs," he replied and made for the door. "I'm only doing a flying visit myself. I'm totally knackered," he called back.

"Send him my love," Grace called after him.

Hunter rode the lift up to the third floor of the District General hospital. Mike was on the surgical ward after his operation. Following the signs, he strode down the corridor, entered the ward and passed the nurses' station towards the six-bedded unit where Mike was. At the glass partition he stopped and scanned the room, until he spotted Mike sitting up in bed. But he was with a woman and the sight of her caught Hunter by surprise. He had only ever seen Chief Inspector Janet Dobson in uniform. He knew from his visits to Headquarters that she was in charge of the Prosecutions Department. But here she was in civvies, leaning across Mike's bed chatting to him and holding his hand.

Hunter smirked. *Well you crafty old bugger. All that time I felt sorry for you, thinking you were alone. And you've been knocking off a Chief Inspector.* Hunter retraced his steps. *You don't need me tonight for company, Mike Sampson.*

He was about to get back in the lift when he felt a tap on his shoulder. He turned to see Pauline Darbyshire. She looked drained.

"I thought it was you," she said.

He picked out a note of nervousness in her voice. "Have you just been visiting Alan?" This felt awkward.

"Yes, have you just come to check on how he's doing?"

"No, I've just called to see a colleague."

"I hope it's nothing serious."

"No he's fine. Just had an operation." He wasn't going to expand on that. He didn't want her knowing what had gone on since her husband's arrest.

"I'm glad I've caught you, DS Kerr. Alan said he'd like to talk to you."

Hunter was puzzled. "What do you mean?"

"He's finally told me what's happened. He's in a right state. He knows it's pretty serious, but he wants to get it sorted out. He said he wanted to talk with you." She touched Hunter's arm. "I think he trusts you. Go and have a word with him will you? He's only just down the corridor."

"But I can't speak to him Mrs Darbyshire. I can only do that in a proper interview. I can't do it here in hospital."

She gripped his coat. "Please, DS Kerr, he sounds desperate."

Hunter sighed.

"Please," she repeated.

He was about to politely refuse until curiosity kicked in. A quick chat with Alan Darbyshire was not going to harm anything especially if he documented the conversation tomorrow. He knew it could be a point of debate at court, but he decided to cross that bridge when he came to it.

Hunter patted Pauline's hand still gripping his coat, "Of course I'll have a chat with Alan."

He followed her back in the direction of the surgical ward, but before they got there the corridor branched off and took on a detour towards the admissions ward.

Pauline pointed out where Alan was and left Hunter at the door.

Darbyshire was propped up in his bed, hooked up to a beeping monitor. He looked surprisingly well, given that he'd had a heart attack only twelve hours earlier.

"Gave us quite a scare there Alan," he opened.

"They've said it was a warning for me to change my lifestyle, blah,blah,blah. You know, the usual routine. A couple of days and I'll be out of here and back in your cell." He gave a reluctant smile.

Hunter really wanted to say 'It's only what you deserve.' Instead he said, "Pauline told me you wanted a word?"

Alan Darbyshire gesticulated for Hunter to sit down. "If you wouldn't mind."

Hunter sank into a high backed chair. "What can I do for you?"

"Look, I know from yesterday's interview that you've got enough on me for perjury, but I think I should explain how things are."

"You can do that when we interview you once you get out of here."

"Oh come off it Hunter. You'll get the version I want to give you in interview. Don't you really want to know what went off?"

Hunter eyed him curiously for a few seconds. Then he said, "I'm listening."

Alan Darbyshire stared back. "I'm not as bad as you think, you know. Sure, I've strayed a little, but that's what we all did back in the seventies and eighties. Dodging and weaving with a job ran with the territory. I include Jeff in that as well. It was just how we worked as a team." His look hardened. "But Jeff didn't deserve this. This has gone beyond what I thought would happen." He paused and took in a deep breath.

"I'm still listening."

"Look, I was never into Peter Blake-Hall for anything, neither was Jeff. We were not on the take, like you're maybe thinking. True, Jeff and I got a new car, and a holiday at Peter's place in Benidorm, but we paid for those. We got them at cost, that's all." He blinked and dabbed a finger at the corner of each eye. "You probably know that Peter was my snout. I came across him as a young man, just setting up his own mechanic's business. He knew who was into ringing motors and doing bits of handling and he helped me put a few villains away. It was a good little number I had going with him. It helped me get promoted and stay in CID, and in return I helped him out when he got that club. I advised him how to run it and how not to get caught out, especially with it being a strip club. I mean he wasn't doing any harm, was he? Just that it was a different climate back then." He chewed his bottom lip and said, "Getting round to Lucy, Peter rang me that day when she went missing. Jeff and I went to see him and we really did believe what he told us. We really did all those enquiries that are on the file and from what the people said we genuinely thought at first we'd find her at Daniel Weaver's house. Of course when we saw those scratches to his face and no sign of Lucy we thought he'd harmed her. Finding Lucy's bag in his shed just sealed it for us."

"You really found that bag in the shed then?"

"On my honour yes, I promise. Jeff and I firmly believed Danny had done something to Lucy. Especially when we found out he'd been having an affair with her over the past six months and that she was pregnant with his child. We just assumed he'd flipped that Friday night and killed her, and Jeff and I wanted to find what he'd done to her. As you know he didn't confess. But we were absolutely convinced he'd done it, given the argument in the market place, and then her unexplained disappearance and so that's why we did those extra notes." His eyes glassed over again. He shook his head. "When he was found guilty, we still believed we'd got our man. Jeff and I visited him in prison with the aim of finding out where he'd buried Lucy, and even when he continued with the innocent act, we thought it was just a show."

"When did everything change?"

"They didn't, at first. Then we started to get a few whispers about Peter and his mate Ronnie Fisher bringing in drugs. And then there was that accident where the undercover officer got killed in that reporter's car. Which, as you know, was covered up by crime squad. I saw him, you know, at Peter's club, but I didn't know he was an undercover cop. In fact I was with Peter on the night he got killed, so I knew he wasn't involved in that."

"And Ronnie."

"Now he's a different kettle of fish. Ronnie is a nasty piece of work. I believe it was Ronnie who did Jeff and it wouldn't surprise me if he'd been involved in running that reporter's car off the road that night. Nothing would surprise me about that man."

"What makes you say that?"

"I've got to know him these past dozen or so years. I've seen what he's done to a few who've upset him at the club. Ronnie is a psycho."

"So what happened before Jeff got killed? Did he tell you about the notes he had kept of Daniel's interview?"

"He didn't say he had the notes. In fact, I thought those were long gone. I watched him burn them, or at least I thought so. I never knew he'd kept them all these years. He just told me he had kept evidence."

"So what happened?"

"A couple of weeks before he was killed, right out of the blue, he rang me one night. He said it had been preying on his mind about what we'd done to Danny Weaver, and that maybe Peter had really killed Lucy. I told him he was just feeling low."

Alan broke off and licked his lips. Then he continued, "He'd told me about his cancer and that he'd not got long to live, so I just said 'Jeff what's done is done.' And he told me he wanted to make amends and was just letting me know he'd kept some evidence to help Danny get his conviction overturned. I told him to think about what he was doing - meaning the consequences for me but he just repeated he'd thought about it a long time. He thought Peter was responsible for Lucy's death and maybe a new investigation would prove it. I asked him again to seriously think about what he was doing. Then he hung up on me."

"And you told Peter."

Alan slunk low on his pillow, he looked defeated. He nodded back. "Yes, those are what those photos are all about. I didn't know of course that the reporter had been sniffing around Peter's club. I didn't know about them until you showed them to me yesterday. I'd phoned Peter and told him that I needed to see him urgently. I went to his club and told him exactly what Jeff had said to me. And I asked him straight out if he'd killed Lucy."

"And what did he say?"

"He denied it of course. But like you DS Kerr, I've been a detective a long time and I could tell when I looked him square in the face that he'd done it, or at least knew something about it. And by that I'm thinking Ronnie. He was the one who kept saying I needed to do something about it. Make sure the evidence disappeared. I'll never forget what his face was like when he told me that either I sort it or he'd sort it for me. I'm telling you, I think Ronnie killed Jeff."

Hunter wasn't about to tell him that post-mortem findings indicated that the likelihood was that two people had been involved in his ex-colleague's murder. He asked, "And what about the girl Jodie Marie Jenkinson?"

"I didn't know about that. It was Peter who rang me and told me that a reporter was bugging him, and asked me if I'd said anything to anyone. I told him I wasn't that stupid. Then he told me that this Guy whatever his name was knew an awful lot, and that if it wasn't me then someone had to have overheard our conversation. The only two people in the club that morning besides me, Peter and Ronnie, were the bar manager and a girl stocking up the bar. I told him not to do anything stupid."

"You know the girl was found murdered in the old Barnwell Inn, don't you?"

"Yeah, I saw it on the local news. But I swear that is nothing to do with me. That's down to Peter and Ronnie."

Hunter leaned forward, rested his forearms on the bed and for a few seconds scrutinised Alan Darbyshire's face. Then he asked, "What are you after Alan? Telling me all this?"

"Look, I know you've got enough on me for a charge of perjury, I'm not stupid. Those notes Jeff kept have sunk me, but at least I can broker a deal."

"A deal?"

"Yes." He grabbed Hunter's sleeve. "Do you know, DS Kerr, I wish I could turn the clock back. I really do. And believe me, recently I've not been able to sleep over it, but I can honestly say that at the time I believed Danny Weaver had murdered Lucy"

"But he didn't, did he?"

He looked shamefaced. "That's why I need to make amends. I'll stand up in court and give evidence against Peter and Ronnie about those photographs you have of us. I'll tell the court what that meeting was about, just before Jeff and that girl's murder. It'll be enough to swing a jury. And in return I want a reduced sentence in an open prison. That's the deal."

- ooOoo -

CHAPTER SEVENTEEN

DAY SIXTEEN: 9th December.

"He doesn't deserve it, but I think CPS will go for it. Evidence in a murder, or in this case four murders, outweighs a twenty-five-year-old perjury charge. And also don't forget the press coverage on this one. Everyone's under immense pressure at the moment because of the miscarriage of justice appeal," Detective Superintendent Michael Robshaw said, having listened to Hunter's version of the previous evening's chat with Alan Darbyshire. "I'll speak with CPS first thing this morning and run it past them." He rubbed his hands together and then gave them a loud clap. "Okay everyone, we pick up where we left off yesterday." He pointed at Hunter. "You and Grace re-interview Peter. The clock on him runs out at two pm today. Hit him with the photographs which Guy Armstrong took and Kerri-Ann Bairstow's statement. Let's see what he says about those. I've asked the techies at Headquarters to examine the memory of his phone today, to see if we can put him anywhere near our murder sites and also check if he has any incriminating texts. If I get that information back in the next couple of hours, then we can hopefully squeeze in another interview before the end of his detention. Given what Alan Darbyshire has said, together with Lisa Aldridge's statement, I'm going to see if CPS are happy with what we've got so far and get them to agree to a holding charge for the murder of his wife Lucy." Next he turned to Tony Bullars. "Tony, I want you and Carol to take Jessica out to her father's house and see if anything comes of it. It's a real long shot, but I know of cases where it has worked. The psychologists call it recovered memory therapy. Let's keep our fingers crossed it works in our case." Then his eyes scanned the room. "Good news, everyone. Mike came round yesterday afternoon and except for a few war wounds he's none the worse for wear. And he's identified his attacker as Ronnie Fisher. We've got him bang to rights on one thing at least. Now, the rest of you have your tasks for the day. We have the search of Peter's club and we have some new addresses to check for Ronnie Fisher." He clapped his hands again. "People let's make today count. Good hunting everyone."

* * * * *

Peter Blake-Hall, now sporting a fresh shirt and pair of jeans, looked relaxed as Hunter and Grace entered the interview room and sat opposite.

His solicitor sat beside him, legal pad and pen at the ready.

"Found Ronnie yet?" Peter asked smugly.

Hunter slowly opened his folder and took a deep breath. "This interview is about you, Mr Blake-Halll. It does not concern Ronnie Fisher."

"I take it then that you haven't found him," Peter said with a wide grin.

Hunter felt himself tense.

Grace toe-tapped one of his ankles, her reminder to him to stay in control. Then she started the tape machine and went through the opening procedures before the interview could commence.

When she had finished, Hunter said, "Peter, this morning I want to talk to you about an incident which went on at the front of your club on the morning of the tenth of November just over a month ago. You and Ronnie Fisher had a meeting with a man called Alan Darbyshire, a retired police officer." He watched the smirk disappear from Peter's face. "Or rather, I should say disagreement. Do you remember that?"

"No."

"Well, let me help you remember." Slowly, for dramatic effect, Hunter opened his folder and slid out the A4 photographs Guy Armstrong had taken. He had chosen three. One of them was the shot of Peter stabbing Alan Darbyshire in the upper chest with his finger. "Take a look at these carefully, Peter. You'll see they are timed and dated. Do these help?"

Blake-Hall's head was down, his eyes on the photographs, but Hunter could see the colour draining from his face.

He mumbled, "No comment."

"Now I've shown you these photographs, can you recall what was said during your meeting?" He exaggerated the word 'meeting'.

"No comment."

"I can help you there as well. Because I've been chatting with Alan Darbyshire and he says he came to see you that morning because he had a phone call from an old colleague of his, who had evidence relating to the murder of your wife. That ex-colleague was a man called Jeffery Howson and he had evidence, which he had kept hidden for twenty-five years, which would exonerate Daniel Weaver, and blow the whole case wide open again. And I understand you were not too happy about that and threats were made with regards Jeffery Howson, together with suggestions that the evidence should be made to disappear."

Peter Blake-Hall raised his head. He looked livid.

"And a couple of weeks after this meeting, Jeffery Howson was found murdered at his home. Do you know anything about that?"

Blake-Hall chewed on his lip.

"I would appreciate an answer. In your own time of course." Hunter sized his prisoner up across the table. After several seconds of silence, he repeated, "An answer please, Peter."

Through clenched teeth, Blake-Hall replied, "No comment."

Hunter leaned back in the seat. "Did you expect Alan Darbyshire to keep quiet about this Peter? Well, unfortunately for you see he's decided to see the light and he's in the process of making a deal with CPS. Also, he's not too happy about his friend being killed."

"Detective Sergeant Kerr!" The solicitor intervened. He tapped his pen sharply on the table. "Kindly stick to the proper methods of interviewing, if you wouldn't mind."

"Sorry, Mr Wilkinson I thought I was."

The solicitor scowled.

Hunter put on a false smile and returned his gaze to Blake-Hall. "Peter, have you ever been to Jeffery Howson's house or near Woodland View where he lived?"

"No."

"You're absolutely sure of that?" Hunter studied his face. Blake-Hall seemed to dwell on his question for a good ten seconds, before he answered.

"I would know if I'd been to his house, wouldn't I. No, I haven't."

"Okay, thank you." Hunter played with the photographs, straightening them along the table. "I just want to take you back to these photos. I've already mentioned Alan Darbyshire's take on this meeting. What if I also tell you that your conversation was overheard by a girl who was working that morning in your bar. What if I tell you that she told a friend of hers that she overheard you talking about the murder of your wife Lucy, and that person has made a statement about your conversation between yourself, Ronnie Fisher and Alan Darbyshire."

"Is there a question there officer?" the solicitor said.

Hunter fixed him with a hard stare. "There is, if you'd let me finish." Hunter looked at Blake-Hall. "Did you know that a girl called Jodie Marie Jenkinson, who worked for you behind your bar, overheard your conversation that morning?"

"No comment."

"And that she then contacted a reporter called Guy Armstrong, who I know you do know, because he was at your house that day we came to visit you, and that she told him of the conversation. Were you aware of that?"

"No comment."

"Was that why he was at your house that morning when we came? He wanted a comment from you regarding the conversation Jodie had overheard. That was why we caught you arguing and pushing him away, wasn't it Peter?"

He jutted his chin forward, "No comment."

"Jodie was found dead about three weeks ago in a pub called the Barnwell Inn, which is currently undergoing renovation and we're treating that death as murder. Have you been to that pub in recent weeks?"

"No."

"Sure about that Peter?"

"Definitely."

"Peter, we seem to be going nowhere here. I've explained that several people have either given statements against you, or are about to give a statement, which puts you in the frame as our number one suspect for the murder of your wife, Lucy. Would you like to say something in your defence other than answer no comment?"

"No comment."

"What about the murder of Jeffery Howson?"

"No comment."

"Do you want to say anything in relation to the murder of Jodie Marie Jenkinson?"

"No comment."

Hunter shuffled the photographs together, stacked them one on top of the other and slipped them back into his folder. He said, "This interview is over."

Grace took the tapes out of the machine and as was customary procedure, allowed Peter Blake-Hall to select one. Then she sealed both cassettes, let Peter sign for them, dropped them into her jacket pocket and made for the exit.

Hunter picked up his folder and followed. As he got to the door Peter Blake-Hall called out, "How is your colleague, detective?"

Hunter swivelled. A menacing stare was targeting him. He spat out, "Sorry?"

"Your colleague? The one who was stabbed outside my club?"

"Why, do you know something about that?"

The edges of Blake-Hall's mouth curled upwards. "It's a dangerous place out there detective. In the words of the sergeant from Hill Street Blues, 'be careful out there'."

Reading the underlying threat in what Blake-Hall had just said, Hunter stared back. He wanted to smash that smug grin right off his face, but instead, he replied, "Thank you for your concern, but I'm a big boy now Peter, I think I can look after myself."

* * * * *

Jessica and her grandmother arrived at reception ten minutes before their appointed time. Carol Ragen nipped downstairs to meet them, and then showed them outside to the front of Barnwell police station, where Tony Bullars had brought an unmarked car into the visitor's car park.

Carol opened the passenger side rear door and Jessica and Margaret slid into the back seat.

As they belted up Tony thanked them for coming. He noticed that Jessica, looked very much like her mother, Lucy. She even had the same straw blonde hair, though in Jessica's case, it was slightly longer. It was swept back from her face, cascading down the back of her quilted coat.

He asked. "Your grandmother's explained the purpose of your visit today?"

Jessica nodded. She glanced at her grandmother and grasped her hand.

"And you're okay with everything?"

"I think so, yes."

"Before we take you to your father's house…"

She interrupted Tony, "He's not there, is he?"

"No, he isn't."

She breathed a sigh of relief. "Good."

"Before we go there, I just want to ask you a few questions Jessica. If you are uncomfortable at any time with what I'm asking, you just tell me, okay?"

She nodded.

"When we spoke with your grandmother the other day, she happened to mention that you had seen a psychiatrist…"

"Only until I was fifteen. I didn't think there was any point after that."

"Okay, fine. And you had been seeing him I understand because of the dreams you were having?"

"Nightmares. And I still have them, but I can cope with them a lot better now. They're just part of my life."

In a soft and steady voice he said, "Jessica, I just want to ask you what you see in these nightmares. We haven't spoken with your psychiatrist, and I appreciate this is confidential and personal to you, but it might just be of help to us."

"I don't see how it can."

"Well, you never know. We've completed a lot more enquiries now that were overlooked in the original case when your mother went missing and we've learned a bit more. It might link in with something. After all, something in your past is responsible for triggering them. Don't you agree?"

She shrugged.

"Can you just tell us what happens in them?"

She squeezed her grandmother's hand tighter. "They always seem to start off with either a scream or a moan. Sometimes it's both. And then I'm in this long corridor and then suddenly I'm standing in a doorway and when I look down..." she paused and stared blankly through the windscreen, before continuing. "It's like an out of body experience, you know? Weird like. Well, then I'm looking down at my feet and blood's coming up through my toes." For a couple of seconds she remained transfixed, staring out. Then her focus was back and she said, "That's it. Almost the same thing, every time."

"So you don't see anyone in these nightmares?"

She lapsed into a thoughtful silence for a few seconds and then replied, "No, I don't think so. Though I do see shadows."

"Shadows?"

"Just shadows. That's it I'm afraid."

"Okay, thank you." Tony twisted back and engaged gear. "Right, let's get you over to your dad's place."

They had only travelled a mile before Jessica piped up from the back. "Where are we going?"

"To your dad's house." said Tony.

"But you're going the wrong way."

"No, this is the way to Hooton Roberts."

"Hooton Roberts?"

"Yes! Where your dad lives."

"No, we didn't live there. Me and mum. We used to live outside Wortley."

Tony slowed the car and pulled into the kerb. A car behind blared its horn.

Turning around, he said, "You're saying there's another house?"

"Another house? No I'm saying the house that I know, and where I was brought up, was a cottage between Wortley and Birdwell. Dad was doing it up when mum disappeared."

Glancing sideways, Tony's surprised look mirrored his colleague's. He turned back to Jessica. "We've been searching the wrong house. We thought Peter's current home was where he lived when your mum disappeared."

"No I've never been to that house. He got that house about eighteen months after Daniel's trial."

Tony slammed into first gear, wrenched hard on the steering and spun the car around onto the opposite carriageway. He managed a u-turn in one manoeuvre.

"Right Jessica, Wortley here we come! You point out the way to the house when we get there."

From the Dearne Parkway, Tony picked up the Stocksbridge bypass and then took the signposted lane into Wortley.

It was a small village; one pub, one church, the grand Wortley Hall, which was now owned by the Trade Unions, and a few dozen cottages.

It was the first time Tony had taken notice of the place. He thought of the many times he had travelled this ridge-backed road, through God's Own Country, to one of his favourite places Holmfirth, where they filmed 'Last of the Summer Wine' and all that time he had missed seeing how pretty this village was. The next time he was here, he told himself, he'd call in at The Wortley Arms. He'd noticed that it was now a restaurant and it looked pretty damn good.

Passing the church, Margaret pointed out Constable Row, where she and her husband used to live. Then a hundred yards further on she called out again, "Turn right, just ahead, that's where the house is."

The signpost indicated the road to Birdwell. He turned into the junction and found himself driving along a narrow road. Skeletal trees lined the first two hundred yards of the route and as he left them behind the view opened out to farmland either side. The only cottages he could make out seemed to be those on the hillsides, miles away. As he came out of a left hand bend, Jessica called from the back,

"It's just along here."

Tony spotted the cottage up ahead, slightly set back from the road. It was larger than he had imagined; a solid Yorkshire stone farmhouse, with a stone slated roof. He had to mount the grassy verge at the front of the house to park, otherwise he would have blocked the carriageway.

Turning in his seat he said, "Just give me a couple of minutes. I'll see if there's anyone in and if I can sort something out." He turned off the engine. "This'll be the oddest request I've ever made," he added, opening the driver's door.

Five minutes later he returned to the car and stuck his head inside. "There's someone in. It's a woman, her husband's at work." He grinned. "She was a little surprised when I told her why I'd come, and what I wanted, but she's kindly agreed to let us in and have a look round." He set his gaze upon Jessica. "Are you still okay with this?"

"I think so yes."

Tony opened up a rear door to let out Jessica and Margaret.

For a few seconds Jessica stood and stared. Her grandmother wound a protective arm around her.

She said softly, "Are you okay love?"

"Yes thanks, Gran," she answered, tapping her grandmother's hand and easing herself from the comforting restraint.

Tony led the way and the other three followed him along the path, skirting around the side of the house, to the rear. At the back door a well-made lady, in her early fifties, was waiting. She opened the door wider to allow them in. She looked perplexed and Tony wasn't surprised, given the strange request he had made.

Tony turned to Jessica and asked, "Anything?" He watched as Jessica's gaze darted around the kitchen.

She said, "Most of its how I remember. The units look familiar, though there wasn't a table and chairs here." Pointing to the far wall she added, "And that dresser wasn't here." She stepped into the middle of the floor and slowly turned her head. She looked at the woman who owned the house, "Do you mind?" she asked, pointing at a door which connected with the hallway.

"Be my guest," the woman replied. She still wore a bewildered expression.

Jessica walked to the doorway, spent a few seconds looking around the hallway and then pirouetted on her heels and faced back into the kitchen. Suddenly she clamped a hand over her mouth.

"Oh my God!"

In that instant her face paled. Then she started to sway.

Tony got to her just in time as her legs buckled. He caught her under the arms, and then half-dragged, half-carried her to a chair Carol pulled out from beneath the kitchen table.

He lowered her into the seat and supported her.

Jessica's face was waxen and a band of sweat had gathered on her forehead.

She took a deep breath. "I saw my mother!" she gasped. "She was lying just there!"

A Welsh dresser, shelves laden with blue and white decorative pottery, stood on the spot where she was pointing.

Tony Bullars stood on the back doorstep of the renovated farmhouse; the place which, twenty five years ago, had been Jessica's home, and in which, only ten minutes earlier, she had unlocked the memories of her past. She was still back there, in the kitchen, being comforted by her grandmother and supported by his colleague Carol.

He'd already called and spoken to DI Scaife and been told to hang fire there - Detective Superintendent Leggate was on her way.

Within the next few hours, this place would be swarming with Scenes of Crime Officers and a forensics team. He wondered what the owner would say; she already seemed dazed by it all.

He dug his hands deeper into his trouser pockets and stared out across the rolling countryside. Although he had just got a good result, he was still feeling pretty low. He had left Mike alone. If only he hadn't gone for that supper, he thought. Somehow, he needed to redeem himself.

A sharp gust of wind whipping across the barren landscape, stung his cheeks and brought him back from his reverie as he shivered. He was glad that he had kept his overcoat on.

Admiring the scenery sharpened his concentration. Beyond the low garden wall, he noted that the field dipped away. He could make out the tops of trees in a small wood. There his gaze stopped.

Now if I'd just killed someone here, that's where I would bury them.

* * * * *

"Bingo a result!" Hunter called loudly as he read what was displayed on his computer screen for the second time.

He shot a glance across at his partner. His announcement had caught Grace's attention.

"Got him!" he said. He returned back to his computer, selected the print menu and clicked the mouse. Behind him, the printer whirred into action and he picked out each page the moment it fell into the feed tray. Spinning back to his desk, he fanned out five A4 sheets like a deck of cards, and then glanced between the paperwork and what was on his computer screen to check they were the same. He patted the sheets together and picked up the phone. It rang a good dozen times before the custody sergeant answered. After a few pleasantries, Hunter said, "Can you rouse Peter Blake-Hall's solicitor for me please? You can tell him I've got some good news for his client."

As he hung up he slid the five pieces of paper across his desk to Grace. "Feast your eyes upon those goodies." He checked his watch and said, "Good timing. We've got another hour before his clock runs out. Can you help us knock some charges together? I'm going to give Peter Blake-Hall an early Christmas present."

Clasping a handful of rolled up papers, Hunter skipped across the rear yard to the Custody Suite like a child released from class at the end of the day. Grace was on his coat-tails. As they entered reception, Hunter saw Peter Blake-Hall had already been released from his cell and was standing beside his solicitor.

As Hunter and Grace approached, the solicitor tapped the face of his watch. "DS Kerr, in twenty minutes my client's time is up and you will have to either release him or charge him. So if you're thinking about going in for another interview?"

"Thank you for pointing that out to me Mr Wilkinson, I am fully aware of that. And no we're not going in for an interview, that will not be necessary. This will be short and sweet."

"Then you will be bailing Mr Blake-Hall?"

"On this occasion, no." Hunter slowly unfolded his paperwork, never taking his eyes off his prisoner. "You remember we seized your mobile phone, Peter?" He searched his face for a reaction. "Well I don't know if you are aware, but those things hold such a vast amount of information. It logs every call you make and every text even if you delete them..."

"Is there a point to these deliberations, detective?" asked the solicitor."

"There is, if you'd kindly give me a moment." Hunter rocked and flexed his neck. "There is also a magical thing called cell-site analysis, which can be done with mobile phones. We can pick out every location you have ever been to with your phone. Not only can we accurately map where you have been, we can also time and date those visits." Hunter saw Peter Blake-Hall's face drain of colour. "And I can tell you, Peter, that from your mobile we have been able to log you as being on Jeffery Howson's street at ten-fifty-two pm on the night of Saturday twenty-second of November which was the night he was murdered. But then, of course you would know that." He paused for a couple of seconds, hoping for a response. When there was none, he continued, "We also have you logged at the site of the old Barnwell Inn on the afternoon of the fifth of November. That is the location where we found Jodie Marie Jenkinson's body a week later. Finally, we have you logged at various locations between Wentworth and Harley on the night of first December, which is when Guy Armstrong was run off the road and then murdered in his car." He watched Peter Blake-Hall's jaw drop. "Peter Blake-Hall I am charging you with the murders of Jeffery Howson, Jodie Marie Jenkinson and Guy Armstrong." As he cautioned him, Hunter thought to himself that there was just one more murder now to resolve –. the one that had triggered this whole dramatic chain of events - that of his wife, Lucy.

- ooOoo -

CHAPTER EIGHTEEN

DAY SEVENTEEN: 10th December.

The Major Incident Teams office was packed. Task Force Officers had been drafted in to search for Lucy's body. There were bums on seats and on desks, and uniform and plain clothed officers even stood shoulder-to-shoulder in the aisles for morning briefing.

The previous afternoon, Scenes of Crime Team had visited the cottage where the Blake-Halls once lived. In an area behind the present owner's Welsh dresser, traces of blood were found in the gap between the floor and the skirting board. That sample had been transported by a police motor cyclist earlier the previous evening, together with a comparison DNA sample from Jessica. If it was Lucy's blood, they would soon know. The house had been sealed off as a crime scene and the shocked owners had been shipped out to stay with relatives. A Forensics team had been working through the night examining the kitchen; floor tiles and part of the skirting board had been removed and additional dried blood patches had been found - every indication that they had found the spot where Lucy was murdered.

The forensics work was continuing that morning.

The focus of that morning's briefing was to find Lucy's burial site, and the gardens of the farmhouse and the nearby woodland were centre-stage in that search. A police expert in body search techniques was leading the briefing.

The slim, dark-haired Inspector, dressed in blue coveralls, addressed the assembled group. He said, "I visited the farmhouse yesterday afternoon and the woodland below the house is the most probable location where Lucy's body is buried."

Turning sideways, he tapped his splayed fingers over a large-scale ordnance map, of the Wortley area, Blu-tacked onto Lucy Blake-Hall's incident board that morning.

"I have identified three key sites in the woods as ideal locations." He prodded three areas of the map. Each of the sections had been marked by red felt pen lines drawn into oblong shapes. He pointed to the lowest box. Focusing on the uniformed officers, he said. "This will be our first search quadrant this morning. If we get an indication that it is a burial site, then we will fix the area and call in forensics."

Some of the Task Force officers nodded.

"The weather forecast over the next few days is in our favour and the winter terrain on the ground is thin at this time of the year, so that is also an advantage. However, what is against us is the length of time Lucy has been in the ground, so everyone has to move extra slow within the search grids and keep their eyes peeled." He wound up by saying "If you find something, call me."

* * * * *

While members of the MIT department were consigned with the task of finding and detaining Ronnie Fisher, Hunter and Grace's assignment for that day was to prepare the Peter Blake-Hall remand file relating to the murders of Jeffery Howson, Jodie Marie Jenkinson and Guy Armstrong for the local CPS. His first court appearance was that afternoon and they already knew that his solicitor was not going to be contesting the remand. Nevertheless, the file they presented before the magistrates still had to contain all the relevant evidence from the major witnesses, together with the forensic information which had sealed Blake-Hall's fate.

Later would be the harder work, when they had to prepare the case papers for presentation before the Crown Court.

Hunter had a pile of witness statements in front of him and was making a précise of their content. Grace was going through the exhibits and putting them in order.

Grace's desk phone started ringing. She let it go for a few seconds before picking up. Not taking her eyes away from her pile of documents, she cocked her head, trapping the handset between neck and shoulder and answered.

It disturbed Hunter's concentration and he turned to his partner.

Her head jolted upwards and her surprised gaze met his as she pointed excitedly at the handset. Snatching up a piece of scrap paper, Grace began scribbling as she listened intently.

Hunter tried to make sense of the one-sided conversation. He could tell from Grace's reaction and wild note taking that it had to be important.

Finally, after ten minutes, she slammed down the phone. "You'll never guess who that was?"

Hunter opened his hands and shrugged.

"Kerri-Ann Bairstow. And guess what?"

"Grace!"

"Okay, okay, I'll tell you." Grace glanced at her notes from the telephone conversation. "She thinks she knows where Ronnie Fisher is, or at least where he's going to be later today."

"Bloody hell, Grace."

"Exactly. Isn't that a turn-up for the books? Who'd have thought Kerrie-Ann would grass someone up?"

"Well, it is someone who more than likely killed her friend."

"Yes, I suppose there is that to it. Anyway, she says the info's come from a mate of hers who used to buy their smack from Ronnie. He's got his head down in a flat at Lundwood, but he's booked on board a ship tonight to Amsterdam. He's sailing from Hull at midnight. But before that he's got to collect some cash stashed in the safe at Peter Blake-Hall's club. He's going there some time later today before it opens." She took another look at her jottings. "A guy called Scott Riley is picking him up and running him out there."

* * * * *

It was a Gold Command-led Operation and Detective Superintendent Michael Robshaw was running the show from District headquarters.

Scott Riley hadn't been hard to find; he'd got plenty of form. And they had found a red Vauxhall Corsa, which was registered to him, behind his flat.

Now all they had to do was wait for it to move.

To help with the capture of Ronnie Fisher, the Force Surveillance Team had been brought in and they were currently parked up in various streets around Scott Riley's address. They had every road and side-street around his home covered; the moment he drove away, someone would be tailing him.

At Peter Blake-Hall's club - Ronnie's destination, according to Kerri-Ann Bairstow the police were waiting. A four-man Task Force Firearms team, together with a dog-handler, were hidden behind garages three streets away, and Hunter and Grace, with Detective Superintendent Leggate, were in an unmarked car, parked behind a derelict warehouse on waste ground at the rear of the club.

Hunter was in the driver's seat, shuffling uncomfortably, his fingers rapping away gently at the steering wheel. They had been parked for almost an hour and a trickle of nervous excitement ran through him. It made him recall his Drug Squad days - then, he had frequently savoured the same experience.

He stared out through the windscreen, his eyes settling upon the rear of Peter Blake-Hall's club. The light was beginning to fade; a faint orange glow had replaced the pale blue horizon. It was only mid-afternoon, but day was giving way to evening.

As he checked his watch for the umpteenth time, Hunter's personal radio crackled into life. The Surveillance Team were breaking their silence. The crew in the 'eyeball' vehicle announced that two men had just got into Scott Riley's red Corsa, but they were unable to identify the occupants.

A woman's voice announced "Target vehicle is off, off, off."

Hunter gripped the steering wheel - the waiting was over. If it was Ronnie Fisher in the car, then in another twenty minutes he would be here and within his grasp.

Within five minutes the commentator's voice had changed - the first car had fallen back and a new lead car was now on the Corsa's tail. Hunter could make out, from the directions and landmarks being broadcast, that the target vehicle was indeed heading their way. For a couple of seconds he could hear the blood rushing inside his ears and felt the muscles in his legs and forearms beginning to tighten. The adrenaline had kicked in.

Ten minutes into the unwavering commentary, Hunter heard the sentence he had been waiting for - Ronnie Fisher, their target, had been identified as the front seat passenger. He felt a tap on his shoulders from the back seat. Detective Superintendent Dawn Leggate was giving him the starting orders. He turned the ignition and revved the engine. The car rocked.

The next ten minutes seemed to fly by. From the radio chatter, Hunter determined that the Corsa was heading their way.

As the red car entered the final section of small side-streets on its way to the club, the chatter over the airwaves increased.

A couple of the tail-end cars from the surveillance team convoy would now be peeling away, increasing their speed, ready to block off any escape attempt by the driver of the Corsa. In a few minutes he would be boxed in and going nowhere.

"It's a stop, stop, stop, outside the Le Chambre Rose,'" came the cry over the radio, quickly followed by, "Target is out of the vehicle and heading for the front doors."

Detective Superintendent Leggate issued the order, "Strike, strike, strike."

Hunter gunned the engine. The car's rear wheels spun and slid momentarily, churning up loose gravel. Then they gripped and Hunter tore towards the back entrance of the club.

A hundred yards from the rear of the premises, the call of "He's doing a runner," blared over the airwaves. Hunter saw the emergency double-doors explode open. Ronnie Fisher came out of them so fast, he almost fell over. He managed to balance, then spun away sideways and picked up his sprint.

Hunter yanked the steering wheel hard, hitting the brakes, and the car skewed. Before it had even jerked to a halt, Hunter threw open the driver's door and launched himself out.

Ronnie was twenty metres ahead but Hunter quickly made ground, snapping close to his heels within seconds. He barked out the order "Police, stop." It had the desired effect - Ronnie skidded to a halt.

Before Hunter could get within striking distance, Ronnie had turned and dropped into a rugby tackle squat. Hunter didn't have time to stop, but before he made impact he threw himself side-on, catching Ronnie full in the chest with his shoulder. They hit the ground together, though Hunter's momentum rolled him away. As he leapt to his feet, Ronnie was mirroring his actions, outstretching his arms to do battle. In that instant, Hunter locked eyes with someone who had the look of Frankenstein's monster.

In the blink of an eye, Ronnie reached down snatched something out of his right boot.

"I'll fucking kill you," he growled.

Behind him, Hunter heard Grace scream, "He's got a knife."

He jerked back. And only just in time, as a glint of metal flashed before him. The blade had missed him by a few inches.

Ronnie slashed forward with the knife again. This time Hunter was ready. He swung his left arm across to deflect the blow. It wheeled Ronnie to one side, exposing his ribs. Hunter hooked in his right fist, putting his whole weight behind the punch. A bone-jarring crack resounded and Ronnie screamed in pain as the air exploded from his chest.

He toppled, instinctively flinging out an arm to prevent himself from hitting the ground. Hunter brought his elbow crashing down onto the top of his skull like an executioner's axe.

Ronnie was out before his face hit the ground.

A sudden weakness overcame Hunter and he felt light-headed. Bending double, he clawed in long gulp of air.

Detective Superintendent Leggate and Grace approached. He could hear other detectives spilling through the emergency doors, scrambling towards them.

Everyone stopped and encircled the unconscious Ronnie Fisher. Blood was trickling from his mouth and nose.

Hunter raised himself up to his full height and took in another deep breath. He was beginning to shake. The first thing he saw was the bemused look upon his SIO's face as she viewed their grounded, bloodied target.

Straight-faced he said, "Reasonable force, boss!"

- ooOoo -

CHAPTER NINETEEN

DAY EIGHTEEN: 11th December.

After receiving treatment for two cracked ribs, a busted nose and a split lip, Ronnie Fisher was released from hospital at 3.30am, in handcuffs, with a police escort, and transported across to Barnwell Custody Suite, where he was bedded down for the night.

* * * * *

Hunter found it hard to drop off to sleep – he was still so high, long after climbing into his bed. And then when he finally dozed, he slept fitfully. He awoke just before 5.30am and after half an hour of tossing and turning gave up, switched off his alarm and climbed into the shower. He drove into work in the dark, on quiet roads, his thoughts drifting towards the day's work ahead.

At the rear door, he bade good morning to the day Sergeant.

He sprinted up the back stairs and at the top almost collided with his partner Grace, coming out of the ladies toilets.

Catching his balance he said, "You're in early."

"Couldn't sleep. Been putting on my face for the day." They were the first ones in the office and while one made the hot drinks, the other put bread into the toaster. They had polished the toast off and replenished their drinks before the first of the other team members arrived.

As they savoured a second round of drinks, prior to briefing, the pair discussed, checked and doubled-checked their evidence, and made a start on the drafting of preparatory notes, ready for their first interview with Ronnie Fisher. They had Mike's statement, identifying Ronnie as the person who had stabbed him, and they had recovered the knife which he had attempted to use on Hunter. They were confident Mike's DNA would be on it. Ronnie was already looking at charges of attempted murder for Mike and the attempted murder of Hunter. There was also a charge from earlier in the investigation when he had assaulted Hunter at Jodie's bed-sit.

The weight of those three charges would be enough to hold him, giving them sufficient time to collate the evidence relating to the murders of Jeffery Howson, Jodie Marie Jenkinson and

Guy Armstrong. And they were very hopeful of getting a result from those as well - like Peter Blake-Hall, Ronnie had kept his mobile phone and that had been seized for examination.

The morning briefing was led by Detective Superintendent Leggate. She congratulated everyone on the previous evening's success, and followed up by announcing that as of today she was running everything - SIO Michael Robshaw had been called across to the Force Headquarters in Sheffield to discuss his promotion and new role with the Assistant Chief Constable (Crime), and to organise a full press conference to hail the success of their investigation. She then moved on to the real purpose of the briefing - the collating and preservation of evidence against Ronnie Fisher. A search of the red Corsa had turned up several bags of clothing, shoes and trainers, and in Scott Riley's wheelie-bin they had found a pair of woollen gloves, smelling strongly of petrol or other similar accelerant. With a wry smirk, she raised a laugh by adding that it had not been hard to persuade Scott that it would be in his best interest if he gave a statement outlining that he had seen Ronnie dump them.

She reminded everyone that woollen fibres had been found on Guy Armstrong's petrol cap, at the homes of Jeffery Howson and Jodie Marie Jenkinson, and at The Barnwell Inn the site of Jodie's murder.

"If these are the same gloves, then we've really got him bang to rights," she said proudly, and after a slight pause, continued, "It doesn't end there guys, I got another phone call late yesterday, forensics have come up trumps as well. The DNA sample, provided by Jessica, has helped us identify that the dried bloodstains in the kitchen belong to her mother, Lucy. It looks as though Lucy was murdered there. SOCO and the forensic team at the farmhouse are currently extending their examination into other rooms." She broke, her eyes exploring the faces of the detectives. "We are almost there everyone. All we have to do now is find Lucy's body."

* * * * *

A solicitor from the firm of Grant, Harding and Wilkinson was representing Ronnie Fisher, and as Hunter stepped into the soundproof interview room he had already prepared his thoughts for a challenging interrogation, most likely a battle of wills between himself and a 'pain in the arse' defence solicitor.

Seeing the legal representative, Hunter took in a deep breath and let it out slowly. This one had an appearance even smoother than Peter Blake-Hall's solicitor. He looked to be in his mid-fifties with a good head of neatly trimmed silver grey hair and wore a dark blue pinstriped suit, which appeared handmade. A white Oxford, button-down shirt was teamed with a dark blue monogrammed tie.

This man was no legal clerk, thought Hunter, as he dragged out one of the chairs opposite. His appearance shouted senior partner.

Hunter dropped his folder onto the table and lowered himself slowly into the chair.

Grace took the seat beside him, next to the tape recording machine.

Hunter made the introductions and flipped open his folder of notes.

"Mr James Harding." The solicitor replied.

Guessed right.

Ronnie Fisher was silent. He half-sat, half-lazed on his seat, legs out straight, arms folded, his chin resting on his chest. He didn't acknowledge them with even a glance.

Hunter couldn't help but notice the ugly red graze across his forehead, and his badly swollen nose and mouth. He fought back the urge to smirk.

He waited for the tape machine to kick in and then cautioned Ronnie Fisher. "Do you understand what I have just said, Mr Fisher?"

Silence.

"I first want to talk to you about the attack on me last night, when you tried to stab me."

Silence.

For almost forty-five minutes Hunter fired round after round of questions, firstly regarding the attack upon himself and then the stabbing of Mike Sampson. Ronnie Fisher refused to speak. Hunter would have preferred to have engaged in verbal combat, but he knew how it would look when it was put to a jury and he let out a satisfied sigh as he finished the last question.

As the first tape came to an end, Hunter closed his folder and half rose from his chair. Leaning across the table, using his arms as supports, he announced in a strong formal voice, "Ronnie Fisher, I am charging you with the attempted murder of Detective Constable Michael Sampson and the attempted murder of myself. Would you like to say anything about that?"

Ronnie Fisher raised his head and gave him a hate-filled stare.

* * * * *

The Task Force Specialist Search Team who were combing the woods for Lucy's body had finished exploring the first marked-out grid section shortly before eleven am.

The nature of the work had been tedious and laborious and so when the call came for them to have a break, there was an almost unanimous sigh of relief.

Police Constable Craig Darrington was busting. For the past hour he had needed a piss, so when the shout went up he immediately scampered away from his group to a holly bush he had spotted earlier, just outside the search grid.

Quickly, he released the waist belt containing his equipment, and unzipped his coveralls, gasping with relief as the stream of urine left his aching bladder. At first he stared around him, checking no one could see what he was doing, but then, as his jet-stream of piss turned to a trickle he dropped his gaze to the ground, ready to zip himself back up and return to his team. For a brief moment he studied the area where he had urinated. The unusual undulation of a small section of the woodland floor caught his attention. His eyes drifted around the uneven oblong shape for a few seconds and that was when he spotted a discarded cigarette butt. For a further few seconds he studied the uneven surface and came to the decision that he needed to explore this, if only to satisfy his curiosity. He reached out for his metal 'sniffer rod,' which had been resting against the holly bush and set it atop the mound. With an almighty strike, he thrust it through the top layer of soil. He heard a muffled crack from beneath the earth and the most awful putrefying smell drifted out from the centre of the hollow pole. The hairs on the back of his neck bristled and then he yelled, "Sir, over here!"

* * * * *

Detective Inspector Scaife took the call from the Task Force Inspector and immediately informed Detective Superintendent Dawn Leggate of the search team's discovery.

Hunter and Grace entered the office after their interview and the SIO met them.

"Drop what you're doing. You two are coming with me," she ordered. She filled them in as they headed downstairs to the exit. They piled into a spare car and raced up to the scene.

Hunter drove at break-neck speed. At one stage, coming out of a bend, close to the public entrance into the woods, he had to brake sharply to avoid hitting a photographer dashing from between the trees.

"It hasn't taken the press long," the Detective Superintendent said, as a posse of them swarmed towards their slowing car.

As Hunter weaved a course through, he saw a couple of uniformed officers were doing their level best to corral them back.

Hunter jockeyed the unmarked car between the ruts of a thin winding path for another few hundred yards, until he spotted a caravan of parked and marked Task Force vans and Scenes of Crime vehicles lining the narrow track. There, he stopped.

Quickly suiting themselves into protective coveralls, the three detectives left the car, and tramped the small distance, over damp and springy ground, to where a white tent had already been erected. Uniformed officers were putting the finishing touches to the setting up of a sterile perimeter using blue and white crime scene tape.

The team had worked fast, thought Hunter, as he ducked beneath the plastic tape and headed towards the forensic tent. Outside of it, two white-suited members of the Forensic Team were sifting loose soil onto a small pile.

Inside, three forensic specialists were on their knees, using hand trowels to scrape away lumps of soil. Duncan Wroe, clipboard in hand, was supervising things.

They had already removed a good couple of inches of topsoil.

Duncan levelled his gaze at the SIO. "You've already been updated ma'am?"

She nodded, "The task force Inspector rang the office half-an-hour ago. He said that they think they've found a body."

"It's certainly looking like that, unless someone's buried their pet here."

Another hour later, soil scraping resulted in a six-inch dip in the earth. The loose dirt had been emptied into plastic containers and carried outside to be sifted for evidence - a slow but necessary job.

Hunter was just checking the time on his watch - his stomach was telling him it was long past lunch-time, when he heard a rustling from the ground.

He glanced down, just as a member of the digging team pushed themselves back from the hole.

A young woman's voice announced excitedly, "I've found something!"

* * * * *

It took the forensic team another two hours to fully unearth the remains of a body, wrapped inside semi-transparent extra strong plastic sheeting, the type used by builders.

It took another half-an-hour of careful handling before they loaded it into the private ambulance so that it could be safely transported to The Medico Legal Centre for a post-mortem.

* * * * *

Professor Lizzie McCormack had been called out to carry out the examination of the human remains, and by 3.30pm, she and her technician, together with Hunter, Detective Superintendent Leggate and SOCO supervisor Duncan Wroe, had all assembled inside the autopsy room at the Centre.

The pathologist sliced open the heavy duty plastic sheeting which contained the cadaver. As she worked, she talked; the in-built microphones picking up everything she said, relaying her words back to state-of-the-art digital voice recording machine.

Duncan Wroe was filming everything using his digital camera.

As he watched and listened, Hunter tensed. He had waited for this moment for so long. He hoped it was Lucy's body.

Carefully, Lizzie peeled back the first membrane of semi-transparent sheeting. There was another layer beneath, and she cut through this and repeated the process. Slowly, the covering was pulled away and the body was revealed. Its flesh was gone and only a dirty brown skeleton remained. A stained and dirty, blue satin, knee-length nightdress covered the torso.

"Definitely female," announced the Professor, in her soft Scottish burr. "And I think this goes a good way to help identify her." She reached down and hooked a finger around a thin metal chain, which encircled the corpse's neck, raising it slightly. It was a silver necklace with interlinked lettering. There was no mistaking what the lettering spelled -'Lucy.'

"Bingo," said Dawn Leggate through gritted teeth.

Lizzie McCormack smiled. She rested the necklace back onto the bones and then moved a hand down towards the pelvic area, lifted her head and peered over the top of her spectacles. "And this definitely proves it!" She pointed into the pelvic area and drew a circle in the air. "This young lady was with child. Not full term, but there's enough bone and cartilage to determine it was over the twenty-four weeks' stage." She pursed her lips. "And I can see straight away the cause of this young lady's death." She moved her hand away from the pelvis, up towards the skeleton's skull and pointed to the right temple.

Duncan Wroe leaned in with his camera.

Hunter stepped to one side to get better sight of what the Professor was pointing to. He got a good view over Duncan's dipped shoulder. An irregular-shaped hole, the size of a two pence piece, had been smashed into the head.

"Fracture of the skull," Lizzie continued, "And looking at the area of damage, and its position, that would have caused death within a few seconds, or at least would have rendered her immediately unconscious and she would have died within a very short period of time. A lot of force has caused that injury and the object would have had a sharp edge."

"Like a knife, for instance?" Hunter said.

"Ooh no. Something far more substantial than that. A hammer is the more likely object."

Hunter was just about to ask another question when the light-bulb went off inside his head. He hadn't spotted its significance at first.

He said, "Got him!"

His eyes met those of the Detective Superintendent'.

"When Peter Blake-Hall made his original statement, the day he reported Lucy missing, he described her as going out wearing a yellow smock dress and a fawn cardigan. And the witness Lisa Aldridge, states in her statement that she saw Lucy being dragged into her husband's car and the yellow dress stood out in her description of Lucy. If that's the case, how do we account for this body here wearing a nightdress? The only way that could have happened is if she went home and got changed into it."

Detective Superintendent Leggate nodded in agreement, "And that would fit in with why we found blood at the

276

farmhouse and Jessica's recollections from her nightmares. Peter dragged her into his car that night and brought her back home."

"She got changed out of her clothes and into her nightie."

Hunter and his SIO put their thoughts into words.

"And they had an argument over her meeting with Daniel Weaver. Remember, he had asked her to run away with him?"

They finished the last sentence together, "And that's when he struck her and killed her!"

* * * * *

Turning away from the bar, clutching the round of drinks he had just bought, Hunter felt a hand on his shoulder.

"Are we friends?"

He met Detective Superintendent Dawn Leggate's questioning look. "We were never enemies."

She removed her hand. "No, but we didn't get off to a good start did we? You're in my team now and I just want to know that things between us are good for the future?"

"Things are good, boss."

She smiled. "Good. I feel like a drink now." She pointed to the three drinks he was holding. "I see you've got yours already."

He laughed. "Not all for me boss. One's for Barry Newstead and the other's for Grace."

"And I'll stand the next round when those have gone. Everyone's earned this. That was a good result, Hunter. Finding Lucy's body was the icing on the cake."

"Yes. And it's especially good for Mr and Mrs Hall, and for Jessica. They can finally have closure after all this time."

Their conversation was interrupted by a shout of "Mike's here," from Grace.

Hunter looked towards the door. Mike Sampson was being helped through by Tony Bullars. He stepped in gingerly, his right arm clamped to his side, shielding the area where he had been stabbed. Mike raised his free hand in a gesture of thanks and then headed off towards his team mates, Grace and Barry, who were in the process of dragging seats around a table. Tony followed behind like his minder.

Detective Superintendent Leggate spoke into Hunter's ear. "I'll get their drinks. I'll bring them over."

Hunter acknowledged her with a nod and then edged his way to his crew.

He slid the drinks onto the table, pushed a pint towards Barry and handed Grace a white wine. "The gaffer's treating you two," he said to Mike and Tony. Mike seemed be having difficulty getting himself settled in his seat. He turned to him, "I've told her to get you an orange, you're on antibiotics."

Mike wagged a finger at him and they all chuckled.

Hunter raised his glass, said "Cheers," and took in a good mouthful of Timothy Taylor beer.

"Cheers," came the reply.

Wiping his mouth with the edge of his hand Hunter focused on Mike again. "I came to see you the other night."

"Oh, yeah? I can't remember. Was I sedated?"

"No, you were otherwise engaged." From the look on Mike's face, Hunter knew he'd made the connection. He took another sip of his beer.

A moment of silence ensued, until Grace piped up "What's this then?"

Hunter nodded at Mike, "Are you going to tell them, or do I let the cat out of the bag?"

Sheepishly he replied, "You mean me and Janet Dobson."

Grace's jaw dropped. "You mean Janet Dobson, as in Chief Inspector Janet Dobson?"

He affirmed with a quick dip of his head, his face coloured.

"Well you've kept that a bloody secret. When was this?" Grace asked.

"Just over a year."

"And you've kept it to yourself all this time?"

"We wanted to keep it to ourselves for a while longer." He added, "I've no bloody chance of that now, have I?"

Everyone laughed.

"How did this come about then?" asked Barry.

"I knew her husband. I used to go match-fishing with him. He collapsed and died of a heart attack three years ago while we were out fishing. Nothing I could do to help him. I helped her get through things, and then I used to go round and keep her company and we just hit it off."

With a sardonic grin Barry added, "You ought to be ashamed of yourself, taking advantage of a vulnerable widow."

Grace gave Barry a friendly punch to the arm. "You leave him alone. I think it's wonderful." She raised her glass. "I hope you'll be very happy."

Hunter flopped back against his high-backed seat. The warm atmosphere, the relaxing effects of the beer and lack of sleep over the past few weeks had all taken their toll.

As his team's banter drifted into the background, he was thinking about home.

He finished his beer and checked the time, reaching into his pocket for his car keys. He'd spend a couple of hours with Beth and the boys, have a warm bath and then he'd collapse in his bed.

It was always the same at the end of an investigation.

-ooOoo -

EPILOGUE

24th December.

Stepping through the last security door into the visiting room of Wakefield Prison, Daniel Weaver unclenched his fists and stuck his hands into his jeans pockets. He paused for a second to check out the room, thinking that he'd never viewed it before from this angle.

The view was much better from this side, he decided.

Then he caught sight of the prisoner he had come to visit. He picked up his step again, passed a couple of tables where felons were engaged in conversations with their loved ones and then plonked himself down on a seat opposite the man.

He never took his eyes from him.

"It's you," Peter Blake-Hall said. "I wondered who the fucking smart-arse was who'd given my father's name on the visiting sheet."

"Nice little touch, don't you think?" Daniel studied Peter's face for a second and then said, "It's about him I'm here."

"What the fuck do you mean? What the bloody hell have you got to do with my father?"

"He died here you know, Peter."

"Yes, I fucking do know he died here. Some cunt slit his throat."

"But they never found out who'd done that, did they Peter?"

Daniel watched Peter's expression change,.

Daniel pushed himself up. "Well I won't say it's been nice visiting you. And before I go, I want to leave you with something. During my time here, all twenty-five years of it, I made a lot of friends, good friends, and each of them know how you stitched me up." He let his last sentence trail off, and then added, "Oh, and before I go I just want you to know I only have to give the word and I'll have the best Christmas present ever."

The flash of panic in Peter Blake-Hall's eyes brought a smile of satisfaction to Daniel's face as he straightened his back and turned towards the exit.

- ooOoo -

Lightning Source UK Ltd.
Milton Keynes UK
UKOW05f1610310714

236117UK00002B/14/P